The Architects

STEFAN HEYM

DAUNT BOOKS

First published in Great Britain in 2012 by
Daunt Books
83 Marylebone High Street
London W1U 4QW

1

Copyright © Stefan Heym 2000

First published in Germany in 2000 by C. Bertelsmann Verlag

Afterword by Peter Hutchinson
© Northwestern University Press 2006

ISBN 978 1 907970 09 2

Typeset by Antony Gray
Printed and bound by
T J International Ltd, Padstow, Cornwall

www.dauntbooks.co.uk

PROLOGUE

They would soon reach Brest, he heard one of the guards mention. The guards were playing dominoes, noisily banging the small black pieces on a board laid across their knees, and smoking Machorka. The car swayed and rattled, and the stench of sweat and agony refused to lift despite the open vents and door.

Brest, he thought. Since last year – this much had penetrated taiga and prison wall – the town and fortress of Brest had been Soviet. Beyond them lay the border, lay Germany bloated with Nazi conquest.

The blurred anxiety, his since being told he would be deported, now came into focus; it took energy to assure oneself that nothing more terrible lay ahead than a transfer from the frying pan into the fire. He had settled with life. The death of Babette, cruel though it was to think of it this way, was the finish to a worry; fear for Julia remained, but even that was blunted by the hope that Sundstrom, with his talent and connections, might have escaped arrest and be taking care of the child. His own road ran in a straight line: the forthcoming ceremony at the border – that act of friendly international cooperation by which one police force handed an inconvenient Communist to another – led to a new jail and further questioning, though no longer by Dmitry Ivanich or Ivan Dmitrych, and then to a camp, German this time, and reunion perhaps with comrades he hadn't seen for seven years, since 1933, survivors like himself.

The car lurched; the segment of landscape in the open door swayed. His heart contracted in sudden shock: what would he tell them?

This was a new angle; it held its own particular terror.

Tell them the truth? That he and Babette had been arrested like enemies of the people, at four in the morning – four ten, to be precise – and imprisoned, and starved, and beaten, and kept from sleep during the day and questioned at night, night after night, till their nerves screamed and their brains sagged? That they had done everything to coerce him into signing a confession to something he had never done, Ivan Dmitrych and Dmitry Ivanich shoving that sheet of yellow lined foolscap at him over and over again, hour after hour? That he had been left to rot in a cubicle of solid putrefaction, jammed in with an ever-changing number of men – Men, how proud that sounds, Gorky once had said – men confused and stupefied, staring blindly into space or slashing out over a drip of kasha, breaking into shrill hysterics or dying dumbly; men, like himself, left to wait for a decision that was to be made by some authority unknown at some time not scheduled?

Tell this truth to people who had suffered equal horrors and had kept their spirits alive and intact by the fierce, unquestioning faith in the country whose territory now ended beyond Brest and in the idea that gave birth to this country and in the bright, beautiful, glorious future that that idea radiated? Tell it to men in Sachsenhausen, or Buchenwald, or Dachau, who would have to weigh their belief and their faith against what they knew of him, Julian Goltz, Communist, member of the Reichstag; who, at the pain of losing what held them together in their time of trial, could only conclude that he was what he had refused to confess to Dmitry Ivanich and Ivan Dmitrych: a traitor?

It was a new angle that quite pardonably had escaped him in his fear for his child, Julia, whom he hoped was with Sundstrom; in his sorrow over Babette, dead in the wintry cold of her cell; in his revulsion at the monstrosity that his party had become. He admired the devilishness of the police mind that had dreamed up this new torture by dilemma, this tearing of a

6

man's conscience by his own loyalties, and he wondered if it had been a German or a Russian police mind. Or perhaps the thing was done without design: an incidental outgrowth, minute in proportion to the greater issues, of a pact signed at Moscow and toasted in champagne. The situation was not without humour. He had resented that his day in court, permitted the ordinary criminal, had been denied him by the methods of Dmitry Ivanich and Ivan Dmitrych. Now it would be granted him – inside a German concentration camp, with his own comrades his judges over an issue whose truth they would have to deny.

In the Soviet Union, they would have to say, no man is arrested without cause. Human error? Granted. But any investigating magistrate would clear that up. And could he answer: that's what I believed, too? Could he give them a thumbnail sketch of Dmitry Ivanich, elongated, emaciated, grey-skinned, with pale eyes and moth-eaten hair; droning out the same questions from 1:00 a.m. to 5:00 a.m. every morning; punctuating the intervals with the crack of his ruler on the bare wood of his desk; waiting, patiently, for the assault on your shuddering nerves to take effect; and, when his voice grew tired, turning the questioning over to Ivan Dmitrych. Could he adequately describe Ivan Dmitrych – short, stocky, smooth-shaven skull, shining bluish eyes impersonal behind thick lenses, tongue sucking at brown stumps of teeth? Who would believe in the possibility of their routine and what it did to a man?

But his judges had had similar experiences, hadn't they? Well, not quite. Their hell had been at the hands of a police who did not claim to stand for the cause *they* stood for; the ordeal by interrogation had not been visited upon them by individuals who claimed to defend the socialism *they* dreamed of. No, theirs had been a different hell, lighter, almost pleasurable. That's why his judges would not admit that Dmitry Ivanich or Ivan Dmitrych existed; nor the rulers cracking like whips against your sanity; nor that people – thousands? Hundreds of thousands? – were

7

being ground in this mill. Nor would his judges accept the boots tramping the corridors of that Moscow hotel before dawn; and the listening, the sweat cold on your face; and the prayers that the boots pass by your door this one more time. And it was better they disbelieved . . .

He listened to the sounds around him. The clanging of the wheels was unchanged; the dominoes hit the board with undiminished fervour. The prisoners were talking in subdued tones – small talk, as far as he could make out. He hoped the thought that had been tormenting him would never occur to them.

Outside the square of opened door tall birches swayed slowly by, slender white trunks, the October leaves golden yellow; then a low-roofed peasant house. The pastels of the horizon pronounced the distances of this country, this land he had loved since his first step on its soil, since his first word of greeting to the first Soviet soldier he had encountered, the brotherly word *Tovarich*. He had come on Party orders; he had gone to the Crimea to cure his lungs, ruined in nights of hugging the moist ground of the border forests between Germany and Czechoslovakia.

He stared at the passing landscape and smiled tiredly. How simple things had seemed in those days: a clear front with clear issues, his only doubt the *why* of a defeat that had turned him – whose voice had roused the masses on the public squares of a dozen German cities, whose biting words in Parliament had driven his opponents to frustration – into a specialist on smuggling and illegal frontier crossings. It had taken painfully long for him to accept the fact that nothing was clear-cut. Even after Dmitry Ivanich and Ivan Dmitrych had become fixtures in his life, he was still trying to convince himself that it was administrative error or enemy cabal. He had begged for pen and paper to write to his friend Arnold Sundstrom and the comrades prominent in the German émigré party organisation. At one time he had wanted to write to Comrade Stalin: not an individual

8

complaint, but a calm summation of principles that acquainted Comrade Stalin with the arbitrariness of his police, the distortion of justice, the mockery of socialist law, so that Comrade Stalin with one authoritative dictum could wipe out this nightmare.

But as he came to know Dmitry Ivanich and Ivan Dmitrych, he saw that they had no personal axes to grind and were small wheels in a big machine that ran along fixed lines and by central directive. He abandoned the idea of reform by petition and concentrated every nerve and cell on a stubborn determination to survive.

On further thought, there was no need to jeopardise Arnold Sundstrom by writing to him. Sundstrom would do what he could, without nudging. As one after the other comrade they knew and trusted disappeared, he and Babette and Sundstrom had talked of certain eventualities – offhandedly, never quite admitting reality and its threat. But there was the child, and Babette had finally jumped the hurdle. 'You would take care of her, Arnold, wouldn't you, if anything happened to Julian and me?' Arnold Sundstrom had lifted the table lamp so that the light fell on Julia, asleep in the small bed at the foot of the large one; he had gazed at the child's loose curls and sleep-flushed face and said, 'I promise! – Unless, of course, I am prevented from it by force majeure . . . '

He tried to visualize Arnold's exact expression at that moment. But his friend's features remained disconnected, in the abstract: the eyes that usually exuded a slight overdose of whatever emotion they were to convey, the noble nose, the ample lips over the imperial chin, the lionesque mane. Force majeure? . . . Arnold Sundstrom, architect and revolutionary, was not the person to bow to any force majeure; he usually found ways to twist the arm of fate, or if not the arm, at least the finger. The child would be safe, in good hands; that was one less care; and he hoped that Babette had died a shade less horribly in that icy cell for the knowledge of it.

9

The rattle of the wheels against the rail ends assumed a different, hesitant rhythm; a few grimy brick buildings moved into view; farther off a mound, grass overgrown, rose out of the flatlands like a prehistoric chieftain's tomb: an outlying fort, probably. The guards picked up their dominoes, and then two of them, rifles unslung, took up position at the door. 'Brest!' someone said again, and the last talk of the prisoners died down.

He closed his eyes against the sudden sting in his heart. It wasn't fear; it was the recoil of his nerves from the questions that awaited him, questions his judges would ask, more difficult than any posed by Dmitry Ivanich and Ivan Dmitrych. And what of his own secret questions; what of that moment when the beating of the rulers across the desktop had become sweet reasonableness with Dmitry Ivanich and Ivan Dmitrych explaining that to sign the proposed confession was his revolutionary duty, when a blinding clarity in his otherwise numb, exhausted brain demanded of him whether this was still a revolution gone astray or an unprecedented counter-revolution on the rampage.

The train jolted to a halt. The steam from the engine hissed gently; the noises customary to a railway station were muffled and soon faded out as if the people on the platform, the railroad workers, the porters had agreed on a cordon of silence about this one, specially guarded car. Any second now, he expected to hear the hoarse '*Davay! Davay!*' and to feel his ribs prodded by the muzzle of a gun, but the guards continued to lean against the doorjambs, the wrinkled shafts of their boots crossed leisurely.

Those shafts brought back to him the nightmare that had haunted him so long: shafts like these, with the reflection of a single light bulb on their dull lustre, in another doorway. They moved aside, and he saw the steel cot, and the filthy blanket outlining the gaunt figure, and Ivan Dmitrych flicking the blanket off a face that had no resemblance to Babette's, thank God, except for the shape of the ears and for the characteristics of the teeth gleaming from between tautly stretched lips, and Dmitry Ivanich saying to him in a voice suitably solemn, 'Your obstinacy killed her, Comrade Goltz.' But the anticipated shock effect and the benefits deriving from it failed to materialise. Death is an inferior artist; the masks he leaves show only their estrangement from living memory.

The car was being uncoupled; he heard the train moving off, then another engine approaching slowly, then the clang of the buffers. The transfer, apparently, was not to take place in the station: what fine discretion and tact the authorities had!

There's always a first, he thought; he had never before found them to be sticklers for form. One night, after an especially vicious sally by Dmitry Ivanich, he broke out, 'But you haven't a shred of evidence against me!' Dmitry Ivanich, more amazed at the naïveté of his comment than at its impudence, stared palely and answered, 'Do you wish to imply that the security authorities of the Union of Socialist Soviet Republics prosecute people without good and sufficient reason?' The reply had sounded standard, and Ivan Dmitrych seemed to sense that it lacked conviction. He placed his pudgy fingers on Dmitry Ivanich's arm, thus indicating a desire to take over, and asked, 'What about those telegrams, Comrade Goltz?'

'What about them?'

The bullet-shaped, bluish skull lowered belligerently, but the voice held to an infinite patience. 'In 1935, in Prague, you received a telegram informing you of your father's death, Comrade Goltz?'

'Yes.'

'And in 1939, this time in Moscow, another telegram reached you from Germany containing virtually the identical message?'

'But—'

The ruler crashed down and cut him off from repeating the true, logical explanation he had given both Dmitry Ivanich and Ivan Dmitrych he didn't know how many times.

11

'How many fathers did you have?'

'But—'

The ruler, again. 'Will you kindly reply to what you're being asked?'

'One.'

'Well, then!' Dmitry Ivanich, injecting himself once more, had risen to his full, gangling length, half threat, half self-righteousness. But Ivan Dmitrych's hand on his forearm restrained him, and Ivan Dmitrych himself, impersonal behind his thick glasses, pronounced the one statement of principle that was made during the entire course of the hearings. 'Dmitry Ivanich and I,' said Ivan Dmitrych, 'are a good team; one of the best, I might say, in this field. Let me assure you, Comrade Goltz, that we have extracted confessions from people like you on a lot less evidence than we possess in your case.'

He thought of how this statement would sit on his judges awaiting him at the end of this journey, and he felt for them. Why had he spent all that effort on survival; why hadn't he done Ivan Dmitrych and Dmitry Ivanich that small favour – a stroke of the pen – and finish? A fine choice was left him now: to knock the props of existence from under himself or from under his comrades . . .

He tensed. The car had begun to move. Between the two guards in the door, he saw the end of the platform; a peasant woman staring, kerchief tight about her head; the last station sign, *Brest,* lettering blurred. Then came a clatter and rumble as engine, tender, car rolled over a number of switches. One of the female prisoners in the semi-darkened end of the car wept hysterically, her shrieks rising with the acceleration of the wheels. The guards at the door uncrossed the shafts of their boots. 'All right now,' one of them said. 'Get your things.'

His bundle was small enough. There is a time in a man's life when all that he values is carried within him. He watched as the hysterics spread. A guard swayed over and indiscriminately started kicking at the bodies on the straw. The wails and pleas ceased; people scrambled up and stood shadowy, lurching with the motion of the car, one seeking support from the other. He saw each detail, coldly etched: the wood on the floor, worn and splintered from a thousand loads; a woman's feet, misshapen, discoloured, last winter's frostbite; a pair of eyes, dulled to the point of opaqueness; and outside the door a landscape changed into one vast, desolate field of fire for invisible guns, not a house, not a tree, not a bush, and the slope toward the leaden band of a sluggish river. He saw it all and yet he didn't; his mind was frantically clustering about one single thought: there must be an answer I can give, a valid explanation of how this could come about and how a man can keep his belief in himself and in his cause despite all the Dmitry Ivaniches and the Ivan Dmitryches – not only can but *must*! Must! But the answer wouldn't come and the explanation eluded him; and the brakes screeched into his search; and he was thrown against someone who started cursing.

What happened then was a jumble: getting pushed off, stumbling about, being herded together, blows, cries, shouting, '*Davay! Davay!*' There was a bridge, steel, rusted in places; a railroad track running along its centre, catwalks along the sides, low railings; at the other end of the bridge a group of men, armed, helmeted. He walked as in a daze, his soles mechanically seeking the reality of the thick wooden ties between the rails. Suddenly he chuckled as this new idea hit him: there was the bridge, every square inch of it, plastered with memorial tablets like those set into the Kremlin wall, and one of the tablets carrying his name, *Julian Goltz,* and the date, *12 October 1940.* Beyond the tablets he saw the river, rock-strewn, and the men from the other end of the bridge advancing. The answer, he thought. Where's the answer?

And then he thought of Julia, the sleep-flushed face, the curls soft and loose on the pillow. He swallowed, breathed deeply, and broke into a trot.

Shouts. He reached the railing, swung one leg across. He saw the clouds reflected in the water, one white, one pink-rimmed from the hidden sun. The bridge seemed very high.

He wondered from which side the first bullet would come; then he felt it, one huge pain.

CHAPTER 1

She loved this fur.

It was as if it had a life of its own. Julia hugged it about her, nestling in it and feeling the warmth of the coat and the warmth of her body merge. It gave her a sense of being protected, something that went back to dimly remembered times: being tucked in a soft blanket, a cocoon to curl up in, and voices whose tones she no longer could recall whispering forgotten words to her.

The snow, which had been coming down since late afternoon, had stopped falling. It glistened under the arc lamps, turning the street and the parking lot opposite into a silver plain on which the automobiles gliding up soundlessly and turning off to be ranged by green-caped policemen drew curved patterns. People moved over it as if it were a thick rug, converging on the broad sweep of stairs that led to the entrance of City Hall. Through the glass of the door Julia saw the non-committal faces of the two black-clad young men who inconspicuously scrutinised those entering. But even this was part of the festive atmosphere and belonged with the segments of light streaming through the Gothic latticework of the high windows, with the red and gold of the flags set against the crisp, clean white with the swish of the women's taffeta and the rustle of their Chinese brocades as they passed her.

Julia saw Arnold waving at her from the parking lot. He was stepping gingerly so the snow wouldn't get into his patent leather shoes. He wore no hat; indeed, he didn't own one; on the few days when the weather in this part of the world turned really cold he put on the old fur cap he had brought with him from Moscow. His hair was as full as ever; a few years ago it had turned grey at the temples – diplomat's grey, he called it, making of it no more than he did of the difference between her age and his. She watched his progress across the street from which all common traffic was blocked: the policemen, whether they knew who he was or not, saluted him; and a number of the guests who, in view of the hour, had been displaying a sort of well-tempered hurry, paused to greet him: 'Good evening, Comrade Sundstrom!' or 'How do you do, Herr Professor!'

Watching it from the broad steps of City Hall, Julia was aware that some of this was deference, and very German, yet she gloried in it: the city held enough evidence in stone and concrete of *his* right to recognition. She loved him very much at this moment, and not for his success and the general respect he enjoyed, but because he was so certain of himself, so strong and self-contained. And so entirely hers as he came up to her and lightly placed his fingers in the crook of her elbow and told her, 'You look positively radiant, dear.'

The two black-clad young men held the door open for them. He acknowledged the service with an affable wave of his free hand and steered her to the ground-floor cloakroom. The little old woman behind the counter left other people unattended and rushed to take his overcoat and then waited as he removed Julia's fur wrap. With a brief check at one of the huge mirrors on the line-up of his medals on the black of his tuxedo, he offered Julia his arm, and, repeating, 'Positively radiant!' he guided her up the wide, carpeted stairs.

She was conscious of the glances following them, the eyes that swerved from him to her and remained fixed on her. She had intended to be no more than background and tried to control the swing of her haunches.

'Happy?' he asked her.

'Very.'

He looked at her. Did she know how desirable she was?

'Shouldn't I be happy?' she said. 'This is your day!'

He frowned, half irony, half deprecation.

'And there are the lights,' she went on, 'colours, people. There's a difference between an architect's conception and the way a room looks when it's filled with life. That's when you see if you've worked well or not.'

She was a little too eager, he thought – naïve, you might say, like the youngsters who came streaming upon the Party's appeals to break new land in Siberia or rebuild the ruined cities of the Ukraine. It showed the education they had received, always with the common cause, the common goal in view. 'And this,' he, enquired, 'measures up, in your opinion?'

She stopped a few steps below the landing for a slow, sweeping survey. She had done part of the work on the interior designs of the reconstructed City Hall, which had been half demolished by the bombings. She saw the purple lines of the drawings emerge through the marbles and bronzes, but he gave her no time to find her answer; he appeared, in fact, to have forgotten his question – up ahead, their faces creased in frozen welcome, waited the hosts of the evening.

The Lord Mayor, Comrade Riedel, gazed at Julia from drooping eyes; his bluish lips and receding range of chins moved as if he were speaking while he limply shook her hand; his wife remained a pale blotch of face. Then Julia moved on to Elise Tolkening. Dumpy to the point of deformity, her barrel shape defeating the cleverest dressmaker, Elise had held Comrade Tolkening through all those years when other comrades, back from exile or rising from lowly jobs, turned from the arthritic hands and age-lined faces of the companions of their former struggles to marry their secretaries.

'Perhaps, Comrade Sundstrom,' Comrade Tolkening was saying, 'we can find a few minutes for one another during the evening.'

Tolkening had a way of beaming at a person shrewdly, as if they shared a common confidence. This time, the beam included Julia. Her heart gave an extra beat: Berlin had decided! As through a haze, she saw a fresh batch of guests move toward the banquet hall – wasn't that John Hiller among them, the sarcastic mouth, the narrow, boyish shoulders? – had Arnold arranged for his invitation? Then she was swept into the banquet hall and jammed into a mêlée of bodies that, though rooted as if by magic, were straining toward a common objective.

This wasn't her first reception. The initial crush would ease as soon as the official speeches were made and the official toasts drunk; but she hated the undignified pressure toward the long rows of tables laden with saddles of venison, and huge platters of crab meat and smoked ham, and bowls of oranges and bananas that had been imported for the occasion. Arnold, an old hand at public functions, braced himself against an onslaught of uniformed chests and balanced the two glasses of wine he had retrieved. Julia tried to get to him. She felt the corner of the table jabbing her hip. She saw a blue-veined, red-nailed, be-ringed hand scoop up three, four, five oranges and drop them into a large, gold-embroidered bag. Then the loudspeakers bellowed inarticulately, the intermittent crescendos recognisable as Comrade Tolkening's rhetoric. The answering speech of the leader of the Soviet delegation, hidden from Julia by the crowd, was briefer, but not brief enough; a good many people, determined to get their share, had grabbed silverware and plates on which they were piling mounds of food.

A familiar voice spoke of feeding time at the zoo. Julia turned to find Axel Von Heerbrecht grinning at her. What did *he* know, she thought – this spoiled man whose slick commentaries on the radio devastated the actresses of the city's drama theatre. What did he know of the hunger of people, which she had experienced the larger part of her life? . . . how many years was it since the war? Ten, going on eleven. Of these ten, how many had been lean ones? And those people gorging at the tables – how many of them had been stunted not by a few years of doing without but by a lifetime of it!

'Hello there!' Heerbrecht's eyes were roving over her. 'We've organised a niche where you can at least stand without being jostled – Käthchen Kranz, and Warlimont of the Youth Organisation, and your friend John Hiller . . . '

She suppressed a wince. John Hiller had his desk in a studio adjoining hers, but she didn't count him among her friends. 'I had better wait here for my husband,' she said.

Heerbrecht bowed slightly. 'Shall I look for him?'

'Thank you! It won't be necessary — ' Julia saw Arnold extract himself from the crowd, the two wine glasses, still full, in his hands. 'Oh Heerbrecht!' he greeted offhandedly and offered Julia one of the glasses. 'I tried to get here,' he shrugged, 'but I was engulfed and ended up at Comrade Tolkening's table . . . '

Heerbrecht wrinkled his short, stubby nose into a snort. 'Then may I congratulate you?'

Sundstrom was piqued. 'I didn't go there to *sit* at the table; I was thrown against it.'

'You misunderstood,' Heerbrecht said coolly, 'I was referring to the new honours in store for you.'

Sundstrom hesitated. Then he smiled and handed the glass he had reserved for himself to the commentator. 'Cheers!'

'Cheers!' Heerbrecht, face impenetrable, clinked glasses with Julia and smiled back at Sundstrom. After some polite moments, he left with an equally polite apology.

Julia glanced at her husband. The flat taste of the wine still lay on her tongue, and she was afraid that her sense of happiness had become a bit scuffed. Arnold's colouring, perhaps, was more florid than usual, but his calm expression reassured her. 'Shall we eat?' he said.

The rush for the food had abated. The majority of the guests stood about, struggling with the problem of how to hold their plates and simultaneously cut the roast beef. Arnold took a roundabout lane to one of the centre tables. Dispensing greetings and smiles, he threaded his way past Karl-August Mischnick, the poet laureate, who combined the pompousness of a public figure with the dirty skin and noisy manners of a bohemian; past the internationally recognised physicist Professor Louis Kerr, who, slightly besotted, was followed about by his sad-lipped, sapless wife; past Comrade Leopold Bunsen, chief editor of the Party's district paper, whose narrow, fat-embedded eyes winked with deceptive merriment. Meanwhile, from a balcony loge, a regimental band began trumpeting, the red-and-white-striped shoulder pieces of the musicians moving in rhythm to the silver-tasselled conductor's precise baton.

'Arnold?'

'Yes, dear?'

But she kept silent. She supposed that this had to be, and had to be done in this manner; she was part of his life and his life was part politics.

'You'll feel better once you eat,' he consoled.

But the tablecloth was littered with crumbs, drips of mayonnaise, orange peels, dirty dishes; the skeleton of a roast hare, bare but for bits of gristle, completed the melancholy still life. He managed to scrape up some food for her and himself: a spoonful of herring salad, a few slices of wurst, a quartered pickle. 'They'll bring around frankfurters later,' he said. 'And I can tip the head waiter when I find him. The personnel always keep some choice bits in the kitchen.'

'We didn't come here for the food, did we?' she said.

He took her plate, put it aside, and kissed her hand, emotion mingling with an old-fashioned gallantry that somehow suited him. Julia let her hand remain in his. A few seconds passed before either grew aware of the sudden space about them.

She looked up. Comrade Tolkening was beaming at them, flanked by Elise and by two Russians from the Soviet delegation in whose honour the reception was being given. A nondescript young man, probably the interpreter, tailed them.

'Sorry to interrupt, Comrade Sundstrom,' Tolkening gestured

a feigned regret. 'But I should like you to meet the leader of the delegation come to visit us—'

'Oh, I know Comrade Krylenko!' said Sundstrom with a nostalgic smile. 'The years have been kind to us both . . . ' Hands outstretched, he wanted to advance to the red-haired, rotund man whose smooth face had betrayed no reaction whatever to his greeting.

Tolkening stopped him. 'I should like you to meet Comrade *Popov*,' he said pointedly. And turning to the other Russian who stood beside him, dark eyes motionless above deep rings, Tolkening continued, 'Comrade Popov, may I present Comrade Professor Sundstrom, chief architect of our city, and his charming wife.' The interpreter was mumbling along. 'Comrade Sundstrom, as you may have understood,' this was all the riposte he chose to administer after the faux pas, 'has lived for some considerable time in the Soviet Union.'

Julia felt her checks burn. But then she saw that Arnold was extending his hand to Popov and smiling with his usual calm. Popov shook the hand and told Tolkening in Russian, 'I am acquainted with Professor Sundstrom's work.'

The statement, neatly translated, seemed to impress Tolkening. 'So you have seen his World Peace Road? It's our showpiece here.'

'As yet, I haven't had the opportunity,' Popov explained. 'It's on the delegation's program, I am told.'

To all intents, the awkwardness of the Krylenko incident was forgotten. Julia, relieved, listened to Elise Tolkening solemnly expounding, 'This is the street on which Peace came to this city in the person of Comrade Stalin, on his way to Potsdam. That's why we chose it as the first to be cleared of rubble, the first to rise from the ruins, wider, airier, more beautiful and splendid than any street this city ever had, the first street of socialism. That's why we renamed it World Peace Road. Our Karl-August Mischnick wrote a poem to commemorate the day the street's first building was finished. On the suggestion of Comrade Tolkening, the poem was set to music, and choral societies all over the Republic are singing it. I'm sure Comrade Tolkening can arrange to have recordings given to the delegation and a set of photographs that show the changing face of the street . . . '

Popov heard the translation through. He thanked Elise and assured her that the delegation appreciated any information that would help it to get a full picture of the great efforts of the city's working people and their Party. 'As to Comrade Professor Sundstrom's work,' he reverted to his subject, 'I have studied some of the designs he did in Moscow.'

'You're a colleague?' asked Sundstrom in Russian, not waiting for the interpreter. 'Architect?'

Julia wondered at the weariness in his voice.

'Construction engineer,' Popov informed him.

'In the Ministry?'

Popov, the lines sharp on his face, appeared not to have heard. He turned to Tolkening. 'I've always admired Comrade Professor Sundstrom for his many-sidedness. You rarely find so much of it in an architect.'

Comrade Tolkening studied the interpreter as if something beyond the translation should be read from the young man's bland expression. 'Ah, well,' he said then, having made up his mind. 'Comrade Sundstrom?'

Julia knew that the moment had come for the promised disclosure. Everything in her tensed.

Suddenly she felt Elise Tolkening's surprisingly light hand on her wrist. 'Come, child!' Elise said, sympathy in her low voice. 'The men want to be alone . . . '

Like a short, stubby tugboat, she nudged Julia along. Julia didn't know whether to laugh or cry. In the end, gratitude won. There were times when you sensed the woman's personality behind her unfortunate appearance.

*

22

Elise Tolkening dropped her among a covey of officers' wives, German and Soviet, who had been instructed by their men to show an interest in one another. She tried to listen to the stumbling efforts at conversation, but her mind kept revolving about the other thing. For months now, ever since Arnold had told her that Tolkening had mentioned a possible National Prize, she had waited for the decision. Outwardly, Arnold was indifferent; he insisted the prize didn't count – the work did, and he made her feel like a child hankering after a bauble. But it *was* important – public recognition, encouragement! Not only for him. For her, for the entire collective that had built the Road, for everybody, from architect and draftsman down to the hod carriers. There were always the voices you couldn't pin down, denying what was obvious to any person of honesty and good will: that the Road combined the spiritual essence of the people's aspirations with the best traditions of the past and symbolised something noble and worth the struggle.

She saw Heerbrecht approaching, Käthchen Kranz on his arm. Without curbing the slight sneer in his voice, he called, 'You look lost, Julia Sundstrom!' and his free arm gathered her up. She laughed. Everything seemed suddenly funny – the .women from whom she had been carried away. Heerbrecht with his silly nose and his owl-like glasses, Käthchen Kranz: Käthchen wore a towering hairdo and false eyelashes; she was officially permitted to look as westernised as she pleased because with her tap dance routine and her songs veering from the folksy to a sort of baby-voice jazz she was the local personification of what Comrade Bunsen's paper called The Gay Muse.

'With your figure and your looks, Mrs Sundstrom,' Käthchen was weighing her effect on Heerbrecht, 'you should be seen around! . . . You work? You're an architect? You're married? . . . How deadly! I thought that Axel and I could put you in circulation, couldn't we, Axel?'

'My dear Käthchen,' Heerbrecht patted her without relaxing his soft pressure on Julia's arm, 'Mrs Sundstrom has ideals.'

'And I haven't?' protested Käthchen. 'Haven't I launched the true socialist-realist hoopla, also named the Lipsi, and don't I believe in you and Comrade Warlimont and Comrade Bunsen and Comrade Tolkening?'

'People will think you're being sarcastic,' said Heerbrecht.

Julia's amusement ended as abruptly as it had started. She found herself at the niche Heerbrecht had described earlier in the evening. It seemed still occupied by its initial crew, including Comrade Warlimont, blue shirt open at the collar, and John Hiller.

Hiller stepped out in greeting, a half-empty cognac bottle dangling from his fingers. 'I warn you, Julia' – his tongue had trouble with his consonants – 'I will be drunk and disorderly.'

'You will not!' she said more heatedly than she had intended. 'You will behave yourself.'

'Why should I? Give me one good reason, Julia. Because of you?'

'Because you're at an official reception. Because you represent the City Architects' Bureau—'

'The collective, eh?' He squinted at her. 'The rank and file?'

'The collective,' she said. 'The rank and file.'

Käthchen Kranz had rested her hairdo against Comrade Warlimont's fatty chest. Warlimont was slipping her a cognac. Heerbrecht, while not relinquishing his claim on Käthchen, felt sorry for Julia; he hadn't counted on Hiller's becoming belligerent on a little alcohol.

'Why don't you quit acting the temple virgin, Julia!' Hiller resumed. He rubbed his hair; part of it fell dark over his forehead and made his face, ordinarily quite sensitive, appear gross. 'Be your age! Your great Sundstrom will get what he's been pushing for. Warlimont knows it. Everybody knows it. Comrade Tolkening was sure to see to that – if only so as to have drippings of

24

the glory grease his own curly head. So . . . !' He pressed the bottle on her.

'No, thank you!'

His eyes grew moist. 'Julia,' he pleaded heavily, 'have a little drink. Just one. With me. On that prize. On all those little turrets we stuck on all those roofs, and on all those little columns we pasted on all those fronts . . . '

He saw her face go white. He dropped the bottle. It crashed.

'Oh, Julia . . . '

Warlimont was saying something about the dragging in of Comrade Tolkening's name, and that cadre files should be checked regularly. Käthchen Kranz made clucking noises of regret at the rift in the *Gemütlichkeit*.

'Heerbrecht,' demanded Julia, 'will you please take me to my husband?'

*   *   *

Sundstrom lit a fresh cigarette from his old one and stuck the butt, glowing end downward, into the moist earth of the potted palm. The palm was part of an arrangement camouflaging the kitchen entrance; it gave a semblance of privacy to the talk he sought with Krylenko.

'Trust Tolkening to make the most of it.' His Russian was flawless, but his irritation brought out his accent. 'And I can show you the item in the paper: it said you would head the delegation.'

Krylenko shrugged. 'It was a last-minute thing. Do you suppose I liked the change?'

Sundstrom crumbled the dried-out tip of one of the palm leaves. 'I really should try to get to Moscow, if only for a few days. One loses touch. Here everything is second-hand . . . information, policy . . . There've been quite a few changes recently, haven't there?'

'Things change constantly.' Krylenko had the sort of eyes that always seemed to look past you. 'That's in their nature.'

25

'Pavel Grigorich!' Sundstrom curbed his impatience. 'An earthquake is also a change. But I can try to run from its epicentre.'

Krylenko laughed. 'I don't think we're having an earthquake or are going to have one. We couldn't afford it.'

The statement was given in the authoritative tone that Sundstrom appreciated. But the fact remained that Krylenko, judging by this delegation, had slipped from the position of authority. 'Who is this Popov?' Sundstrom enquired. 'Where does he come from?'

Krylenko's red brows rose imperceptibly; Sundstrom's thought sequence had been apparent. But Krylenko kept it light. 'Oh, Popov knows his field. You needn't worry on that account.'

'Do I need to worry?'

'You?' Krylenko snorted. 'At this distance from the epicentre?' Krylenko stopped: the smile, so apt, had tempted him into admitting something he wouldn't admit even to himself. 'I told you there won't be anything like an earthquake,' he said angrily. 'We may be having some slight subterranean tremors in the establishment; they occur when a huge structure resettles into place.'

This sounded sensible, and Sundstrom wanted to believe it. The great man, on whom so much of the structure had rested, had been dead almost three years; and though a number of his top aides had lost their footing in the shuffle and had tumbled from their pedestals, nothing demonstrably basic had occurred, none of those upheavals that did no one any good.

'But tell me, Pavel Grigorich,' he said, 'couldn't your tremors indicate a more violent process, a rumble in depths that no responsible person would wish to see stirred up? Why was this Popov suddenly placed over your head? Who is he?'

'Well,' Krylenko moved uncomfortably, 'the man has had a raw deal!'

'Oh, one of *them*!'

'Yes, one of *them*, Arnold Karlovich.' The shadow of a palm leaf threw a striped pattern over Krylenko's flat, unemotional face. 'They're dribbling back into Moscow. I don't know from where, and I don't want to know. I never asked Popov, either. They get their allotted footage of space, and a job, if they're well enough for one, or a sanatorium cure . . . '

'But that's—' Sundstrom checked himself. 'I mean, you'll never be able to keep this quiet. It'll seep through. There are too many of them.' He noticed that his hand was shaking and that Krylenko had seen it. 'Haven't you thought of the consequences?'

'I?'

'You. Everybody.'

'You know whom I ran into a week or so ago,' Krylenko appeared to be changing the subject, 'right on Arbat?'

Sundstrom lit another cigarette. If I don't watch out, he thought, I'll become a chain-smoker. Krylenko was patently evading an answer to his question although it touched them all, the whole movement, worldwide.

'There, on Arbat, looking at a store window – Daniel Yakovlevich.'

'Wollin? . . . ' A hoarse whisper, as if a sudden blight had settled on Sundstrom's vocal cords.

'Your friend Daniel Yakovlevich Wollin,' confirmed Krylenko, 'in the flesh. Snow-white, but otherwise chipper, as far as I could see. Well, he's the sinewy type; they bear up best. He immediately asked about you.'

Krylenko was observing him. Sundstrom felt dizzy. The blood had rushed from his head to his heart; Krylenko must notice his pallor.

But Krylenko continued evenly, 'I told him you were alive, and where you were living, and that you had married the little Goltz girl. At first Daniel Yakovlevich refused to believe she was that grown-up; then he did a quick count of the years – those he had been away, and those a child needed to become a wife. He was very happy for the two of you, and he said to greet you.'

'Thanks.'

Sundstrom was grateful that his voice functioned again. The National Prize, Tolkening had said in the presence of Comrade Popov and Comrade Krylenko, was a sure thing. And now Daniel Wollin, out of nowhere, being so happy and sending him regards. A great evening this was turning out to be. 'It certainly is a miracle!' he said.

'Miracle?' asked Krylenko. 'What did you expect?'

Arnold Sundstrom swallowed. What had he expected? His blood, which had filtered back into the tissue of his brain, again threatened to rush toward his heart. Nothing. He had expected nothing; he had never thought things through to that point. Mercifully, his mind had always been able to switch off in time.

'Why should I have expected anything?' Sundstrom said finally. 'He disappeared, that was all. What could I do? Or you . . . or anyone?'

Krylenko kept a non-committal silence.

'Did Wollin tell you of his plans?' Sundstrom went on asking. 'What happens to those people? Can they do what they please, move about, talk with whom they like?'

'Why, yes, I suppose so . . . '

Krylenko sighed. His patience was wearing thin. He had been through this long ago. When he walked behind the catafalque, from the Hall of Columns, through the grief-stricken stillness of the Moscow streets, he had seen it coming. They had played Beethoven over the loudspeakers. Beethoven!

'But why?' This came deep from Sundstrom's chest, like a rale. 'Why, Pavel Grigorich? Whom does it help to pull the skeletons out of the closet? The Party? The Soviet Union? Socialism?'

'Calm yourself, will you! What would you want us to do, maintain the old abuses?'

Sundstrom frowned.

'After all,' Krylenko gestured tiredly, 'most of those people were entirely innocent.'

28

'I've never known you to set personal ethics above the good of the revolution . . . ' Sundstrom bit his lip. He was going too far. Krylenko, even if demoted, remained a power. 'Of course, injustices must be liquidated!' he covered up hastily. 'But a Wollin here, a Popov there – how many of them, I ask you, appearing in how many places! . . . you'll hear whispers first, then talk, then it'll be shouted from the rooftops. And then what is to become of . . . of the others?'

'Personal ethics,' Krylenko quoted back at him. 'Injustices. Skeletons – I wish, Arnold Karlovich, you would cut this subjective approach.' The corner of his mouth twitched. 'Yes, subjective. Matters will be handled with discretion I hope – no rush, no fanfare: who wants to point a finger at himself? But it *has* to be done.'

He paused; Sundstrom kept on braiding one of the thin strips of palm leaf around his fingers.

'Because it's historically necessary!' Krylenko answered the unasked question. 'Because along the old track lies collapse – economic, moral, political. If you'd stayed on in Moscow, you, too, would have felt it. The world's in change, our own world; the only force that held it in its groove . . . He. But we carried Him to the mausoleum. I tell you, Arnold Karlovich, more lies were embalmed on that marble slab than a withered body in a marshal's uniform. As long as He was around, everything was clear and easy, every equation worked; and if it refused to, you damned well knew how to make it work. And now—'

He broke off.

'But these aren't your problems,' he consoled. 'No anxiety is called for on your part; nothing like it ever happened here, in this neat little Republic of yours . . . I see your wife coming.' And slightly bowing his head to her, 'My dear Julia Julianovna, you must forgive me for depriving you of your husband.' He nudged Sundstrom. 'Don't you think you might tell her?'

Sundstrom managed to give his eyes sparkle and to make his

29

face light up; all warmth, all joy, he took both her hands in his and said, 'I've got wonderful news for us, wonderful!'

'The prize?'

'Yes, dear, the prize.'

The snow had turned to slush. The car skidded. Sundstrom cursed.

'We should have had the driver,' Julia said, nestling at his shoulder and watching his broad, capable hands on the wheel. He handled the car expertly, but he was tired, tense and tired. 'We could have sat holding hands.'

'Let the man have his evenings,' he grumbled. 'I don't like people calling themselves socialists who let their drivers wait about while they consume cold chicken and push their careers.'

Julia nodded. She loved this in him: he hadn't forgotten who paid the bills, and though he was a public personage with a right to a certain share of the public funds, he scrupulously avoided using a penny of them for his own comfort, his own benefit. Some men grew lax with sudden luxuries thrown their way – not her Arnold. Being a Communist, he once told her, long before they were married, is a way of life. He had explained to her that corruption included using your power for anything outside the precise purpose for which it was given to you. Cases of this sort brought out the fighter in him: he had the cook in the work's canteen fired for short-changing the workers on the butter allotment, but he also had the director of a building trust brought to court for padding the figures on his plan fulfilment and pocketing the bonus. He would personally collar the sales-man in a state shoe store for selling a shoddy pair of boots to a bricklayer and demand the money back or else, but he didn't shy back, either, from speaking out in Comrade Tolkening's presence when one of Tolkening's chief aides assigned top priority to his typist for a two-room apartment with bath so the two of them could conveniently sleep together. A Communist,

30

he had impressed on her ever since she could think politically, must be intolerant of the sluggish mind, the lukewarm heart, the *laissez-faire*, the one-hand-washes-the-other, and the let's-let-it-ride; your thought and your action must be as clear-cut and scrutable as the drawing on your board. He wasn't always loved for his principles, but his sense of justice and the integrity of what he said were respected.

'The prize,' she said, 'do you think it'll be for just you, or for the collective?'

He hadn't heard her. His eyes were fixed on the road ahead or on something even farther off than the reach of the headlights. His abstraction, his frown, brought back to her a tinge of the discomfort she had felt, the unpleasantness in the niche, the little turrets and the little columns – the collective, represented by John Hiller, of all people!

'Arnold!'

He started. 'Yes, dear?'

She repeated her question, and heard, to her own dismay, her slightly nagging tone. She saw his hands grip the wheel. 'That's all academic,' he was saying. 'The award is months off! And what difference does it make? The money?' He flared up. 'The world's in change – and you worry about *that* . . . '

She felt cold despite the fur wrapped about her, the nice, new fur coat he had given her for Christmas. 'What have I said that's wrong?' she asked, and continued like a recording with the needle caught in the groove. 'You were so happy about it and so was I – I don't understand – Don't you want to tell me?'

He patted her knee. 'Sorry,' he said. 'I forgot.'

His eyes no longer held that distant look.

'What did you forget?' she asked.

'That you're still a child in more ways than one.'

She winced. 'I don't think I said anything particularly childish.'

'I didn't say you did. Do you remember what I told you about the prize?'

31

'That it wasn't the prize that counted but the work.'

'Ah.' He nodded. 'You see?'

'But haven't you *wanted* it? People even say you pushed for it . . . '

'They do?'

Her lips tightened. People – that was John Hiller.

'Would you mind telling me who said that?'

'I heard it said. In passing.' She was lying now, and not doing it well. Why on earth should she protect Hiller? 'People say all sorts of things, especially against persons who're above their gossip. Against – against great persons.'

She meant that. He *was* great: as an artist, a thinker, and a human being. But again he wasn't listening. His eyes were riveted on the far end of the white cones that the lights cut out of the road; his face worked, his jawbone twitched.

'We're home,' he said finally. 'Thank goodness.'

While he garaged the car, Julia went inside and switched on the light. Frau Sommer, the housekeeper, apparently had gone to bed; but the radiators were still hot, the steam in the hallway radiator singing cricket-like; a mechanic would have to come. Where would you get one and how long would it take him to do the job? It was the little things that ate at your nerves. She hung up her coat and, for a moment, thoughtfully caressed its sleeve.

Slowly she walked down the hallway and up the stairs. The house was kept in warm tones, a sombre warmth, dark reds prevailing; the stillness about her was overwhelming. She was very conscious, at this moment, that it was *his* house: he had chosen it among three or four offered him; he had picked the colour scheme, the panelling, the carpeting, the chairs, settees, and tables, and had the bookshelves and wall closets built to his design. They had left their Soviet furniture behind, taking with them only the rugs – Arnold had collected some very fine Bokharas – and their *objets d'art*: Georgian rams' horns trimmed with silver, Palech boxes with their shimmering miniatures on black lacquer, hammered brass from Samarkand, silver-work from Tula, and paintings – a Levitan among them showing a brook in the spring, water gurgling about the last ice that clung to the roots of the shore, and about the white of the birches that luminescence of bright leaves yet to be. The paintings made her homesick, forestscapes with the light streaming diagonally through the trees, those unmistakably Russian trees, infinitely tall, in an unmistakably Russian forest; and a picture of an unmistakably Russian street, deeply rutted, leading past unmistakably Russian houses half sunk into the ground, the wood about the eaves caved like filigree.

She stopped at the thin whimper. Then, running up the rest of the stairs, she rushed to the child's room, tore open the door, and with a comforting 'Julian!' gathered the boy into her arms.

She turned on the light bracketed above his bed. She felt his ribs shaking against her breast, the pumping of his heart; the eyes, dark grey, velvety – her eyes – were wide with the after-pain of fear.

'Does it hurt, darling? Where?' Any illness of his threw her, and there wasn't one that passed him by: mastoid, measles, mumps, a conspiracy to keep him pale, underweight, and susceptible.

'The man!' he said, tensely. 'Julia,' he had called her Julia from the first and they had never corrected him, 'the man came again.'

'What man?' There's no man here.'

'The man with the red hat. He has long arms and no face. Sometimes he has a big suitcase, to carry you off in . . . ' He swallowed a sob. 'He comes every night. Well, not every night, but lots of nights.'

'There's no such man. Nobody wants to carry me off. Nobody wants to take me away from you. You've been having a bad dream.'

'I've been awake all the time. And I can see him with my eyes closed, too.'

She felt his forehead. It was sweaty. 'You don't see him now, do you?'

'No. But he was here. Julia?'

'Yes?' She was tucking the blanket about him.

He freed his arm and held on to her hand. 'Why does he wear that red hat?'

'But if there's no such man, how can he have any kind of hat?'

'A red hat, with no brim.'

'If you were lying awake, and frightened, why didn't you call Frau Sommer?'

The child sat up. Julia turned. Arnold had come up behind her, all smiles, benign, solicitous. He held out his arms. 'You're awake, son?'

She told him of the dream, the man with the red hat without a brim.

'Where does the child get such ideas!' he grumbled. 'I must have a word with Frau Sommer.'

Julian was huddled against the backboard, the blanket pulled up to his chin. Arnold Sundstrom sat down on the side of the bed, gazing at his son. Why had the child moved away from him?

The boy, jawbones twitching as his father's sometimes did, shook his head. 'I want the man to go away!'

Shoulders hunched, Sundstrom leaned forward. 'Only one person on earth can make him go and never come back. Only one person is strong enough for that.'

The child looked at his father, interested but sceptical.

'You,' said Sundstrom.

The blanket slid from the boy's shoulders. His wrists, narrow, stuck out from his pyjama sleeves; he slowly moved his thin, long fingers. An ache sat in Julia's heart like a foreign body.

Sundstrom put the blanket around him and gently made him lie down. 'You're stronger than the man,' he was saying.

Julian was listening, still with a certain reserve. 'He's too big.'

34

'I've had to fight people all my life,' Sundstrom went on, stroking his son's small hands, 'and some of them were twice even ten times bigger than me.'

The child nodded; he seemed to be waiting for the nostrum that would make him expand to the size needed for the struggle. Julia thought back: when she was a child and Arnold sat down at her bedside, everything in her had strained to him, her heart had opened up, grateful for any caress, any proof that she wasn't alone.

'A person's strength depends on what he fights for and whom he fights for,' Arnold Sundstrom coiled the boy's fingers into a fist. 'See? . . . When the man comes, the man with the red hat and no face, whom are you going to fight him for?'

'Julia,' said the boy, closing his fist tightly.

He said it almost without tone. Julia saw the veins, bluish, shine through the thin white skin of his neck; she saw Arnold rise, an odd expression distorting his mouth; she knelt down at the child's bed, covering his face with kisses and at the same time gripping Arnold's hand as if she were trying to form the link between the two of them, her husband and her son.

'Will you sleep now, darling?' she asked gently.

The boy reflected, a tiny line creasing his brow. 'Will you leave the door open?'

His glance indicated the door he meant: the one connecting the parental bedroom to his. Julia saw Arnold motion in irritation; but she said, 'Of course, darling!' and, getting up and patting the child once more, she shook her head appeasingly at her husband.

She took Arnold's arm as they descended the stairs. In the living room, she sat him in the big armchair at the fireplace.

'You mustn't give in to the child's every mood,' he stated.

She dimmed the lights, went to the corner cupboard that opened into a miniature bar, and poured two large brandies.

'If you count on closing the door later,' he continued, 'forget it. I know him. He'll wake up immediately and lie awake the rest of the night. He won't whine; he won't protest; he'll just lose trust in you – and in me.'

She sat down on the armrest, handing him his glass.

He stared at the logs that lay, gnarled and dry, on the andirons. The fireplace, though it worked perfectly, was rarely lit; we never have time for ourselves, he thought, and when we have, we can't get away from our problems. 'You may believe me,' he said. 'I have more experience than you in bringing up a young person, and my methods have shown results.' His fingertips explored her thigh, which, taut against the broad armrest of the chair, was firmly resilient.

'I had no intention of closing that door,' she said, clinking her glass against his and holding the brandy on her tongue. The distortion of his mouth was back again, that odd expression. 'You aren't jealous of Julian?' she asked, with a tiny laugh.

'You don't help him by holding open the door to our bedroom.' He was angry; his insistence was making an issue of nothing. 'Man with no face and a red hat!' he said. 'What next?'

She opened his black tie, unbuttoned the starched shirt-front, and slid her hand along his collarbone and down his chest. He raised his face; his lips had softened. 'You were very beautiful tonight,' he smiled. 'Everybody commented.'

She kissed him; his lips tasted of brandy.

'Very beautiful,' he repeated, slipping her dress off her shoulders. Her shoulders were smooth, warm, young; he drew her close to him; a faint tinge of the perfume she had put between her breasts had remained through the evening; her skin excited him, the shape of her breast, the salmon pink of the nipple set off against the pastel of the flesh. It was those breasts budding that, years ago, had first made him aware of his changing feelings toward her – a hot summer's day, outside of Moscow, shortly after the war; Julia wearing nothing but a cotton shirt and shorts, climbing barefoot over the mossy rocks in the bed of a brook; slipping; a scream; his helping her out, holding the frightened girl protectively; and the transparency of the cotton shirt wet through and through. He had been thoroughly shaken – what was he, a monster? – and there was the holy obligation he had toward Julian Goltz and Babette; until he reasoned it out: she no longer was a child, was becoming a woman, breasts, hips, shanks, hair growing in her armpits and on the mound that began to swell at the onset of her thighs. She, too, sensed the change that had come about; later, she as much as admitted this to him, though she was too young, of course, to understand the complexities of their relationship. She became coy and reticent; the uniformed life of school and pioneer organisation helped, the unattractiveness of it, the puritan uprightness, all straight surfaces; but underneath: the nights, the turmoil! He travelled much in those years as a member of a commission of experts on the reconstruction plans of the cities destroyed; he was relieved each time he could leave her and unhappy the moment he had left; he longed for her, the features of her small face that seemed to have grown more delicate at each return, losing their childish proportions; he was jealous, of teachers, coaches, fellow students, Komsomol secretaries; he dreamed of her, of tearing the starched white collar, the cheap brown cloth of the unflattering school uniform, and sweated in anxiety at his own desires. He dreamed of her, too, when he was back in Moscow. They lived in one room; a large one, true, with use of a common kitchen and a bathroom in which two of the other tenants parked their bicycles. They slept separated by a ramshackle clothes closet and a curtain suspended from a steel wire; he could hear her every move in her bed, her breathing; he couldn't help seeing her in her moments of partial undress, or brushing up against her as they sat down at table or moved a suitcase or as they came in the door or went out. She continued playing the good little girl, but she couldn't know the full depth of the pitfalls, and so could switch from the loaded silences between man and woman to the brightly meaningless chatter of a near-child. Until one day, on a stopover in Riga, someone offered him a second-hand party dress, black, low-cut, with sequins. He bought it, and in Moscow he bought the accessories: silk stockings, high-heeled shoes, a small, but fine, necklace. That evening, he told her to take off her school uniform and put on his presents, and undo the two pigtails that stuck away from her head, stiffly, and comb out her hair and let it fall to her shoulders. He waited behind the clothes closet, listening to the swish of the taffeta and to the rustle of the silk as her fingers smoothed the fit of the stockings. Then, as he stepped through the curtain and saw her standing before the mirror above the washstand, her elbows raised as she patted her hair in place at the back of her head, his mouth went dry. Dragging his feet, he stepped up behind her, put his hands to her ribs, and softly, softly brushed his lips against her temple. He had almost no voice as he said, 'I shall marry you, Julia,' adding, hastily, a sort of reassurance to Julian Goltz and Babette, dead these years, and to the law, 'as soon as you're *fully* grown-up.'

And now she was grown-up and the mother of his child, and still in some ways very much as she had been then. He kissed her breasts. 'Julia?'

'Yes, dear?'

'I've wanted you all evening.'

This wasn't quite true; a number of matters other than making love to his wife had been on his mind: World Peace Road, Tolkening, the prize, Krylenko – and Wollin. But now he wanted her.

'I've wanted you, too.'

This wasn't quite true, either. She had been restless, nerves quivering; there had been the soft warmth of the fur and her joy blazing in to nothing; the niche with its blatant rivalry between Comrades Heerbrecht and Warlimont – for Käthchen Kranz, and the outbreak of insults from John Hiller. She had wanted – she didn't know what. But now she wanted him.

With a twist of her torso, she helped him to slip her clothes down to her hips. His eyes caressed her – the curve of the flank the seashell smoothness of the skin taut over the muscles, the grace of her, the youth, the sensuousness.

He levered himself up from the low cushion of the chair, then lifted her, one arm about her waist, the other underneath her knees and carried her to the couch set against the opposite wall. Easing her down, he again gazed at her, thinking: the miracle of it, happiness; whoever would have believed that happiness could grow out of all that had been, but there it was; she moved slightly, raising herself so that, fingers clumsy, he could strip away her dress and underwear and stockings, and she lay there, nude, every hollow familiar and yet a challenge. Happiness, he thought again; wife; young wife, child, position, work, money; and with a sudden stab of fear that took his breath away his heart felt the threat to this.

'Arnold?'

'Yes, dear?'

Gently, 'I love you.'

'Yes, dear.'

He threw off his clothing, not caring where things fell. Eyes riveted to her body, he was aware of his flabbiness. He pulled in his stomach, straightened his shoulders. Diplomat's grey, he thought. And thought: I shouldn't be thinking at all now; not of me, not of hanging trousers across back of chair, not of happiness, not of Wollin; what sort of happiness is it when you must think of it as happiness in the abstract; abstraction is the death of everything round, flesh-toned, three-dimensional.

She laughed softly.

He shivered. 'What're you laughing at?'

'Not at anything.' She had raised one of her knees and lay, relaxed her right arm behind her head. 'I laughed because I feel so . . . so wonderful. May I not? . . . '

He threw himself beside her. She felt his kisses, the strength of his shoulders, his hands on her, the tangle of her nerves, and

39

thrilled to the force that racked her. Her fingers found the back of his head and she pressed his face to her, closer, closer – and her hands went limp.

'I'm sorry,' he said.

She didn't understand. She lay quite still. Questions milled in the back of her mind, refusing to sort themselves into sequence and meaning. And weighing down everything a horrible sense of shame – her nakedness the sign of some unfathomable guilt, her passion shrinking into itself, her palms moist with the cold sweat of panic.

'Forgive me, Julia,' he said miserably.

'What is it?' She looked at him. 'Was it my fault?'

He cowered before her, the blanket that had been lying at the foot of the couch half pulled across his groin. She reached for the other end of the blanket and covered her legs and belly.

He forced a laugh, 'These things will happen, you know . . . ' He was relapsing into his fatherly tone and despising himself for it; but he couldn't help it, not now. 'We're just lucky it hasn't happened before.' He must talk, fast. When had things started to go wrong? When had that burrowing started behind his forehead, and that fear, fear of failing that brought failure, an unbroken circle, vicious, a trap? 'There's mind, nerves, glands. Sex is the sum total of them all. If one thing's disturbed, none of it works properly. But the worst is post-mortems, harping back to it. Let's forget it. Sleep.'

Julia listened as if she were hearing his words in retrospect. He had sounded calm, self-confident. 'Is it that I was . . . ' she hesitated, looked down at herself, pulled the blanket higher, 'too eager?'

'Why don't you try to understand . . . ' This was a mild reproof. 'It could be any of a thousand things. Julian insisting on our keeping that door open, or that awkwardness with Popov, or the car skidding. Human complexities . . . whoever can get to the bottom of them?'

He broke off. Piffle, he thought. It's me, I'll lose her. And, groaning inwardly, he cursed that nameless thing that he had buried for so long and that cropped up on Arbat and was threatening his life, his career, his very potency. And thought of the cruel irony of a vengeance that used as its instrument his own young wife, the creation of his own emotions, his compassion, his atonement.

He put his face to her naked shoulder. She was slowly caressing his back. He spoke into her shoulder. 'No, it isn't you. It's neither of us. It's this day, the excitement of it, the strain. I was simply tired. It'll pass.'

'What did this Comrade Krylenko tell you?'

He raised his head. She kept caressing him; her face seemed utterly at peace. 'Why? Nothing,' he said. 'Just local Moscow gossip.'

CHAPTER 2

The long table was stacked with papers – blueprints, sketches, line drawings. Each time somebody dug one out to underscore an argument, they fell into a confusion of ashtrays, pencils, notebooks, paraphernalia.

The arguments had been kept to technical points, as usual on these mornings; Arnold held ideological lectures to a minimum in his work meetings. He once had explained why to her: in a good collective, he had said, principles should be clear; no need to thresh out aesthetics and theory when you want to decide the length of a crossbeam.

Then why, frowned Julia, was he breaking his rule? Why, in the middle of replying to a perfectly legitimate, factual question from Waltraut Greve, was he laying into capitalist architecture and its modernism? Waltraut's voice and her thin lips and the air of superiority with which she compensated herself for a flat chest did irritate you, but that couldn't be Arnold's reason now.

He had risen from his seat at the head of the table and was pacing along the designs tacked to the wall – designs that were the opposite of the bare, cubistic forms he was condemning.

'Not one architectural idea to their functionalism!' he exclaimed, his eyes searching, testing the faces that lined the conference table. 'The same façade in structure after structure, naked, a desert stretch from ground floor to roof, with not an oasis for the eye!'

The decadence of it, he explained, lay in the denial of the human need for beauty, for dignity. A building was more than a container; it represented permanency, a monument people set to their ambitions, dreams, ideals; only a class like the bourgeoisie, which no longer had any ideas and was deeply permeated by the sense of its own futility, could advertise their ugly slices of concrete as an achievement.

'The work of the bourgeois architect, of course . . . ' he stopped pacing and smiled ironically, 'is greatly facilitated. He has no need to think about aesthetic division and balance, or arrangement and form of windows, ledges, balconies, gates, ornamentation . . . '

He had ended, triumphant, chin jutting. Most of the heads along the sides of the table nodded in agreement; Waltraut Greve, whose question ostensibly had unleashed the torrent, held hers lowered as if a blessing had come down over it. And he was in splendid form, Julia thought, after a night in which sleep had evaded him. She had been awake herself, listening to his irregular breathing, his restless heaving from side to side, his half-suppressed sighs. She had waited for him to call to her; he hadn't; she had waited to crawl to his side of the bed but had kept to her own, staring through the dark at the square of deeper dark that was the open door to the child's bedroom.

Yet, at the breakfast table, she saw that the night had left no apparent trace on him; the shadows under his eyes were no deeper than usual. He was even-tempered, friendly, joked with Julian and Frau Sommer, and seemed to have entirely forgotten the previous evening, the reception, the prize, the homecoming, and what followed.

Julia pulled her thoughts back to the meeting. Arnold had resumed his place at the head of the conference table and was dealing with deadlines, supplies, who was to attend to what. He conducted the meeting with his customary ease, allowing time for proposals and criticism, yet keeping everyone in his assigned place and within the limits of his function in the collective. Everything went smoothly; the hurdles enumerated by the men in charge of the various sections under construction were no greater than on other days, and traceable to the usual shortages of material; you would have to telephone, find substitutes, arrange, improvise; had Marx, Engels, Lenin, or Stalin ever promised that the road to socialism would be straight and well paved? He had the golden touch, that approach to a situation, even the most addled, which made it appear less difficult, its solution within grasp; and he dropped the news of the prize – it would be for the collective – so casually, so self-effacingly, and yet with such psychological timing that you thought you could physically feel the flagging spirits soar.

Still, that tinge of discomfort hovering inside her refused to dissolve. He had his people so well in hand; work was progressing satisfactorily; he had the certainty of the prize – why, then, had he felt the need to defend what needed no defence, to praise what had proved its value a thousandfold, to advocate the architecture that was socialism's own: from the streets and squares of Vladivostok on the shores of the Pacific to the last building site of World Peace Road, here in this city? Was he fighting the shadows of his long-buried Bauhaus past – those late twenties with their now-scorned notions of art and architecture that had led to intellectual bankruptcy? Or what shadows?

Julia realised that he had moved on to criticism of himself. Self-criticism, he liked to say, keeps the rust off your mind; he demanded it from everyone in the collective, but he set the example as he did in everything he demanded of others.

'It's my fault,' he was saying, his nervous energy again forcing him to get up and pace. 'I am to blame that the preliminary plans for the extension of World Peace Road are not yet finished. We've talked about it often enough, we've discussed the problems ahead . . . the unity we must create in an ensemble in which public buildings and residential structures open upon the city's centre with its multi-storey tower to house Party and district government, and its plaza for marches and demonstrations, tangible expression of the people's power . . .'

He paused to catch his breath. His gaze rose above the heads

44

along the table, into the distance, as if he were seeing the finished ensemble and the vista of cupola-crowned tower and tribune and people swirling down the plaza, banners fluttering, small children perched on shoulders to glimpse the great leaders and organisers of socialism. Julia knew the vision; he had described it to her, his voice vibrant; sketched it for her, his head close to hers; the road, the plaza, the tower assuming dimensions under his capable, broad-fingered hands.

The vision vanished at the chance encounter of her eyes with John Hiller's; angry at herself for not brazening out the query in them, she looked down at the table, then reached for her pencil to try recapturing on her notepad the big lines of the project. ' – should have organised – work on preliminaries – ' In patches, as through fog, Arnold's words reached her. ' – plans – last night – after pleasant news – reported to you – Comrade – Tolkening enquired . . . ' Julia forced herself to listen. 'Comrade Tolkening asked about those plans. He's solidly behind us and our ideas, but we may not be the only ones submitting plans. You must understand: World Peace Road and its extension are no longer solely a local street. We have put it on the map. It has become a national issue; it is being studied and examined, east as well as west; it has grown into a symbol of socialist re-construction and a leading example of our aesthetic conceptions in architecture.'

He stopped his pacing, his skull framed by the detail design of the capital of a column. 'It was embarrassing, I can tell you, to hear all this from Comrade Tolkening and to be unable to reply, 'Tomorrow, Comrade Tolkening, you'll have the plans on your desk.' We know Comrade Tolkening and his interest in archi-tecture and his understanding for the difficulties of the creative artist. But just because he is that sort of person, he has a right to demand the greatest effort from us. I repeat – whatever our failing, I am at fault. But I plead with you to help me. I am sure that, together, we can work it out . . . '

45

Everything in Julia impelled her to jump up, wave her hand, pledge her enthusiastic support. But again, her eyes caught John Hiller's; fish eyes, cold, not a spark of emotion in them. She determined to have it out with him as soon as possible: any man without sense for another's heart bared to him, for the sweep of a moment that should carry you forward, was out of place in a collective dedicated to constructing the future. Or perhaps, in this Germany, people always held back, gauging what was in it for themselves.

'So, in the name of all of us,' she heard her husband say, 'I promised Comrade Tolkening that we'd have the plans for him . . . ' he paused ' . . . within ten days.'

Silence. This was more than the silence that commonly followed the main speaker's words – the physical drain involved in a ten-day effort to ready the architectural designs for nearly a mile of street was frightening.

A tiny gesture of Arnold Sundstrom's. 'Yes, Voukovich?'

'We can get up some designs. There's no doubt in my mind' – as always when Voukovich was agitated, a heavy Croat accent larded his German – 'in less than ten days, if you'd want us to, Comrade Sundstrom!'

Julia saw the quick change from thoughtful determination to smiling approval on her husband's face; he seemed surprised at such quick support from an architect as conscientious as this young Yugoslav. Perhaps, thought Julia, Edgar Voukovich was showing his gratitude: his father, ex-partisan leader and Yugoslav attaché in one of the eastern capitals, had chosen to side with the revolution when Tito reneged; he had died shortly after, leaving Edgar unable to return to Yugoslavia. Arnold, maintaining that men must be judged on their merits and nothing else, had taken the young man on to his staff despite tongues clucking against any Yugoslav.

'But Comrade Sundstrom,' Voukovich was continuing, 'didn't you exhort us only the other day to think of fresh approaches to the project – approaches even more representative of the new time and the new man creating it?'

The smile about her husband's lips seemed stony; his lids were half closed; it was the only sign Julia detected of wariness.

'We would like to find those new approaches,' Voukovich said. 'We, too, are conscious of our World Peace Road having more than local significance – but within ten days? You can't develop new ideas in that time. You can only rehash the accustomed, reshuffle old elements, repeat and regurgitate.'

He seemed justified. Julia tried to, but couldn't, avoid John Hiller's oblique glance as he settled back in his chair and began pulling at the lobe of his ear – a habit Julia had observed in him, not very pretty. She knew that Voukovich roomed on the same floor as John Hiller in a half-bombed-out house on the southern outskirts: had they arranged this backhanded attack on Arnold between them, Voukovich fronting for John Hiller? Hiller might have known of the ten-day deadline; he had been at last night's reception . . .

'Regurgitate!' she said icily. 'Wouldn't it be better if we applied ourselves to the job with all we've got? There are no easy solutions, ever.'

'Julia!' he said gently. Arnold Sundstrom had come halfway around the table. 'Voukovich has a perfect right to his doubts and to voicing them. I shall always welcome an honest opinion.' He resumed his pacing. Voukovich's objection gave him a chance, he said, to expound on the difference between the New and the *New*, dialectically. The new element that socialist architecture searched for was not the sensational, the outlandish, the experiment in form, the new-at-any-price; the aim was not to shock, but to accord with the sense of beauty innate in the working people, and to help further and develop it.

His words were like a warm bath; you sank into them, drowsy, unresisting, a tiny thrill passing through you from the back of your skull to the base of your spine.

He had stopped. He was gripping the backrest of John Hiller's chair, addressing himself over the young man's head to all of them but to her, Julia felt, particularly. 'The conception of the New I have in mind does not grow out of some architect's whim, or a striving to be noticed, or a need to sell ideas. It rises organically out of the great experiences of mankind – what Goethe, in his *Faust,* called the harmonies of the spheres. This concept derives from the works of geniuses like Michelangelo, from our German Baroque masters, and from Schinkel, who caught the pure lines of the ancient Greeks and translated them into proportions we can grasp. But it also comes from the motives of our folk art in which the plain people express themselves and from which we all can learn . . . '

His eyes were shining. 'This road we are building, these palaces, as certain people say with half sneer and half envy . . . ' He permitted himself one large gesture. 'We're not building for ourselves. There's a patron for whom we are working and to whom we're responsible . . . '

The people, whispered Julia. The reservations that had been plaguing her were gone. She once more abandoned herself to that sweep of spirit instilled in her from her earliest day by storybook and radio voice, by teacher and organiser, and by the man who gave her love, father's love, lover's love: how fortunate we who, for the first time in history, are free to build for the people; being of them and for them, part of their creative effort, their struggle, their dream.

Arnold's manner had changed again. He was talking lightly, familiarly, as if taking everyone present into his confidence. 'I recall a small incident – but typical. When we exhibited the scale models of the first section of World Peace Road and people came to examine them and give us their comments and suggestions, I overheard a plain, simple woman saying, ' "But are these houses for ordinary people like us? . . . " ' He winked at Julia, fellow worker, fellow conspirator. 'I'll confess that, for a moment, I was stupefied. Then a man, a building worker to judge from his denims, answered her. "Why, ordinary?" he said. "We're not ordinary . . . " and he looked at all of us standing about the models of our dreams " . . . we're extraordinary people!" '

He sat down, lit a cigarette, and inhaled deeply. The punchline of the story still held; he had this knack of using the right phrase at the right time. Julia was proud of him, with a resurgence of her feeling of the night before when she had watched him cross the snow-covered street to the salutes of the police. No, her pride was more impersonal now: it encompassed sharing his work, being an architect like him, creative, able to convert a wisp of fantasy into the neat, harmonious outlines of a blueprint and make this blueprint, in turn, take on dimensions in stone and steel and glass that would last – some architects' dreams had outlasted the ages.

The wave of optimism that she had churned up for herself broke as the talk along the table penetrated her mind: general agreement with Comrade Professor Sundstrom's pledge – some cheery yeses – very few buts, and these on questions of detail. She had an ear for the undertones. It was as if everyone was going through some kind of ritual: slow, solemn motions following old-established rules, words whose meaning had long grown obscure. The ritual petered out. One more voice, like a straggling Amen – then, finish – except that Arnold sat there lapping it up, smiling broadly, the lion having feasted on the antelope, letting the afternoon sun bake his sleek skin, not a growl, not a claw. Didn't he notice?

And the thing she had been suppressing all morning burst into consciousness. She suddenly understood: he was trying to live down last night. That's why he had been impelled to lecture on the fundamentals, condemning the feebleness, the decadence, the lack of creative ideas in others. That's why he was forcing himself and his collective to an almost impossible

49

task instead of reasoning with Comrade Tolkening for an extension of time.

Abruptly, he closed the meeting.

Julia was one of the last to leave the conference room. The air, stale with tobacco smoke, lay heavy on her; the white light of the fluorescent tubes cast a pale haze over the disarray of abandoned chairs. Waltraut Greve was scurrying about, gathering the papers that littered the table, rolling them up, bundling them. Julia felt the glance of the myopic eyes, hostile, disagreeable.

The hallway, semi-dark, was a relief. There were the bulletin boards crowded with outdated announcements, photos of honoured workers, a yellowed editorial. The studios, as the cubicles were euphemistically called, lay behind a provisional wall, rough planking interspersed with doors loosely hinged and closing badly. Sounds of voices and movement, muffled, from all along the hallway; the barracks-like structure afforded no privacy, but at the moment Julia was glad for the nearness of people.

She slowed her steps. Her own studio was a few doors down the hallway, cosy and with a few personal touches as far as the sobering presence of drawing board and filing cabinet and reference books permitted. She should be going there, to get together the bits and scraps, the notes and drafts she had made on Arnold's suggestion, and partially in collaboration with him, of the extension project. Maybe, if you put them all in some system and sequence, you had a basis from which to proceed – and maybe again, nothing; just repetition and regurgitation, as Voukovich had termed it.

She could hear Voukovich from beyond the planking. He was laughing; not an unpleasant laugh: full-throated, from the heart. Happy fellow, to find something to laugh about with what was facing them! Or someone had told a joke, John Hiller probably; he had an arsenal of jokes, corny mostly and some quite cynical, though she knew she was spared many of them: she was the boss's wife and, politically, too true to the line to be held worthy of the real beauties. Hiller actually was talking; she couldn't understand what he was saying, but he seemed to be enjoying himself; his words were entwined with guffaws; someone was slapping his thigh.

Resentment rose in Julia. The echoes of the lectures and reprimands of her lifetime collected within her and became a moral necessity; what during the conference had crossed her mind as a likely idea became a must. With three or four long steps she was at the door to Hiller's studio.

The two started up as she tore it open. Voukovich, at the drafting table, still held the thick pencil; next to him, only half visible, lay a large book, open, and the beginnings of a draft, vertical projection, in perspective – view of a road with the first buildings partly sketched in.

Hiller was the first to regain composure. He reached over, closed the book, title downward, and nonchalantly rolled up the sketch.

'Secrets?' she said from the doorway.

'Beautiful Julia . . . ' Hiller knocked the paper roll against the palm of his left ' . . . we have our secrets.' His eyes grew thoughtful. 'We do not wish to burden your pretty little mind.'

Voukovich silently offered the chair on which he had been sitting and held out his pack of cigarettes.

She sat down and crossed her legs and saw that Hiller was studying her knees. While she accepted a light from Voukovich and blew out the first curl of smoke, she pulled down her skirt.

'Beautiful Julia,' said Hiller, 'we are at your disposal.'

'You were revolting last night,' she said. 'Making a show of yourself and pulling me into it.'

'I'm disconsolate. Broken-hearted. I shall go down on my knees to you.' He made a move as if he were actually going to kneel, but stopped halfway and turned to her, voice raised. 'Don't you see I really am! – disconsolate, I mean. Why do I drink? Why do I

51

behave like a sot? Three guesses. Because of you! . . . you! . . . you!'
And, sentimental once more, 'Ah, beautiful Julia . . . '

'You're a fool,' she said.

'He *is* a fool,' confirmed Voukovich. 'But even fools suffer.'

Julia killed her cigarette though only a quarter of it was smoked.
'He's been talking to me like this ever since he joined the City
Architects' Bureau. I don't know what kick he gets out of it.' She
looked up at Hiller. 'I'm not Waltraut Greve or any other of your
girls. I'm a married woman, with a child. I am Frau Professor
Sundstrom.'

'Frau Professor Sundstrom.' Hiller put aside the paper roll. 'I
happen to be in love with you.'

She took up the roll and was about to open it.

'No, please!' Voukovich reached for it. 'I mean it. It's not
finished. It's not even properly begun. It's . . . a joke.'

A motion of her hand held him off. 'I'm becoming *very*
interested . . . ' She hesitated. Voukovich's lips twitched in embarrassment; John Hiller looked at her curiously, something
provocative in his remarkably light, hazel eyes.

Julia had a premonition. She could let the matter slide, replace
the roll on the drawing board, say a few non-committal words,
leave – and all would be as it had been: no complications, no
heartache, not a crack in the smooth surfaces. But she wasn't
that sort of person; if you wanted to build a new world you
couldn't shy from the unknown. And last night precluded
retreat: somehow things were no longer the same after last
night.

She did return the roll to Voukovich, but that was a gesture.
'I've wanted to talk with you anyhow,' she said. 'The two of you.'

Voukovich nodded, resigned; John Hiller was again gazing at
her legs.

'Listen to me!' she said angrily. 'You're easily the two most
talented men on this collective. Don't you see the obligation you
have?'

'Beautiful Julia,' John Hiller bowed with a grandiose sweep of his arm, Shakespearean. 'We'll do anything you ask of us.'

'You'll not frustrate *me*!' she countered. 'I'm serious about this. I have the work at heart.' But she felt a helpless rage fill her throat. Please, dear God, she thought, don't let me bawl now, not in front of these reprobates.

'We haven't refused you a thing,' Hiller said kindly, 'have we, Edgar?'

'I can't forget the days' – the flutter of emotion was in her voice – 'before all this was built, when there was nothing but rubble, the remains of houses. And we called on the people to help. We showed them the first drafts of World Peace Road, a few lines only, the rough of an idea, and we asked, "Won't this be beautiful?" . . . Remember, John?'

He leaned against the drawing board, arms crossed, shoulders hunched, and frowned. 'I remember.'

'And the people came – voluntarily, after work. By the thousands.' She paused. This hadn't been so long after their return to this country, and she remembered herself at Arnold's side, in the floodlit moon-landscape, with people like black ants climbing over the ruins, working away with pickaxe and chisel, passing the salvaged bricks from hand to hand, cleaning them, stapling them. This, too, was Germany; these, too, were Germans. 'Where have there ever been architects,' she asked, looking from John Hiller to Voukovich and back, 'building on such a foundation?'

They were silent.

She turned her hands, palms up, as if to say: that's all; I've made my point; it's up to you. The last trace of irony was gone from John Hiller's face; it had grown soft and resembled, suddenly, a small boy's, listening to a fairytale. Voukovich was fingering his pencil; he blanched a little as she picked up the drawing, unrolled it, and gave it a first glance.

'But this is . . . ' she interrupted herself, squinted to get the full impression of the perspective ' . . . this *has* got something! Sweep . . . proportion . . . '

'Has it?' Voukovich's voice was strangely small, toneless.

Waltraut Greve came in. She dumped a bundle of rolled-up drafts on top of the filing cabinet and stood, the reflection on her glasses hiding her eyes.

'Have a look at this, Waltraut!' This, though Julia told herself that no support was needed, and certainly not from Waltraut Greve. 'It's a rough – but can't you feel the possibilities in it? This grouping here, with the colonnaded front in the centre . . . '

Waltraut Greve held the drawing to her face. Julia noticed the girl's short, chewed-off nails and frowned. Waltraut never committed herself if she could help it; she was wonderful at applying a small detail, a rosette, a panelling; she was a batik printer more than an architect.

'Believe it or not, Waltraut . . . ' she laughed awkwardly ' . . . I came here to give the boys the needle . . . '

Waltraut replaced the drawing. It slowly curled into a roll and lay pointing toward the large oblong of the book.

'Ten days,' Julia was saying. 'Nearly a mile of street. It needs this and that and the other thing . . . I'm ashamed to admit, John . . . ' A blush crossed her cheeks. 'After last night . . . but here it is. You started, and it has such promise. May I take it along – to Arnold?'

She toyed with the roll, then with the book. Her fingertips, nervous, found the edge of the bookmark. She got up. She finally wanted to see what was between the worn brown covers of that tome. She noticed Voukovich blinking, John Hiller growing tense. 'My God,' she said, half anxious, half annoyed, 'what's this new secret?'

John Hiller placed his hand on the book's back cover, holding it closed. As he did, his body pressed against hers.

For a moment book, table, walls faded. There was only this awareness of the touch, the pressure. Julia's knees went soft.

He withdrew quickly. 'Beg pardon,' she heard him say, hoarsely.

Then things returned to focus. She wondered faintly if Vouko-vich or Waltraut had noticed anything. I must find a crutch, she thought, something to busy fingers and mind. I'm a married woman, with a child at home, Frau Professor Sund-strom – suddenly going aflutter at a male brushing up against me. Absently, she had opened the book, at the page marked. Unseeing, she gazed at the double-spread illustration.

'I told you it was a joke,' Voukovich repeated, painfully apologetic. 'I warned you. Why don't you women ever listen?'

She was conscious of Waltraut's glasses, no longer blind, the eyes behind them watching her. Julia shook her head, trying to clear it. The lines on the double-spread picture began to connect, took shape, fell into perspective. She deciphered the caption: *Design for Reconstruction of Charlottenburger Chaussee.*

Again those watchful eyes. Waltraut was like a toothache that radiated from your jaw to the last convolutions of the brain. John Hiller had pulled his head between his shoulders as if he stood in a cloudburst. Charlottenburger Chaussee, thought Julia, lay in West Berlin. Voukovich was still making dejected noises.

Julia spread out his drawing and held it next to the double page in the book. He hadn't even bothered to add anything. Hands flying, she leafed to the title page; the paper, heavy, glossy finish, slipped from her fingers.

'You don't need to bother,' she heard John Hiller say hoarsely. 'This book is the famous *Neue Deutsche Baukunst* by Herr Albert Speer, Hitler's chief architect. I found the thing in a second-hand bookstore. The Ministry of Culture boys forgot to clean it out. I thought it was quite instructive.'

'I hate you,' said Julia, resentment at what had been her glands' reaction blending with her angry frustration at having let herself be trapped. 'This is . . . ' she pointed at the drawing ' . . . vicious!'

'Why?' asked Waltraut Greve.

Why? thought Julia. Because it was Nazi. Anyone knew . . . knew what? Had *she* known?

'Why?' Waltraut repeated, her voice grinding at Julia's nerves. 'Because it is copied? What isn't? Michelangelo, the German Baroque masters, Schinkel – didn't your own husband, less than half an hour ago, give us a whole list of people from whom to copy?'

'Herr Speer isn't Michelangelo. Herr Speer is . . . ' Julia broke off. She stared at Speer's design for a reconstructed show street in a reconstructed victorious Nazi Berlin, at the grouping with the colonnaded front in its centre.

'What does it matter who Speer is – or was – ' Waltraut stood, flat, angular, relentless 'as long as it fits . . . '

'*What* fits?'

But the question was pure despair. And Waltraut knew it. 'This,' she shrugged toward Voukovich's copy, 'and that . . . ' with a vague motion of her hand in the direction of World Peace Road beyond the walls of the cubicle, the office, the barracks.

'That's a lie!' Julia pulled the sketch close to her, almost tore it. She searched for the flaws she must have overlooked, for the ugliness that must have escaped her, for the horror that must be embedded in it somewhere. 'This is tainted!' she insisted.

'Where?' asked Waltraut. 'It's a big street with big buildings; pompous, maybe, but representative.'

She didn't say of what, and Julia didn't enquire. She sensed the joy Waltraut Greve felt at laying her out for the men to sneer and laugh at: the joy of the woman ill-endowed at jabbing the knife into a body with good curves. And she was defenceless: you needed only to select a few elements from Gorky Street and the Kremlin crenels, plus a cornice or two from old German peasant houses in nearby villages, mix them in with this Charlottenburger Chaussee, and you had a genuine Sundstrom Road with the National Prize built into the perspective.

Julia felt her nails digging at her palm. No, this wasn't all. It couldn't be. She hadn't lived a lie, all these years, nor had Arnold, nor all those professors with whom she had studied in Moscow and who had taught her the principles of aesthetics and how to differentiate between right and wrong, good and bad. There was another side to it. There must be.

'Julia,' Voukovich was ruffling his hair 'you mustn't take this to heart. I'll tear up the damned thing—'

'You won't!'

'It's *my* sketch . . . ' But he made no move to take it. He looked at John Hiller as if expecting a cue; as none came, he said, 'The point is, Julia, that architecture is amoral. There are ugly buildings and those that for some reason please us – all other values have been read into the thing.'

'It is un-Marxist,' Julia said heavily, 'to separate form and content. Socialist architecture has socialist content; Nazi architecture . . . ' She couldn't finish her sentence. Speer's Charlottenburger Chaussee and Sundstrom's World Peace Road – she was caught if her theory held.

'But beautiful Julia,' John Hiller leaned against the filing cabinet, the corner of his mouth curled, 'form is secondary, sort of superstructure, isn't it? And we know what time it takes for changed forms to develop analogous to changed content . . . '

He had emphasised the *we*, including her. Yet she suspected him: he had used all the right terms, but were they in the right sequence? 'You mean to say everything depends on who lives in a building and who works in it . . . '

'Exactly.'

' . . . and who owns it.'

'Yes.'

Julia nodded. She could bring some examples of her own to support that point of view – say, the uniforms of army and police that closely resembled the Nazis'; yet it was a proletarian army and a workers' police – but did she have to like the uniforms?

'Edgar?'

57

Voukovich looked up.

'You said you wanted to tear up your sketch.'

'Yes, Julia.'

'Would you let me have it?'

His eyes questioned.

'I want to show it to Arnold.'

Waltraut Greve laughed.

'What for?' asked Voukovich. 'To get us in trouble?'

'But if I hadn't seen this,' Julia nodded at Speer's design in the big book, 'I would have shown it to him with joy in my heart. Now . . .'

John Hiller grinned, pulling at his earlobe. 'And if he finds out that you came to him with a heart not full of joy but of ulterior motives?' Before anyone could stop him, he was back at the drawing table, grabbed the sketch, and tore it to pieces.

Julia saw the bits of paper flutter into the wastebasket. It looked final, an incident closed; no more to be said. She wished it were that way. But there was last night and its residue of uncertainty. And now her work had become questionable – her work, the collective's – Arnold's. Hadn't Arnold known of this likeness between the lines and planes that formed under his wonderful hands and the conceptions of the glorifiers of Auschwitz and Buchenwald? If he did know, how could he explain it? And if he didn't, how come the resemblance, and what were its meanings?

She turned and left.

John Hiller moved to follow her, but Waltraut Greve held him back. 'Your heart-throb's in a mess there,' she said, 'eh?'

He looked her over, from the bangs on her forehead to her low-heeled shoes that made her feet appear flat and large. She knew he was seeing through her clothes and she blushed: blotches of red on unhealthy white.

He was on the telephone as she entered his studio. He seemed animated; what the voice at the other end of the wire was saying

58

obviously pleased him; he looked at her, eyes bright, welcoming; a wave of his hand invited her to sit down.

Julia remained standing. He continued talking, apparently unaware of the distance she was leaving between her and himself.

'At four o'clock,' he said, 'we'll take them through . . . completed buildings, building sites, planning department, studios; everything will be prepared and waiting for them, you may rely on that.'

She knew that tone: slightly metallic and yet smooth; assuring, authoritative; the range deep. He was talking to someone he considered his equal or slightly above him, someone with status.

He was listening now. Then he said, 'You may tell Comrade Popov not to worry. We'll show him the real thing, not villages à la Potemkin. And he may talk to architects, technicians – to *any*one.'

He stressed the *any*. Julia was hearing the undertone. Was there obsequiousness? Or was he bending over backward to be democratic?

He was laughing now, his good, old, manly laugh. 'No, no, no, Comrade Tolkening! I know you didn't mean to imply that. Nor did Comrade Popov. I just wanted to avoid misunderstandings. Not on your part, Comrade Tolkening, of course. On Comrade Popov's.'

He raised his brows, listened. So the delegation was coming this afternoon, thought Julia; there would be commotion enough. Arnold was glancing at her, winking: you and I, we have our job cut out for us now. She would have to be charming and factual, hostess and fellow worker; she was good at that, he had told her more than once.

'Popov?' he was asking. 'Ah, I've had certain information.'

Julia was suddenly conscious of her hands. They were sweaty, sweaty and empty. John Hiller had destroyed the sketch, all right; but the book was there, *Albert Speer, New German Architecture*, on the drawing board in his studio. Why had she left it? Why if she had wanted to confront Arnold with the Charlottenburger Chaussee – World Peace Road kinship?

'I'll tell you when I see you, Comrade Tolkening!' He was expansive now, his inner peace and contentment showing through every pore. 'One of *them*, yes, naturally.' And after a few seconds, 'Thanks again. It was good of you to have called me. Goodbye.'

He returned the receiver to its cradle. His eyes narrowed, his smile evaporated. 'Julia?'

She fidgeted.

'What's wrong, Julia?' He rose and came toward her. 'Something upsetting you?'

She raised her face to him. From his worried eyes he spoke his love for her, shaming her to the roots of her being. 'I . . . I had come to ask you—'

'What, Julia?' His voice was vibrant, warm.

Her mind's eye was frantically searching for the points of similarity between that execrable drawing in Herr Speer's book of Nazi trash and World Peace Road, creation of the man who stood before her and whose whole heart seemed to be going out to her. Those points were escaping her now, though she was sure they hadn't been imagined. She wished she had brought the book and was glad she hadn't, both. She wished she had thought more about the matter instead of rushing into this like a fool. She wished she had had the sense to deny the slander: Who were they – Voukovich, Hiller, and that misfit Waltraut Greve – and who was Arnold?

He took her into his arms, held her. She felt his hard chin against her cheekbone; he was kissing her eyes, first one, then the other. 'I know . . . ' he whispered. 'It hit you . . . '

She sighed deeply, as after a crying jag. Thus he had held her when she was a child, and had dissolved her apprehensions.

'This thing last night,' he resumed, 'I know. It's nothing a woman gets over lightly.'

He felt her wince, held her more tightly. 'Help me!' he said.

60

She nodded into his shoulder. He smelled of something tangy: an eau de cologne she had given him for Christmas.

'A little too much has hit me these last days.'

The moment of closeness was passing. 'Yes, Arnold,' she said.

'I may not look it,' he smiled, 'but I, too, have nerves.'

'Yes, Arnold.'

His fingers pressed against her back; then he released her. 'About that delegation,' he said. 'You'd better go home and change.'

'I'm going home,' she said, 'but to bed.'

'I thought you wanted to help me?'

'I don't feel well. That's what I came to tell you.'

'I see.'

He returned to his desk and sat down behind it. Then he buried his face in his hands. She saw his hair, full, wavy, the diplomat's grey at the temples. She saw the skin at the back of his neck, lined, red, leathery, and his broad fingertips supporting his buckled forehead. She saw these details with frightening clarity and thought how much one didn't see ordinarily, even on those closest, and how much one didn't know, and wasn't it better one never knew?

CHAPTER THREE

The Sunday paper ran the full keynote address of Comrade Tolkening at the district party conference. A two-column picture in the upper third of the front page showed Comrade Tolkening, his wife Elise, and the chief architect of the city, Comrade Professor Arnold Sundstrom, gazing at the top of a near-finished building on World Peace Road.

Sundstrom leaned the paper against the coffeepot and studied it while buttering his slice of bread.

'He looks as if the Holy Ghost was about to descend on him,' remarked Julia from the opposite side of the table.

'Comrade Tolkening?'

She nodded.

'That's the camera angle,' Sundstrom said. 'The photographer should have known better, or the editor. If I were Tolkening, I'd have them both fired . . . I don't cut a bad figure, though,' he added. 'What do you think?'

'You're photogenic, dear,' she replied.

He threw her a quick glance. Was she being sarcastic? That would be something new. But she was calmly wiping a smear of soft-boiled egg from Julian's chin and sending him off to play.

'Listen to this,' he said, 'from Tolkening. "Architecture, like every art, will fulfil its social function only if it directs itself toward forming people imbued with socialist culture and love and understanding for the arts, and toward shaping their surroundings in the most consummate manner." He lifted the paper away from the coffeepot, placed it flat on the table, pulled a pencil from the breast pocket of his Chinese silk lounging jacket, and marked off the quote. 'Interesting, eh . . . ' And, after a pause, 'Most cogent.'

Julia kept stirring her coffee. These last weeks, she had almost succeeded in repressing the image of the double spread in the book on John Hiller's drawing table; only at rare moments it re-emerged, its lines growing fuzzier each time. This was one of those moments. 'I wonder,' she mentioned uncertainly, 'if Comrade Tolkening really *knows* that much about all the subjects he speaks on.'

Arnold Sundstrom pocketed the pencil. He supposed it couldn't be helped: in her Soviet past, Julia never asked that kind of question; but this wasn't some province behind the Urals; this was Germany, East Germany, Republic with wide-open borders toward the West from which the doubts came flooding into even the stoutest hearts. He would have to watch her; a crack like that from her, if expressed in the wrong company, would net him no end of trouble; the education of a young mind was a permanent job; you never finished with it.

'With Comrade Stalin it was credible,' she went on, 'but it takes a genius always to supply the correct answer to problems of agriculture or linguistics, politics or art.'

'It isn't that difficult,' he snorted ironically. 'Every one of us has the guide that Comrade Stalin utilised to determine his approach – the teachings of Marx and Engels and Lenin, dialectical materialism, a whole body of economic, political, and philosophical thought that serves you and me as well as Comrade Tolkening.'

He took a large bite of his slice of bread and chewed and swallowed. She observed him. The grouping with the colonnaded front in the centre interposed itself between her and him, a transparency through which his large, florid face shone like part of the design. 'How is it, then,' she asked, a little uncomfortable at her insistence, 'that Joseph Vissarionovich was always right, and never the others? Didn't they have that body of thought at their disposal? So there *is* something to the genius of a man . . . '

Arnold Sundstrom thought of the dark eyes of Comrade Popov

scrutinising him from above deep rings, of the deceptively kind questions during the guided tour through World Peace Road – nothing tangible, and yet a threat – and decided not to commit himself on the genius issue. 'There are advisers, specialists . . . Part of being a leader is picking your advisers. As regards architecture, I'm happy to say that to a certain extent Comrade Tolkening relies on my judgment.'

He waited. She appeared satisfied; at least she said no more on the subject. The trouble was that he no longer could gauge all of her reactions; this was new; it dated back to the night of that damned reception; a number of things had mounted up and affected it; it was a fine example of the leap from quantity into another quality, dialectics in actual operation, in operation against him, Comrade Sundstrom.

The doorbell rang. He was almost glad of it, though he hated people breaking in on his Sunday morning peace. 'Who do you think that is?' he asked, careful to keep to his note of annoyance.

She listened. Downstairs, Frau Sommer was shuffling toward the door; Frau Sommer had arthritic feet and wore felt slippers that took on the shape of her crippled bones. Julia straightened her napkin and folded it with quick, efficient moves; she wasn't keen on having John Hiller and Voukovich and Waltraut Greve drop in today, as they had on the Sundays when work was being rushed on the extension drafts for Comrade Tolkening; the designs, done up as prettily as the brief time permitted, had been handed in; the usual house fronts, proportioned symmetrically, with windows and doors corresponding to their mates up the street, but with some new conceptions for cornices, and with a bas-relief frieze that symbolised the people's new attitudes toward work under socialism, running below the fourth-floor windows of the central building of the extension project. And nothing had been heard about it since. Wasn't it always that way, rush-rush, everything complete within ten days,

64

or five, or three, and then wait. I'm becoming a malcontent, she thought; and with a last, angry pressure, her hand put the final crease into the napkin.

Frau Sommer appeared in the door. 'Telegram, Herr Professor,' she said.

He hastily rose and took it from her and said, 'Thank you, Frau Sommer.'

Frau Sommer shuffled off.

Julia, relieved, lit a cigarette. Telegrams came all the time: Arnold Sundstrom received telegraphic invitations to out-of-town meetings and conferences, to plenary and not-so-plenary sessions.

'Arnold!'

He had lost colour.

She dropped her cigarette. 'Is it bad news?'

He waved her off, managed a tight laugh. 'Good news,' he said. 'Very good news.' He ran the back of his hand across forehead and eyes. 'Wollin is coming.'

'Wollin?'

'Daniel Yakovlevich.' He had forgotten that she might not remember. Or couldn't remember, thank goodness; she had been so young. 'Daniel Wollin was – is an old friend of mine,' he corrected himself.

She took the telegram from him. *Arriving Sunday 5.45 p.m. Central Station,* it read. *Can you meet me.* And the signature. It had been sent off in Moscow three days before. God knows in what office it had been held up.

He was at the large glass door that led to the terrace and was staring out at the landscape – trees bare, the ground littered with last year's leaves, the smoke of some invisible factory in the distance refusing to rise. It was one of those dismal Sunday landscapes that occur between February and March: the winter gone but spring not yet arrived, everything in mute suspension. It wasn't true, he thought, that Friday is the unlucky day of the week; Sunday is. On the seventh day the Lord was finished creating this world and took a rest, and that's when the whole misery started.

'An old friend,' she was saying, 'from Germany? From the Soviet Union?'

The next question would be, he thought, *Why haven't I ever heard of him?* And the horrible thing was that whatever he said might turn out to differ from Wollin's version: one couldn't constantly hover about the two of them, censor every word, observe every gesture.

'Daniel Wollin,' he said, still staring at the uninspiring grey beyond the terrace, 'was a fortunate man.'

'Was?' she asked.

'Was . . . is . . . what's the difference?' And thought: fortunate – by God! To be able to pop up on Arbat, in the year 1956 – with that history! – 'Everything came to him,' he said. 'There are such people. They don't go after the fish; they don't cast their net; the fish follow *them,* big fish, little fish . . . ' He turned and faced her. 'That's true genius!'

Julia had lit another cigarette and was waiting. She had on a pair of tight-fitting slacks and a turtleneck sweater, black and silver, which emphasised her figure and lent a deeper hue to the warm grey of her eyes. His hands twitched.

'We were both students at the Bauhaus in Dessau,' he said, controlled. 'But he was the favourite. Gropius, Mayer, Mies van der Rohe – they all prophesied a great future for him . . . '

He shrugged. Considering that this moment had been hanging over him like a cloud ever since Krylenko had told him of the encounter on Arbat, he wasn't doing too badly.

'And he's been in Moscow,' she said, 'since when?'

'Of course,' he went on, 'you must consider that Gropius and the whole Bauhaus school were formalism pure and simple. But they did know talent when they saw it.'

He glanced at her to check the effect of his story; he rarely had talked to her of his Bauhaus past, and then only in terms that stressed his remoteness from the aims and methods of that time.

'And you haven't seen him in all these years?' she asked uncertainly. 'Then why has he picked us to come to?'

'Because he's got nobody . . . ' He stopped. And broke out, 'Can't you let me tell anything consecutively! It's hard enough . . . ' He searched his pockets, couldn't find his pack of cigarettes. 'Could you . . . ?'

She lit two cigarettes, one to replace her own, which had gone out, forgotten, in an ashtray; the other for him.

'Thanks,' he said as she placed it between his lips. Then, holding her wrist, he pleaded, 'I'm sorry. But you mustn't interrupt with questions. If you must question, do it after you've heard me through. I'll tell you as much as I can. As much as . . . '

Again, his words remained hanging in midair. Why, why, why, he kept thinking. Why had they done this? Why not let the dead stay buried? He would never be through telling; there was no end to it once you started unravelling that tangle, and every inch of the thread was dipped in blood.

'Don't you want to sit down?' she said, gently freeing her wrist.

'I'm sorry,' he repeated, this time apologising for his grip. I'm making this much too dramatic, he was thinking. Keep it light. Light and unobtrusive. An old friend coming to visit; a bit sudden, true; but what of it? 'I guess I will sit down. It's been so many years. Let me figure – yes, sixteen. 1940, I saw him last. You were a child . . . ' Why bring that up, he thought; a bad year for her, too; for all of us. 'I couldn't even tell you now,' he said, 'exactly what he looked like.'

He did know, though; every detail of face, stance, gesture, that last time he saw him; the voice, soft, calm, hardly changed from the ordinary as he said, They'll be coming for me, Arnold, tomorrow at dawn or day after tomorrow; you won't believe any of the charges, will you; we've been friends for so long; you must tell the German comrades, perhaps they can do something, explain, intervene, take matters to the higher-ups – And all this without once raising his voice; Jesus in Gethsemane showed more temper; just those eyes, sad – no, bitter – and his fingers, long, sensitive fingers, lacing and unlacing.

'What I had to work for,' Sundstrom said, 'in the sweat of my nights, Wollin grasped instinctively. He had an amazing eye for proportion, for a new solution . . . surprising at first, but once you studied it, the only logical, the only possible solution . . . always, of course, if you based yourself on Bauhaus fashions, which at that time I did.'

He seemed to be talking to himself as much as to her; Julia suspected that the visit of this Daniel Yakovlevich Wollin, of whose existence she was learning at this late date, was somehow linked to the complex of events, reflections, and emotions that had started to dog her life and her husband's.

'Daniel Wollin,' he was saying, 'made a Communist out of me.'

She frowned slightly. 'He did?'

'You, Julia, were born a Communist.' He laughed. 'Not every-body is!'

She had always seen him: Arnold Sundstrom, hewn out of one piece of rock. That he ever could have been something else, and that there was someone before him who had fashioned him – reasonable though it sounded – required thought. And this someone was now emerging from the dimness of that past, casting ahead of him the shadow of new unrest, new questions.

'This, too, had come to him easily,' Sundstrom said, the nostalgic tone of retrospect tinged by the faint echoes of an old resentment. 'Intellectual problems stumping other people for months or even years seemed to solve themselves in the face of his logic. Modern architecture, he used to tell me, requires modern industrial methods; modern industry requires a modern form of society; that's why architects, modern architects, are predestined to be Communists.'

'At the Bauhaus?' she said, returning to the table and lifting the cosy off the coffeepot.

And this, he thought, is only the beginning! 'There's no contradiction,' he said, repressing his annoyance. 'At that time we honestly believed that glass and steel and concrete and straight lines were the expression of the spirit of our day.'

He watched her pour the coffee. She was settling herself comfortably, damn it, attentive to his every word and intonation: the interrogator in his own home, at his own table, in his own bed.

'One lives and learns,' he said. 'Soviet architecture was the great teacher. Actually, ours was a leftist deviation, petty bourgeois radicalism; the working class is not destructive; it takes over what is of value in past achievements and moulds it to its own purposes . . . ' He paused. He must find something strong, final, settling the issue once and for all. 'Today I know,' he concluded, 'the artificial cubist constructions derived from the teachings of the Bauhaus professors are in essence negative and soulless, anti-humanistic . . . and repugnant to the healthy instinct of our working people.'

You couldn't put it more damningly. But it was hard to argue against buildings – they stood there. Wasn't it Frank Lloyd Wright who once said there was only one thing to do when an architect made a mistake: grow ivy? Ivy! The solution of a jester who all his life dealt with some moneyed eccentrics wanting their homes to be different from the next-door neighbour's; the *bon mot* of a wit who never had known a wrong approach in the arts to cost a man's head. And how much better off the other arts were than architecture! A symphony was ended after its last squeak, a poem could be forgotten, a painting burned – but the mute testimony of stone and brick might embarrass their author for decades. Ivy? – Dynamite!

And the worst was that Julia wasn't responding to his words as she used to, though his reasoning was as good and his emphasis as marked as always. She was nodding agreement between sips of coffee, but she was not fooling *him;* he had a sixth sense for these intangibles, and especially with her whose mind he had shaped. What was she saying? . . .

'And Wollin, too? . . . '

Arnold Sundstrom did some rough calculating. The train was due at 5.45 in the evening. Provided it was on time, he was left to face seven hours and thirteen minutes of this, with the likelihood of worse to come.

'Wollin, too, changed his views on the Bauhaus style?'

'Mannerism,' he corrected. 'Bauhaus mannerism. Oh, I suppose he did change them. You couldn't help changing them once you were in the Soviet Union and saw what was being done there and got into the sweep of things. Unless,' he shrugged, 'you wanted to be an outsider and starve.'

He noticed the slight turn of the head, the sideways glance. She had always heard him speak of people being persuaded by the authority of the Party, the weight of its arguments; never by hunger. I'm slipping, he thought – too many balls to keep spinning: Wollin's fate, Julian and Babette Goltz's, mine, hers; and all this juggling at the brink of no return.

'In fact,' he laughed again; he was laughing too much, 'it was he who kept me from starving more often than vice versa. We both escaped to Prague after Hitler came to power. I had only the pittance paid by some refugee aid committee while he got jobs . . . small ones, but jobs nevertheless – and I must say he loyally cut me in on most of them. I worked on the technical details while he would do the overall design. I never saw a man put over his ideas with so little effort. To hear him talk to one of those tight-fisted Czech businessmen who wanted to have his storefront remodelled or to a moneyed Prague Jew torn between the idea of emigrating to Palestine or adding a second storey to his villa was an experience: he'd throw out a hint or two and soon they would tell him exactly what he thought should be done. This I learned from him . . . a good architect must be a

70

master psychologist. Under capitalism, that is,' he added, 'under capitalism. In a socialist society, the relationship between the architect and his client is entirely different. The client is the people!'

He said this with a certain amount of solemnity, as if he had an audience of at least a couple of dozen persons instead of Julia, who had been brought up on that thought. He felt a little pained though she once more nodded her obedient yes. Then, to take the curse off the thing, he sighed a nostalgic 'Prague . . . For two young architects with little to do, an absolute paradise. Gothic, Renaissance, Baroque, rococo, Empire – in any variety and com-bination, intermingled and dovetailed, jewels, jewels, jewels . . . I tell you, Julia, once this is over – I mean, once we've welcomed Wollin and made him feel at home and set him up in his work somewhere, you and I will go for a wonderful, long stay in Prague and we'll retrace, together, the walks I took in those days; just the two of us; Frau Sommer is perfectly capable of taking care of Julian; a second honeymoon, not our first. We never had a real honeymoon, Julia; those few days in the borrowed dacha can't quite count . . . '

'Prague . . . ' she said. 'I only remember big trees, and chestnuts on the ground, brown and shiny in their burst, prickly shells, and the sound of water rushing over a weir, and sunshine as far as I could see, and my mother taking me by the hand, at least I think she was my mother, and the man next to her my father. I can't recall their faces, isn't it terrible?'

He had a thin, high ringing in his ears; the blood, probably, that was draining from his brain, leaving him slightly dizzy. He had known that this would come; he had sought to avoid it as long as he could: Wollin led to Goltz as inevitably as the brook to the river. Then he felt a sudden rush of pity for her – she at least had harmed no one. He came to her and with trembling fingers stroked her hair, and in a voice hoarse with ill-controlled emotion said, 'Oh, Julia, Julia . . . we've got to find one another again . . . '

71

She held his hand to her cheek. Find one another, she thought, and said, 'You're very good to me. You've always been.'

'But is that enough?' he said, letting a sigh follow the question. Three years, he thought; she must have been about three when she picked those chestnuts in Prague; how much does the brain of a three-year-old retain? Or for that matter of an eight-year-old? She was eight, just about, when those boots came tramping down the hallway in the hotel. Sundstrom frowned: a minute later, Wollin had broken into his room and gasped out the news – the Goltzes were arrested, both of them; even the child had been carted along, dumb with fright, by the NKVD; the men had turned everything upside down and inside out, shouting where was that telegram – that telegram – that telegram.

He shrank. After so many years, the words still echoed within him. He had tried to hush Wollin, in vain. In his turmoil and frustration, Wollin kept shouting, aping the police voices; then he had broken into sobs; a man sobbing, a Communist, it was awful. If they could arrest Julian Goltz, Wollin had cried out, then who was *not* a traitor in their eyes? Julian, their party organiser in their Prague time, their teacher, mentor, friend? And this, while the NKVD still roamed the hotel. In vain his warnings, his pleas; Wollin refused to understand that even thinking this question was enough to hang a man.

How much does a child of eight perceive? How much remains etched in the substrata of her mind, to re-emerge when you least expected it? All these years, he had tried to find that out, had tried to cover it over; and there were hours when he asked himself whether all that he had done for her, including marrying her, hadn't been to keep her within reach, easy to observe; he had always denied it, but he was realist enough to admit that his sense of solidarity, his pity and charity, his love, his finest emotions, had happily coincided with the practical necessities of his life.

He grew aware that the silence had lengthened intolerably. Why didn't she go on? Why didn't she continue talking about her parents, ask questions?

'In Moscow,' he said, sounding tentative, 'in Moscow I was able to recompense Wollin for all he'd done. In Moscow it so happened that *I* got the commissions – nothing big, you understand, but enough to live on and to help him earn a living, too.'

Nothing big, he thought; this wasn't the impression he had given her in the past. That rest home he had built overlooking the river near the road to Kashyra was no small project; nor the miners' club at Stalinogorsk or the series of village schools for six, eight, and ten classes. Big, small – Wollin's arrival was creating a vortex; the more he worked to free himself, the deeper he was being sucked in.

'Moscow,' she said, 'was different from Prague?'

'My dear,' he said, 'you know *that!*' And sensed, too late, that the difference she had in mind was none of the obvious differences – the twisted-onion towers on St. Vassily's instead of the Prague Gothic on Thein Church; socialist austerity in place of coffee-house *laissez-faire*. She was putting her finger on that cardinal difference which explained that now it was *he* who could talk the client's language and hit the client's taste and adjust to the client's mood, no longer Wollin; Wollin appeared to have become rigid, his ideas out of line, his proposals too intellectual, his solutions unacceptable. Wollin would work, though; he worked hard; all you needed to do was give him the general outlines of what was wanted and he would perform the rest, in top-notch quality, and always with that little something added that made his designs stand out from the rest – a certain delicacy, an extra neat proportion.

'When did he go to Moscow?' she asked.

'1936.'

'The same year as you.'

'The same month,' he said. 'We all went on Party orders.'

'Yes,' she said, and fell silent.

Arnold Sundstrom suffered another twinge. *We all* had been too comprehensive an expression for just two young architects making their cautious way toward the capital of socialism; *We all* included the Goltzes: Julian, Babette, and the child; *We all* was another slip-up in the succession of mistakes he was making. It was as if he could hear her demanding: *We all*: you, and Wollin – and who else?

But she said, her eyes troubled, though not too greatly, 'And how come you lost sight of him?' And, as his answer failed to come promptly, she continued apologetically, ' I mean, you had worked so closely with one another, first he with you, then you with him . . . '

'He disappeared.'

'Just like that?'

'The Soviet Union is a large country,' he said. 'You've travelled through it. You know.'

He saw her toy with a cigarette. She didn't light it; she crumpled it slowly, and let the crumbs of tobacco fall on a saucer. He loved her tapered fingers, her narrow hands. She's all I've got, he thought, all I've got after a lifetime of struggling and wheedling and crawling and working; I'll fight before I lose her, and I don't care who gets hit.

'Didn't you ever make enquiries?' she said. 'Where he might have gone? And why?'

He turned and faced her, full. 'There are cases when one enquiry is enough.'

'Oh,' she said.

Just like my father's and mother's? It had to come. He was waiting for it. He had given her explanations, one after the other, each carefully geared to her age and understanding, each carefully weighed to agree with its predecessor, each carefully balanced between the permissible, the probable, and the bearable – until, after the birth of their child, the matter was no more touched on,

74

as if Julian the son had obliterated the last memories of Julian the father. And now, as of this moment, none of those careful explanations would do any longer. Wollin would smash them, had already smashed them, by existing. Why hadn't he died? So many opportunities to exit quietly – in the jails of the NKVD, in Siberia, beyond the polar circle, God knows where – exit without leaving a trace instead of clinging to life, a leech, an incubus, nightmarish.

He stopped, thought. That was some snake pit he had in his breast. He moved his hands, a reflex, as if he were stuffing it all back and pulling the lid tight.

'Why don't you talk openly?' she said.

'Openly?' He laughed, differently this time – no longer his previous forced laugh; this one had a life of its own, like a spasm.

'Openly,' she repeated. 'Your friendship for Wollin is no discredit to you. Don't you think I know?'

'You do?'

'Didn't Comrade Stalin teach us?' she said. 'The class struggle becoming increasingly sharp after the proletariat takes powers . . . If men could turn traitor who carried some of the biggest names in revolutionary history, why not an architect, even a good one? They would have taken you, too, at least for investigation, if they had suspected you of being involved. Your record is clear; you don't have to hem and haw because he was your friend.' A little of the rigidity with which she had spoken left her; her lips quivered. 'You're broad-minded to receive him into our house after all that. I suppose you feel he has atoned; and I agree with you, it's not up to us to be more unforgiving than the law . . . '

He began to understand. 'Julia,' he said, a trace of bewilderment still in his tone, 'my dear, wonderful Julia!'

She took this as a compliment, and replied, 'I'm not as wonderful as all that. I just believe in socialism and in the ideas I was brought up by . . . and in you . . . '

She broke off. The Charlottenburger Chaussee design, shadowy but insistent, shoved itself across the field of her inner vision. But this was just the point, she thought: a colonnaded front under socialism differed basically from a colonnaded front in a Nazi triumphal road; the same was *not* the same; everything depended on the what-fors and by-whoms. A load dropped off her.

'Julia!'

'Yes, dear?'

'You're daydreaming. I was trying to tell you . . . '

He had been trying to tell her that there was such a thing as mitigating circumstances, and that under certain conditions of very complicated political nature the dictatorial powers of the proletarian state might be applied more severely than in others. He hadn't made much sense, however; both the shock at her straight-laced, uncompromising, almost bigoted approach and his relief over it still throbbed within him; at the same time he was amazed at himself for having omitted to factor in the force of education: a whole generation spoon-fed on a single doctrine day in, day out – he hadn't a damned thing to worry about.

'I meant to say that we must be thoughtful of Wollin, always find the right tone: kind but not too kind, hospitable but not commiserating. The best would be to act our ordinary selves – best for him, and for us.'

'Of course,' she said, and rose. 'That would be best.'

A shade too quickly, he asked, 'Where are you going?'

She looked up in surprise, 'To Julian! I promised I would play with him after breakfast.'

Nevertheless, it was an unlucky Sunday.

His own fault entirely. He saw it, and he couldn't help it. He couldn't let sleeping dogs lie; he had to go stirring them up; it was like a curse.

He sat in his big chair, trying to read the Sunday paper. The letters arranged themselves into words, the words into sentences; yet, when he had come to the last line of a column, he had no idea what was in it, and thought next time he saw Comrade Bunsen, the chief editor, he would let him know his opinion – bores, all of them, making newspapers in the most critical time of history in the most difficult country in the world that no one could read.

He dropped the paper. The wind had come up, and he stared across the terrace at the bare trees swaying in it. The sky was darkening. Soon it'll start raining, he thought, oh, God, will there never be an end to it; and then he thought of that line of Lady Macbeth's that had stuck in his mind for months after he had seen the performance in the City Drama Theatre – a mediocre performance, but even the mediocre talent could not quite kill the horror exuding from the play –

> . . . things without all remedy
> Should be without regard; what's done is done.

I must reconstruct it, he thought, in sequence, all I told her: first to the child, and so on, through the years; contradictions, now, would be fatal. Yet contradictions were unavoidable if you had to adjust a story of this sort and of these proportions to the varying degrees of understanding of a young, growing mind. *They had gone with these uncles but would return soon, yes, very soon.* Why had the uncles shouted so and taken her to a different place? *The uncles were very, very busy people and had grown impatient.* And later, explaining to her what it was to be dead and that her father and mother would never return but had loved her very much and wanted her to stay and live with her uncle Arnold: *They had done nothing bad; how can you think that of your father and mother?* In school they said so. *They don't know everything in school, how can they?* And later, again, she was thirteen, by then, and the war was over, and they had returned to Moscow and the school registrar had been asking: Your parents killed in the war? – *You must understand, Julia, those years were difficult, more difficult, perhaps, than now; a person could blunder*

77

into things without ill intention, just by associating with the wrong sort of friends, for instance: no, I don't think they did anything bad or forbidden – But why, then? *As I've been trying to tell you: the class enemy is wily, capable of using people for his purposes without their even knowing that they're being used.* But if they didn't know, how could they be guilty? *Perhaps they knew, in the end, but were no longer able to get out of the enemy's clutches?* And then, as this seemed a little above her, not quite convincing, he used the argument to end all arguments: *Do you think, Julia, that the Soviet government, the Party, which has taken the place of your father and mother and wants you to grow up a good Communist and fighter for a new world and the rights of the people, could commit such a wrong?* Or, maybe, this had not been said in the course of one talk, but in several, spaced over months, years; or the nuances had been different; or he hadn't said it at all and had wanted to say it – who kept record of conversations with a child? At any rate, it no longer mattered. Regardless of what he had said or not said, there would be Wollin, survivor Wollin, who knew – how much? One must get to Wollin, explain to him, convince him that this was another time, another country, the very people he remembered no longer the same people: don't disturb what has grown, don't dig up the old roots rotting away under the new grass; look at the future we're building, look at World Peace Road – do you want to rock all that to its foundations? He was afraid, though, that Wollin would not understand, or would understand too well. Was there a common ground on which he and Wollin could meet, a common interest between the prosperous, much-honoured official and the alumnus of one of those camps in the tundra?

He didn't hear Julia until she was almost at his side. She was dressed to go out, the fur coat over her arm, the lipstick emphasising the ample curve of her mouth.

'Time already?' he asked, levering himself out of the chair. Beyond the barren trees, the first gas lamps were spreading a sickly white aura. 'Fog,' he said, 'in addition to everything else,' and shivered in anticipation of the clammy outdoors.

'I've prepared the guest room,' said Julia. 'Do you want to see it?'

He shook his head.

'I re-hung the pictures.'

His eyes queried.

'I put the eighteenth-century maps we bought last year in place of your designs.'

'I never was quite happy at your insisting that those old designs should be hung – even in the guest room. It's a little like Heerbrecht having portraits of himself all over his apartment . . . ' He sighed, then smiled. She had not forgotten that it might hurt an architect after sixteen – was it so many? – sixteen years of enforced inactivity to have another man's buildings stare at him from the walls of his room. Julia was thoughtful that way – a great asset, ordinarily. Ordinarily.

The fog was down in patches. When you ran into one, your own headlights glared back at you, causing your spine to ache from concentration. And on top of it her prattle – Arnold Sundstrom could have shouted at her but didn't dare: he, too, had to be thoughtful.

Huddled back in the corner of her seat, she was smoking, utterly relaxed and wondering out loud what he would look like: Daniel Wollin, ex-convict. Was he tall? Not especially? Ah, so – Apparently, a tall, angular man with huge hands and gangling limbs would have fitted better to the hard, leathery face she imagined, wind-bitten, narrow-eyed, thin-mouthed – composite of exile and pioneer, criminal and scout.

Like tired beetles, the cars coming at him groped their way through the soupy grey. Sundstrom glanced at his watch – there wasn't much time left unless the train, too, was delayed. Then, abruptly, the driveway lay ahead of him, swept clear, black shiny asphalt. The four-pronged electric street lamps threw each detail of the house fronts in bold relief, sharply delineating ledges, entablatures, jambs, capitals: World Peace Road. He didn't know whether to take the lifting of the fog at just this point as a good or bad omen; he stepped on the accelerator; the car shot forward, the buildings floating by like outsized stage sets, the cranes on the construction sites looming up like gallows. On the return from the station, Arnold Sundstrom promised himself, he would take a different route – thoughtful, one must be thoughtful.

The station, still partly without roof from the war's last bombings, came into view. Julia had stopped talking, he didn't remember how long ago; he only now had grown aware of her silence. 'I think we made it!' he said, the cheer in his voice too artificial to weigh against the drab ruins about and the fog that wanted to close in again.

The echo of the car door banging shut rang across the empty square. A lone taxi stood farther off, its driver gone. 'We should have brought flowers,' Julia said. 'But on Sunday . . . ' She sounded forlorn.

He hastened her up the stairs, past a sleepy railway guard, to the platform. A tinny loudspeaker gave off unintelligible noises. An engine hooted; a hollow trembling reverberated from the rails. Sundstrom stared at the oncoming train, his hair wind-blown, his jaws twitching. Then a cloud of steam from the engine, then the cars floating by. He tried to scan their windows for the white blotch of face nine-tenths forgotten.

'There!'

Among the half-dozen passengers getting off the second to the last carriage, a frail man in an ill-fitting long overcoat struggled with a cloth-covered suitcase.

'Wollin! . . . Daniel! . . . '

Julia felt herself propelled along. The frail man set down his suitcase and turned, removing his broad-rimmed Russian velour hat. A slow smile crept across his face, halted a moment, threatened to break.

'Daniel!' Sundstrom breathed heavily and spread his arms.

But Wollin was gazing at Julia as if he were trying to recapture a memory long gone, elusive and yet unmistakable. 'The image of Julian!' he said, and shook his head. 'His eyes, his mouth . . . Well, the shape of her face is her mother's.' And, to Arnold Sundstrom, 'There's something, at least, to latch on to.' And added, 'Besides you, Arnold of course, of course.'

Then he permitted himself to be embraced and kissed on both cheeks by Sundstrom, Russian manner; they had lived there too long not to revert to it, and it helped to get over the first few seconds of a new life. Finally he placed his hat on top of the suitcase, took both of Julia's hands in his, and said, 'I hope you haven't been waiting too long.'

Sixteen years, it shot through Julia's mind. He looked so entirely different from what she had imagined: paled out, fine wrinkles at the sides of his eyes, his hair white above a broad, intelligent forehead; and despite what he must have gone through, a face whose warmth forced you to respond.

'Not two minutes!' Arnold Sundstrom was assuring him. 'We hardly had reached the platform when the train pulled in – the fog, you know, we're having fog, couldn't see ten feet ahead in places . . . ' He interrupted himself, picked up Wollin's suitcase. 'Nichevo! Is this all the baggage you've got? How are you? After all these years . . . you look wonderful. A little tired, perhaps . . . The trip? . . . A rest cure is what you need, I'll speak to the comrades, it's no problem . . . You've had a rest cure? . . . Well, we'll discuss all this later. We have time, lots of it. This is a good place to be, we've been making progress, and you, too, will find your niche . . . '

Julia suspected that Daniel Wollin wasn't listening. He had put his hat back on and was walking beside her, down the long platform, in step with her, as if he had walked that way all his life – letting Arnold cart the suitcase. Julia was in a strange mood: she was conscious of Wollin's record, yet she couldn't pull away

81

from him, nor did she want to; the whole arrival was steeped in an atmosphere of unreality with the fog drifting in through the gaps in the station roof and mingling with the steam of the engine. Off and on, a terrible curiosity compelled her to look at Wollin: could everything – his guilt and his punishment, the inner conflicts, prison treatment, and finally his return to life – have passed him by without permanently marring his face?

Nor did her mood change as they left the station and got into the car: without thinking she chose the rear seat next to Wollin, leaving Arnold to his chauffeur's job but fixing her eyes on the back of his neck as he threaded his way through the shapeless grey of the streets.

After a while, Wollin turned to her. Patting her hand, he said, 'I don't wear tusks, you know. I'm quite a normal human being . . . '

Arnold had warned her – *the best would be to act our ordinary selves* . . . 'It's just that I thought . . . ' She broke off, embarrassed.

' . . . that I'd look different? Beaten? A shadow of myself? . . . Oh, I've seen people go to pieces. But being a Communist helps, even though it complicates matters . . . ' He stopped. That wasn't what he had wanted to say. He had no idea how much Julia Sundstrom knew of his fate and that of her parents, of the whole sordid story, and it wasn't his job to enlighten her. But if she believed he was some sort of ogre, a convicted enemy of the people . . .

'Why don't you two relax?' Arnold Sundstrom switched on the windshield wipers to rid the glass of the layer of greasy moisture. His head ached from trying to see the road and, simultaneously, to catch the undertones of what was being said behind him. The wiper, wagging right, left, in maddening rhythm, kept pulling his eyes from the few yards of pavement he could distinguish; he sounded short as he said, 'Can't you postpone the heavy stuff until you've had a drink?'

Wollin pressed his hand on Julia's to forestall her giving an answer that might force him to commit himself. Then, after a brief silence, he said, 'I have no wish at all to talk of . . . of the heavy stuff.'

'I didn't mean to be rude,' said Sundstrom.

'I'm not that touchy . . . I've been housebroken . . . ' Wollin's lips thinned. There: his mind was circling the same old thing. He thought he had dispensed with all that in Moscow; it was miraculous, when he first came out, to see that millions of people were going about their business without the least regard for the events that had shattered his life and whose effect, to a greater or lesser degree, must have touched upon the lives of each one of them. That's when he had decided to forget – not forgive but forget – if he could and if he were permitted to live out his days undisturbed by the big, hollow words. But apparently he couldn't. The moment he set eyes on Arnold and on Julia, the past rushed back at him, roaring with the old echoes. He glanced at Julia. No, he wasn't sorry that he had come – and he couldn't very well tell Arnold Sundstrom to turn the car around and take him back to the railway station.

They were washing their hands for supper at the large pink double basin: Arnold Sundstrom at the right one whose shelf was garnished with his toothbrushes, lotions, shaving soap; Daniel Wollin using the left one that was clearly Julia's. In the mirror, which ran the length of both basins, Sundstrom furtively studied the image of his old friend, trying to find in it the face he once knew. That face was superimposing itself on the present-day countenance – a kind of overlay, disquieting because of what it conjured up.

Viewed soberly, there was no reason for any greater disquiet than the general situation warranted. Wollin – the Wollin of now who was slowly, contentedly drying his hands – was no threat, except in conjunction with other circumstances that one must seek to avoid. True, as Wollin had said in the car, he was not a beaten man, but the network of fine wrinkles on the almost transparent, sagging skin showed how tired and worn he was, and the paled-out blue of the eyes bespoke their disillusionment. Ashes, ashes; if there was any fire left in him it was buried deep, and all you had to guard against was the gust of wind that might kindle the flame; most important, the spirit was gone; interrogations, prisons, camps, God knows what else had snuffed it out; Daniel Wollin no longer was the man who had walked into the hearts of people and fired their minds with his imagination.

One last glance at the mirror, this time encompassing the both of them. They were no match. Though the same age – Wollin, in fact, was a few months younger – the one was old, colourless, his juices thinned out, while the other stood at the summit of his life and success, strapping, robust, flourishing, his keen eye on the opportunities that a period full of great opportunities offered. He had nothing to fear, Sundstrom assured himself; he could, in fact, afford to be magnanimous once he established the line that the guest would have to toe.

Sundstrom folded his towel and hung it on the rack. Then, placing his arm about Wollin's shoulders, he said, 'Before we go into the dining room, I'd like you to keep in mind that Julia knows nothing . . . '

'Nothing?' Wollin gently freed his shoulder from his friend's clasp. 'But Julia was old enough at the time to register how her parents were taken, and by whom!'

'And?'

Wollin searched his pockets.

'Cigarette?'

Wollin accepted the cigarette and the light Sundstrom held out to him. 'But then . . . she must think that Julian and Babette . . . that her parents were . . . traitors . . . criminals . . . '

Sundstrom shrugged. 'I didn't put it quite that hard to her.'

'And she must think . . . that I am . . . well . . . '

'There isn't much choice, is there? You either believe in socialism or in . . . *that* . . . I preferred that Julia have faith in

84

socialism. I also thought that would be more in agreement with her father's intentions. And I wish that you—'

'—that I conduct myself accordingly.' Wollin returned to the basin and let cold water run into a glass. He drank slowly, apparently savouring each sip, and then wiped his lips. Finally he said, 'All right, let's go.'

Julia had changed into a wide-sleeved robe, a kind of hostess gown open at the throat and emphasising the lines of her body. Her hair was smoothed back and held in place by a barrette. Wollin hesitated. The décor of the room and the beauty of the woman in it hit him and for a moment he saw himself back in his hutment, filthy, stubbled, the grey cotton padding sticking out of his torn jacket, methodically chewing a hunk of sticky black bread so as to get the maximum value out of it; and he thought, I don't belong here; and then thought, you see what you can have if you play it right; perhaps I did make a mistake somewhere, or did I?

Julia gestured toward the table on which a tray with vodka and *zakusky* was set out. 'Like home,' she began, and remembered that to Daniel Wollin, émigré existence in the Soviet Union might not have had that connotation. Awkwardly, she pointed at the dabs of long-hoarded black and red caviar, the slices of sturgeon in aspic, the pickled cucumbers. 'You see,' she apologised, 'Arnold and I carry big clods of Soviet soil on our soles.'

Sundstrom poured the vodka. Wollin raised his glass, 'To that soil – and may it bear the fruit we hope for!'

A spark seemed to light up his tired eyes. Sundstrom noticed it and felt a momentary uncertainty. But Wollin had already changed the subject. He was asking Julia about Julian, regretting that he had arrived too late to meet the child. He loved children, he said. And paused. He was gazing at her, as he had on encountering her at the station, and he said more to himself than to her or Sundstrom, 'Absolutely like her father. His eyes, his expression . . . '

He caught Sundstrom's quick glance. 'But you'll hardly remember your parents, Julia,' he added. 'Forgive me.'

'You knew them well?' said Julia.

'Of course he did,' Sundstrom interjected with finality. 'And so did I.' And to Wollin, 'Julia and I have built a good life for ourselves, as you can see. This fills us completely,' he turned to her, 'doesn't it, dear?'

CHAPTER FOUR

He started up with a jolt; the shock of awakening was with him always, persistent, even though the time was past when raucous curses pulled him from his sleep and clawing hands tore him from his cot.

He sat up, supporting himself on his elbow. Soft sheets, soft blankets, soft pillows, and against the muted tones of the wall-paper three neatly framed eighteenth-century maps, hand-coloured, the heraldry exquisite. There it was again, the knock at the door, less a knock than a scratching. Instinctively, Wollin closed his pyjama top and ran his palm across his stubbled chin.

The door opened.

Wollin let himself fall back against the pillow. 'And who might you be?' he asked, inclining his head sideways and squinting at the small figure.

'I'm Julian.'

'Good morning, Julian. Won't you sit down?'

The boy looked at Wollin, trying to gauge the man and the meaning of his invitation. 'They wouldn't let me stay up to meet you,' he said: no complaint, a statement of fact. 'But I saw you from the window.'

'Your window opens on the driveway?'

'Uh-huh.' The boy sat down at the foot of the bed, hands in the pockets of his striped bathrobe. 'Your name's Daniel Wollin?' And, without pausing for confirmation, 'You've come here to stay.'

The eyes, thought Wollin. Julia's eyes, and Julian Goltz's. Sensitive face, probably an imaginative child; pale, though; thin. 'How do you know all that, Julian?' he asked. 'Seems you know almost everything.'

'Frau Sommer.' The boy shrugged. 'She talks. Julia talks too but not so real. Do you dream much?'

'Off and on.'

'Do you ever dream of the man with the red hat and no face? He has long arms, and there's no brim to his hat, and sometimes he has a big suitcase to carry Julia off in. But you don't look like him.'

Wollin shook his head. Imaginative! – God knows what problems and complexes the little fellow carried around with him. The sins of the fathers . . . a blatant injustice, but there it was. 'No,' he said. 'Nor do I own a red hat. Mine is dark blue, and it has a broad brim. Do you want to see?'

Julian nodded.

'Look in the wardrobe. On the lower shelf.'

The wardrobe opened easily. Julian returned; this time he sat down nearer Wollin and his scrutiny was less loaded with suspicion.

'Do you have any children?'

'No.'

'None at all?'

'None.'

'Then you can come and play with me sometime. Do you like to build houses?'

'Yes,' said Wollin. 'How do you build them?'

'Blocks,' said Julian. 'Don't you know? You take blocks, square ones and long ones, and round ones and short ones and you fit them to one another so you get different-shaped buildings, always from the same parts.'

Elementary, thought Wollin, who in his long Siberian nights had played the same game; why do we leave the technique to the children? He smiled at Julian. 'You understand a lot about architecture.'

'My mother is an architect.'

'So is your father, isn't he?'

'He built World Peace Road,' answered Julian, as if by rote. 'And two hundred big houses in the Soviet Union.'

'Two hundred . . .' repeated Wollin. Had it been that many? Then he remembered that two hundred was probably the largest number the child knew – and yet, if he had said two hundred thousand, or two million, the boy would have been just as right: Sundstrom built them all, or men like Sundstrom did in the same image. Wollin patted the small, somehow fragile hand. 'Two hundred. And World Peace Road. Your father is a very famous man.'

'Aren't you?'

'I'm afraid not.'

Julian inclined his head, as he had seen Wollin do, and squinted at him. 'Why not?'

'That's a long story,' said Wollin. 'But where would we be if everyone were famous? Who would do the ordinary work like washing dishes and sewing bathrobes and laying bricks?'

'I don't want to be famous. I want to be strong.'

'Your father is strong, too.'

'I want to be stronger than he is. So I can drive away the man with the red hat when he comes and wants to take Julia.' He seemed to be contemplating. 'You never had any children?'

'Not that I know of,' said Wollin.

'Why not?'

'Because I never was married.'

'Oh.'

Again the pause for thought. Wollin felt the small body press against his knees as the boy leaned back to gaze at him pensively.

'Then how come,' Julian asked finally, 'you talk with me so . . . so—'

'As if we were old friends?'

'Uh-huh.'

Wollin frowned. What tone did Sundstrom use toward his son? 'I'll tell you, Julian,' he said, then, 'If I ever got married and had a little boy, I would want him to be about like you. And that's why I can talk to you as if we had known one another for a long time.'

Julian had jumped up. He was at the door, hanging on to its handle in a last moment of hesitation.

'And where are you off to?' enquired Wollin. 'What's the sudden hurry?'

'I've been here an hour and a half.'

Wollin involuntarily glanced at his wristwatch. Eight minutes had passed since his being awakened.

The door handle snapped up. 'And I've got to say goodbye to Julia!'

Wollin stared at the door long after the bright-striped small figure had vanished. He didn't feel too happy at the visit. He was beginning to get involved, he thought, and from an undesirable angle at that.

The word *niche* assumed increasing importance in Arnold Sundstrom's thinking.

It had popped up, spontaneously, as part of the welcoming; Wollin would find his niche, or one would be found for him. *Niche* contained a sense of something snug, warm, comfortable; you could hole up in it and spend the rest of your days well cared for, your problems solved, a happy vegetable; also you were at least partly walled in; your own troubles ended, you could make no trouble for anyone else.

He asked John Hiller to his office and explained how Wollin should be guided to his niche. 'I am picking you for the job,' he said, 'because you have a head on your shoulders. My old friend Wollin is a man of great talent; he studied with me and for a while we worked together, but due to circumstances beyond his control he's been out of his field for a number of years. Quite a number of years,' he added significantly, 'you understand, John?'

John Hiller pulled up his brows. 'I think I do, Comrade Sundstrom.'

But Sundstrom felt the need to elaborate. 'There are times,' he said, 'when the path is narrow and the going rough. A man can stumble easily then . . . why don't you sit down, John?'

Hiller complied, crossing his legs and lacing his fingers behind the back of his head. He knew that his chief frowned on laxity, but Sundstrom seemed not to notice.

'You see, John,' Sundstrom was saying, 'I feel some personal responsibility toward Wollin's finding his niche. But it'll have to be handled with great tact and psychology: I want him to *want* a place in this organisation. You follow me, John?'

Hiller nodded. These last few days, he had seen the frail, white-haired man occasionally drop into the barracks, poke his nose in Julia's studio, remain with her for a while, then briefly visit Sundstrom's, and leave again as quietly as he had come; and he had wondered about this Wollin.

'It's not just that I feel he could make a contribution to the collective,' Sundstrom went on. 'I also think it's the best way to get him to adjust.'

'Certainly.'

Sundstrom glanced up. He did not particularly like those non-committal answers; there always was, in Hiller, a residue hard to look into, a certain reserve, but the all-out yes-sayers were no good for this case; they would scare off Wollin by the clumsy, blundering embrace of their enthusiasm; and he wanted Wollin about, a Wollin tamed and under his control.

'I imagine,' he continued, 'you and Mrs Sundstrom will start off by showing him around the studios, explaining to him our set-up, our methods of work, our . . . Are you listening?'

Hiller started up. 'Of course . . .' And thought – you and Mrs Sundstrom.

He and Mrs Sundstrom, he learned, would then take their ward to City Hall, where the long-range plans were kept for the reconstruction of the entire city and for its future growth – the giant drawings of the skylines of 1965 and of 1975, and the plaster model of the projected centre of town, with the Government and Party Building as it would tower cloudward, its Gothic conception appealing to the very emotions in man that the creators of the ancient cathedrals aroused in their contemporaries. And after Wollin thus was prepared to see today's effort in its great context, he was to be shown today's achievement: World Peace Road, both the completed parts and the sections under construction.

'The big tour, in other words,' said Hiller, and thought: why Julia? Why does he want Julia along to watch Wollin? To watch me?

'The big tour, if you want to call it that,' smiled Sundstrom, showing his teeth. Nice, strong, even teeth that won't easily let go of what they've bitten into, thought Hiller. 'However, don't forget,' Sundstrom was saying, 'that my friend Wollin is not to be considered a visiting dignitary, but a future fellow worker. Let him have a good look, let him test for himself, let him ask questions. Faculties long disused tend to atrophy, desires long stunted to shrivel; I want you to help reawaken in him the creative urge that for years has been buried under all sorts of debris.'

Hiller unlatched his fingers and dropped his hands. There was obviously more that Sundstrom wanted to say.

Sundstrom was toying with the slide rule he kept on his desk. 'I believe I told you that I feel a certain personal responsibility toward my friend Wollin . . . ' He turned his head from side to side; his eyes ranged beyond John Hiller's shoulders as if he had picked up a suspicious scent; then, as all was quiet, he said, his voice low, confiding, 'Political responsibility, too.'

'Ah,' said Hiller, and nodded.

Sundstrom put aside the slide rule. 'I know you as an intelligent and discreet young comrade, John, one of our most promising. It can't be too hard for you to pick the essentials from what a man says or only half says . . . '

Hiller uncrossed his legs. ' . . . and report those essentials?'

'We want to help Wollin. In order to help a man, you must know his problems.'

'And Mrs Sundstrom will supplement my report?'

Sundstrom swallowed. But when he spoke, he sounded light enough. 'I don't expect this will be necessary. I have full confidence in you. I am sending Mrs Sundstrom along because, aside from myself, she is the only person who represents a tie to my friend Wollin's past. He knew her as a child . . . '

'That will make it easier,' said Hiller, leaving open what it was that would be facilitated. And thought: the decoy, she's going to be the decoy; I wonder if he has told her; but she didn't even have to know; her presence would be sufficient.

'So I can rely on you?'

John Hiller knew he could no longer avoid Sundstrom's searching glance; what gullible fools people were, to assume they could see into another man's mind and heart. He calmly looked back at his chief.

'I could make this a Party order,' Sundstrom resumed. 'But I prefer the direct channel. In this case especially: for my friend Wollin's sake – why involve third persons?'

John Hiller rose. 'When do we start?'

Julia wanted to refuse. But what reason could she give – that she had doubted that World Peace Road was one of the finest examples of socialist architecture and that the doubts kept recurring? Nor could she object to John Hiller's joining the junket unless she brought up Herr Speer's Charlottenburger Chaussee project and how she had chanced upon it. And there was Daniel Wollin, the melancholy about his eyes for once replaced by animation; she didn't want to disappoint him.

That evening the grand architectural round-trip suddenly

assumed a new aspect. Supper over, she finally finished the nightly problem of putting Julian to sleep – the separation from her, which the child did not mind during the daytime, he resisted when it grew dark; but remembering the loneliness of her own childhood, Julia didn't have the heart to turn off the light and leave the boy to his fancies and fears. She returned to the men as they were concluding a discussion that apparently had dealt with questions of principle: her husband was outlining the ideas he followed in building the Road.

'Socialism,' he was saying with no more than a brief welcoming glance at her, 'juxtaposes to the policy of turning human relationships into those of material nature the opposite aim: turning material relationships into human ones.'

A month or two ago, Julia would have wholeheartedly applauded that statement or any other, equally deep, that came from her husband. Now, she found herself waiting for a comment from Wollin.

None came. She heard the slight edge to Arnold's voice as he continued, 'To a conception of man as an irrational being, socialism opposes the perspective of man's all-around physical and mental development. That's why, along with the growth of socialist consciousness, you will find arising an architecture with ideological forms corresponding to socialism – that is socialist-realist architecture.'

Wollin was fingering the grape leaf design of the greyish green soapstone ashtray before him – the gift of a Chinese delegation that had been led through World Peace Road. Julia felt as if she were having one of those dreams in which you walk and walk and yet remain mired in place. Perhaps I'm being unjust, she thought; you can't judge a man's philosophy by a few concluding phrases; and then, with a stab of panic, she thought: *a* man's? – Arnold's! Who am I to judge?

Wollin pushed away the ashtray. 'In all those years,' he said gropingly, 'I never gave much thought to theory. I *built*.'

'You . . . what?' Sundstrom was startled.

'I built. I populated the steppes with great cities, out of the tundra rose my future settlements – bright, airy, planned sensibly, organised to the needs of man, symphony in greens and silvers . . . '

He had changed. The weariness was gone; the skin of his face tautened; the vision seemed to have pumped new energy into his sinewy body; despite his white hair, he looked youthful, eager, springy.

'You mean all this,' Arnold Sundstrom's laugh sounded not quite genuine, 'was in your imagination?'

'I mean I'm a practitioner,' said Wollin. 'I look at a building or a complex of buildings and I try to gauge how they measure up to the purpose for which they were constructed.'

'That's all?' frowned Sundstrom.

'I see a wide range of purposes,' countered Wollin.

'Ah, so.' Sundstrom relaxed. 'Then we agree, don't we?'

They didn't agree, thought Julia, of course they didn't. And she realised, with a shock, that Wollin's past and whatever guilt he might carry mattered less to her than the cities that the man's imagination had planted in the tundra.

The streak of bad weather had broken. A robin's-egg-blue sky, after the rains, cast its sparkle over the pastel-shaded tiles of the house fronts and set off each detail to its best advantage – the intricate balustrades delimiting the roofs, the cornices above gates and windows, the mosaic friezes and the knobs and rhombs that ornamented the space between floors. Together with the reflections of the light in the narrow windows of the street's sunny side, this variety of small forms helped to lighten the heroic proportions of the blocks of building and created a mood that encouraged Julia. Why should a sight that a few brief weeks ago she had found beautiful have lost its lustre? Why should the aesthetics on which she had been brought up have lost their validity?

She eagerly turned to Wollin. 'Impressive, isn't it? You must see it from here!' She had chosen a spot from which the Road, with the cranes at its end jutting skyward, showed to advantage.

'From here you'll recognise the groupings, the turrets that punctuate, as it were, the distance. There was argument on those turrets, and some of us,' she emphasised the *some* in an oblique reference to John Hiller, 'still aren't convinced. Finally Comrade Tolkening decided to have turrets.'

Wollin smiled.

'Comrade Tolkening takes great interest in our work.'

'So he should,' said Wollin, the smile still hovering about his lips. 'Architecture, more than any other art, is the business of the People. They pay the bill.' He fished from his pocket the small, dog-eared notebook he had brought along and jotted something down. 'Shall we go on?'

This left everything up in the air. But Wollin had followed that policy from the inception of their tour – accepting her friendly efforts but never committing himself at least this far. Julia knew that this was his way of drawing information from her, even information she had no intention of giving, but she couldn't stop trying to prove the Road to him, its designs, its purport.

Wollin seemed to sense her need for that. His manner began to assume an element of indulgence, the doctor at the patient's bedside; it frustrated her. Even more frustrating was his notebook. She wouldn't squint at the notes he took, and she hesitated to ask about them; so she tried timing his notes with whatever he was interested in at the moment; but there was no apparent pattern.

Nor was John Hiller of help to her. John rarely walked where she could observe his face; coat collar turned up, unconcern in his very gait, he kept himself either slightly ahead of or slightly behind her and Wollin – always within listening distance, always ready to reply to Wollin's questioning, his replies carefully sticking to facts and figures.

Wollin was steering toward the last of the completed buildings. The concrete slabs for the sidewalk had not yet been laid; you walked on planks to get across the mud to the large entrance gate. Wollin stopped to study the grillwork above it: black wrought-iron leafy branches, heavily intertwined, at their ends pinecones, idealised versions daubed in gold.

'Have you any idea what this cost?' asked Wollin.

Julia saw the golden pinecones stick out as if they were about to shed their seeds on the heads of the two men and on her own. Hiller was coolly explaining that the bills did not go through the City Architects' Bureau; the Bureau was concerned with getting the work done and with its artistic value; this grill was fashioned by the top man in the field, a name internationally famous . . .

Julia's irritation mounted – whether at the tour-guide tone John Hiller was using, or at the fact that the cones reminded her of certain juvenile drawings, or at Wollin's shrug as he passed underneath the grillwork to enter the building.

'I find you offensive, John!' she broke out, glad that the heavy door had fallen closed behind Wollin.

Hiller, who had been about to open the door for her, turned in question but changed his mind as he saw her lips curled in bitterness. His supercilious smile vanished; his eyes pleaded. 'You know, Julia, it's not my aim in life to be offensive to you.'

'Then why . . . ' She broke off. He had taken her arm to help her from the planks to the entrance, a few steps; she felt the reluctance with which he let go of her.

'Maybe I'm antagonising you, Julia,' he said, 'because I don't dissimulate as much as the others.' He pushed open the door and held it for her.

Wollin was standing at the stairwell, studying it as they came up to him. 'I'd like to see it from the top floor looking down,' he said. Together, they crossed the marbled hallway with its mosaics on one wall and the brass mailboxes built into the other. The elevator was located at the far end. After a while, it came creaking down and a snub-nosed boy, whistling and swinging a pair of roller skates, emerged.

The whistling stopped. The boy gaped.

'Well?' said Hiller, half jokingly. 'You find us so extraordinary?'

The boy was suspicious to the point of hostility. 'What do you want?' he asked.

'Just looking about,' said Hiller. 'Any objections?'

'That's *our* house!' said the boy

'Ah, leave him be,' said Julia.

'One moment,' Wollin interjected. He bent down to the boy and said, 'I've come from far away to see how you live. You live here, do you?'

'Uh-huh.'

'Where?'

'Fifth floor.'

'How long?'

'Two and a half weeks.'

'Where here did you live before?'

The boy named a street. 'Near the freight yards,' Julia said 'Slums. Half bombed out.'

'What's your father?'

The boy was growing impatient. 'Carpenter,' he said. 'Building trades. Can I go now, mister?'

'Did he work here? On World Peace Road?'

'Mister – they're waiting for me.'

'Your mother – is she at home? Or does she work?'

The boy had squirmed away. The entrance door crashed into its lock. Wollin stepped into the elevator.

'This,' said Julia as the elevator doors closed behind them, 'is the real greatness of this street: the people who are moving in.'

'Top floor?' said Hiller.

'Top floor.' Wollin nodded. And to Julia, 'But this increases our responsibility.'

The floors glided by, a foot of grey, unfinished concrete, a steel door, then concrete again. The three in the elevator were silent, very conscious of one another.

Then a sudden jerk: the elevator stopped in mid-shaft. Julia laughed in embarrassment, a shade of worry sounding through. Elevators did fall down shafts, breaking people's bones.

'Jammed!' Hiller tore open the narrow wings of the inner door. 'These things always jam, I've been told. And we're between floors . . . ' He pressed the emergency button. From the bottom of the shaft a bell rang noisily but stopped as soon as he took his finger off the button. He rang again. 'Somebody's bound to hear. Or someone will want to use this contraption.'

'At this time of day?' asked Wollin.

'Maybe that boy's roller skates will break down, too,' Hiller offered.

'How about the trapdoor?' Wollin pointed to the ceiling of the cabin. 'I could climb on your shoulders or you on mine—'

'—and crawl out into the grease on that cabin roof?' Hiller rang once more. The shrill clang seemed to increase the tension.

'Something has got to be done!' Julia's apprehension had given way to anger. She had been proud of the boy with the roller skates; he had come so opportunely, illustrating a point; this silly mechanical failure was erasing the illustration and leaving a blot of discomfort.

'We can't just sit here!'

'Why can't we?' Hiller closed the inner elevator door, leaned against it, and pulled out his cigarettes. 'Have one? . . . '

For a minute or so, they smoked in silence, the small bluish clouds wafting ceilingward and escaping through the air vents.

'Why can't we just sit here, Julia?' Hiller resumed. 'Don't you know that you're the girl I'd most like to be marooned with in an elevator?' He paused. 'Or on an island. Or anywhere.'

Wollin opened his too-long coat. 'You forget I'm marooned along with you.'

'Oh, we'd find a niche for you,' Hiller countered lightly.

'Niche!' Wollin had become sensitive to that word. And there was the thought that Hiller could have meant it, that the young man's brashness was a thinly camouflaged pass at Julia. 'Look, Comrade Hiller,' Wollin bristled, not because of the pair of horns that one day might decorate Sundstrom's forehead, but because of Julia, 'let's not overtax a stupid joke in a stupid situation.'

'And who's doing that?' enquired Hiller.

'You are, with your island plans . . .' Wollin broke off. Where had he let his temper manoeuvre him? 'There are things that go back over the years . . . that have shaped Julia into the woman she is . . . and you might respect that—'

'Oh Daniel!' She realised she had called him by his given name. 'I beg you . . .' And to Hiller, 'And you . . .'

Neither of the men spoke.

'Perhaps we *should* try the trapdoor,' she said diffidently. Then, without looking at the switchboard, she groped for the emergency button and pressed it.

No bell sounded. Instead, the elevator slid smoothly, soundlessly, downward. Julia stared. Her finger still held on the button marked *Ground Floor*.

'There's that boy again!' said Hiller as they got out. The boy was standing under the mosaic in the hall, one skate on his foot, the other, minus a pair of wheels, dangling from his hand. Julia wanted to laugh. The boy looked at them resentfully. Hiller turned to Wollin. 'Do you still want to see that stairwell arrangement?'

The vista beyond the crenellated wall rising from the sixth-floor level was astonishing. Below, the Road stretched, wide, handsome, built for the traffic of the future – toward the right, the two long rows of buildings completed or in varying stages of construction.

Julia, who had seen it often enough – if not from this, then from another vantage point along the project – never failed to be moved. There was poetry in the sight; not Mischnick's, the poet laureate's; not poetry you could put into words; but a poetry that converted itself from stone and space directly into emotion.

On Wollin's face, too, she caught a reflection of this inner glow; she pointed at the old slums to the left and on either side of the Road, the half-destroyed, grimy factory buildings, the bombed-out tenements that were waiting to be torn down. 'It was *all* like that,' she said. 'I remember it so well. I was in the first months of pregnancy when we started clearing the rubble for World Peace Road . . . we: Arnold, I, everybody; the people. My son is not yet five now, and look at this! Were there ever architects to build with such material?'

The crane above their heads was swaying over and lowering a load of bricks. The foreman of the floor's construction team guided it in place next to one of the bricklayers who, without looking up, kept working, rhythmically, slapping down the mortar, putting down the stone. As the foreman unhooked the load and the heavy cable swung away, Wollin stepped over to them. 'May I?' he asked, and before either of the two could demur, he had taken the level that stuck out of the foreman's pocket and was holding it against the window jamb on which the bricklayer was working.

The man snorted.

Wollin removed his overcoat, folded it, and laid it on an overturned bucket nearby. 'May I?' he said again, and held out his hand for the bricklayer's trowel.

'Another one, huh?' the man grunted.

'Another who?'

'Time-checker!' the bricklayer said in Wollin's face and relinquishing the trowel to him, added sarcastically, 'Help yourself, Brother!'

Wollin pulled down his tie, opened his shirt collar, and began working. The foreman, Julia, and Hiller stood around him and watched; the worker, in apparent indifference, lit the stub of a cigarette; from elsewhere, the other men of the team occasionally looked over at the stranger setting brick on brick. Wollin had hit a steady pace, not as fast as the bricklayer's, but the jamb rose visibly under his hands – neat, straight, no mortar slopping over, each stone in perfect alignment to the wooden frame that gave the width of the window.

'And?' said the bricklayer, stamping out his stub. 'What d'you want to prove?' He almost tore the trowel from Wollin. 'That we're God-damned parasites doing a slipshod job on the people's money? Where've you been laying bricks? . . . Siberia, you say? Ah . . . How much time they gave you for the square meter? And how much money?'

Wollin's lips tightened.

The man, furious, paid no attention to the telltale silence. 'We've learned our trades, too!' he rasped out. 'But we're on piece rate, see, and I first've got to hit my quota and then start hustling to see real money. Siberia! . . . That's where they work for love, do they?'

The foreman was trying to calm the worker.

The man pushed him away. 'All right, all right . . . I know she's Mrs Sundstrom and I'll be reported . . . '

Julia shrank.

'I don't care.' And to Wollin, 'You think *I* waste the people's money when another man has to chip down my bricks for the windows to fit? What'll you say, mister, when I tell you that whole walls've got to be broken open because someone didn't project the pipes in time, and that thick concrete floors have to be chiselled through because the electricians found out too late where to run their cables? Why, half the floors of this building went up without the proper blueprints, and if Barrasch here,' he pointed his thumb at the foreman, 'wasn't so good at guessing the proper thicknesses of wall, we'd have to tear down most of the work and start from scratch!'

Wollin glanced at Hiller. Hiller nodded discreetly. Julia heard him say something to Wollin, an explanation, apparently.

But Julia knew. She knew all the complaints the enraged bricklayer recounted; she knew more: that a lot of those pretty tiles that were pasted to the outside walls would fall off when the frosts came next year or the year after because they couldn't be anchored properly; that there were constant improvisations and substitutions of material, necessitating changes and refittings; that costs mounted beyond every estimate; that there weren't even any serious estimates; that everything was done by fits and starts, planning, blueprints; and that they were bogged down by dozens of echelons in dozens of institutions and offices that had to give their seal and signatures to every toilet seat installed. She knew it all and yet had been able to repress it because – because of Arnold? – because of the excitement of seeing the Road grow? – because these were the difficulties of anything new and untried?

The foreman had shoved his burly frame between the bricklayer and the three visitors. 'At any rate,' he was mediating, 'it's going up, isn't it? We'll manage, Mrs Sundstrom, we'll manage all right.'

'And we're quite proud of the Road, Comrade Barrasch!' said Julia, gripping at the straw.

Muttering, the bricklayer had gone back to his work. Barrasch waited to be dismissed. Wollin was waiting, too – and so was John Hiller. It was as if by tacit agreement the men were leaving the next step to her. The shadow of the crane's arm moved across her. The sky seemed cruelly bright.

'Comrade Wollin!'

He saw the honey-coloured strand of hair that the wind blew onto her forehead. She was slowly walking to the edge of the storey, away from everybody. He followed her.

She remained frighteningly close to the edge and once more pointed at the wide street, at the buildings, an ornate file on either side of it, at the broad driveways with the stripe of incipient green between them, at the few cars moving past and the people no larger than dots.

'This is terribly important to me,' she said, unable to conceal her turmoil. 'I'm sure you've reached an opinion. Will you work with us . . . with Arnold and me?'

'It'll be hard.'

'You don't like World Peace Road?'

'Julia,' he said gently, 'must I answer?'

She sounded harsh. 'Yes. For my sake.'

'It isn't only the eclecticism of the thing,' he spoke without turning to her, 'the scavenging of detail from a period that, in turn, lived off previous periods architecturally. Nor are the structural mistakes and backward methods decisive; they can be corrected. It's the basic conception that I find difficult to take . . . '

'But this was approved! – not just by the best architects of the country and the highest functionaries – by the people! By the people who cleared the rubble with their own hands and then came to look at our designs and models. I've talked to them; I swear to you they were pleased and happy as children . . . '

Wollin stepped behind her and took hold of both her elbows as if to steady her against the wind and the height. 'An old-fashioned corridor street,' he said, 'but pretentious. Designed for triumphal processions that lead from nowhere to nowhere, in the middle of nothing.'

'You saw the long-term plans. The city will be built up.'

'Like this?'

'Comrade Wollin, you've lived in the Soviet Union; I don't know exactly where and how, but you've seen their work. We're building along their lines . . . '

'That's why,' he said.

She whipped about, faced him. 'That's counter-revolutionary!'

'And I'm a counter-revolutionary, you mean. And I was where counter-revolutionaries by rights are sent.'

'Daniel!' Again she had used his given name.

John Hiller looked toward them, his expression querying if he was needed.

She lowered her voice. 'But if this,' her hand motioning toward the Road, 'were wrong, then other things Soviet might also be wrong?'

'They might,' Wollin said firmly.

The world began swaying. Julia felt the trembling in her knees. Beyond the edge of the floor, demarcated by a thin line of bricks, were six storeys of sheer wall.

Her hand reached for Wollin. 'Then you mean to say . . . you might have been . . . sent away unjustly . . . '

'Possibly.'

The floor had steadied. The sky was in its accustomed place; John Hiller, the foreman, the bricklayers, the crane and its load slowly lowering were back in proper perspective. 'But then my father and my mother—'

She saw the quick movement of his Adam's apple, but he said nothing.

'My father and mother might have been . . . They were arrested, taken away . . . ' Her voice trailed off, then returned, her words tumbling. 'I saw it, you know . . . the men coming . . . boots, faces . . . the bed torn up . . . my mother holding me in her arms . . . then one of the men . . . I scratched, screamed . . . my father telling me I must be a good girl . . . '

Her eyes widened; their grey had turned almost to black.

'And you . . . ' She shook her head. The piece wouldn't fit in the puzzle. 'I remember only flashes of that time. It is as if for me a consecutive life began only after Arnold fetched me from that children's home. He was so good to me. Always.'

'I'm sure,' said Wollin.

She gazed at the Road stretching at their feet. 'Wrong, you say?'

'Hypocrisy in brick.'

Her laugh was brittle. 'Sometime, I'll show you the design for another triumphal road. You'll be quite amused, Daniel.'

Hiller was approaching.

Julia moved back from the edge of the story. 'John!' she called out and met him half way, arms outstretched.

'John, we're through with the grand round-trip and inspection tour. Where can we have a good, stiff drink?'

'Château Hiller!' he proclaimed, with a sweep of his arm. 'D'you like it?'

Julia looked about while Hiller helped her out of her coat and told Wollin where he might wash his hands. Her first impression: *could* one live that way? Was it even permissible? Those contrasting colours; the use of the naked brick wall; the nonsensical paintings and the Baroque angel; the wide black couch, funereal but for the bright scatter pillows; the Biedermeier cupboard, slightly chipped, in one corner, and in the other John's private bar, roughly put together of old crates and plastered over with lewd front covers of West German and American magazines – the impudent mixture of the thing, the very casualness that made you suspect a careful design behind it. Her second: what a two-faced liar this man, who lived in this fashion at home and who worked along quite different lines in the studio.

'D'you like it?' he repeated, motioning her into the room and onto a barrel-shaped, surprisingly comfortable chair. Through the large window you saw the bombed-out walls of the building and a couple of young birches that had taken root in the piles of rubble; you could just about sense the green of the buds.

'Why bother her?' asked Wollin, lighting a cigarette and squatting on a corner of the couch. 'Don't you understand it puts her into a conflict of conscience?'

'But I do like it,' Julia protested half-heartedly. 'It only seems unusual at first.'

'It could stand the feminine touch,' John Hiller admitted,

squinting at the wide-bellied old glasses on the bar into which he was pouring the brandy. 'There, now, that'll help us over the World Peace Road blues.'

Julia swallowed at the sacrilege. Her doubts and premonitions rushed back at her; she had to force herself to answer lightly, 'Doesn't Waltraut Greve supply that touch?'

John Hiller handed out the drinks. 'She does come by occasionally,' he said. 'Are you comfortable, Brother Wollin?'

Wollin held out his glass for a refill. 'I may have done you an injustice, John Hiller. I suspected that you were sicced on Julia and me. But you're not the watchdog type.'

'Watchdog?' Julia sat up. 'Sicced on us? By whom? What for?'

Hiller laughed noisily.

'I'm sorry.' Wollin shook his head. 'I've had to be on my guard for too many years.'

Julia stood up. The alcohol, after the exertion of the day had gone to her head ; she held on to the back of her chair. 'Daniel Yakovlevich Wollin – that's contemptible. We've opened our arms to you, Arnold and I, and our hearts. Yes. And you haven't a single good word for Arnold. You call his work a hypocrisy. You cast aspersions on him as if he . . . as if he had anything to hide . . . '

John Hiller, who had been about to pour himself another brandy, remained motionless. She was very beautiful in her anger, in this last bucking against something that he felt she knew was becoming the new reality of her life. A tiny vein showed blue under the white of her temple; her eyes shone; she threw her head back to set her hair that gleamed like bronze in the light streaming through the window. Should he tell her that Wollin was right – uncanny Wollin – and that Arnold Sundstrom apparently had something to hide, God knows what? – No. She'd had enough today; she was groggy; what she needed was another drink.

'Julia baby,' he came from behind the bar to fill her glass and filled his own, too, and forced her to drink with him, 'what's the purpose of being mad at Wollin when you're really angry at yourself? Is it his fault that you're beginning to look at things from another angle?'

He ruffled her hair, and she let him; she saw his brows that were grown together over the root of his nose, and his eyes that were free of his usual irony. 'Don't call me Julia baby,' she said, and thought: perhaps he has the understanding I need; he's different today, probably because he's within his own four walls, and what about Wollin? 'I'm no baby,' she insisted. 'I'm nearly as old as you—'

'—and the mother of a child and the wife of Comrade Professor Arnold Sundstrom,' he finished.

'Amen,' said Wollin. He had settled back on the couch, a couple of pillows propping up his back, and he was warming his glass in his two hands. He wasn't clear whether he should be jealous on his own account or guard his friend Sundstrom's property or simply relax and let matters take care of themselves. 'Someday, Julia,' he said, 'I'll tell you about the tundra. That's an architect's dreamland, nothing on it, a plain on which you can raise the shapes and dimensions of the future. Comrade Professor Arnold Sundstrom has had that chance – a whole city district three-quarters bombed to bits. God, what he could have done, even with the limited materials available!'

'Why don't you tell him!' she said.

'Do you think it would help him?'

'No.' She paused, frightened at the sudden discovery of the distance she had let separate her from her own husband. 'Or . . . if *you* feel . . . ' she added weakly.

'Julia baby!' John Hiller was offering his dose of cheer. 'I'll now prepare supper. You'll stay, the two of you. This is just the beginning of a memorable evening . . . You want to help, Julia baby? Brother Wollin, I leave you in charge of the bottle!'

The kitchen was neat, bright, compact, a dollhouse kitchen

with hardly room enough for one person to move about. He really didn't need help; he was one of those men who liked to cook and who went about it deftly and economically, no fuss, no wasted motion. Perhaps he brushed up against her more frequently than the cramped space necessitated; each time a not unpleasant sensation that she knew she must struggle against tingled through her blood; but when she tried to leave, his hand on her arm stayed her, and she no longer objected.

Between slicing and frying and carving and mixing – those spices, she thought, definitely never came from the state-owned stores – he kept talking: of Voukovich's flat into which they could look through the kitchen window, except that it was dark over there, Voukovich being away on a trip, business, official; of himself and Voukovich finding this part-ruin and seeing its possibilities; of getting the workmen to help them reclaim it, after hours – with filched material, she thought – of painting the rooms and fitting in cupboards and doing the hundred and one things to make this a livable place and of the thousand and one difficulties. He kept up his patter. He thought: Mrs Arnold Sundstrom, rigidly corseted views, rigidly corseted morals, socialist teacher's pet; but one little crack in her monolithic personality and all of it would crack; it always does with that sort of person; I'm catching her on the rebound.

He held out his finger with some of the patty dough. 'Taste?'

She laughingly licked his finger, and then stopped laughing. He drew her to him; his lips closed in on hers; she fended him off. 'I don't make love that readily and that easily.'

'Julia baby,' he said, 'I can wait.'

She leaned against the doorjamb, feeling pleasantly dizzy, and wondered at her layers of emotion, her capacity to absorb shock: the scaffolding of her beliefs was crashing down about her ears, deep clefts of doubt were splitting the earth, and she was licking the dough from this man's finger.

She saw the wide, intelligent curve of his skull; the smooth

109

skin of his neck; the play of muscle on his naked forearm. She said, 'Why should I make love to you at all?'

'Because you're due for it physically, psychologically.'

'You're crazy. I won't destroy my life.'

'Isn't it destroyed?' He shoved the patties into the stove, each one containing its portion of ragout. 'What's there to hold you back? That phoney of a husband?'

'Our child.'

'A child never stopped anybody,' he said. 'A child belongs to the mother.'

She suddenly came to. 'What are we talking about!' she protested, managing a laugh. And opening the kitchen door, 'You don't need any help . . . '

'Set the table!' he called after her. 'Dishes and silverware are in the cupboard!'

Wollin looked up. He hadn't moved off the couch, but the level of the brandy in the bottle was considerably lower. 'Had a good time?' he enquired, a trifle heavily. 'He's a bright boy; he'll make his way.'

Julia spread the tablecloth. 'Are you recommending him?'

'Not for you.'

'He can cook!'

'Julia . . . ' he broke off.

'What are you thinking of?'

'A great many things. My head's in a whirl. Faces, people, buildings. How much you resemble your father! – of course, everything translated into the feminine: the eyes, the mould of the chin. Julia, I'll never say a word to hurt you. I may be drunk, you understand, but this is the sainted truth: I have only one urge, to protect you.'

'From what?'

He rose unsteadily. 'From falling to pieces,' he said.

His eyes narrowed. 'There's something basically correct about Arnold's having spun that cocoon about you. You should be

110

protected. But Arnold does a bad job of it. Can't help himself, I suppose. A tug at the proper end of the thread, and off comes the whole web. *I*, on the other hand,' he spread his arms, forgetting that he still held the bottle, 'I would . . . '

'Food!' John Hiller announced. He stood in the doorway that led from the kitchen, a large tray in his hands. The smell of meat and spice, pungent, made Julia's brain as cloudy as the drinks had. She sank onto a chair and waited to be served.

Julia knew she should at least phone home, but she postponed it. After supper, she thought; and then, after this drink, positively; and then we'll be going soon anyhow; and then it was too late. Wollin, drunk, was moaning and swaying his head like an old Russian woman in misery and reciting the names of comrades she'd never heard of. 'Dead,' he kept saying, 'all dead,' his fist hitting the table so that the dirty silverware clattered on the dirty dishes. Through the fog in her mind, she waited for the names of Julian Goltz and Babette Goltz on the roster, but he either had forgotten them or never got around to them. He got up clumsily, his eyes no longer focusing, and broke into a babble of curses – in Russian, curses of a brutality she had never before heard – and then raised his hands before his face as if warding off a volley of blows.

'Daniel!' she cried. 'Daniel Yakovlevich!'

He started. His arms fell. He stared at her. 'You're so beautiful,' he said. 'You're the hope.'

Then he sank, face forward, among the dishes.

Hiller tried to pull him up by the collar; Wollin's head lolled back. Hiller slapped his face.

'Don't!' Julia's lips quivered. 'He's been through so much.'

'We can't let him lie there!'

'I'll help you.'

Though Wollin was surprisingly light, it was an operation since neither she nor John was quite steady on their feet. They hitched

111

his limp arms over their shoulders and lifted him up; and Julia suddenly thought how ridiculous the three of them must look as they struggled against the force of gravity and how outraged Arnold would be if he saw the scene, and she suppressed her giggle. They managed to carry Wollin into Voukovich's flat and onto Voukovich's bed. John took off Wollin's shoes and she – this she remembered distinctly – covered him with Voukovich's blanket.

The next thing she recalled was the insistent ringing of the telephone. That was back at John's place, John's hands underneath her armpits half guiding, half caressing her.

'It's Arnold!' she said, frightened.

His eyes questioned; his fingers lay on the receiver. She hesitated. The ringing stopped.

'Julia baby,' he said, 'what're you afraid of?'

She was too drunk, or too excited, to detail her reasons. She only knew that everything had become uncertain: her marriage, her work, her beliefs. She felt his hands on her body and heard him say things that were good to hear and that might, or might not, be true.

How long he had been waiting for this, months, years, ever since he first saw her entering the studio, so young, and with a grace that drove the blood to his head; how often he'd undressed her in his thoughts and held her, not close to him, not at first, rather at arm's length to give his eyes a chance at her shoulders, her breasts, her hips, her thighs; and only then took her, gently, gently, waiting for her responses, waiting until she begged him—

'John . . . John . . . '

'Yes, baby?'

'D'you think there's something peculiar about me?' He held her, no longer at arm's length, but close to him, his fingers tearing at her clothes. 'What makes you ask?'

She couldn't tell him – Arnold's explanations, the vicious circle, mind, nerves, glands.

'I'll prove there's nothing peculiar about you!' He laughed. He placed her against the pillows of the couch, adjusted the lighting, and announced, 'This is a very exciting colour scheme – the flesh tints against the black and the russet and the chrome. Once an architect, always an architect, eh?'

The room was slowly circling about her head. She closed her eyes; her thoughts seemed to lose their edge; her tensions eased.

Then she felt him, gently, gently, as he had promised. His lips toyed with her earlobes, her lashes, her mouth; in between kisses, he whispered of the discoveries of his fingertips. It was a pleasurable game, with none of the darknesses she had known and the blinding flashes; it was as if they were long familiar with one another, perhaps, she thought, because he had rehearsed it all in his mind.

The telephone rang.

She tightened up; her heart raced. 'Relax,' he said, 'relax baby.' One hand kept caressing her as the other reached for the receiver. 'Oh, it's you, Waltraut!' he spoke into the phone. 'So late? . . . You called before? No answer? . . . How too bad . . .' He took the receiver and held it to Julia's ear. Its pitch more tinny than ever through the transmission, the voice nagged. Julia couldn't follow its drift; the very ludicrousness of this two-level situation suddenly translated itself into a gush of desire that made her cling to him; she hardly heard him say into the phone, 'You go to hell, will you,' and put down the receiver; she held on to him as if he was life and strength and love and world, and then fell back spent, happy, smiling.

She lay there, she didn't know how long, her consciousness three-quarters switched off. John was idly caressing her, light and shadows changing the planes of his face and his shoulders and chest. She saw his tousled dark hair which, in conjunction with his rounded forehead and his slightly aquiline nose, gave him a somewhat Roman appearance. Now I'm an adulteress, she thought, and mechanically began listing all the moral and

113

political tenets against which she was sinning; but none of this penetrated beyond the surface, and she continued feeling comfortable and at peace.

Until she heard the soft creaking of the door and heard fumbling steps and saw, in the doorway to the room, darkly outlined but for the almost luminous white of his hair, Daniel Wollin.

He stopped, swayed slightly, muttering an apology before John had time to throw a blanket over her and himself.

Then he was gone.

'Damn it . . . I must have forgotten to lock that door!' John Hiller caressed her, but she remained rigid. 'Wollin couldn't have seen a thing!' He tried to set her at ease. 'His eyes were glazed like a church window. And even if . . . he'd be the last one to babble I assure you . . . '

She turned from him.

'What's to become of me?' he heard her ask in a thin, strange voice.

It made him feel like a rapist, hateful.

CHAPTER FIVE

As she sat in the child's room watching him eat his breakfast cereal and drink his milk, it seemed inconceivable that her world should have come out of joint.

There hadn't even been a scene. Arnold had been telephoning when she came home. He broke off whatever he'd been saying, turned to her, his face a mixture of relief and suspicion, and changed his tack toward the person with whom he had been conversing. 'It's all right now,' he spoke into the phone. 'I'll be at the meeting.'

Julia had been prepared for a volley of questions, a bristling reproach. There was nothing. He said, 'Julian and I waited up for you. He fell asleep on my lap.' Then, his eyes bloodshot from fatigue, he said, 'The District Party Committee is meeting this morning. Comrade Tolkening has asked me to come to it, at least for one of the points. I'll be back as soon as I can. Will you wait for me?'

And he grabbed his coat and was gone, carrying himself as upright as ever.

'Julia?'

'Yes, darling?'

'Where is Uncle Wollin?'

'In his room, I suppose . . . resting, or freshening up. Don't forget to eat your egg.'

Julian obediently stuck his spoon into his egg cup. 'Uncle Wollin is a good man, isn't he?'

'Oh, yes.' And after a pause, 'What makes you ask, darling?'

The shadow of a vertical line appeared on the child's forehead; his eyes darkened in thought, and he suddenly looked un-childlike. 'Daddy said I mustn't worry. Uncle Wollin was with you.'

She took the small hand in her own. She wished that by closing her eyes she could shut out all that had happened.

'Julia?'

She felt the thin arms about her neck. The child was weeping. Her mind raced: oh, God, what *can* I do?

'But I'm here, darling. Why are you crying?'

'I thought you went away.'

'But where? Without you?'

'I don't know. I thought you left me.'

'Left you!' She tousled his hair. 'Don't I love you the best – more than anything?'

'More than Daddy?' He gave a last sob.

'The very most.' And thought, I'll throw myself on Arnold's mercy – if only he doesn't take the child from me. She would confess to everything – her doubts of his work, of the Road; her thought that her father and mother could have been taken away wrongly; her feeling of being trapped, helpless; and her night with John, which was a reflex action, beyond the control of reason.

'Daddy told me stories.'

'What kind of stories, darling?'

'Oh, of the peasant Nikolay and the horse that could fly, and of the three little foxes, and of the big broken bell in the Kremlin and how to build a house, and he would teach me how to be an architect so that I could build houses, bigger houses than any he built and more beautiful . . . '

The thought of the two of them waiting up for her hit her anew. It put her so terribly in the wrong: the wanton wife off with her lover; husband and child at home, sorrowing – and yet there was something not quite true in that picture – it was posed somehow. Arnold wasn't that guileless; he couldn't afford to be, considering his position in public life. Until now she hadn't credited him with ulterior motives; she had entrusted herself to his guidance, believing implicitly in his integrity.

No, she wasn't trying to find excuses for what she had done. There were none, but there were reasons.

'Those were lovely stories your daddy told you,' she said finally. 'Do you really want to become an architect?'

He smiled, and his eyes grew large and bright. 'You're an architect, Julia!' he said.

The night receded with its tangled events, and there was only the face of the child, her child, all hers.

What transpired at the meeting largely passed him by. In the brief moments when he was aware of the others present, he suspected that everyone must be noticing his distraction; he made an effort to follow the proceedings but simply couldn't; his thoughts kept circling about the same spot like crows about offal.

'Are you ill Comrade Sundstrom?'

He started.

'Don't you feel well?' This was Tolkening, his narrow-set eyes gauging. 'You know I would rather our leading cadres didn't over-exert themselves. A sick revolutionary is a useless revolutionary.' He paused. He prided himself on his aphoristic mind and liked to hear his sayings quoted on the lower levels of the apparatus. 'Perhaps you had better go home, Comrade Sundstrom, and take care of your grippe?'

Sundstrom didn't care to contradict Comrade Tolkening's diagnosis. He was getting away lightly, at that. He had seen other comrades withered by a rebuke from Tolkening for less than the crime of inattention; he muttered something of having a frightful headache, his skull about to burst, and gathered his papers and left.

He drove slowly; he didn't feel safe at the wheel with his mind constantly wandering off. Underneath the velvet kindness with

117

which Tolkening had dismissed him he could feel the claws. Sundstrom frowned; having to leave the meeting forced him to face the answers he hated facing to questions he hated putting.

Then why ask any? Wasn't the horror of last night enough, the minutes ticking off, the half-hours, the hours? With each passing hour the fear in his mind had taken on a more tangible shape – and nothing he could do to ward off what he had seen coming since the visit of his friend Krylenko and that ill-fated Popov. Really nothing? He should have packed off Julia and little Julian and sent them somewhere, anywhere, before Wollin came; or he should have given up the Road, his work, everything, and gone into hiding with wife and child, as the sensible man hides before a tidal wave. But he hadn't been sensible. He had been too big for his britches. Last night had taught him.

And last night was only a foretaste of the hell he was in for. His wife turning away from him was the beginning; then they would all follow, the friends alongside whom he had risen to prominence and power; when the pinch came they couldn't afford to uphold him, although, in one sense or another, they were as guilty as he was – or perhaps *because* it was so.

He didn't bother to garage the car. The fatigue of the whole night caught up with him as he dragged himself up the garden path and into the house. His body ached for sleep; at the same time his nerves were so taut they seemed to quiver. He needed a drink, or coffee, or one of those pills.

Julia was in the living room, waiting for him as he had requested. He mumbled a greeting but passed by her and made for the wall closet in which the bottles were kept. His trembling hand stretching for the vodka, he quoted, in a sort of gallows humour, a nineteenth-century German rhymester,

> It is an ancient saying, Vicar,
> that man in trouble takes to liquor . . .

And added, 'Drink?'

Julia shuddered. 'No, thanks.'

He downed one vodka, poured another, and then eased himself into his big chair.

Julia was studying the design in the rug. It can't be so difficult, she was thinking; just tell him; one, two sentences, thirty seconds, sixty at most, and you've said it all. 'I must talk to you,' she began, and stopped, her breath giving out.

Arnold looked up at her, heavy-eyed. His mouth curved downward. 'Can't you wait for the gong?' he asked. 'Let me come out of my corner, at least . . . '

She watched him toy with the stem of his glass; his face was slack, almost baggy. If he would only reproach her, rage at her, threaten to beat her – anything was better than this loaded silence.

'I can't live with a lie,' she began again, tortured. 'That's not how you brought me up.'

He raised his hand. 'One moment, please.'

She understood him. He wanted to savour the last few moments of illusion before he heard the brutal details of a truth he could guess at.

'Perhaps I've brought you up in too straight-laced a manner.' He nodded. '*Let your communication be, Yea, yea; nay, nay* . . . But it doesn't work that way . . . Julia . . . whatever it is that has come between us, let's not forget that there are motives in life that are beyond a person's control, that we are driven more than driving.'

'This is kind of you,' she said. 'You want to make it easier for me.'

'And for myself,' he emphasised. 'And for myself.'

There's my chance, she thought. He had given it to her; she need only take it, say that something beyond her control had carried her away – the brandy, the day's exertion, an emotional upset, his having failed her; there were dozens of explanations for the sudden spark of a short circuit; she could pick any one of them and construct a case for herself. Did he want that?

119

She saw the wariness in his eyes. She hesitated. One, two sentences, thirty seconds, sixty at most – but there was the finality of it. Did he want *that?*

'What did Wollin tell you?'

'Wollin?'

'Wollin!' he said. 'You spent the whole afternoon with him. And the evening. And the night. You might have called by the way; we have a phone. I sat staring at that phone till it wavered before my eyes. Where were you?'

'At John's . . . John Hiller's,' she corrected herself, noticing his indifference to the name.

'A party, huh?'

'A party, sort of.' She felt her knees giving and found a chair. The confession she had wanted to give from a full heart was turning into an interrogation – her own fault; everything was her fault.

'But what did Wollin tell you?'

'Tell me about what?'

'Julia,' he leaned forward, the plea in his voice overshadowing the anxiety, 'I appreciate your wanting to spare my feelings, but my feelings would be better spared if you would stop skirting the issue. Why don't you come out with it . . . for my sake, for ours. I'm sure that you and I, together, can work out some answer. We did love one another, we still do, I'm sure . . . '

His fingers dug into his scalp; his face was distorted by an inner pain. They give you an anaesthetic when they operate on you, Julia was thinking; why wasn't there an anaesthetic for this sort of operation?

'John Hiller,' she said, 'John and I—'

'Don't evade!'

'But I'm not!'

He rose. The glass, empty, clattered to the floor. 'I am not interested in John Hiller or any of his clever tripe. If I want to know from him I'll hear from him directly. But what did Wollin say? You don't want to infer that you spent hours with the man and he kept his mouth shut like a Trappist monk? What did you talk about?'

'Architecture.' She said it mechanically, and mechanically laughed; she had struggled with all her might to break open the door that barred her way and found it led into a void.

'Architecture? Only architecture?'

'It's a big enough field!' Julia felt her face harden. A stubbornness that was new to her appeared to be freezing out her remorse and sentiment.

'And because of what Wollin said about architecture you forgot where you belong? Forgot even to telephone?'

'No.' Julia sounded sullen. 'Not quite.'

'Ah, you see!'

Sundstrom settled back. Gradually he was getting at the truth, he thought, fateful though it would be. But better to have the truth and be able to take measures than continue in that uncertainty. What he had before him was an equation with two unknown factors: how much did Wollin know, and how much of what he knew had he told Julia? Of the two, the latter factor seemed easier of solution. Though Julia was resisting him she couldn't play hide-and-seek forever – he was too experienced in dealing with people and he knew every fibre of her mind.

'But architecture was at the root of it,' she resumed defensively.

'Suppose you tell me,' he suggested, and thought, if that's the tack you want to take, go ahead.

'I will tell you.' She shivered slightly. She grew aware that she was bathed in sweat. 'I'll tell you everything.'

'I wish you would.'

'But you must promise—' Her lower lip began to quiver; for a moment the tinge of obstinacy that had marked her face was gone; she seemed more than contrite.

To him, however, the fact of her posing conditions outweighed all else: she had the whip hand, and she was using it. 'What must I promise?' he said warily.

'To let me keep Julian.'

He made a move to rise. He should grip her by the shoulders and shake her, shake her till she was as limp as a rag doll, her self-will gone and with it the threat to him that she represented. But he couldn't even get up. He sat, panic laming his limbs, and stared. She wanted the child. She was going to divorce him. She knew.

'Wollin's been lying,' he finally managed to say, a weak attempt at preserving something out of the wreckage.

Julia didn't understand his harping on Wollin. But she saw how he felt; he was taking it badly; and the past rushed back at her, the moments of his tenderness – tenderness toward the child Julia and then toward the wife Julia. What was it that had driven her into John's arms last night? Disappointment? Uncertainty? Glands? And would she be able to resist it another time if now, for the sake of the man huddled before her, she chose to lie?

'All right,' he said, 'I'll promise.' His glance guarded, his head moved from side to side, the wounded lion trying to take the scent of the hunter. The few seconds' hesitation on Julia's part had been enough to revive some of his resiliency; let's find out first, he thought, and then decide; you've been in worse spots, Arnold Sundstrom; ethics, or the lack of them, never killed a man.

'You promise that I'll keep Julian regardless of what I tell you?'

'Uh-huh,' he nodded.

Julia took a deep breath. Then she closed her eyes as if she were about to dive off the board, and said, 'It's that I've begun to doubt.'

'Doubt what?'

'World Peace Road. Everything we've done . . . '

In a way, it did Julia good to recount, step by step, the stations that had led her to the humiliation of last night. Only by this did she see that those doubts went back further than she had assumed – further than the evening of the reception for the

Soviet delegation, back to the first occasions when she noticed the disparity between the noble phrase and the actual performance, between design and purpose, cost and achievement.

These processes, she saw, begin unnoticeably, one minor item threading itself to another till you have a small chain, but long enough to curl itself into a question mark. Even then, you can repress the question inside you and make enough noise to silence others daring to raise it. But ultimately the answer superimposes itself, reduced to a single word: *hypocrite!* And then you sit, faced with the shambles – a drawing in an old Nazi book, for instance, or the gilded pinecones of a wrought-iron grill.

No, no, no, you're not finished; you don't give up in minutes the beliefs of years, common experiences, ties, the trust and confidence that grow from love. The issue is still open; everything hangs in balance, but the weight of the doubts keeps growing heavier; you seek the oracle. Ordinarily, the oracle would have been Arnold, broad chest at which to nestle, strong hands from which to receive guidance. But he's a party to the case, and the doubts corroding her beliefs corroded his image. The oracle, therefore, is named Daniel Wollin – predestined to give his verdict by virtue of parallel experiences and longstanding friendship. 'Perhaps the pattern of my thoughts is childish,' she concluded, 'but that's how they run.'

'Oracle!' he snorted. 'You picked the right man.'

'He isn't?'

An angry gesture of the hand. 'An architect who for sixteen years hasn't built as much as a *pissoir*, a man who has been shut off from life that long will be full of resentment. What did he say? Briefly, his conclusion, please.'

'He called our World Peace Road a hypocrisy in brick. And later he said that you knew how to build better than that.'

'And you believe him?'

'I must have . . . yesterday.' Yesterday, she had seen the macabre in the false fronts, in the capitals and cornices pasted on, the

123

balconies on which no one could step, the pomp that no one could use; yesterday she had fled into John Hiller's bed.

'And today?'

'Arnold,' her tongue felt dry as a withered leaf, 'how do you explain the frightening similarity of the Road that you and I built to the Nazis' Charlottenburger Chaussee project?'

God, he thought, she certainly was choosing a roundabout way to reach the point he was waiting for. Or was it all one in her mind – the architecture and the arrests, the forms of art and the forms of government – and did she want to unroll, in her way, the whole grand picture of the hell that people dragged themselves through just to survive?

'It was you,' she said, 'who taught me to see the connections between content and form. What is there in both our way of life and the Nazis' that makes for nearly the identical expression in stone and mortar?'

This was outrageous, heresy of the worst sort. She had gone a long way in a short time, and he hadn't even noticed, riveted as his thoughts had been on his own troubles. And it was ridiculous, too – being forced into a highly academic discussion on the social origins of architectural forms when his mind and soul were centred on one single, vital point: did she or didn't she know about the actual why and how of her parents' end?

'Why is it that important, Julia?' he asked. 'Where does it get us? Why don't you tell me without subterfuge what Wollin said to you that shook you up to the point of your staying away from me the entire night?'

'But everything proceeds from there!' She made a step toward him, two, then stopped, her hands pleading. 'Why don't you want to understand?'

'Proceeds from where?'

'Architecture,' she said. 'The ethics of it.'

He rubbed his chin. I forgot to shave, he thought; I'm in bad shape, and perhaps because I'm seeing ghosts where there aren't any. Architecture, its forms and content, well and good; it was her life, or part of it; but would she keep dwelling on it if she had even an inkling of what was haunting him?

'Those similarities that seem to perturb you are superficial,' he advanced cautiously. 'Where they can be proved at all, they're the outcropping of the client's taste.'

'The client? Which client?'

The weakness in his joints was disappearing; he was beginning to feel himself again. If it was just a case of her having the socialist-realism blues, he saw no reason to maintain an untenable fiction for the sake of sparing her feelings. 'Hasn't it ever occurred to you that the architect isn't the boss? The poet needs only a sheet of paper, the painter a piece of canvas, the musician a piano, or at most an orchestra – the architect, in order to realise his ideas, must have an organisation: workmen, land, materials, machinery. That organisation costs money, much money . . . do you have it? Or do I?'

She had never heard him talk that way. The at-oneness of artist and people, under socialism, had been his constant.

'You want turrets, Comrade Tolkening?' he asked, his voice rising. 'I'll put up turrets for you. The authorities want World Peace Road to look like a cross between the Kremlin wall and the Parthenon, with some Baroque thrown in? I'll build it to specifications . . . '

He waited for her to speak, but she seemed to find no words, her lips tight in shock, her eyes large with grief. 'And you're blaming me!' he said angrily. His years of frustration broke through. 'Why don't you investigate, as a Marxist should, the origins of our clients' bad taste? Look at the life these men led, the limitations of their minds, the power suddenly thrown into their hands; enquire into what shaped their sense of beauty, if any, and their dreams of the monument they wish to erect to themselves . . . and then you'll see, I hope, that World Peace Road could have been a lot worse than it is!'

'But this is . . . this is . . . '

'Cynicism?' He rose and advanced toward her almost threateningly. 'Once upon a time I, too, thought that in socialism the fetters were smashed that tied the architect to building pyramids. Then I learned that I couldn't do both, build as one should and eat, follow one's artistic convictions and live . . . Or should I have chosen to fashion my cities out of clay on a wooden board, in a Siberian penal camp?'

'But why did you feed me those illusions? Why didn't you ever tell me?

'Your oracle told you, your Wollin, didn't he? *Hypocrisy in brick!* . . . And what else did he tell you, about himself, about you . . . about me?'

She stood there, shoulders hanging, head low, among the shambles of her world. All of it had been lies; he had confirmed it when he was confronted with the facts; he himself had furnished her justification for her escapade with John Hiller; the hypocrisy in brick was only one of many. And what remained, then, that you could believe in?

'Well?'

She looked up at him uncomprehendingly.

'Stop play-acting, Julia! Didn't he complain to you of unjust arrest, protest his innocence, yammer on about his years in camp?'

'Should he have?'

'Did he or didn't he?'

'No.'

'Julia . . . listen to me. I may have lied to you about architectural questions and matters connected with them in this or that way. But I swear to you: each lie stemmed from my love for you, was designed to protect you, help you grow into the wonderful person you are, the core and content of my life. And now that I've made a clean break of it, won't you tell me the truth, too . . . for our sake, for the sake of something beyond those lies, something that always was true and will remain true . . . '

He broke off. He hadn't known that he still had this power in him, this eloquence that came from the heart, but he saw the effect of his words: her face had grown soft and her eyes, the eyes that he loved, spoke to him from their depths.

'John Hiller . . . ' she began.

'Oh, for God's sake!' He gripped her wrist. 'Stick to the point will you!'

It was as if a shutter had come down between them.

'Wollin!' he urged. 'What did *he* say?'

'Why don't you ask him?'

'Because you're my wife and I'm asking you.'

'Wollin was drunk.'

'Drunk . . . ' Sundstrom bit his lip. Drunks said all sorts of things.

'Let go of my wrist, please, Arnold. You're hurting me.'

'I'm sorry.' He relaxed his grip. 'Did he mention any names?'

'He muttered a lot. I couldn't follow him, and I didn't listen. Arnold – what is it you fear he might say?'

'Fear? I fear nothing. You keep that in mind – not a thing!'

'Yes, Arnold.'

Her answer came too readily. He fumbled for a cigarette, lit it. 'There was a time, Julia, when fear sat in the back of one's neck like a goblin.' He hesitated, but the need to explain at least some of himself was greater than the voice that told him to shut up for heaven's sake. And a degree of frankness perhaps would help, would counteract the drunken mutterings of Wollin. 'That was the time when our friend Wollin got himself in trouble, as did some other people.' His eyes sought Julia's and held them. 'Yes, your father among them, and your mother.'

She should speak up now, he thought; say something, ask. But she didn't. She moved away from him, a step or two, but kept looking at him as if he were an insect pinned under glass. He felt that control of the situation was slipping from his fingers; indeed, positions had switched already: she, the questioner, and he, the examinee.

'You can't claim I kept that from you' – his voice neared a dangerous pitch – 'I didn't. Fear!' He dragged at the cigarette, coughed, forced himself to a calm that he knew was costing him his last nervous reserve. 'But one learns. It's a narrow path, Julia, that leads upward; you have to know where you step, and you have to be sure-footed. You understand?'

Julia pressed her hands to her head as if the veins underneath her temples wanted to burst. She saw herself standing on the open sixth-floor level, World Peace Road swaying below her; she was once more caught in the terrible logic of things: if one feature of the great, life-spending, future-holding system of thought was faulty, then another might be faulty as well; if socialist architecture as taught and practised was a sham, then socialist justice, too, might have been applied wrongly.

'Do you mean to imply, Arnold, that my father and mother' – her hands fell, and her painted mouth seemed too red and too large for her paled-out face – 'but that would be murder.'

'I implied nothing!' The cigarette had dropped from his fingers; a circle, dark brown on the cream of the rug, slowly grew about its burning end. 'But I want to know if Wollin did.'

'He didn't, I swear to you. It's all in my mind.'

'It is?'

He desperately wanted to believe her. But even if Wollin, this one time, had not spoken, what would he say tomorrow, or the day after?

'If it's in your mind,' he said harshly, 'forget it. The idea is crazy, diseased . . . and that's the mildest way to describe it. Or do you, who grew up in socialism, actually claim the police of a socialist state and its judges and all of us who tolerated and supported them are guilty of conspiracy to murder innocent people?'

It was unimaginable, the way he put the question. Julia shook her head.

'Oh, the rug!' he said. He groaned as he bent to pick up the cigarette. 'We'll have to have it mended.'

'Yes,' she said, 'I'll attend to it,' and thought that she would too, as if nothing had changed, and responded with an absent-minded 'Come in!' to the knock at the door.

But it wasn't Frau Sommer coming to enquire what to serve for lunch and completing the return to the everyday routine. It was Wollin, in hat and overcoat, the weight of his cloth-covered suitcase giving him a lopsided stance.

'Come in!' Sundstrom repeated after his wife. His jovial 'Where d'you think you're going?' didn't quite cover up the renewed surge of panic.

Wollin put down the suitcase, took off his hat, ran the back of his hand across his forehead, and came in, somewhat diffidently. 'I've taken a room,' he informed. 'I've been looking for one these last days.'

'Why the secrecy?' Arnold Sundstrom glanced suspiciously from him to Julia and back. 'What made you think you've outstayed your welcome? Forget that room. Stay with us – as long as you want! Right, Julia?'

Julia kept studying the hole burned into the rug.

'I know I'm welcome here,' said Wollin. 'But it's simply time, after sixteen years, that I settled down in a place of my own. By the way, Arnold, you won't get rid of me that easily' – a faint smile accompanied his little joke – 'because I'd like to work with you. Yesterday, Julia asked me if I would. And you've talked about that niche for me . . . '

Arnold Sundstrom swallowed. Then he forced himself to extend both hands and to walk the few steps toward Wollin.

'Daniel,' he said, managing to sound full-throated, 'old friend and comrade – I hoped that this would be your conclusion after you saw World Peace Road. Of course, I know the shortcomings of the Road as well as you do . . . ' He turned to Julia. 'We were just discussing that weren't we?' And back to Wollin. 'But these are the manifestations of a transition period.'

'Certainly,' said Wollin. 'May I call a taxi?'

129

'You insist on taking that room?'

'Please—'

'Then I'll drive you there.' Sundstrom laughed, slapping Wollin's shoulder. 'You won't get rid of me that easily, either!'

CHAPTER SIX

Edgar Voukovich always grew depressed when he saw a fellow creature suffering. And Waltraut Greve was suffering with abandon; she threw herself on his couch and buried her face in his pillow.

'I can't hear you,' he said.

She turned her head sideways. Her eyes were swollen and reddened, her lipstick smeared. 'You don't want to hear me,' she sobbed. 'I have no friends.'

'If you would stop muffling your voice in that pillow—' he suggested.

'He's a beast.'

'He isn't really,' said Voukovich in half-hearted defence of his friend. 'He's just weak and maybe unprincipled.'

'I understand,' she said with a wan smile that deepened his sense of futility. 'The great friendship. Pylades covering up for Orestes. All right, I have no claim on him; he gave me no promise and he didn't take my virginity, I assure you. But to do his climbing via the boss's wife's behind—'

'—a not unpretty behind—'

'If you like them fat and floppy! . . . ' Waltraut tossed herself around and lay on her back, one knee up. 'It absolutely disgusts me to hear that poor old cuckold crooning: John Hiller this – and John Hiller that! One ought to report the whole thing to the Party. The Party is very much interested in its members' morals!'

Edgar Voukovich contemplated the bare patch of unsmooth skin above the top of her stocking. She might actually blab out of jealousy. He groaned. Women!

'Edgar,' she said, 'come here.'

He got up from his chair, stuck his cigarette into the bill of a brass duck hovering over his brass ashtray, and sat on the edge of the couch. She pulled him down to her, stroked the back of his neck, and kissed him, and he was aware of her cold, roughened fingertips and the eagerness of her thin lips, and he grew furious at John Hiller for having created this new complication.

Finally she let go of him. Her head motionless on the pillow, she stared at some spot on the ceiling and said, 'You're all the same. All you men.'

Voukovich pulled out his handkerchief and dabbed the lipstick smear off his mouth. 'Beasts,' he said.

'Beasts,' confirmed Waltraut.

Voukovich wished he felt like a beast; she was a hot lay, this much he knew from John Hiller. But he couldn't get over the misery of the situation: gawky, unfulfilled, looking for re-assurance, why didn't she pick on someone else! That's what the poets always forgot to write about – the characters stumbling off toward the wings when the great lovers fell into each other's arms.

'You don't really love him Waltraut.' Voukovich hoped that his matter-of-fact tone would reduce things to matter-of-fact proportions.

'Love?' Even Waltraut's laughter had a nagging quality. 'how can you love him? He's got only his you-know-what. The rest is calculation, manner, ice.'

'Well, if that's the case,' Voukovich's Croat accent grew heavy, 'you'll get over it.'

She started to ruffle her hair but gave it up. Voukovich fetched his cigarette from the duck's bill. It had died, and he lit a new one. Waltraut didn't want to get over it. She wanted to nurse her grudge and make grief out of it, and nothing short of his making love to her would deflect her. But he was in no mood for that. He thought of John Hiller and Julia Sundstrom and the complications *that* story would bring, and under his breath he cursed Hiller and his you-know-what.

Waltraut sat up and studied herself in the mirror pasted to the flap of her pocketbook. She grimaced at what she saw and, rummaging through the pocketbook, found a sheet of cleansing tissue. But before she could clean off the lipstick, her hand started trembling, her body shook, the pocketbook dropped to her lap.

'Waltraut!' He grabbed her shoulders to support her. 'You want a drink? I'll make coffee . . . '

'Leave me alone.' The nagging had vanished from her voice; her grief made it sound as if something had cracked inside her. 'I want to go home.'

'I can't let you go home in that shape.' But he helped her to get up; he was damned lucky she had made up her mind; it saved him a lot of gyrations. 'Stay a while, why don't you? Get hold of yourself.'

'You don't mean it,' she said with a clear-sightedness that made him cringe. 'And I prefer having my breakdown in privacy.'

Voukovich sighed. For a moment he toyed with the idea of trying to give her what she had come for; there wasn't much to her that was alluring, especially not now, but a good deed carried its own reward. Then he thought that he would be saddled with her and it might have the opposite effect and bring back her hysterics: and then it was too late to do anything.

She had slipped into her coat and was gone.

'Would you mind explaining to me why you had to tell her?' asked Voukovich.

John Hiller hooked his elbows over the backrest of the chair he was straddling and looked dreamily at Voukovich's head of dark, self-willed, short curls. 'Why didn't *you* apply yourself to her needs?' he said captiously. 'It used to be a toss-up between you and me; and I'm not so sure she didn't toss you, once or twice, on the side.'

'She didn't, actually – but that's not the point.' The shade of Voukovich's depression changed from dark blue to a near-black. 'I thought I'd let you know that Waltraut threatened to take the whole thing to the Party. A morals case involving Comrade Professor Arnold Sundstrom's pretty young wife and assistant architect Comrade John Friedrich Hiller – what joy! For Julia's sake, at least, I hoped you'd keep your mouth shut.'

'There was no other way to get rid of her.'

'Except by bragging?'

Hiller pushed the chair away from under him, marched up to his friend, and took him by the lapels. 'Have a good look at me, Brother Voukovich!'

Voukovich didn't react.

'What do you see?'

Voukovich shrugged.

'You see a new man. I'm in love, if people like you are capable of imagining such a feeling. For Julia, I could beg, steal, kill – sacrifice! Take my quivering heart from between my ribs and hold it out to her: accept it! I could . . . Why do you shake your head? Because sentiment's out of order in this age and place? Because this is romanticism and it sits badly on me? But I'm only the shell of my old self. We're so blasé, so sordidly sober. The only time we permit ourselves some leeway is when we play back a tape we stole off the air and rock and roll our bodies into contortions. I tell you, I feel strong enough to challenge Sundstrom . . . and I do mean more than just the man. I could—'

'If you could do so much for your love, couldn't you have tried to spare her the trouble into which you're heading?'

Hiller raised his finger to his nose and wrinkled his brow, which gave him the odd look of a small boy trying to imitate his teacher. 'I grant you, Edgar,' he said, 'that this wasn't my intention. A one-night stand, yes; a feather in my cap, because of her position and because she always struck me as so prissy. But

134

now, as to my best friend, I tell you' – his face brightened, his eyes seemed to have a light of their own – 'I wish you one day in your life with one-tenth of what I feel. It would be enough to hold you for a while. Let Waltraut broadcast her news from the top of one of those towers on World Peace Road . . . I'm in love and I don't care who hears of it.'

'People might not take such a happy view of it.'

'People – I suppose you mean the Party – will be satisfied if I stick to the accepted forms. I'm willing to marry Julia, if she'll have me.'

'I know.' Voukovich grinned. 'You mentioned sacrifice.'

'Hell, no!' Hiller sounded annoyed. 'I *want* to marry her.'

'You had her only once,' mentioned Voukovich. 'Or—?'

'But what a once!'

'All right, all right . . . ' Voukovich squirmed.

'It was sensational!' Hiller was saying. 'This closeness, this . . . understanding . . . She's a woman who is everything, from sky to earth—'

'—and back?'

'And back. Sit down, man. You think I'm an unconscionable fornicator, don't you?'

Voukovich went over to Hiller's bar, climbed on a stool, and began munching on some old crackers he found in a tin box. His tongue struggling with the crumbs, he said, 'I'll confess my views of you ran along those lines.'

'What's in the touch of a hand?' Hiller asked. 'The touch of *her* hand as she left me in the morning . . . I knew, then, what she was going back into . . . she's so sensitive, so completely in the power of that Sundstrom. I wanted to beg her to stay, but she wouldn't have done it.'

The few yards' distance from the bar to where Hiller stood, outlined against the raw brick of the wall, offered Voukovich a better opportunity to gauge his friend. The qualitative change from eternal scoffer to wide-eyed romanticist seemed genuine enough, but then any mood of Hiller's was sincere in that he gave himself to it fully while it lasted.

'So I brewed myself a coffee,' Hiller was saying, 'and settled down to think. And I came to a surprising conclusion.'

With a determined twist of his wrist, Voukovich closed the tin box. 'Taste like old socks, those crackers,' he explained. 'What conclusion?'

'That Sundstrom will do anything rather than create trouble for Julia . . . or for me.'

'You don't think he'll consider those horns you put on him ornamental, do you?'

'I just don't think the horns will be his biggest worry.'

'Ah.' Voukovich slid down from the stool but kept toying with the tin box. 'What makes you believe that?'

'The fact that he's made me his chief stooge and confidant!'

At least, thought Voukovich, this approach was more in character.

'Why did he pick me to play the alternate tourist guide for this fellow Wollin?'

'Well, why?' said Voukovich.

'Why was Wollin that long in the Soviet Union? For the fun of it? Or was he held there? And why did he return just now, and come here, and join this office?'

'How do you know so much about Wollin?' asked Voukovich.

'Innuendo – mostly from Comrade Professor Sundstrom. But anyhow, wouldn't you think Julia was sufficient to shepherd the mysterious stranger around?'

'Perhaps Sundstrom thought two are better than one,' suggested Voukovich.

'And why are two better than one?' Hiller's face creased into a sly query; he was a different man from the one who, not two minutes ago, had spoken so nobly of love. 'Because one can report on what the other said . . . and heard.'

'You didn't!'

A contemptuous wave of the hand disposed of that question.

Voukovich came closer. 'But what *did* Wollin say that, to Sundstrom, was worth the trouble of taking you into his confidence and having you gumshoe his wife?'

'Not much, really.'

'You're dreaming it up, John!' But Voukovich didn't sound quite certain. 'You have a crush on a woman and you're making up plots.'

Hiller grabbed Voukovich's right hand, raised it. 'Swear! Swear to the memory of your dead father that you will keep this a secret as long as I don't release you from it.'

'Stop that kid stuff.'

'Swear!'

'If you insist—' Voukovich's hand came up reluctantly. 'I swear.'

'There's something fishy about the great Sundstrom. Specifically about his past relationship to Wollin . . . possibly even to Julia. You think that's farfetched? But what except the past could the two talk of that would be of interest to Sundstrom . . . the weather?'

Voukovich knew from his father, dead of a broken heart, that there were more things in heaven and earth than were taught in Marxist study courses. He began to believe that his friend's suspicions might have a foundation. And if, as Sundstrom had hinted to Hiller, Comrade Wollin's lengthy stay in the Soviet Union was not quite voluntary, a whole barrage of questions opened up – questions as ticklish as they were complex.

'Architecture!' Hiller threw up his hands. 'They stuck to architecture, strictly . . . Comrade Wollin is a careful man. Only as he got into his cups, things started bubbling up from wherever he had them locked away inside him; and even then I suspect he kept a couple of barriers down between his unconscious and his tongue.'

'That doesn't give you much to go by,' Voukovich said doubtfully.

'On the contrary! It was enough to tantalise Sundstrom. He was torn between relief and doubt like a fish who's swallowed two worms, both of them on different hooks. He finally pleaded with me to stay on the job . . . as if I needed convincing to accept a free permit to keep close to Julia.'

'You'll lose your permit quickly enough when Waltraut opens her mouth.'

Hiller's shrug was pointedly indifferent.

Voukovich sat down and seemed to immerse himself in a study of the scuffed tips of his shoes. 'Do you really believe, John, when it comes to a showdown you can say to Sundstrom: lay off me and Julia, pal, because if you don't I'll tell on you?'

'Perhaps not that crudely. If you've observed Sundstrom, you'll know he has an ear for half-tones.'

'You worry me, Hiller.' Voukovich's toes had lost their fascination. 'If what you suspect is true, if there are in Sundstrom's past dark pages on which you threaten to throw light, he'll find ways of getting rid of you faster than you can cry for help.'

For a minute, Voukovich's warnings took effect. Hiller walked to the window and looked outside as if the answer might come from the young birches that had taken root on top of the rubble. Then he laughed. 'If he still were as powerful as he was! But is he? You haven't heard the latest!'

'Rumours! Rumours! If you hate a man sufficiently you take any wishdream as fact.'

'The latest is that, in Berlin, the World Peace Road extension plans have hit a snag.'

'Come back here and say that again,' said Voukovich.

'*Our* extension,' confirmed Hiller, the *our* containing the full dose of his sarcasm. 'Seems things aren't running as they did since Comrade Popov and his delegation arrived. I don't claim these signs and portents have a common root, necessarily . . . the delegation, Wollin's arrival, the second thoughts in Berlin. Sundstrom's obvious uncertainty. But suppose the rumble, the

138

faint flashes indicate a storm: what then of Sundstrom's borrowed power? Because borrowed it is, and from Comrade Tolkening; and Tolkening will drop any man who becomes a source of embarrassment. That's his method . . . always has been.'

Smart figuring, thought Voukovich. Hiller was not yet thirty and was marshalling his facts like an old hand at politics – dirty politics at that. How did that jibe with the lover willing to sacrifice everything, to tackle anyone, for the sake of his love?

Voukovich had been thrown into this part of Germany with all the encumbrances of a refugee, but also with the advantage of such a person: distance. He saw that there was a whole generation of youth who, in their struggle to survive, wriggle through, get ahead, seemed to have cheated themselves out of their share of heart and enthusiasm – people with a built-in double bottom, with two sets of feelings, two sets of values: one for public profession, the other for private consumption. The strange thing was that whichever set they happened to be protesting, they appeared unconscious of the existence of the other – a schizoid state not yet described in any psychology textbook he knew of.

Voukovich pitied Julia. He didn't hate Sundstrom. He knew that Sundstrom, primarily and always, looked out for Sundstrom; yet the man had ridden over all objections to the acceptance of a young Yugoslav into the City Architects' Bureau.

'So you see my position isn't half bad,' Hiller was concluding, rocking from the balls of his feet to his heels and back.

'Well, yes,' admitted Voukovich. 'But I don't like an affair of the heart so deeply interlaced with God knows what rotten politics.'

Hiller whistled softly, serenely. 'Those are the times we live in, Brother Voukovich, the times.'

For Julia time seemed suspended, a state of neither-nor; a slight hypertension of her nerves her only indication that she was in the radiation area of some cataclysm developing outside her, beyond her influence.

She did her eight hours of work, avoiding John Hiller as much as she could and showing indifference when an encounter proved unavoidable. She directed her household; Frau Sommer had never known her to be so efficient, not a detail forgotten, each chore attended to. She spent more time than ever with Julian, inventing new stories to feed his insatiable imagination, enveloping him in her love. All of it helped to delay decisions she felt unequal to, but it also gave her life a dream quality – one of those dreams you have in the early-morning hours, shortly before coming awake; dreams containing snatches of reality oddly enmeshed with your own fears and desires.

She no longer expected that it would be Arnold who forced the decision. Outwardly, at least, Arnold appeared as satisfied as herself at the return of calm and routine: the guest room upstairs once more unoccupied, the traces of Wollin removed from the house. Arnold was again at his accustomed ease, his voice sounding sure, his laugh carefree.

At odd moments Julia wondered about him. That he had forgotten seemed impossible: Wollin's presence at work was a constant reminder of doubt and disturbance. This left the conclusion that Arnold's restraint and accent on cheerful indifference were design. Perhaps he believed in letting sleeping dogs lie, or he hoped that some of the outward peace he maintained would trickle through to the subsoil areas where the magma of conflict simmered.

She was willing to play along. She had no intention of provoking another crisis, although she felt that this calm couldn't last, that a break would come in the surface smoothness as the days passed and the strain mounted. There was that night when he resolutely closed the door to Julian's room and crossed to her side of the double bed and, his hand trembling, almost tore her pyjamas off her. She had known that this would come; it was

140

part of the attempt to restore the old façade on a patched-up structure.

She hadn't denied herself to him. She felt his heavy body, his hairy shoulders, his pumping chest; she observed his lids compressed in concentration, the frown on his forehead, the will that propelled him; and when, finally, resting his weight on his elbows, he managed a questioning smile, she gently patted his shoulder in silent confirmation of his manhood.

He slept deeply afterward – like a stevedore she once had seen in the noonday heat at the Volga, sweated, leaning against a bale, slavering from the corner of his half-open mouth. She listened, wakeful, to the relentless clicking of the alarm clock, the distant clang of a railroad train being shunted, the rattle of the trucks on a cobbled street, the wail of a fire siren. The sounds of the night, which once gave her a sense of snug comfort underneath her blanket, now tugged at her nerves. She forced herself to lie still, fearing to disturb Arnold; she knew she would start screaming at him if he woke up and so much as asked her why she wasn't asleep. She tried to get to the root of the thing that was boring inside her like a cancer, but she could find only outcroppings which refused to fit themselves into a pattern. She tried to drag from the crevices of her mind the patchwork of images that went back to her childhood and link these to Wollin, to Arnold, even to the red-haired Comrade Krylenko with his vapid, protruding eyes, who had come and gone and left unrest in his wake. She saw her father, looking very slender and young as he held her and swung her high up in the air, laughing and saying things she had long forgotten but she remembered they had made her laugh, too; behind him, the sun had speckled a lake, or was it a river? Involuntarily, she compared the picture of the young man throwing his child in the air with the man druggedly asleep at her side, her father looking young enough to be his son; but he was her husband – the equations of time introduced strange factors. She couldn't recall Arnold as a young man, hard as she tried to conjure up an impression of him in that period; he must have changed over the years since he and her father were friends, since that hotel on Gorky Street, since Prague; her image of Arnold had always been the same, more fatherly than her own father, as if he had entered her life only after her parents were gone. Which was patently not the fact. She did remember that he was in their hotel room when the squat women who always sat behind the desk in the hallway brought in the telegram – Julia frowned: did she know at the time it was a telegram? Or when had she learned it was one? – and she remembered that her father had opened it and said that *his* father had died. Her mother was there, too; Julia could see her, but only in outline; the details of her mother's eyes, face, hairdo, dress were dimmed. Clearly etched in her mind, however, was her father, telegram in hand, sitting down on a chair; and a pervading sense of sorrow; and herself climbing on his knee and trying to console him. But Arnold's face remained a blank, though his shape was distinctly present, broad shoulders, broad hands – a figure like a cut-out on which the child dresses a paper doll. Arnold was *not* there when the boots came. This was later, though – weeks? – months? That's when, for a moment flashing by, the dim outlines of her mother came into sharp, three-dimensional focus – the straggling hair, the disarrayed robe, the eyes large and dark in fear, the cry of 'Why?'

Julia was jolted upright by the alarm going off. So she had slept after all, but she felt as if she'd been broken on the wheel. Arnold, after a yawn and a stretch, was up and stomping about; then she heard his whistling from the bathroom, a Russian marching song, full of that high-pitched, optimistic gaiety that had been so much a part of her own makeup so short a while ago. 'Aren't you getting up?' he called from under the shower.

Luckily, Julian was demanding her attention; it gave her the chance to busy herself until Arnold was out of the bathroom. Later, at work in her studio – she didn't work well, the pencils broke, her hand was uncertain, her mind a haze – she couldn't recall how she got through breakfast and through the ride with Arnold into town. He kept making cheerful noises; he seemed to have grown an inch overnight, an inch and a half, maybe; the world, to him, was back in place, each man and woman, each tiny insect crawling in their proper orbit.

Later, she could remember nothing previous to the moment when, the light waning, she had switched on her desk lamp and saw John entering. It was an undramatic entry: he was carrying the papers that were his excuse for coming, quite genuine reference material. But she felt the blood heavy in her veins, each heartbeat reverberating in her ear like the bang on a kettledrum; a sweet and numbing sensation immobilised her joints.

She saw his papers drop to the floor. Then she felt his body against hers, his lips on hers, and thought, God, if someone were to come in now, and then she no longer thought of anything.

Even as they separated, they still seemed to cling to one another.

'This is unbearable, Julia,' he said, his voice grating. 'I can't live without you. You must come to me. Tonight . . . ' He took her silence for an answer. 'Then tomorrow night . . . This happens to people once in a lifetime. Please, don't move. Let me look at you. I love the shape of your face and the way your hair grows at your temples. I love the back of your neck, the small hollows there, and your lips and your tongue; there isn't anything about you I don't love, down to your feet, the narrow instep; did anyone ever tell you how exciting your foot is?'

He was talking hastily, his words tumbling, as if his feelings would escape him if he didn't express them all in this one minute.

'Please, Julia, don't think it's only bed I want, though I long for you. It's more than that, it's in here, in my heart, or wherever the psychiatrists say a man's love is located. Believe me, Julia, please.'

'I believe you.'

'Ah.' He seemed relieved. He knew he sounded hectic, but he needed that, he thought, to sweep her off her feet, and himself along with her. 'Because I must have you, Julia, not just for one night or two, but for nights and days. For *always!*' he added, weighing the word and finding it fitting. 'Let us *live* together, you and I . . . ' His mind conjured up the image of the *you and I*, two people walking down a straight road between poplar trees; where had he seen this, a dream, a motion picture? 'If not in this town, then elsewhere. The world is big, Julia, and even this Republic is larger than one provincial city, one World Peace Road. We'll marry, if you want to.'

She smiled. She took his hand, her light, sensitive fingers caressing. He felt happy that he had said it; he didn't know how it had come about, but now that it was said he wanted a *yes,* jubilant or at least emotion-filled; of course she must get a divorce, there was that to think of.

'We'll marry!' he repeated, pulling her closer and kissing her eyes. 'Getting married will stuff their mouths . . . We're young, we've got brains, the world is our dish, we don't have to depend on anyone's good graces. Simple isn't it? And beautiful. Oh Julia . . . ' His voice, warm, wooing, tapered off.

'Kiss me,' said Julia. 'No, properly. As you would kiss the bride.'

He laughed and complied. 'Well?' he said then.

'And they lived happily ever after,' she said, her eyes darkening, a slight, bitter curve to her mouth.

'I told you no fairytale,' he protested. He noticed the papers on the floor, picked them up, placed them on Julia's drafting table. 'The two of us making love was no fairytale,' he went on harshly. 'That was reality! The livest thing that ever happened in our lives. What changed your mood?'

She couldn't have said what it was. Up to this moment she hadn't been aware of any change. Perhaps it was fear of the unknown, of breaking a pattern: she still saw herself in need of the guiding hand, Arnold's hand. Or lack of imagination: John the lover was credible; John the husband, the father replacement remained unreal.

'One doesn't easily jump one's track,' she said vaguely, beginning to feel guilty toward him as well. 'You must have patience with me. There's Arnold, there's the child. There's the Party the Work, the Road . . . '

' . . . the whole treadmill. If you wanted *that* why didn't you think of it before?'

'Before our night? Oh, John, that was the end of a strange, terrible day. I don't ever want another like it . . . I once saw a scaffolding collapse, with men on it. That's how I felt. I don't want to have to face decisions, at least not now—'

'You want to live with your feelings shut off?'

'I must rest again, sleep again, settle down again. Don't think it's only you who are upsetting me; you're part of it, but there's more to it . . . '

Hiller sat down at her table and lowered his head into his open palms. 'And you think you can undo what's been done? Un-live what's happened? Blind yourself to what your own eyes have seen?'

'I loved it, John. I loved the picture of life you outlined for the two of us. But as I listened to you, I said to myself: one of us has got to keep his balance.'

'What's so unbalanced about that picture?' He raised his head and looked at her accusingly. 'Why shouldn't it be real?' The more he realised that he was being let off the hook, the more deeply he believed in his sincerity. 'All right,' he said, finally. 'I understand. Sundstrom would make it very unpleasant for you, and you love the child. But there are ways, arrangements . . . '

For a moment she appeared puzzled.

'My God,' he said, partly impatient and partly amused. 'Socialism or no, half the wives I know have lovers!' Again, his imagination lent wings to his words and he felt that catch in his throat. 'In some aspects it's a lot better than the legitimate way that sooner or later is bound to become routine. You'll have a second, secret home; a second, secret life . . . a life unburdened by the day's details, with the high points of feeling compressed within a few hours . . . '

She reached over, her fingers brushing his lips. 'Let me hear some more,' she said with a smile, 'of that second, secret life.'

He kissed her fingertips. 'What do you want, Julia? I've offered you everything. I've spread myself for you to walk on. Shall I get out of your life?'

'Oh, no,' she said quickly, drawing him to her. There were steps outside in the hallway. Someone called, 'Mrs Sundstrom!' And after a while another voice stated, 'She's probably gone home.'

Julia waited tensely, getting a foretaste of her second, secret life. John was speaking to her gently, urgently; she understood only the last of what he said. 'I've given you as close a recipe as you'll ever get on how to have your cake and eat it, too. What *do* you want, Julia?'

For a moment the image of herself lying flat and without feeling rose in the back of her mind; then she thought, even that may get back to normal, I must give Arnold a chance; but how could she? There were girls who easily accommodated two or three or four men during the same period in their lives and enjoyed them all, but she was a one-man woman; and she said, 'Does it have to be the occasional bed, John, the haste, the sordidness? Can't we just keep what we feel for one another on a different level?'

'And pine?' he sneered. 'And moon? And masturbate?'

She winced.

'I thought we were both grown-up. No, my dear, that schoolgirl romance doesn't go. Not in this day and age, and not with me . . . Come here.'

She obeyed, and stood before him in her rumpled white smock, arms hanging motionless, lips slightly parted.

He held her between his knees in a vice and grasped her elbow so she couldn't move. 'You can't play the Young Pioneer, not with that body of yours and your glands. I've tasted you; I *know*. I understand your wanting to keep things above board, but *you* know it doesn't pay to scruple, not for the sake of the great Sundstrom – that four-flusher, that hypocrite and opportunist, with his pompous mouthings and his bastard architecture, who would sell his comrades, his brother, his own wife for power, position, influence . . . '

She struggled to free herself.

'You will hear me through!' John Hiller said grimly. Her nearness excited him; her refusal was a challenge; her rejection of him released him from responsibility. 'I don't accept your no. I'll prove to you and to everybody what manner of man you are sticking to. I'll,' he hesitated briefly, 'I'll submit a design of my own for the World Peace Road extension, and every line of it will expose the fraud that's been committed here in the name of architecture . . . Oh, Julia.' The grip of his knees relaxed and he leaned his head against her. He had overextended himself. He had neither the ideas nor the experience, nor the political strength, to carry out his threat. Then he looked up at her and saw the light in her eyes and thought: of course she would like that . . . a duel in blueprints over her . . . what woman wouldn't?

'How would you approach it?' she was saying, both captivated by the proposition and relieved that it detoured them from the pull of their desires. 'What would be your basic conception?'

He let go of her, leaned back comfortably, and lit cigarettes for the both of them. A deep quiet had settled over the flimsy building; everyone, it seemed, had left; the day's work was done. 'On second thought,' he said, 'it might be shooting sparrows with cannonballs. There are easier ways to prove my point.'

Whether it was the quiet that had set in or the switch in tone, Julia sensed the inherent threat. The cigarette tasted flat; the sharp shadows on his face were distorting it; she wished she could break away, but her feet were rooted.

'There's only one person, anyhow, who needs to have the point proved: you.'

'I want to go now,' she said. 'I'm expected home.'

'Only you,' he insisted. 'Do you know why I came along that day, on the grand round-trip and inspection tour? To spy on you, you and Wollin. To listen to what he was saying to you, and how you were taking it, and what you were asking him – not just the words, but what lay implied in shade and intonation. I was intelligent and discreet, your husband told me, with a head on my shoulders . . . ' He nodded as if to demonstrate that a head was hinged to his trunk. 'I was the man for the job, he said, the man to report the essentials to him, reliably and promptly.'

She heard herself breathing. The shadows on John's face lengthened; the white in his eyes gleamed, mother-of-pearl.

'Julia?'

'Yes?' almost at a whisper.

'Don't you want to know why the precaution?'

'Perhaps he was jealous?' She laughed brittlely. 'Not without reason, as it turned out . . . '

'Jealous of Wollin? You don't believe that yourself, Julia.'

She saw Wollin standing close to her, holding her, six storeys of precipice behind her, the Road swaying, the walls – the moment of truth. She had felt then that Wollin, in all his frailty, had an inner strength to which you could hold on.

'Oh, no. *That* was political. The great Sundstrom, my dear Julia, is much too filled with his own importance to suspect that a woman could prefer someone else to him. Strictly political. What could he have feared that Wollin would tell you?'

Julia felt a wave of hot panic rise from her heart through her throat to her brain. 'The Road,' she managed to say. 'Maybe he feared Wollin's judgment.'

'He has no illusions as to the Road,' Hiller snorted. 'You've got to do better, Julia.'

'But I know more of Wollin and what happened to him from

148

Arnold than from what Wollin ever told us. He spent years in Siberia, by some unhappy conjunction of circumstance – or even by a miscarriage of justice . . . '

John Hiller's cigarette glowed up one last time, very bright; then he threw it on the floor and stepped on it. 'If he told you that much,' he asked slowly, 'what is it he fears that Wollin might know and tell you, inadvertently or not? Were others exposed to the same unhappy conjunction of circumstance? Persons you knew,' he seemed to listen into the room – 'loved?'

'John . . . ' Her voice, strained, seemed not her own. 'Let me go now, John, I beg you.'

'And if so, why does he fear you might learn of it? In what way is he concerned?'

'John!' A surge of hate made her voice shrill. 'This is monstrous!'

'What is? . . . The monstrosity is in your mind, taking on shape from what was there long ago.'

She turned. In the doorway she stopped, unable to go on, and leaned against the doorpost.

He caught up with her and took her in his arms. 'I'm here for you,' he said, his mouth seeking her hair, her eyes, her lips. 'Always.'

She pushed him away and stumbled off.

CHAPTER 7

Everything in Comrade Tolkening's office was designed to create a solemn, sombre atmosphere: the gloom of the wainscoted walls; the huge oils of a steel mill interior and of a workers' demonstration with red transparencies against a low-clouded fateful sky; the heavy drapes; the umber-coloured carpeting; the glass-enclosed bookshelves with their long rows of the classics bound in dark leathers; and in the anteroom, seated on a low, oaken bench, Comrade Kloppermann, his eternally glowering personal secretary, like a watchdog collared by an invisible chain. Comrade Kloppermann made the wait for admittance to his chief a most unpleasant experience.

Comrade Tolkening, then, was all cheer and affability. He hurried from his desk to greet Sundstrom, ushered him to a long conference table, and seated him catty-cornered to himself at its head.

'You don't mind my having lunch?' he enquired, opening the waxed paper that contained rye sandwiches, thinly buttered, and two green apples. 'My days are so crowded I have to squeeze in my lunches when I can.'

Sundstrom wasn't sure that he should feel pleased at the display of familiarity; he restricted himself to a mutter that could be interpreted as approval, or as a denial of his competency to decide the timing of Comrade Tolkening's modest meal.

Tolkening noticed his glance at the apples, which were not to be had in the stores, and, peeling one deftly with a penknife, explained, 'From my own garden. They'll keep if you put them on layers of wood shavings, in crates, in a dry cellar. You didn't know I knew about that, did you? You didn't know I have a

150

small garden, outside of town, and raise some of my own vegetables? I come from small people and I stick to them. A man mustn't cut his roots.' He chewed. 'Besides, it keeps your arteries from clogging up. I intend to live . . . to a ripe old age.'

Sundstrom watched the apples being sliced and the sandwiches being munched, and he wondered if he should ask Tolkening for the use of the phone so he could order a cup of coffee from the buffet downstairs in the Party building – at his own expense, of course – but he thought better of it.

Suddenly Tolkening shot over one of his piercing glances and said, 'You don't live right, Comrade Sundstrom!'

Sundstrom winced. In his present position, the remark could have several meanings.

'I noticed it the other day. Do you exercise, ever? Do you walk? What sports do you do, regularly, I mean? . . . Ah, you intellectuals: all day at your desks and smoking. Then the Parry wonders at the number of infarcts!' He wiped the blade of his knife, snapped it closed, and pocketed it. 'Is there something worrying you, Comrade Sundstrom? I don't like those rings under your eyes, those hollows in your face, those little red veins. Any trouble with the wife?'

'No!' – brief, almost disdainful.

'With your work?'

Sundstrom contemplated the question. Tolkening didn't ask people to his office for a chat or to spout advice on their health; and there had been that silence from Berlin. Sundstrom had been in the movement too long not to know the danger signals of non-committal replies from central authorities, or of no replies.

'I don't think it's my work,' he said finally, and added a significant, 'subjectively speaking.'

'That's it!' exclaimed Tolkening, obviously happy at the familiar groove of familiar terminology. 'Subjectively. That's it. No one in Berlin who knows your work has anything against it or blames you in any manner.'

151

Sundstrom took cognisance of the fact that, if no censure of him rested on subjective grounds, something must be happening to upset the delicate balance of that power structure commonly referred to as *objective circumstances*. But that was worse. Subjective failings or what went for them could be righted by a corresponding dose of self-criticism expressed in the right terms and on the right occasion. Objective circumstances lay beyond the individual comrade's ability to correct; they victimised you before you knew it, your status gone, your job a joke, your years of loyalty a waste of time.

'Shall we talk openly, Comrade Sundstrom?'

Sundstrom saw the Party secretary's smooth face beaming at him: confidence deserves confidence; we're comrades, friends. 'I wish you would,' Sundstrom replied, feeling the cold finger of fear at the back of his neck. Somewhere, somehow, people were conspiring against him; and he was in the dark, groping, unable to see them or strike back. 'Among comrades,' he stressed, 'open language is always best.'

'I don't want you to feel, Comrade Sundstrom, that the situation is in any way precarious. There isn't a comrade in Berlin who hasn't the friendliest feelings toward you and doesn't wish you well. Furthermore, they themselves have approved everything you did on World Peace Road . . . '

Sundstrom noted the careful manner in which Tolkening excepted himself from any of the dealings, architectural and otherwise. When Tolkening said he would talk openly, you had to watch every intonation to catch what he hinted at and what he hid; but that wasn't easy with your mind racing in circles – what did they know? What threads were being spun: Popov, Wollin, and now Tolkening?

'The extension plans were handed back to me.' Tolkening gathered the apple peels into the waxed paper. 'Comrade Kloppermann out there will return them to you when you leave.'

'But why?' Sundstrom blurted out. 'Why?'

A frown of Tolkening's narrow-set eyes drove the remaining colour out of Sundstrom's face. 'I'm sure I don't know, Comrade Sundstrom. There were comrades who suggested a competition so as to have more ideas to choose from. Mind you, this isn't directed against you, personally; no one even questioned the achievement of the completed parts of World Peace Road or that the National Prize should be given for it . . . '

'Well, for God's sake, how do they want me to build?'

Tolkening grew icy. 'I'm no architect.'

Sundstrom immediately saw his mistake; in another moment, Tolkening would turn about and accuse him of trying to shift the blame for his own shortcomings onto the Party. Sundstrom felt that his nerves were like open cables whose inside strands sprawled in disorder, red, green, blue, yellow; you had to splice them somehow, bundle them, so as to re-establish communications between the numbed brain and the fluttering heart. He wished Tolkening would let him light a cigarette; but Tolkening would never permit that: concern for your fellow man; save him from premature infarct.

'Comrade Tolkening,' Sundstrom managed to hit the proper mixture of trust and submission, 'you and I know that I am building exactly to specifications that are part of a general picture. And you and I . . . ' he desperately emphasised the twosome of himself and the district secretary, 'you and I have been through too much not to know that a switch in those specifications cannot be considered a separate phenomenon.'

Tolkening gently shook his head; his lips stretched into a thin smile. 'There was some talk of new techniques, prefabricated parts, complex building methods . . . '

'New techniques!' When it came to his own field, Sundstrom had the arguments at the tips of his fingers. 'I don't deny they may be more economical, after the huge initial investment in plant and machinery – but they lead straight to formalism. Are the Berlin comrades prepared to take that step?'

153

Tolkening reflected. He didn't know why the use of pre-fabricated parts should lead to formalism, but the mention of the taboo and Sundstrom's axiomatic certainty made him hesitate.

Sundstrom pursued his advantage. 'Did they give anything definite? Any line? Any principle?'

Tolkening began to explain. But what had been said in Berlin was hazy in the extreme, and since he himself had only the haziest notion of things until he was carefully briefed by his experts, he soon sensed that he failed to be convincing. He broke off with an angry 'Well, they want *some* change. You find out what change; that's your problem.' Then, as suddenly as he had flared up, he broke into his usual shrewd beam that encompassed Sundstrom and the length of the conference table as if he were taking into his confidence the ghosts of all who had ever sat at it.

'Change,' repeated Sundstrom, and again his thoughts filtered back to Wollin, and then to Julia. 'Which is the root change, Comrade Tolkening, the change from which all other changes derive? Find that, and you and I will have a line to guide ourselves by.' The *you and I*, by now, was insolence; the probability was that Tolkening knew very well what source the trouble sprang from; would he accept being yoked together in this with his chief architect?

'The root change?' Tolkening crushed the waxed paper and the apple peels; his normally controlled face was torn by anxiety; Sundstrom had never seen him like that. 'The Great Man is dead, that's the root change!'

'But he's dead three full years,' Sundstrom mentioned.

'The powerful take a long time dying.'

Sundstrom listened: perhaps some of the puzzle pieces that plagued him would fall into place now.

'He was only human, it turns out. What a demotion!' The beam that Tolkening wanted to display failed to light up. 'And he must be demoted further for the new men to rise to stature.

154

You're an architect, Sundstrom: what happens if you break the keystone out of an arch?'

A quick look at the expression of those narrow-set eyes convinced Sundstrom that as much of Tolkening's guard was down as ever would be; the man was as genuinely troubled as himself – hadn't he warned Krylenko of what might develop if you let Wollin and thousands and hundreds of thousands like him re-emerge? 'You'll have to do some fancy propping,' he answered finally, 'and do it fast.'

'That Moscow Congress,' said Tolkening thoughtfully, and more to himself than to Sundstrom, 'will stick in our craw . . . '

Sundstrom held himself in check. He leaned forward, tense, his fingers laced – he knew that Tolkening had taken him to the source of all the changes that were affecting his life, from his public status to his bed; the queries kept crowding his tongue, but he knew any one of them would shutter the window through which he was being permitted to peek.

'I don't say the Soviet comrades didn't act properly in setting out to right old wrongs and correct old abuses, especially if you evaluate what confidential information has come through to us from the deliberations of the Congress.' Tolkening paused. 'You've heard about that, haven't you?'

Sundstrom managed to keep his jowls from twitching. The old fear was back, but with new prongs that dug into his guts: if they uncovered things in Moscow, where would they stop?

'Ah, well.' Tolkening seemed to take his indiscretion lightly. 'You lived in Moscow during those years, Comrade Sundstrom. You know anyhow.'

So had Tolkening lived in Moscow! Sundstrom straightened. Were the two of them, sitting at this table with nothing between them but a foot or two of dark-grained oak, secret allies? Did Tolkening want to test their mutual positions now that matters had been set into uncontainable motion? Did he want to find out how much his chief architect knew of personal details? And how

155

much – Sundstrom's jowls did start to twitch – how much did Tolkening know of *him?*

Tolkening permitted himself a brief sigh. 'We who've experienced the pressure of those Moscow years can appreciate how lucky our Party is and how upright the character of our leading comrades that they prevented anything of that sort from happening in this Republic. We've had no forced confessions here, no sham trials, no executions of innocent men . . . ' He flashed a beam at Sundstrom. 'We have a clear conscience.'

'A clear conscience,' Sundstrom repeated, trying to find the right medium between emotional affirmation and statement of fact. The *you and I* had led to the *we* – a great word, the greatest of all: just see to it that you remain part of *we,* your virtues no bigger, your sins no worse than those of your fellow man, and you'll always have a measure of protection.

'I'm glad you understand the situation,' said Tolkening, 'and that you were able to reassure me on the doubtful points. The rest is tactics.'

Wollin, thought Sundstrom. Julia. Tactics. The ghosts of the past didn't share Tolkening's house or his office. Perhaps Tolkening had no ghosts, or was thick-skinned enough not to notice them.

'Do I interpret your thoughts correctly,' Sundstrom forced his mind onto the matter of tactics, 'if I say that a change in the structure of power would tend to require a change in the structure of building?'

'I wouldn't put it that crudely.' Tolkening showed his teeth, a fine dental job. 'I see in this development renewed proof of the accuracy of Marxist thinking on art as a reflection *or* life.' He rose and, his arm about Sundstrom's shoulders, walked him to the door. 'I'm sure you'll take that under advisement, Comrade Sundstrom, when you ready the improved designs for your World Peace Road extension project.'

Sundstrom saw Comrade Kloppermann look up from his bench

at his chief and the visitor so closely linked in the doorway. Kloppermann's glowering seemed to assume a different character – the dog had been thrown a bone and, for the moment, was satisfied – and Sundstrom knew that, even if he had not won, his position at least had not deteriorated. The next days, he thought, would tell, what with the project having to be revamped and a hurried trip to Berlin to try to get the inside story: on that earthquake in the Kremlin and the precise extent and effect of its seismic waves.

The speed with which the news travelled through the organisation amazed even Hiller. Wherever he went, whatever studio he entered, people knew – and with a fair amount of exactness – the complications the project had encountered in Berlin. They also sensed that the trouble had a political angle; they had no specific information; they just knew through indoctrination and everyday experience that nothing in economics, architecture, the arts, or personal relations could be seen apart from politics. Only Voukovich, who had been mauled in the clash between the Tito group and the rest of the socialist camp – and through him Waltraut Greve – suspected a definite cause. Hiller frowned: could the unrest spreading through architects' studios and construction sites be linked to a few lines buried in the press – *Comrade Stalin no longer to be considered one of the classics?* Could this be the cause of the shadows he saw hovering about Sundstrom?

Nonsense. One must retain one's sense of proportion.

But Waltraut pounced on him. 'Why do you think yesterday's sure-fire ideas have become today's duds?'

Hiller remained non-committal: the designs were done in the well-known rush, lacked some new gimmicks to stun the Berlin coterie and furnish them the moral justification for their usual enthusiasm over the usual triteness – nothing that couldn't be taken care of with a little thought and imagination, and thought and imagination were exactly what Comrade Sundstrom requested everyone to apply to the matter.

Voukovich shrugged. Waltraut stepped close to Hiller and chucked him under the chin. 'You're a lousy actor, John.' Hiller saw the bangs stringy over her forehead and wished her to the devil. 'And a bad psychologist,' she added. 'Your shielding the husband doesn't hide the fact that you're laying the wife.'

'I just don't permit personal feelings to colour my judgment,' Hiller said testily.

Nevertheless, he grew thoughtful. Sundstrom, in delegating him to help get the revisions of the extension plans in motion, had treated the matter lightly. But if the trouble proved more than a poke at Comrade Sundstrom by envious competitors, then the man's fall, if not imminent, was in the cards, and one's own course of action needed to be considered.

'What's the good of speculating? . . . ' Voukovich grew conciliatory. 'We'll see what we shall see. It's sickening never to be able to do the job you really want to do; again, we'll put beauty patches on old ugliness; we'll even bob a nose or two when what's needed is a new face, a new spirit, a new heart.'

Waltraut had hardly listened to him. The opportunity to let John Hiller taste some of her bitterness was too rare to waste on aesthetics. 'Instead of nice-nellying and playing the boss's glorified stooge,' she told Hiller, 'you should be grateful that he's on the skids; push him, boy, push him; the prize is waiting for you, blonde, soft, lacy, and oh so innocent. Or perhaps you're playing Iago to this deaf, dumb, and blind Othello and forgot to mention your new role to your old friends?'

Hiller took her by the shoulders and shook her, hard. 'Why don't you . . . shut . . . up!'

'That's right.' Her voice had a strange pitch. 'Hit me!' She didn't try to free herself from his grip; she seemed to enjoy it. 'So I can go about saying: look at that bruise, Hiller gave it to me, the great lover. Ah, John, you're so stupid . . . '

He let go of her, not because of her taunts, but because for a moment he had felt the old urge for her. He left without assigning the work he had gone there to distribute.

In the hallway he paused, lit a cigarette, tried to collect himself. The sudden sensation sparked by Waltraut's nearness was not what upset him most: she was a bitch in perpetual heat, exuding whatever it was they exuded. It was the Iago comparison she had thrown out that disturbed him. He hated Sundstrom with a passion commensurate to his desire for Julia, but every day found him deeper in the man's confidence, charged with ever more jobs that required tact, discretion, subtlety. Thank goodness the parallel ended before it reached the gentle Desdemona – To hell with Waltraut Greve's Shakespeare. Every generation, every society had its own brand of villains, and if only half of what seemed to haunt Sundstrom was based in fact, a present-day Shakespeare had his material cut out and ready for him.

Hiller pulled at his earlobe. He suddenly felt frustrated: what really should he tell his colleagues they must do? Sundstrom had been vague; he was simply improvising until Tolkening or Berlin or even Moscow handed down a new ukase to serve him as a new crutch. And Sundstrom's uncertainty was affecting him, too; the previous state of affairs, when a man at least knew exactly which way he must dissemble, seemed preferable.

Hiller stamped out his cigarette butt, frowned at the ancient editorials tacked up on the bulletin board, and decided to break the planned sequence of his rounds. Hands deep in the pockets of his smock, shoulders hunched, he proceeded toward the far end of the hallway, where behind a huge filing cabinet was the door to the niche in which Wollin had been tucked away – the only man who could supply some of the answers – *if* he cared to give them.

But face to face with Wollin, the questions he wanted to ask refused to align themselves. Wollin had those bright, knowing eyes that forbade intrusion; *they* would query if any querying was to be done.

'I'm glad you came,' Wollin said. 'I'm glad someone came. What can I do for you?'

Hiller had no recourse but to state his official business, contradictory though it was – the extension, you know; what can you suggest; new features, new ideas, but growing out of existing lines, of course; continuation, unbroken, and yet an original contribution to the treasure of socialist architecture; building on our great achievements and surpassing them.

Wollin let him finish. He sat, upright, on a straight-backed chair; the large table that served as his drafting board was bare but for a number of pencils. Then, relieving the awkwardness in which Hiller floundered, he said lightly, 'I've been waiting for this, you know.'

A quick glance of Hiller's tried to fathom what lay behind Wollin's waiting: an estimate of the political and psychological situation, architectural convictions, impatience at his supernumerary status, or any two of these, or all of them.

But Wollin didn't enlighten him on his reasons or the extent of his information. Instead he continued, 'And I have prepared for the moment . . . as much as could be done since I was assigned this desk, and as far as I could go with the limited facts at my disposal.'

The decisiveness with which this was said impressed Hiller. Here was a kind of Communist new to him; he had observed Wollin the day of the great round-trip and inspection tour, and later occasionally, and now again: the man's personality excluded ulterior motives; to Wollin, the revolution did not seem primarily a ladder on which you scrambled for position, prestige, privilege.

Wollin got up. From the corner nearest the window he fetched three large sheets, each rolled up separately and held together by rubber bands. 'Shall we go to Comrade Sundstrom now?' he asked from the window, carefully holding the rolls.

'Comrade Sundstrom is in Berlin.'

'Oh.'

Hiller again felt his embarrassment at the part in which Sundstrom had cast him. 'He'll be back tomorrow,' he hurried to assure, 'day after at the latest.'

'Never mind . . . ' Wollin replaced his drawings. 'An architect doesn't work just for one day.'

Hiller said nothing. But curiosity outweighed discretion: Was Wollin as creative a man as he was critical, as imaginative as he seemed solid? And what sort of architecture would he propound after so many years without practice, cut off from any development?

'May I see, at least?'

The rubber band crackled hollowly against the paper as Wollin undid the largest of the rolls. Spreading the sheet across the width of the table, he said, 'As seen from the top of the last building now under construction, looking south.' And stood, holding the paper in place, no sign of emotion on his face; only in the back of his eyes a light glowed.

'The Road!' said Hiller, when he had caught his breath. 'it's there, and yet it isn't! It has been reabsorbed . . . '

'Of course! I have reduced it to what a road should be: a means of getting you somewhere – not a parade route, a triumphal arch in tapeworm shape. The rest is groupings: light, airy, giving people a sense of space and time – and of freedom.'

He fell silent. Hiller needed the silence to bring some order, at least provisionally, into the impressions that flooded him. This was a world in itself, new, a complete break with Sundstrom's Road and the dozens of roads that had been cast in the same pompous image. This was a play with surprising shapes, with curves and contrasts, and yet, if you studied it more closely, you could see the structural simplicity, the unit feeling, a harmony of proportions quite unlike the symmetries that were Sundstrom's permanent standby.

'And what's this?' Hiller pointed at the lower left-hand corner

161

of the sheet, at what seemed to be a row of geometric figures.

'Those?' Wollin laughed. 'They're my building blocks, pre-fabricated, each one of them, to plan and standard. We'll put all this together as a child would, the high, the low, the long, the short. I've done it. For a while I worked in the kitchen, there . . . ' He did not specify the *there*. 'So I had the use of a knife and whittled my component parts. It's only in socialism that we can build that way,' his hand circled over the sheet before him, 'and can plan in space, for generations to come. And economically! I've calculated it. I have on this piece of paper nearly twice the housing called for in the original project . . . plus shopping centres, school, kindergarten, polyclinic, community centre, garages. And for the same money.'

'This is a dream,' Hiller said after a pause, the regret having crept into his voice against his will. 'They'll never accept it.'

'Why not?'

'Because it's reasonable. Because they are caught, sitting on their wedding cake architecture, even if they now want us to chip off some of the icing. After having called *that* socialism, and *this* – a gesture of the hand toward Wollin's grand design – 'soulless, decadent, formalistic, they can't turn about and suddenly declare the contrary.'

'My dear young Comrade . . . ' The network of lines on Wollin's face was pronounced. 'I'll tell you this not so as to disturb you but because I want you to have faith in man: I spent sixteen years of my life in the most horrible jails and camps, for having betrayed socialism, it was stated. And then it was stated just as un-ceremoniously that I had never done such a thing, and that I was free to go.'

He rolled up the sheet and spread the second, the ground plan of this project. 'On this,' he said, 'you'll see more clearly the relation of green to buildings, the access routes swinging off the extended World Peace Road, the new lease on life we give that neglected animal, the pedestrian . . . Formalism!' he suddenly

162

exclaimed as though he had only now understood the charge. 'Define it properly and you will find it refers to form without content, the baseless curlicue, the old rut still being followed although it no longer leads anywhere. Here,' his finger pointed for proof on his plan, 'every form is linked to its purpose. Comrade Hiller!'

Hiller started. He hadn't been this stimulated since his school days, when to his eager mind the great mother of all arts, architecture was not yet a whore, submitting to any customer. 'Yes, Comrade Wollin?'

'You see, I believe in the possibility of this plan because I believe in the power of reason. What's reasonable is beautiful, and what's beautiful belongs with socialism.'

Hiller nodded, not trusting his voice. But underneath his emotion the practitioner reasserted himself, the young man who had learned to live with realities and who discounted the phrases. Not that he believed Wollin was mouthing any: Wollin was sincere, but a dreamer; the miracle was that his dreams had survived – or had *he* survived because he dreamed?

Hiller re-examined Wollin's design for angles and combinations that went beyond the architectural, and he wondered which of its features might be made palatable to men like Tolkening; another part of his mind tried to determine the effect Wollin's plans, or any of his ideas, might have on the shifting relationships of himself to Sundstrom, to Julia, to the unknown forces on the move.

'What were you intending to do with those drafts?' he enquired.

Wollin's shrug was more eloquent than his comment. 'Show them to Sundstrom.'

'But they're a manifesto . . . *against* Sundstrom!' Hiller waited. Wollin seemed to have trouble slipping the rubber bands over the rolls. Finally Hiller added, 'At best, he'll steal some of the non-essentials and incorporate them into the new hodgepodge that he'll have to submit. And he'll hate you for the rest of his life, and one day he'll cut your throat.'

163

'I don't think he loves me as it is.'

'Still, he gave you a berth. You may want to hold that.'

'Believe me, Comrade Hiller,' the crow's-feet at the corners of Wollin's eyes twitched, 'I've had greater temptations to sell out on my principles . . . What would you suggest?'

'*Not* show it to Sundstrom.'

'For sixteen years, I have been building toy cities.'

'Do you think you'll get to build anything through Sundstrom?' Hiller suddenly saw the combination he had searched for; target: Julia. 'We'll submit it in Berlin.'

'*We?*'

'You don't have to trust me.' Hiller forced himself to sit down, leisurely. 'I know the picture you have formed of me: Sundstrom's stooge, not above sleeping with Sundstrom's wife.' He saw the pained line of Wollin's mouth; through all of his experiences, the man had preserved a sensitive heart; people like that had to be shocked into action. 'But I tell you, your plans can be put over.'

'How?'

Hiller thought of Voukovich, of that ostensible aside in the press on the deceased demigod not really having been quite the deity. 'Perhaps not entirely in the shape in which you conceived them: we don't want Comrade Tolkening to burst a blood vessel or the Berlin board to gag. If you'd let me, I'd help you develop the changes that should be made. The situation *is* opening up – this you know better than I do. But I know the local idiosyncrasies: the material, technical, political possibilities; the byways and the shortcuts. Let me be your,' he thought: guide? friend? assistant? None of those fit his own purpose or the mood of the encounter, 'your Sancho Panza.'

'Wasn't Sancho Panza rather an egotist?'

'His master's ego was vastly bigger.'

'Ah, well . . . ' Wollin laughed. 'Let's tackle the windmills, then.'

*

164

Wollin's landlady, Mrs Schloth, entered immediately upon knocking. 'Telephone, Herr Wollin,' she announced. And, opening her eyes significantly, 'Very lovely voice; a lady.'

Wollin shrugged at Hiller. 'You forgive me?'

The door, with Mrs Schloth in it, remained open. Hiller couldn't understand what Wollin was saying; the phone was in the hallway, too far off; and Mrs Schloth kept up her patter on how too bad it was that such a nice gentleman as Herr Wollin should be living so alone, knowing only his work, coming home evenings and hardly seeing what she set before him, and then back to his desk and his pencils and those big sheets of paper, never even taking in a movie; well, they were hardly worth going to, most of them, except for an occasional old film imported from the West; and no pub for him either; the man could frighten you, he was so intent, obsessed, you might say, except he was very mild-mannered and gentle; he must have suffered in his life, hadn't he?

Mrs Schloth dyed her hair jet-black and kept her motherly bosom propped up. 'You're the first person come to visit him,' she informed Hiller.

'And this is the first phone call he's received?'

'First from a woman,' she qualified. 'I hope she's a good and honest sort. He's a lamb, a regular lamb; he's just asking to be roped in. You're a friend of his?'

'I believe so.'

'Then you watch after him. I've been trying to advise him and he sits there listening to me but I tell you I don't know whether he understands the half of it . . . That's a long phone call . . . '

'Isn't it, though?'

'On the other hand,' Mrs Schloth hitched up her bosom, 'they say still waters run deep. I had a boarder once who was as quiet a gentleman as your friend, civil as they come, always said, 'Good morning, Mrs Schloth,' and, 'Thank you, Mrs Schloth,' and punctual with his rent. You could have knocked me over with a feather when the detective came and took him along for non-payment of alimony to four different women, two of them in West Germany at that.'

'I don't think Herr Wollin has been around long enough,' said Hiller.

'Long enough for what?' asked Wollin. 'Would you let me get by, Frau Schloth?'

'To have to pay alimony,' Hiller answered.

Mrs Schloth had disappeared. Wollin closed the door. 'That woman seems to feel that entertaining her boarders is included with the bed linens and the breakfasts . . . ' He returned to his desk and looked at Hiller. 'Julia is coming.'

Hiller felt that extra beat of his heart, a pain; it passed quickly. 'Did you tell her I was here?'

'No.'

'Why not?'

Wollin reflected. 'I don't know. Perhaps I didn't think of it. Does it matter?'

A lamb, thought Hiller. A regular lamb. Like hell.

'She said she had to see me,' Wollin explained. 'Tomorrow Arnold would be back and she didn't know if she would find time then.'

'I can always leave if it's so confidential,' said Hiller, and thought angrily, Who's her lover anyhow?

'We'll see.' Wollin smiled enigmatically. 'Let's get back to work. You said these wavy roof shells on the shopping centre will strike them as insane. But if we fashion a model, don't you think at least some of those men will sense the essential grace of the structure, its gaiety? I want to achieve a psychological effect . . . I want people to *want* to come here: not just to buy what they need, but also to window-shop, to promenade, to congregate; the old idea of the market square, but twentieth century, socialist twentieth century. Do you follow me?'

Hiller frowned. It was ridiculous even to think of jealousy in connection with Wollin. Julia wasn't running from one old man to throw herself at another. She was coming for the very reason that Sundstrom feared: the matter preying on her mind and therefore preying on his. Hiller felt frustrated – and Wollin shut him out!

'John Hiller!' Wollin was calling him to attention.

'I'm sorry.'

'I didn't have the heart to say no to her. If you've known someone as a child and have known her parents – and she *is* troubled . . . '

'You weren't *blind* drunk the night you slept at Voukovich's, were you?'

'No.'

'Well?'

'I wish I thought you were the man for her,' said Wollin.

'What makes you think I'm not? Your own little hankering?'

The pencil Wollin had been holding snapped. 'I'm afraid,' he said after some seconds, 'you and I—'

He didn't finish. Mrs Schloth opened the door. 'You gentlemen were so engrossed you didn't hear the bell,' she said importantly. 'If it wasn't for me, the little lady would still be standing in the cold, or even have turned and left . . . '

Julia, entering from behind Mrs Schloth, saw John.

'Hello, Julia!' he said.

She swallowed. 'Hello, John!'

Wollin came forward to greet her.

'Wollin and I were doing some work,' Hiller was saying. 'I was about to leave. You came here quickly.'

'I found a taxi.' Julia looked flushed. 'You were working? I'm sorry, Daniel . . . Comrade Wollin didn't mention that.'

Wollin helped her out of her coat. 'You're not disturbing anything . . . ' He got rid of Mrs Schloth by asking her to prepare coffee and promising to pay her extra for it. Then he offered Julia the only upholstered chair in the room, his desk chair.

But Julia remained standing uncertainly, glancing from the brass knobs of the old-fashioned iron bedstead to the rug, which had lost most of its nap. Finally she steadied her eyes on the faded wallpaper where fuzzy outlines delimited traces of a burst pipe.

'At last we meet again!' said Hiller with a shade of truculence.

'We've met in the office,' she mentioned, her voice small. 'Nearly every day.'

'This is different,' Hiller replied quickly, and Julia knew he was right. They seemed to be caught in some sort of magnetic field that was as much of her making as of his. If it were not for Wollin's presence, they might have fallen into each other's arms and tumbled onto the floor. As it was, they stood motionless, their restraint tugging at their nerves. 'Different,' Hiller repeated hoarsely, 'more homey.' Then he laughed.

The laugh broke the spell. Julia felt as if she had been dropped from a great height, shocked, exhausted. She heard Wollin's 'I'm sure you'll be interested in what we were working on,' and found herself nodding and went to sit as far away from both men as she could – on the edge of the bed, hands rigidly folded in her lap.

John's presence complicated things. She had wanted to put one question to Daniel Wollin, a single question, but though this question went far back to the past, she now felt that it was somehow connected with John and her night with John.

'We were working on a new version of the World Peace Road extension,' Wollin was explaining in his soft-spoken manner. 'Wouldn't you be interested?'

He was looking at her curiously, as if to test how she was taking this second shock. What she felt was amazement: like a person coming out of the long sleep of an illness and finding that changes have taken place in the life about her – changes made without her. She frowned, trying to fit the new fact into the mesh of her quandaries. She had gone through hours of agony before making up her mind to come to Wollin; she feared the answer to

168

the question and yet she needed it; only her belief in Wollin's utter integrity and calm impartiality, in the *oracle,* as Arnold had contemptuously called him, had decided her. Now she found him less than impartial, involved with her lover on a project that couldn't fail to have an effect on Arnold's life – and her own.

'It's really Wollin's idea,' said Hiller. 'I'm just helping to plane some of the rough edges. It's all very new and surprising, and I think we've got something . . . ' He paused. 'Come here, Julia. Remember . . . I promised I would fight!' He pointed at the sketch.

Wollin stood, apparently indifferent, beside the drawing. 'Nice of you to give me a credit line,' he said.

'I'll even fight with borrowed weapons,' Hiller countered, suddenly aware of the risk he ran in an architectural competition for a woman's heart, and feeling resentful of Wollin and a trifle silly. Then he noticed that Julia, though at his side, was no longer with him.

Julia was gazing at the projected view south from the last building presently under construction, and it was to her as if she had been transported to the site where, not so long ago, she had actually stood alongside Wollin and for the first time had sensed the terrible link between an art that was a lie and the lie in life. But now the field of rubble to the south, the remnants of bombed-out tenements and loft buildings, the whole maze of hopelessness and dust were replaced by this view of the future, this harmony of clean-cut shapes to which her trained eyes gave colour and dimension. If this could be built . . . she stopped.

If this could be built, all that was pressing in on her heart was capable of solution. She couldn't tell why this was so, but she was sure of it, and she was for it – for this new sense of beauty that grew on new attitudes.

'Like it?' said Wollin.

Julia nodded.

'Want to help?' asked Hiller.

Of course she wanted to help. Help build this. But it could

never be built *against* Arnold, as John seemed to dream and possibly Daniel Wollin; only with him.

'We could make it a threesome, Julia,' Hiller urged. 'Imagine their having to choose between the team of Wollin, Hiller, and Sundstrom as against Sundstrom – Sundstrom alone, who has never had a creative idea of his own, a second-rate eclectic doing his architecture by ear, by his ear at the politicians' lips . . . '

Hiller broke off. This was becoming a pattern between Julia and himself like a curse: they set off fine, hardly able to contain their urge for one another, and then fell apart – and over what? It was his eagerness. In Julia's presence all his carefully nurtured sophistication dropped away, and any Wollin who didn't have blood enough in his veins would get a rise at the sight of her breasts and her thighs proved superior to him.

'I think this can wait,' Wollin was saying. 'I think Julia has another matter on her mind.'

Julia said nothing. But the view south on the World Peace Road extension faded before her eyes; she saw the scratched top of the desk again, and the upholstered chair Wollin was offering, and his kind, tired face; and she knew she would break down and go to pieces if she didn't find clarity soon, and that there was only one place to gain it.

'Am I, perhaps, in some way part of that matter?' asked Hiller.

'Yes,' said Julia.

'Then you don't want me to stay?'

Julia saw his distrust, and his pout, at this moment, reminded her of little Julian. It made her feel motherly and enabled her to laugh at him and take his face between her hands and kiss him, lightly, on both eyes and on his mouth.

He turned, half angrily, and said he would wait for her downstairs before the house – the whole night, if it was necessary.

'It won't be,' Wollin cut him short, and called through the door, 'Frau Schloth – we need only two cups, please!'

*

Wollin was very much aware of the fact that, for the first time, he was alone with Julia.

Of course, he had been alone with her when he stayed at the Sundstroms', but those moments had failed to register; Arnold Sundstrom was always there – in the atmosphere of the house, in its furnishings, its colours.

Wollin watched Julia stir the sugar in her cup. She seemed unconscious of the sensualness of her hands, her tapered fingers holding the spoon, the slight motion of the back of her hand, and of her wrist. He wondered if John Hiller was actually waiting for her before the door; he thought of the two of them embracing and tried to blot out the image, though it proved that she was to be had; perhaps that was exactly what he didn't want to think of.

He did have normal reactions. He had established this fact to his own satisfaction while he was still in Moscow. In camp, this had been one of his minor concerns; the act of survival was subdivided into several categories, the prime one being the supply of sufficient calories to keep the organism functioning. But then, as conditions gradually eased up for him and hope grew of an eventual return to civilisation, the other categories became important; he had seen so many shattered personalities, from brutes whose only resemblance to humans was that they walked on their hind legs to snivelling creatures about to exhale the last spark of what kept them alive; and he couldn't have said which was worse: the crippled body or the crippled soul.

He did have normal reactions. There had been Tatyana, revival after sixteen years, hasty night in a crowded flat, the buxom body grown flabby, whispering to him of boredom with a husband off on an official trip to Sverdlovsk, receiving him into her eager warmth; and he, feeling his nervous fears sliding off him, feeling himself inexhaustible and insatiable both, to wake up in the end, a stranger in a stranger's bed. And then, Lyubov, doctor at the polyclinic, no illusions, matter-of-fact, taking off her unbecoming underwear as if she were stripping for an operation and caressing

171

him in a knowing, businesslike manner; then, in a burst of uncontrollably passionate tenderness, her harsh mouth and hard hands trying to make up to him for the lost tendernesses of those years – a stranger, too.

He raised his cup to Julia as if it contained wine instead of coffee. She was no stranger. From the moment he got off the train, she was no stranger. And it wasn't because he had known her as a child, or because there were grafted onto her and transmuted a number of the features of his friend Julian Goltz. It seemed that *this* Julia, this young woman with the troubled eyes and the half-smile, had always been part of his life, part of himself like his hands or his thoughts.

'Here's to you,' he said. 'To us. To friendship.'

The smile materialised. 'I wonder how you held on to this through all your . . . your experiences.'

'Held on to what?'

'To that way you have of putting a person at ease. Of putting me at ease . . . ' She reached across the small coffee table Mrs Schloth had brought in and impulsively took his hand. 'Your plans, your beautiful plans . . . aren't you afraid?'

He raised his brows.

'Of Arnold. Arnold is very powerful. With his connections . . . '

'He's always had connections.'

'And used them?'

'And used them.'

He felt the slight tremble in the hand that still lay on his. She was at the point of saying what she had come to say. He waited.

But the hand withdrew. 'You will never build your World Peace Road extension if you try doing it against Arnold.'

He sipped his coffee. He would have to teach Mrs Schloth how to make coffee for him. 'That I'm here, with you, Julia, is a miracle. If this can happen, even the adoption of decent architecture in this country is possible.'

'Daniel—'

'Yes, my dear?'

'Wherever I turn, I'm faced with new riddles.'

'And none of the answers?'

Julia leaned forward, her head between her hands, and appeared to be addressing her knees. 'Those that I see are so horrible and frightening that my mind refuses to explore them fully. But I can't go on if I keep clinging to the simple, clear patterns that used to explain life. There's John, there's Arnold, there's the Road. There are the people and this whole Republic, with their two truths. And there's you . . . yes, you, too . . . '

He saw the soft light on her hair, reflection of the lamp; he wanted to caress her head, but he didn't move.

'Daniel Yakovlevich, what really happened to my parents?'

She looked up, her eyes seeking his. He remained motionless.

'You see, I *must* know,' she went on, her voice rising out of a whisper with effort. 'If they were killed, why? And by whom? At whose decision?'

Wollin stepped to the window. A shadowy figure was pacing near the streetlamp across the way. He thought he had all the right in the world to tell her; she half knew anyhow. But then he recoiled. It wasn't *his* job; and he wouldn't be there to catch her when the full force of the blow made itself felt and the full realisation of the magnitude of the evil done; or was it that he hesitated at throwing her, for good, into the arms of loverboy waiting down there?

'What did Arnold tell you?' he asked, finally.

What had Arnold told her? – Julia tried to recall the dribs and drabs he had given her at various times. But they mingled with the awful hints John Hiller had dropped, and everything was blurred and unreal except for that one, hard question: *do you think that the Soviet government, the Party, could commit such a wrong?*

'In your person,' she said slowly, 'and by your person you contradict everything he ever said on the subject.'

173

He faced her. 'Then why not let *him* explain?'

He saw her eyes, like those of an animal that has been trapped. He was being brutal, but better this, now, than have her turn against him later.

'I wouldn't know the whole of it anyhow,' he placated. 'They picked me up soon after they took away Comrade Goltz and his wife . . . ' Why did he refer to her parents in that formal manner? He couldn't say, unless it was to make them somehow abstract, and he knew the futility of this. He clumsily stroked the back of her head and her shoulders. 'Half the truth,' he said helplessly, 'would be worse than no truth at all.'

After a while she lifted her face to him. She looked worn and haggard, and two bitter lines led from the wings of her nose to the corners of her mouth. 'My father and mother were murdered,' she said, 'and you're a witness.' She paused. 'Are you afraid of speaking, too?'

'You must ask Arnold,' he replied. Then, his voice rising sharply, 'Ask *him!* . . . *Ask* him!'

CHAPTER EIGHT

Except for a big truck here and there, not a car travelled the autobahn at this time of night. Sundstrom kept the radio going full blast, some Western station with a tired-voiced disc jockey, while the trees came at him in the white cone of his headlights and rushed by, gaunt ghosts disappearing in the wake of his car.

By four in the morning he was at the state-owned roadhouse and stopped for gasoline. A couple of long-distance trailer trucks stood parked in the lot; there was a light on in the dining room; a cup of coffee, thought Sundstrom, good coffee, that's what I need. As he sat down at a table, his fatigue caught up with him. The red-chequered tablecloth began circling, the bottles behind the bar, the display cases; the truck drivers' voices swelled up only to fade from hearing. Sundstrom felt the waitress's hand on his shoulder shaking him. He could hardly make out her question, 'Something the matter with you, Mister?'

'No,' he said, 'oh, no. Thank you.'

He raised his head. The girl came into focus – large boned; the once-white cap on her straw-coloured hair had long ago lost its starch. He noticed that the truck drivers were looking at him and exchanging opinions.

I must be a sight, he thought. 'I'd like a cognac,' he said 'and a mocha double. Do you have something to eat?'

'Soup,' she said indifferently. 'Pea soup. With sausage, if you want.'

'All right,' he said. 'Soup. And sausage.'

The waitress left. Sundstrom felt a pain in his chest and sur-reptitiously reached under his shirt to press his fingers against the vicinity of his heart. If I were to die, he thought, that would

175

solve everything. A blood clot refusing to pass an artery, and Tolkening could chalk up another on his list of infarcts. Or a blowout on the autobahn, at eighty miles an hour; a screech, a crash, flames. He should have stayed the night in Berlin, put some sleep under his belt, or had himself a good time. That secretary in the Academy, with a small flat of her own and those bedroom eyes, had more than once hinted that she was available; perhaps a new woman would make him forget, at least for minutes, the minutes that mattered, and would help him cure some of his trouble with Julia.

From the truck drivers' table, one of the men got up and came over, a heavy, middle-aged gait. He pulled back the chair opposite Sundstrom and sat down on it, spreading himself and gazing at Sundstrom from dull eyes. 'My friend Konrad there says he knows you.'

Sundstrom tried to see the man who claimed his acquaintance, but the angle of the light interfered; in all likelihood, it was a case of mistaken identity. He wished the waitress would bring his cognac and coffee; the big boob sitting at his table was making him nervous.

'Why doesn't he come over,' said Sundstrom, 'if he thinks he knows me?'

'He's kind of shy, Konrad is.' The man, Sundstrom noticed, had an extra thumb on his right hand; thumb tip and dirty nail, it branched off from the main thumb like a small hammer, and the man used it hammerlike, as if he were knocking invisible tacks through the tablecloth. 'He thinks he knows you from Russia.'

'Russia . . . ' Sundstrom felt the pounding of his heart, very hard, very fast, faster than the man's extra thumb was hammering the table. They were five drivers over there; they kept putting their heads together, whispering, gesturing; you couldn't distinguish features, characteristics. It was nonsense anyhow; he had never known anyone named Konrad in his life. 'When was he in Russia?'

176

'Oh . . . he was there a long time!' The man now employed his thumb to scratch the hair on his chest that stuck out from his half-open shirt. 'Say, what's the matter with you? You sick or what?'

'I'm not sick,' Sundstrom retorted, squirming in his seat. Or maybe he was sick; all this running about from Pontius to Pilate took it out of you, and in essence he hadn't learned much more than he already knew from Tolkening or could deduce for himself. 'What's your name?'

'Wilhelm.'

'I wish you'd leave me alone, Wilhelm,' said Sundstrom, annoyed at the lack of authority in his tone. 'I'm sure your friend Konrad has mistaken me for someone else.'

Wilhelm seemed to spread out even more. 'But you were in Russia, weren't you?'

The man Wilhelm's head was too small in relation to his enormous shoulders; he wore his dark hair like a skullcap. 'What business is it of yours?' asked Sundstrom, finally managing to sound tough.

'Hey,' called the man toward the other table, 'he doesn't want to say if he's been in Russia.'

This caused loud chortles tending toward a growl.

'Waitress!' – more a cry for help than a summons – 'Waitress!'

'Yes, Mister!' The waitress plunked the cognac down before Sundstrom. 'The mocha's in the works; the sausage has got to be heated. What's the rush?'

'I want the manager.'

'The manager's asleep. Three and a half miles from here in the village.'

Sundstrom gulped the cognac. 'Then *you* tell this man to go back to his table.'

The waitress looked at Sundstrom and then at the size of Wilhelm. 'I don't mix in customers' arguments,' she decided. 'He isn't hurting you, Mister.'

'He's got an extra thumb.'

Wilhelm raised his hand and wriggled his forked thumb before the waitress's face. 'So he has,' she said. Her giggle sounded odd coming out of her dreary face with its empty eyes.

Sundstrom watched her trudge back to the kitchen. This, too, will pass, he thought: Wilhelm, Konrad, the waitress, everything. Everything passes. The oldest saw in the world – he couldn't recall who had consoled him with it, in Berlin: Krummholz of the Academy Pietzsch of the Central Committee, Wilezinsky of the Planning Board, or someone else; their faces faded into one another, their words, their shrugs. It all added up to the probability that the Moscow events were a passing phase; certain gradual adjustments would have to be made, of course, but no loyal comrade need fear for himself or his position unless he was identified with any of the abuses of the cult of the personality; that's what it was called since that Moscow Congress: cult of the personality. Unless . . .

'If you've been in Russia,' said the man Wilhelm slowly, each word like a weight, 'why don't you want to admit it?'

Sundstrom looked at his empty cognac glass. It had a solid, chunky foot. He imagined himself smashing it through Wilhelm's skullcap and skull.

'Lots of people have been in Russia,' said Wilhelm. 'It's a big country.'

The trouble, thought Sundstrom, is inside me. A man thinks he's seen me somewhere; another asks a perfectly commonplace question – and I jump out of my skin. 'All right,' he admitted, 'suppose I've been to the Soviet Union. What of it?

'Hey,' called the man Wilhelm. 'Now he says he's been there!'

A second man sidled over, shorter than Wilhelm, with watery eyes and a semi-permanent smile that exposed crooked, decaying teeth.

'This is Konrad,' said Wilhelm, his head moving almost un-noticeably on his big shoulders.

178

Sundstrom tried to place the face of this Konrad. He had never seen the man before. Konrad stood arms akimbo, head half inclined, and studied Sundstrom. That's how it must have felt, thought Sundstrom, when you were being interrogated: the impersonal interrogator, the unnamed threat, the innuendos, the questions leading along unknown lines.

'What do you want of me?' he said, his voice squeaky.

'Easy, easy!' warned Wilhelm, and to his friend Konrad, 'Well?'

'It could be him.' Konrad frowned. 'Of course, it's been years. Well, none of us get any prettier, huh?'

'I suppose not,' conceded Sundstrom. Then he gathered up what strength he still had, gripped the rim of the table, and levered himself up.

The small head on the huge shoulders shook. 'You haven't had your food!'

'I'm leaving.' Sundstrom blindly took a bill from his pocket and placed it next to the cognac glass. 'I'm in a hurry. They're waiting for me at home.' It happened to be the truth, too. He was in such a hurry to get home that he had left Berlin without having slept, without anything; home was where the threat lay; or did it lie everywhere, in Moscow, in Berlin, in this godforsaken roadhouse?

'Hey,' Wilhelm raised his double thumb in signal. 'He doesn't want to eat his soup. He wants to get home.'

The other drivers ambled over, hitching up their trousers as they came. Sundstrom was trying to skirt the table, but Wilhelm, enormous though still seated, was in his way. Sundstrom found himself ringed. The smell of leather and grease and sweat and beer was overwhelming.

'I've done nothing,' Sundstrom panted. 'I don't know any of you . . . ' And in helpless protest, 'I'm innocent!'

'Maybe you are,' Konrad's toothy smile grew wide, 'and maybe you aren't. But then who knows what made a man do what he did in those years.'

179

The waitress came, Sundstrom's soup on a tray.

Konrad rook the dish from her and held it out to Sundstrom. 'You never used to refuse a good soup. I've seen you squeal on a man for less than that – for a hunk of bread, in fact, and the bread was mouldy. Or have you forgotten?'

Sundstrom fell back on his chair. He started to laugh – an artificial laugh at first that turned genuine with his relief and finally grew hysterical. Through the tears stinging his eyes he saw the dumb faces of Wilhelm and Konrad and the others. 'For a hunk of bread,' Sundstrom gasped. 'I? Never! I never was in any camp, never a prisoner, prisoner of war, any kind of prisoner. I'm a professor, an architect – I was an architect in the Soviet Union, built some of their great buildings,' his laughter grew controlled, his voice metallic, 'and I'll thank you men to get out of my way.'

They stepped back sheepishly. Sundstrom walked out, erect, his hand brushing back his mane as he went. Only after he had slipped into his seat behind the wheel did he grow aware of his shaking body and his sweaty palms. It's this damned fixation of mine, he thought. A bunch of truck drivers. Ridiculous!

*　　　*　　　*

Happiness.

Happiness was mostly in a person's imagination. Thanks to her imagination, Julia had been a happy child, easily calmed, easily satisfied, despite her great loss. Everybody had said so, teachers, neighbours. Arnold liked to recount how she could make a few pebbles do for a herd of goats one day, or for the population of a village the next, or a classroom full of pupils the day after; or how a few rags knotted together would become dolls whom she named and loved and infused with life and stories. If I hadn't made you an architect, he used to say, perhaps you would have become a writer; they, too, blow a great big bubble out of nothing.

What he omitted to say was that without her imagination she

180

would have gone to pieces, as children do whose love can no longer clot about the accustomed object; or she would have hardened into an unspeakable bitch. As she gazed down at the Road torn by excavators and at the traffic threading its way through the one lane kept open, she wondered how much of the happiness she had had with Arnold was the pebbles substituting for the goats, the rag dolls taking the place of reality. And yet she refused to hamstring this imagination of hers. But for it, last night would have been unbearable as one monstrous thought followed upon the other like a procession of ghouls.

To escape them, she had fled into the plan. Wollin's extension of World Peace Road, worth no more than a pebble if you considered it realistically, was brought alive in her memory and viewed and enriched and taken, victoriously, over all the hurdles – oh, not by her alone; she believed in teamwork, socialism, comradely discussion, in the intrinsic power of the new to rise above the old, and in the understanding and goodwill of those who through long, devoted service had proved themselves worthy of positions of leadership. In her mind, through common effort and selfless labour the plan was developed and made reality by all those dearest to her – Arnold, John, Daniel Wollin. Voukovich, too, would play his part, and the others; and since she was generous she permitted Waltraut Greve to join in the work. In the dark of the bedroom, every nerve taut with foreboding, she visualised the building site and populated it with men and machines; bulldozers moved the earth, cranes swung entire sections of wall into place, the buildings mushroomed up; everything was festive, full of colour and sound; she saw herself walking hand in hand with Arnold, with John, with Daniel Wollin; little Julian was running ahead of them, laughing; he carried one of those celluloid propellers mounted to a thin stick of wood; the thing whirred, red, blue, green, yellow; it was as if the child were drawn forward by it, as if they were all being drawn by it, endlessly, faster, higher.

181

The plan, now, was in her hands. Wollin had lent her a rough of it, perhaps because he sensed that she needed something to hang on to last night as she rode home in the taxi he had called and into which he personally had placed her while John Hiller sulked across the street, the glow of a cigarette briefly lighting his face.

Julia smoothed the unrolled plan against the wind that was trying to curl it. No, she thought, she had not dreamed it. *View South from Last Building Under Construction* – and here she was on top of that building, looking south, and seeing it with her own eyes, in the early light of this April morning, with the bricklayers behind her methodically slapping down mortar and brick and mortar and brick.

She turned at the steps behind her.

'Good morning, Mrs Sundstrom,' said Barrasch, tugging at the purple scarf that lent a note of colour to the grey of his denims and gave his wind-burned face a strange hue. 'Up and about at this hour? I thought you office people don't start work before eight.'

'I couldn't sleep,' she said, 'and I wanted to check on something.'

The foreman looked at her thoughtfully, and then at the plan that she held outspread. 'The Professor usually comes to do the checking,' he said after some moments. 'But he hasn't been around for a while.'

'He's gone to Berlin,' Julia answered non-committally and thought, the man really has a kind face.

Barrasch, without apparent reason, wiped his hands on his trousers. 'If you don't mind my asking,' he said and coughed slightly, 'but I think you'll understand our being interested in view of all the things we've been hearing . . . '

'What have you been hearing?'

The foreman finally succeeded in twisting his scarf into a proper knot. The effort seemed to have made him forget Julia's question.

'What's the sketch you're holding there?' he said, craning his neck. 'The extension?'

Julia hesitated. Once an idea leaves its author's desk, it gains a life of its own, uncontrollable.

'Of course,' Barrasch added modestly, 'if it's asking too much. But I saw your face, Mrs Sundstrom, as you looked out over this stretch of land, and I said to myself: what she's seeing there must be beautiful.'

Julia blinked. The tall man with the huge, callused hands was waiting; she felt as if she could tell him the whole story, from her first doubts to this moment when she clung to this piece of paper, but such confidences were impossible; even if Barrasch were less of a stranger, how could he have understood? 'It's one of the projects we're thinking of,' she said evasively.

'But you like it?'

'It makes no difference whether I like it or not.'

'All right . . . ' The foreman shrugged and was about to turn. 'I didn't want to intrude.'

'No!' Julia hastily reached for his denim sleeve. 'I *want* you to see it. I was just afraid that,' she paused, searching for some plausible excuse, 'that this sketch would seem peculiar to you, unusual. It will need changes. It was designed by a man who hasn't practised architecture for some time . . . '

'May I see?'

She handed him the plan. Eyes squinting, Barrasch began deciphering the drawing and establishing its relation to the landscape deep below his feet. Julia watched his expression. Whenever his head moved and his glance swerved to note another feature, she felt a twinge in her heart. What does it matter, she thought, the man probably has no taste, and anyhow, whatever he says decides nothing.

But the twinges persisted, a nervous shiver adding to her discomfort. She pulled up the collar of her coat and dug her hands into its pockets.

'Cold?' said Barrasch, his eyes still on the sketch.

'A bit tired.'

With almost pedantic care, he spread the sheet of paper on the ledge before him and weighted it down with bricks; then he left her for a moment and came back, carrying a worn satchel. A half-dozen of his men trailed him. He opened the satchel, took out his thermos bottle, unscrewed the top, poured coffee into it, and offered it to her with a surprising grace. His men clustered about the plan in an effort to see as much of it as was possible in a brief glance.

Julia sipped the thin, scalding brew and tried to evaluate their muttered half-sentences, their snorts and nods and sparse gestures. They were elderly men, most of them; two were youngsters with gawky wrists sticking out from the too-short sleeves of their denims; the age group in between had been weeded out by war and the lure of the West. Through the vapour rising from the cup she saw Barrasch's slight smile. 'I thought I'd let them have a look,' he was explaining. 'It certainly is different . . . '

And then she saw, beyond the foreman, the open raincoat billowed by a gust of wind – Arnold.

Julia's first instinct was to cover the plan. But there was no way of getting to it, of hiding it in the folds of her coat; Arnold was coming at her, grey-faced, lips drawn into a forced grin; the plan still lay on the ledge, weighted down, its edges curing and crackling in the wind.

'Ah,' he sighed, part relief, part plea for sympathy and welcome, and then, 'Julia!'

The cluster of men broke up; they stood, not quite at attention, but in an expectant, somewhat at-your-service attitude. Only Barrasch seemed self-assured.

Sundstrom, though disagreeably conscious of their presence, closed his wife into his arms. Julia felt his bristles scratch her lips; he had sprayed some toilet water on himself, but its tang had not entirely dislodged his unwashed odour.

'I drove most of the night.' He still was holding her. 'I thought I'd find you at home. But only Julian was there to greet me . . . and Frau Sommer. You had just left, she told me.'

He let go of her.

'Sorry.' She took his hand. 'I didn't expect you so soon. I was restless. So I rose early and came here.'

'Why *here*?' he asked.

'It was too early for the office,' she said quickly and added a little laugh against the suspicion she thought she heard in his question. Then, to keep him from burrowing further, 'How did it go in Berlin? Is everything all right? Whom did you see?'

His heavy-lidded glance travelled from one of the men to the next and settled on the square of white on the ledge.

'And how did *you* come here?' Julia's voice had an edge to it. 'How did you know where I'd be? Did someone tell you?'

'I wanted to have a look at the area,' he said. 'The extension will have to start at this point. It's been preying on my mind . . . '

He had moved to the ledge. With a slight groan, he bent down, pushed aside the bricks, picked up the drawing. For a time that seemed interminable he held it between his outstretched hands. The grey of fatigue on his face gave way to colour, but it wasn't the ruddiness of his good days; unhealthy livid spots showed on his forehead and cheeks; his hair, dishevelled by the wind, seemed scraggly; repeatedly he compressed his lids as if he wanted to assure himself that what he saw wasn't the continuation of some nightmare.

'Julia—'

She went to him. The wind that came dust-laden from the rubble heaps bulged the paper in his hands.

'Whose is this?' he said.

'Wollin's,' she answered after a moment, and heard herself apologising in confusion, 'It's only a rough, you know . . . a suggestion . . . He would have shown it to you . . . '

His jaws were working frantically. 'How . . . did you . . . get it?'

185

'Please . . . ' Her hand sought his. 'Please, Arnold, no scene! The men . . . '

'The men . . . ' he repeated, as if he were just discovering them. A wave of his hand beckoned to them. 'You've seen this?' he asked of them.

Someone mumbled, 'Yes.'

'Then what do you think of it?' And as they remained silent, he shoved the plan under their noses. 'You can read it, can't you? Tell us, tell Mrs Sundstrom what you think of it! You're the workers; you've built this great Road with your own hands and your own sweat; you're building this country, socialism . . . Tell us if this insanity is worth a single pound of cement!'

They seemed to be ducking under the onslaught. Only Barrasch, who stood slightly to the left of Julia, remained casual. Offering her the thermos bottle he still held, he asked her, 'Want another cup?'

Sundstrom turned toward him, outraged. But the foreman stood his ground, massive, his head appearing too small in proportion to his shoulders, his short-trimmed dark hair capping the top of his skull; and it was Sundstrom who took a step back, frowning strangely, until his free hand, moving across his forehead, managed to wipe away the image of the man with the double thumb.

'You see, Herr Professor,' said Barrasch ponderously, 'it's like this. We build what we get on the blueprints. Everything else is not for people like us to say.'

Sundstrom snapped, 'Then I'll tell *you!*' Pulling the paper to its full width for everyone to see, he almost tore it. 'This is an absurdity! It isn't even functionalism. Squares, curves, cones, circles . . . a geometrical exercise, but not architecture. No, no, no . . . ' He paused, short of breath. 'Some people think their day has come,' he gasped. 'Some people think they can revive their hoary junk. Some people don't know when they're dead . . . '

'Arnold!'

For a moment the horror in Julia's voice seemed to bring him to his senses. It recalled the question she had failed to answer. Waving the draft at her, he repeated, 'How . . . did you . . . get it?'

'Last night.'

'He was at the house?'

'No, I went to see him.'

'*You* . . . went to see *him? Why?*' Sundstrom forgot the men. He saw only Julia, her pale face, the eyes that he once loved and now feared. He crumpled the plan. 'He must have sold you some bill of goods!' And then, suddenly fully aware of what his wife's visit to Wollin must mean, 'What else did he tell you? What else?'

'Nothing,' she said.

'You're lying.'

'Arnold,' her voice broke, 'we're not alone here.'

'What . . . did he . . . tell you?'

'He told me to ask *you*,' she said.

For a second or two, Sundstrom stood quite still. Then the plan fell from his hand. He grasped for his heart. She saw his eyes turn white, all white; he tottered, tumbled back toward the ledge.

She cried out.

Sundstrom lay propped against the pillow. Julian stood next to the bed. Sundstrom raised his hand and ruffled the boy's soft hair.

'No Julian,' he said, 'you mustn't worry on that account. I didn't break anything.'

'Diana broke her arm,' Julian said. 'And she only fell from the seesaw.'

'That's different,' said Sundstrom. 'I didn't fall at all. A man caught and held me.'

The child reflected. 'But you could have broken something,' he finally said. 'You were up on that high building.'

Sundstrom suppressed a shudder. The boy was as insistent as

187

his mother. Then he said, 'If I had had a fall, which I didn't, I might possibly have broken something.'

Julian, apparently considering broken bones an achievement, said thoughtfully, 'Diana wore her arm in a sling . . . for two hundred days. And it's still weaker than the other and she can't throw with it, just a few yards maybe. Why did those men bring you home in that white car, then, if you didn't have a fall and nothing was broken?'

Sundstrom's smile was half pained, half indulgent. 'I didn't feel well.'

'Why?'

'Why!' Julian was at the age when why was the very point of life. Sundstrom sighed. 'Son, I wish I knew . . . ' But he did know. And the child's eyes showed that he didn't accept the plea of ignorance. The hell with it! Sundstrom stretched in the warmth of the blankets. He was ill. They would take an electrocardiogram tomorrow, Professor Bauer had said. Professor Bauer was a very careful man, an old Nazi, but an excellent diagnostician. Illness was a form of protection, too, although flimsy enough and of no permanence.

Julian suddenly flew to the door.

Julia, thought Sundstrom, with a twinge of envy: the boy had an ear for her steps like a puppy for its mistress's.

Julia came to his bed, the child hanging on to her. Sundstrom noted with satisfaction that the fright of his near-death still lay on her face; perhaps a dash of bad conscience was added. To ask *him*, Wollin had told her. Her question loomed like an avalanche about to break loose.

He felt her fingers on his forehead, as if she were testing for a fever they both knew he couldn't possibly have. 'Bauer assured me again before he drove off,' she said. 'He doesn't believe it's organic. Your heart sounded fine.'

Sundstrom lay quiet; only his pupils moved, guardedly focusing on his wife's face.

'Nervous exhaustion, Bauer said,' she concluded.

'Nervous exhaustion,' Sundstrom repeated in a faint voice. 'That can put you in worse shape than an honest-to-goodness heart attack.'

Her fingers withdrew from his forehead. 'I know. You need rest, Bauer said. Plenty of it. A sanatorium, he said, would be best.'

'Sanatorium . . . ' Sundstrom mocked. Shove him off to a sanatorium. He couldn't even afford to go off for two days, to Berlin. 'How can I sit in a sanatorium? We've got to do the extension plans . . . '

'Julia!' Julian was still clinging to her. 'Daddy didn't break his arm.'

She squeezed the boy's shoulder. 'He didn't break anything. And we must all help him to get better quickly.'

Sundstrom contemplated the young woman he had fashioned, his Galatea, except that his material, the bedraggled orphan child, had been more brittle and difficult than the antique sculptor's ivory. It couldn't be that his hand had lost its touch, or his eye its exactness. Maybe Bauer was right: nervous exhaustion. But that didn't come overnight; it built up to its crisis through weeks and months, distorting in the process all proportions and perspectives, until a rough sketch on a sheet of drawing paper seemed like a dagger pointed at your heart, and your own wife, creation of your love and mother of your child, your worst enemy.

'Julian,' he said, taking the child's hand, 'I want to talk with Julia. Run along, will you.'

The boy hesitated.

'Do as you're told, darling,' Julia said. 'I'll be with you in a little while, and we'll play.'

Dragging his steps, the boy went to the door, turned once more in it, and, as neither his mother nor his father recalled him, left, his head hanging.

'He was very frightened,' Sundstrom said when the door had

189

closed. 'He talked of nothing but broken arms and falling from buildings. Julia—'

Julia waited. He would now demand to know what Wollin had told her to ask him, and she wouldn't tell him, at least not now, not in the state he was in. He had tumbled back, ashen faced; she had imagined him plunging, and something in her had listened for the dull thud of the heavy body hitting the ground, and it had taken all her willpower to force open her eyes then and see him hanging limp in the arms of Barrasch and one of the bricklayers.

'Julia, I'm quite ashamed of myself. It was silly to create a row with you . . . and in front of those men.'

He watched her. Her lips were open, incredulous; she hadn't expected this approach. She looked very pretty; surprise softened her face, it seemed.

'Did you save that sketch, Julia?'

'One of the men picked it up.'

'Good. Because you see . . . Julia, this is very hard for me to say . . . you see, underneath all that noise I made I knew there was something . . . something to that draft . . . something we could use, after changes and developments, of course . . . but it might be one way toward a solution . . . '

She wanted to speak. He raised his hand.

'You ask, why, then, the scene? I was beside myself. The Berlin trip . . . no answers, no commitments; just groping in the fog. And then I came here and you were gone. The fears and suspicions, nightmarish—'

Sweat stood on his face. 'You mustn't excite yourself,' Julia pleaded. 'Why do you fear me of all people?'

'I'm not insensitive, Julia: something dark and terrible has come between us. And when I finally found you, I found you with this plan . . . a plan containing not a single idea of mine. And how could it? What fresh ideas have I had these last years? I've been playing for power, power and position; you can't live that way and remain creative. What sort of artist am I now, what sort of architect? . . . No, no, let me finish,' he cut off her protesting gesture, 'you can't possibly know how many thoughts flash through one's mind before it blanks out, and how lucidly you see before you don't see anymore.'

He lay back, his breath coming jaggedly. His hair, on the pillow, had lost its lustre; Julia didn't remember ever having seen it that grey and bedraggled, or his mouth that caved in and thin. She tried to line up in her mind all the reasons she had found for her night with John Hiller; all the questions she had listed to be asked of Daniel Wollin; all the logic that had blocked her feelings for this man who now lay before her, ill and deeply disturbed and in need of her. But the reasons refused to align themselves; her questions remained amorphous; and in the face of his humility her attempts at recapturing yesterday's logic turned into a sense of guilt.

'If only I had had the patience to wait for you at home,' she said, 'none of this would have happened.'

He took her hand in both of his and gently forced her to sit down on the side of the bed. 'Perhaps it was good,' he said. 'Otherwise we might never have had this talk . . . And now, will you let me have a cigarette?'

'But Professor Bauer said . . . your heart . . . '

'Didn't he say it was *not* my heart? Cigarette, please. And light it for me, as you used to.'

She fetched the pack of cigarettes and matches from his coat. She lit a cigarette, herself inhaling the first puff, and then handed it to him, a trace of her lipstick on its end. He carefully took it, his lips almost caressing it where her lips had held it. Julia felt a small thrill, as she had felt at the glitter of the sequins on that dress he had brought her from Riga, years ago, after which she had been conscious of her breasts and her thighs and no longer could wear the starched collar and brown apron of her school uniform without a sense of embarrassment.

'Julia?'

She bore his gaze. She knew its intent and the effect it used to have on her, and she wondered why he tried to burrow in her heart at this moment when she felt for him.

'Will you do something else for me, Julia?'

'Yes. Of course. Anything.'

'Will you invite Wollin for tomorrow night?'

'But—' You ask *him*, Wollin had said. She hadn't asked Arnold.

'There's no sense in postponing this.'

'You're ill, Arnold. You're actually ill. Bauer may call it nervous exhaustion, but I saw you as it happened—' Julia broke off. Everything again had that double bottom. She had seen him tumble, and everything in her had turned to ice; but she was using even that moment of horror as her excuse for not facing the inescapable.

'Don't you understand, Julia . . . I must have that new plan ready and submitted before they get anyone else to submit. If I learned one thing in Berlin, it's that they're drifting – there's no new line, no new principle. So they'll be glad to get anything that promises to be halfway satisfactory . . . '

Her hand, which he had taken again, lay cold in his. 'John Hiller has worked on the plan, too . . . '

'He has?'

'Yes.'

Sundstrom's eyes brightened: his boy Hiller was playing it both ways. But in the end, this would make it easier; his long political experience told him that a man with his finger in two pies has to fear getting them burned twice. 'Then ask Hiller to come along,' he said. 'We need everyone. A team. A collective.'

Julia nodded. It was what she had wanted and dreamed of and recommended to Wollin as the only possibility if the great new beauty was to be realised.

And yet it was not. She couldn't explain why.

CHAPTER NINE

Wollin shut the apartment door behind Hiller then he turned and walked tiredly to his room, past Mrs Schloth, who stuck her bird face out of the kitchen. 'Your guest gone, Herr Wollin? You work too much; you'll be the death of yourself yet.'

He threw himself on his bed and stared at the ceiling. They had worked almost without interruption ever since Julia's phone call yesterday; worked and drunk some vile-tasting brandy that Hiller had supplied along with sandwiches and coffee. Out of the side of his eye Wollin checked the last bottle – about one-third of it was left for emergency use. Mrs Schloth's cuckoo clock in the hallway started chattering. Wollin counted: four o'clock; he had two and a half hours before that supper at the Sundstroms'; you sleep now, Hiller had advised; you have to be wide awake and on your toes for this thing tonight.

Wollin sat up, his feet fishing for his slippers. Sleep! The excitement of creation, which had kept him going for twenty-four hours, grew instead of abating and blended with his apprehensions: seeing Julia once more; the encounter with Sundstrom; the past that increasingly injected itself into everything he thought, said, and did.

He reached for the bottle, poured slowly, noticed with satisfaction that his hand was quite steady, and raised his glass toward the completed drawings, which lay in neat rolls at the end of the table, one next to the other, like church candles. It would be *some* joke, he thought, if they were actually to build this – a giant demonstration in stone against the lies and pretences of the past, a mile-long epitaph to those who hadn't lived to see the future.

Wollin felt his eyes sting. Whenever he was at this nervous pitch, he fell prey to sentiment. He raised his glass again in a private toast to the dead who passed before his mind's eye, a shadowy train, but all of them young; the way he had met them, years ago. There were so many – what devotion to the cause, what energies, what talent had been killed! And if you compared the victims with the survivors, you began to suspect that a sort of negative selection had been made: the mediocrities had lived while the heads of those bigger than standard had been chopped off by the official Procrustes.

He shuddered. He drank.

He could see Julian Goltz as if the man were standing before him – the curve of the forehead, the eyes in which something seemed permanently to smoulder. A working-class leader par excellence, he had that ability to rouse people to action by appealing not to their instincts but to their reason.

Of course, the rage might be so clear because it resembled – transformed – that of the living Julia. Macabre. He slurped the last drops from the glass. Without a toast.

Come to think of it, he had never seen Julian Goltz rouse anybody. He knew him from the hotel in which they all had lived in Moscow, and from their Prague time when Goltz had been in charge of the small group of exiles – no easy job: you're out of the country; you're out of touch with reality; you have to guard against your wishes becoming your guide to action. Goltz had tried to keep intact as many links as he could with Germany; he had family there, too: a father, brothers; Wollin frowned, news of the father's death had come while he and Sundstrom were visiting the Goltzes, a telegram; he didn't recall whether that had been in Moscow or earlier, in Prague. What he did recall was the man's expression, the sadness in it: the same expression he had now seen on Julia.

Julia. As sure as hell she had not asked Sundstrom, and if she had, Sundstrom could be relied on to invent a story.

Julia. The bottle. Let's see if the hand is still steady.

He had come too late. The squat woman who always sat at the

far end of the hotel hallway had looked at him strangely as, fear-stricken, he had rattled the door to the Goltzes' room. The woman had the key in her desk, she told him; the room was free, awaiting the next tenant; the comrades who used to live there – well, you know.

And the child?

The woman's shrug said everything. And a few weeks later, he himself had been picked up.

Again, Wollin felt that stinging in his eyes. The empty glass dropped from his hand; he covered his face. Not even drinking helped him.

After a while he rose, shoved aside the bottle, unrolled the nearest of the drawings, and started checking it again.

Wollin watched Sundstrom pour down his vodka. For someone who yesterday had suffered a sort of collapse, Sundstrom had recovered amazingly; he had colour, his eyes were bright, his ample lips had none of the bluish tinge that indicated a heart ailment. Julia was busy at the sideboard, very much the mistress of the house, with a smile that might be meant for her husband, her lover, or her father-confessor – you couldn't tell. Whether it was her dress or her way of moving or the alcohol in his blood, Wollin felt the excitement of her presence; at the same time he perceived the reactions of the other two men: the tightening of muscle on Hiller's face, the restlessness that had come into Sundstrom's. No, Julia had neither told Sundstrom about Hiller nor asked the question.

Julia was passing the platters with the various *zakusky*. This was a double celebration, she said – of the beginning of their collaboration on the extension project, and of the results of Arnold's medical examination: the electrocardiogram had confirmed Professor Bauer's diagnosis; his heart was perfect, coronaries and everything, but Arnold shouldn't overwork himself, should share his responsibilities.

Wollin loaded his plate. He needed fat in his stomach to soak up the alcohol; he wanted his brain clear for any argument that might arise; he was determined not to let Sundstrom water down his designs; he had already given in too much to Hiller's warnings: this couldn't be done and that wouldn't go through.

'Julia, dear,' Sundstrom rose, glass in hand, 'I want to thank you. Without you, I'd be lost. Having these friends here tonight to help me was your idea, the result of your belief in the essential goodness of people. I drink to you, to friendship, to love . . . '

Wollin studied him quizzically, then shifted his glance to Hiller. Hiller was smiling impersonally, though Julia's hand shook as she raised her glass, spilling some of the vodka. There was something provocative about Sundstrom's display of marital bliss. 'Drink, Julia,' he was saying. 'Finish it, my dear.'

She put down the glass. 'I must stay sober, Arnold.'

'Drink, Julia! So much depends on it for me. So very much.'

'Drink it,' Hiller advised under his breath.

Julia tried to smile, didn't succeed. 'I can't.'

'Why not?' said Sundstrom.

'Leave her be,' Wollin defended her. 'She has a right to her moods.'

'Of course,' muttered Sundstrom, 'of course.' But he was alarmed as he returned to his seat. In his heart, he had hoped to appease the ghosts of the past; his willingness to compromise on the Wollin designs was more than a search for an answer to nebulous demands, it was a sacrifice to the gods who had sent the ghosts to haunt him. 'What makes you think,' he turned to Wollin, 'that you know her moods better than I do?'

Frau Sommer serving the meat course relieved Wollin of the need to reply. Wollin chewed, feeling Sundstrom's eyes upon him: their whites seemed to have hazed over, their pupils to have dimmed. Hiller kept the table talk going; he did a fine job of walking the tightrope from architecture to politics to love; each time he teetered he recovered elegantly. Wollin saw Hiller's intermittent glances at Julia; it was as if the fellow wanted to make sure that she appreciated what he was doing for her, for the two of them.

Sundstrom kept drinking in order to numb the doubts that bored into his skull. What if the sacrifice was in vain; what if the gods, seeing through his subterfuge, refused his offering; what if by some twist his acceptance of the Wollin designs became the cause of his downfall?

'What were you saying there?' he asked, coming back to the present.

Hiller explained obligingly, 'I was disputing, Comrade Sundstrom, that certain forms of society create certain forms of architecture; conversely, that the same styles necessarily trace back to the same kinds of regimes.'

Sundstrom rubbed the bridge of his nose; his brain felt like a lump of lead. 'Do you want to claim, Hiller,' he asked slowly, 'that properly speaking there is no such thing as socialist architecture?'

'The theory has been troubling your wife, Comrade Sundstrom. Because if you compare what the Nazis built with some of what we've put up—'

'John!' Julia had paled.

Wollin wanted to save the evening; if it was to fall to pieces, then let it break up over his designs.

But Hiller was faster than he. 'That's just why I question the theory,' he expounded. 'You find the same empire in Paris and in Petersburg – the one bourgeois, the other feudalistic; the one the expression of a progressive society, the other of darkest reaction. But assuming that forms of architecture could be indifferent to whatever class rules a country, we would eliminate from the outset a number of objections that are sure to be raised against the – the Wollin–Hiller project.'

'Wollin-Hiller . . . ' repeated Sundstrom. By now, he was rubbed raw. Or his mind, after his last day's exertions, was no longer sufficiently agile. 'You think you're smart, Hiller,' he said. 'I've seen too many people in my life outsmart themselves and finish up—'

He stopped.

'In Siberia?' asked Hiller.

Sundstrom's jaws were working. 'And finish up. Period. Don't you think I know you play both ends against the middle?'

'I'm not playing,' said Hiller.

Julia sat motionless. It was like a duel; she wished she could stop it.

'And Siberia is being changed,' she heard Wollin say.

'I see,' Sundstrom said tonelessly. 'Two against one . . . And with an uncertain glance at Julia, 'Three?'

Silence. Julia waited. Ask *him*! Wollin had told her. There was only the clinking of china from the pantry where Frau Sommer was getting ready to bring in the coffee. *Ask* him. Her father and mother had been murdered. There must be an explanation, and only Arnold could give it. After that, everything would be easier. 'Arnold?'

'Yes, dear?'

Her eyes sought his. His head was moving from side to side as if it had received a blow from an invisible hand. She could not ask him, not now; not in John's presence, or even in Wollin's. 'We're not two, or three, against one,' she said finally. 'We're all together in this.'

His head stopped moving. 'That's what I thought.' And added, 'I thought we'd start arguing when we got to the designs, not before.' He paused, brightened at some idea, then refilled his glass. He came around the table to her. Shoving her glass into her hand, he clinked his against it and said, breathing heavily, 'We're all together in this, Julia – and don't you forget it, ever.'

This time, she drank.

*

198

Panic struck as he examined the drawings. Sacrifice indeed! This was suicide.

The devil must have been riding him when he let Julia rope him into this; if ever anything was prearranged! The stage had been set for him up on that building, with the rough laid out on the ledge so he couldn't miss it, with Barrasch and the workers as audience and witnesses.

The devil had been riding him! That he could have imagined a meeting of minds by which the disparities might be worked out, the clash avoided, the threat appeased. These large sheets spread over the piano were no drafts in the rough in which a man could find room to insert his own, well-tried ideas. The thin, sharp lines of these finished drawings – horizontal, vertical, perspective – ruled out any bargaining. Theirs was a categorical clarity. This was yes or no.

The devil must have been riding him when in the shock of his illness he had confessed his weakness to Julia. This, now, was a hold-up – and he had no defence against it: no project of his own, no political support, no ideological guidance. And the worst was that he still was too much of an artist not to see the beauty of the thing. Oh, he could visualise what it would look like; it was as good as anything designed by any of the men who had spilled into the countries of the world from the old Bauhaus; and it was the condemnation of everything he had ever built. After this, he could only bow out. But he refused to do that, to declare himself guilty. He had done what had been demanded of him: call it duty. In a revolution you can't choose – neither your means, nor your people, nor your styles.

'Well?' Julia said tensely.

Sundstrom looked up from the papers. 'I've been thinking,' he said hesitantly. He had himself sufficiently in hand now, he found. This would have to be done calmly, stroke by stroke; in demolishing, you had to pick the spot where the chisel would have the most effect.

'Then you like it?'

It's very interesting,' he said. 'Provocative. And I do mean *provocative.*'

Julia needed a moment to understand him. Then she saw the set of his mouth, and his hands: he was ready to pounce.

'But you saw the rough!' she exclaimed, and immediately felt the futility of whatever she might say. '*You* said we could use it, with changes. *You* wanted this get-together.'

'I did?' Sundstrom found his thumb hammering the drawing before him as if he had grown a branch-thumb like that man Wilhelm's. But he couldn't stop it. 'I'm glad I did. It gave me a chance to see how far this would go.'

Wollin picked up his after-dinner mocha and set it down again. There was in Sundstrom's tone something that reminded him of the interrogations he had had. It froze out any reply.

'Comrade Hiller,' Sundstrom managed to control his thumb, 'a while back you said there was no connection between the forms of society and those of architecture. But you won't deny the influence of a man's thought and character on his work, will you?'

'No.'

'Then will you tell me what these thin-blooded whimsies indicate to you?'

Since Sundstrom was just using him to channel his attack on Wollin, Hiller saw no reason to commit himself. Not being in the main line of fire, he rather enjoyed the fight – it had potentialities.

'A form of insanity?' asked Sundstrom, barricaded, as it were, in the curve of the piano. 'An attempt to out-west the West? A joke on everything that socialist architecture has propounded over the years?'

Julia saw Wollin blanch. 'Arnold,' she said, 'whatever you feel about those designs, you must credit Daniel Yakovlevich's honesty – he's done his best to help us on the extension project.'

'Has he been dripping that into your ear, too?' Sundstrom

straightened like a judge about to pronounce a sentence. 'As Marxists, we have learned to see the entire personality: past and present behaviour, thoughts, political attitudes, self-expression – all compose the whole . . . ' He paused. He was doing fine, bull-dozing any resistance. Wollin's face was withered with wrinkles as if his head had been pickled in vinegar. Julia was wide-eyed; she had never before witnessed a person being crushed; it would be a lesson to her. 'This is a political document,' Sundstrom let his hand sweep over the drawings, 'and has to be judged as such.'

'I agree.'

Julia turned at these first words from Wollin. She thought he must gather up his drafts to save them from being manhandled, but he got up and remained in his place, looking awkward and hunched as he had the day he had stepped from the train and told her she had her father's eyes and mouth.

'I wish it were otherwise,' Sundstrom said, regret coating his censure. 'I wish I could say these were truly the blueprints of our time, our world, our future.' He began to believe what he was saying; certainly he wished he had something to work with. 'I had hopes, because I know your great talent from our student years and I trusted that your years in camp hadn't deadened that talent. I wanted to give you your chance, Daniel. I re-established you in life; I smoothed the way for you, put you in your job. I treated the convict like a comrade.'

'Convict—' repeated Wollin, as under a whiplash.

'Convict!' Sundstrom's voice rose. 'What are these drafts but a graphic detailing of political scheming, factionalism, decadence, cosmopolitanism, and . . . forgive my becoming personal . . . ingratitude.'

Ingratitude, thought Wollin, biting the hand that fed you. As trite as that . . . Sundstrom continued railing; the spirit was upon him; he must defend his holy grail. Wollin couldn't help marvelling at him: the man delivered his accusations without a

201

trace of cynicism; his hackneyed terminology would gather strength as long as he didn't stop talking; it was convincing at least to the orator and had a peculiar effect on him – the voice and words of Sundstrom became those of the sectarian zealot ready to cut down anyone unwilling to follow his major and minor prophets; they conjured up the secret policeman whose growl evinced his secret lust for power. It was frightening; it had to be checked; yet it seemed like an anachronism.

Sundstrom, believing that Wollin was sufficiently taken apart, now devoted himself to the lesser characters in the plot against him. Assuming correctly that the charge of having abused his chief's confidence would be lost on Hiller, Sundstrom commented, 'It's simple to see through you, young man. You think things will change, that you'll get ahead by a well-timed switch from Sundstrom's World Peace Road to whatever you presume will be the fashion.' His tone was bitter. 'Wrong! You forget that the Party, representing the collective wisdom of the vanguard of the working class, makes no mistakes. Therefore, every last convolution on every last ornament on every last building on World Peace Road is one hundred per cent necessary and correct . . . ' His hand shot out, his finger pointing. 'For if you doubt that, you doubt everything, and then you have no business being in the Party, with all that entails. Have I made my point?'

Hiller pulled at his earlobe. 'You have.'

Sundstrom's face darkened momentarily. He thought of his Berlin experience, his futile talks. But his own logic carried him over the uncertain ground. 'That's why, Comrade Hiller, in the end the Party will support *me*. They returned our first extension drafts. They want changes, adjustments, economies? That only proves what I said of their collective wisdom, and we'll submit new drafts – but not these . . . ' His hand struck the sheet before him. 'These, if they were accepted and built, would be an assertion in stone and concrete that the Party made a huge mistake . . . therefore they are anti-Party, and you, Comrade

Hiller, in associating yourself with them, are acting against the Party. Was that your intention?'

Hiller felt Julia's eyes on him. He couldn't afford to have himself steamrollered as Wollin, apparently, had let himself be. He smiled thinly. 'My intention was to help the Party break through toward good, twentieth-century architecture.'

'Good architecture!' exclaimed Sundstrom. 'Twentieth century! What sort of categories are those?'

'This gets us nowhere,' Julia said suddenly. 'You've declined the proposals, Arnold. That finishes it. The work isn't lost. No work ever is.'

Despite this self-consolation she saw the dead end in which they found themselves. Nothing had been decided; nothing had been solved, her own dilemma least of all. She glanced from Hiller to Wollin: neither of them seemed to have a suggestion.

'Julia!' Sundstrom said.

She didn't answer.

'Julia . . . ' There was fear in his voice, the fear that he hadn't broken the front against him; that even Wollin, by his silence, had proven himself stronger. 'Are you siding with them, Julia?'

She felt no pity, no hate – not even guilt, though she had betrayed him, though the man with whom she had betrayed him was present. She just didn't want him to stage another collapse; she wanted no breakdown, no dramatics. 'This gets us nowhere,' she repeated, 'and I'm very tired.'

Sundstrom left the protection of the piano and poured himself a brandy. He could safely break off the evening now; a draw had been achieved, and whether or not Julia approved of the Wollin designs was unimportant.

But it was important to him to discover if he still could whip her in line, this wife who owed him everything.

He drank the brandy. He had been drinking all evening, during the meal and after it, without feeling it. But this last drink did it. It shot straight to his brain. The room, the glasses, the drawings, the two men, and his wife blended into a single menace, and whatever had kept his panic from showing crumbled.

'You're tired,' he picked up her remark, 'and what am I supposed to be? . . . Don't you see I'm trying to uphold more than a conception of architecture . . . a world!' His head swayed toward Wollin and Hiller. 'Against detractors and belittlers, against revisionists and fault-finders: I thought I had a right to expect your support, Julia.'

She stiffened. 'I only permitted myself to feel that the design of Comrades Wollin and Hiller had a certain sincerity . . . and beauty, freshness of approach, generosity . . . '

'This goes beyond architecture, Julia. This is a basic disloyalty.'

She flinched, listened. No, he did not know. He was so centred on himself and his politics that she could have had a dozen lovers without a suspicion entering his mind.

'But for me, you wouldn't be alive,' Sundstrom went on, attacking what he thought was her weak point. 'I took in an orphan; I raised her, made a human being of her.'

'I'm grateful,' she broke in, her voice strained. 'I am, truly. And always will be.'

'Grateful?' He savoured the word. 'I believed it was love. Didn't I watch over it, from its awakening? Or were you, even then, equipped with a double set of morals?'

Julia shut out his voice. As through an opaqueness, she saw John Hiller march up to him; heard John speak sharply, warningly; wondered at his sudden chivalry: John Hiller, the knight errant, was something new.

Sundstrom brushed Hiller aside and turned back to Julia. 'And there's Julian. Do you ever think of the *child*?'

Hiller was now arguing with Wollin, his undertone audible, and Julia heard him insist that they leave and take her with them. Wollin's answer was lost in the sudden 'Julia, my dear!' that Sundstrom had spoken in a voice loud and demanding and, at the same time, pleading.

204

'Julia . . . Remember that first afternoon dress I brought you – second-hand, there was nothing else to be had in the impoverished country. Remember our dacha, the year after, the garden, the light in the trees, the jasmine, the berries . . . '

'Arnold, I beg you!' It was unbearable. The dress was true with its sequins; the jasmine was true, the berries; and his hypocrisy in recalling them had roots that reached into the essence of their lives. 'Arnold,' she sounded strange and brittle to herself, 'John and I—'

'Remember the nights, the white nights that summer in Leningrad, the Neva embankment, the ship gliding downriver in liquid silver . . . '

'John and I—'

'Julia!' The sentiment was wiped off like a glycerine tear. 'I'll tell it to you now, and before witnesses, so you can conduct yourself accordingly: If I'm ruined, I'll pull a lot of people down with me; and you, too, you first. But I won't be. I've had a good thirty years of experience in this; I know every trick in the book, and a few that were never listed. You might take that under advisement as well, John Hiller, and you, Brother Wollin . . . '

Spittle was forming a rim at the corners of his mouth, his face purplish. The opaque sense of unreality in which Julia had been protecting herself broke. This is the end, she thought; the last shred of illusion was gone, Sundstrom the lover the husband the father the artist the Communist; the person before her stood exposed in all the ugliness of his fear. Fear of her, his comrades, himself: a phrase-mongering, power-mad, cowardly, petty tyrant howling at the world because it no longer genuflected to him and his desires.

' . . . you said you loved me.'

His bitterness was too harsh to be completely fraudulent; and she thought, so I did, and was proud of you, and believed in you; she tried to gauge how much of his moral collapse was her fault, and she couldn't. She only knew it had begun the night of that reception, with Comrade Krylenko; but it must have been there dormant, long before, years before, probably always, a cancer silently growing until it had consumed the man.

' . . . falsehood,' she heard him saying, 'and I ask myself, hasn't it been there all along, ingrained, warping our lives? Some people acquire it through circumstance; others are cursed with it from the day they were born . . . '

Julia realised with effort that he was talking about her; she saw Wollin raise his head, his long paralysis apparently ended, and she heard him enquire, 'It's in their blood, eh? The daughter of a fascist agent, isn't she?'

She saw Arnold gasp, but he couldn't draw back; he had pushed himself too far over the brink.

'Unfortunately, Goltz *was* working for them.'

'Just like myself?' asked Wollin.

'There was proof.'

Julia heard the beating of her pulse in her eardrums. Arnold seemed strangely composed. John Hiller leaned forward, tense, as if he were watching a snake about to devour a rabbit.

'Proof?' said Wollin, his tone bordering on the casual.

'Of course. Those telegrams.'

Wollin's brow rose.

'The two telegrams to Goltz, both of them informing him that his father died.'

'Two?'

'Two. Don't tell me you've forgotten!' Sundstrom narrowed his eyes. 'Well, you've had other worries since then and you may have forgotten, or perhaps the coincidence didn't strike you at the time as it did me. Two telegrams – the one in November 1935, in Prague; the other in the summer of 1939 in Moscow.' Sundstrom sounded impatient. 'You were present both times, just as I was: in the Goltzes' Prague flat, we were discussing plans for raising money for a publication; and in the hotel on Gorky Street, Babette was serving coffee. I have a memory for details, always had. *Sorry father died deepest sympathy*; two telegrams, virtually the same wording; how many fathers can a man have, I ask you? It was a code.'

Julia felt her heart freezing. The pulse in her ears stopped; everything seemed dead in her except her mind, which worked like a million bobbins shuttling a million threads spelling out a million times *murder murder murder* . . . Wollin had asked the question she should have asked.

'Anyway,' Sundstrom was saying, 'it's all documented and in the files and Goltz confessed to it.'

'His wife confessed, too?' said Wollin

'I presume so.'

Hiller rose, pulling down the knot of his tie and unbuttoning his shirt collar. The air in the room seemed suddenly to have thickened.

'I do recall now,' said Wollin, his eyes briefly seeking Julia's, 'it was two telegrams. The years . . . As you said, Arnold, I've had other worries since then, and the coincidence didn't strike me at the time.'

Sundstrom began gathering the drafts and putting them together like a lecturer having finished with his notes.

'Also I recall that you and I were the only outsiders present on both occasions,' Wollin continued.

Sundstrom looked up. His eyes appeared to glaze over; his hands mechanically continued rolling up the papers.

'Then it was you who turned Comrade Goltz in,' Wollin concluded quietly.

'Julia!' Sundstrom cried out, plea and panic.

She saw him coming toward her. 'Don't touch me,' she said.

'Don't touch her,' Hiller said, 'or I'll kill you.'

'Julia, open up!'

Again the knocking at the door.

'Why don't you want to let Daddy in, Julia?' asked Julian from the armchair in the corner where he huddled, wrapped in his bathrobe.

'I must talk to you, Julia.' Sundstrom sounded muffled; it was a thick door, solid wood. 'Let me explain to you.'

She went on packing. 'You've explained enough.'

'Why are we packing?' said the boy, large-eyed.

'I'll explain it again,' Sundstrom pleaded, from outside. 'You didn't understand; it's not simple, I know. But you must try.'

'I did understand.' She shut the bag: a few of her things, the boy's. The rest Frau Sommer could pack and send after her. 'I understood exactly. Everything.'

She listened. There was no further comment. Had he given up and gone? More likely he was standing there, behind that door, waiting for her and Julian to emerge as they must.

'Why are we leaving?' said the child.

Julia shook herself. The boy had to be dressed, and warmly; it was a chilly night. 'Because your father and I can no longer live together,' she said, and wondered at her factual tone of voice; it was as if her heart were held together by iron hoops; the bursting point would come later when everything had been attended to and she sat in some hotel, her hands idle; she knew herself.

'Why can't you and Daddy live together anymore?' asked Julian, holding out his bare leg.

'Because—'

Because he had done his revolutionary duty, with a heavy mind and a torn conscience, as he had put it, but what other course had there been for him? He had explained it all, in the presence of Daniel Wollin and John Hiller; the telegrams were more than suspicious, perhaps a provocation; the matter had to be investigated, for the sake of Julian and Babette Goltz as much as for reasons of security; if Julian and Babette were the victims of some plot, who was better qualified to clear the thing up and protect them than the authorities in charge of those affairs? And if not . . .

'I'm cold, Julia,' said the boy.

She hastily pulled up his stockings.

'Julia?'

'Yes, darling?'

'You haven't told me . . . '

'I will.' She felt his thin little body squirm in her hands as she put on his underthings; she looked about for his trousers and the red and blue sweater that she had brought from his room. 'Just let me think . . . '

And if not, Arnold had said to her and Wollin and John, well, then . . . He wasn't telling her anything new, he had said, they *had* talked about it, and more than once: the frightful situation in which the Soviet Union found itself in that period, isolated, surrounded by the enemies of the revolution who didn't shy away from any means, even the most despicable; if people near the very top of the Party could turn agent and traitor, it showed what pressures were used, what temptations. A complicated time; thank God that it was past and done with; what was the good of bringing back its horrors and burdening the present with them when we were working, all of us, hand in hand, to show that the suffering and the blood and the tears had not been in vain?

'Why don't you tell me?' the boy asked, almost in tears.

'Oh, Julian,' she sighed, tying his scarf and buttoning his overcoat, 'it's because your father . . . and my father—'

She broke off. Something within her throat thickened and threatened to gag her. I mustn't become ill, she thought, I mustn't, not now; she felt sullied, physically and spiritually; the two father images in her mind that overlay one another refused to separate and were inextricably mingled with the lover embracing and the murderer strangling her; she wished she could scream to relieve the weight on her heart, but that would frighten the child. In a half-choked voice she said, 'It's because I no longer can love him, Julian. No person can live with someone she doesn't love. If one did, one would become very unhappy.'

The boy nodded wisely. At that moment, the pounding resumed; the child walked up to the door and in a tone shrill with excitement called out, 'No person can live with someone she doesn't love!'

Her eyes began to swim.

'Julia! For the last time, open up!'

She dried her eyes. No, she was not afraid – if she had been, she easily could have held John Hiller in the house, or Daniel Wollin, or both; but she had said goodbye to them and good-night, despite their unwillingness to leave her there; she had stood beside her husband at the house door like a good wife and hostess, and only when the guests were gone had she turned and fled upstairs and gathered her child and locked herself in.

'Julia!' shouted Sundstrom. 'For God's sake!'

She picked up the bag and took Julian by the hand and unlocked the door.

He pulled it open.

'Where do you think you are going?' he said.

'Call a taxi, Arnold, will you please?'

'But I explained to you . . . I thought you understood . . . '

'I understood. I'm not accusing you. I just want to leave, with my child.'

'In the middle of the night? . . . Julia, stay . . . for the child's sake at least. Till tomorrow. Tomorrow I'll let you go if you still want to.'

For a second or two, her resolution seemed to waver. Then she saw him reach for the child.

'No,' she said, 'I'm leaving now. Call that taxi.'

'And where is it to take you?' Sundstrom said, the fight having gone out of him.

Julia, holding on to the suitcase with one hand and to the child with the other, walked past him. She did not know where the taxi was to take her. The future was a blank.

210

CHAPTER TEN

The shuttle bus, bringing the mail and summer guests, swayed across the causeway that linked the seaside resort of Kleinmallenhagen with the mainland. The road was full of holes, and the bus dipped into each of them as if to give the passengers a foretaste of the discomforts of country life.

John Hiller balanced the rucksack filled with his purchases on his lap and gave himself to the lurchings of the bus. He made this trip two or three times a week: the state store in Kleinmallenhagen sold Baltic seashells hand-painted with views of the beach, and colour photos of the boardwalk framed in wooden imitation lifebelts, both inscribed *Souvenir*; also books and bathing trunks, candy and frankfurters, and occasionally Bulgarian tomatoes; but if you needed nails or electric bulbs or canned goods or any of the staples for roughing it in a fisherman's hut, it meant taking the bus.

He had been roughing it for quite some time now, with Julia and the child. The cottage – black beams, red brick, straw-thatched roof – had been a stroke of luck. He had remembered it from one of the last year's weekends with Waltraut Greve; it belonged to a great-uncle of Waltraut's who had moved to the mainland to spend his last years with his son's family; and since the cottage lay quite a distance from Kleinmallenhagen proper, the old man was glad to have found permanent tenants.

The bus passengers heading for the beach and summer happiness looked sullen and hot; the children whined; the women fanned themselves with sweaty handkerchiefs; the men wore their hats pushed back and their shirts unbuttoned. They would be placed in the various boarding houses of West-Kleinmallenhagen, which had been converted into trade-union rest homes; East-Kleinmallenhagen, with its Kurhaus and its quaint, done-over peasant cottages, was reserved for the intelligentsia who came in their own cars and frequented the nudist beach beyond the abandoned lighthouse.

John Hiller shifted the load on his lap. At first the refuge he had found for Julia and himself had seemed ideal; a love nest out of paradise; a calm so deep, with the wind soughing in the pines and the surf lapping the beach, that the cuts and bruises healed over; a beautiful privacy shared by the two of them, the immense black bell of the sky above them. A perfect place – except that Waltraut Greve thought she had a vested interest in the house; she had already visited twice, bringing with her the restlessness of World Peace Road and blatantly offering herself for a quick roll in the hay. And there was Julian, the boy.

John Hiller slapped at the fly buzzing around his head. How could he have said no to Julia when she came to him that night; yes, I'll take you, but no, not your child; though he had immediately seen the catch in it; you loved a woman with your heart and your balls; that didn't mean you loved her brat who nagged her by the hour and when he wasn't nagging her sat looking at you with big accusing eyes as if you had stolen his piece of candy.

But, oh, the love – the love she gave that compensated for everything. Not the night she came to him with the child and he put them up; strange that she came, after the apparent composure with which she had stood next to Sundstrom in the doorway of their house and said her goodbyes and thank-you-for-the-visits; she seemed in a state of shock, having taxied from hotel to hotel; Sundstrom must have done some fast telephoning to block her from finding a place; so she had come to him, suitcase in hand, the boy beside her. He had opened his arms and said, Julia, Julia, Julia. The love she gave him, not that night but later, was obsessive. It rose from some feeling deeper, he feared, than

212

any possible for him; it slaked his thirst and yet left him thirsting for her. A desperate need for life seemed to be shaking her; and once in their fisherman's cottage, neither past nor future existed, only the moment, and the sound of the sea through the open window, and the cool morning breeze on their skin.

That's how it had been in the beginning. And it still could be that way. He had sent Waltraut Greve packing and had shut out the world. He would keep it shut out as long as his savings lasted; after that, he would borrow. He had glued and carpentered and laid wires and painted and turned the cottage into a compact wonder of snugness and comfort; the stove needed a few small repairs; those done, they could sit out the winter. But today again, he had forgotten to drop by the stove-fitter.

The bus shook as if it were about to come apart. The passengers groaned and hung on to their seats and their children. Through the heat haze over the road the first roofs of Kleinmallenhagen appeared with their *fin de siècle* gables and mansard slopes.

Something in Hiller tightened. No – Julia's feelings hadn't changed; the hours when they filled one another's world were still there, when police registration, the mail, the doctor, the radio, architecture, ethics, society, and the boy Julian didn't exist. But there was an aftermath. Julia would sink into an agony of soul-searching, probing an imagined rift between them. When he assured her she was wrong and asked her to take the hour at its sixty-minute value, she would fall silent. It made the spot he was in no prettier. He had gone into this without reservation; his bridges were burned, his job gone, his professional future in this Republic a zero: Sundstrom would see to it that no prospective employer could countenance his cadre file. What more could she ask of him? He thought of himself as a simple person, basically; easygoing; could adapt himself to anyone who gave him half a chance; was ready to enjoy what life brought him, to laugh and to walk around obstacles he couldn't hurdle. She would rather beat her head against the wall.

With a heave that slid people off their seats and tumbled those already standing, the bus halted at the Kleinmallenhagen state store. Shouting, complaining, querying, the passengers alighted. Hiller listened to the footsteps on the roof, the hollow thumps of bags being dropped from the baggage rack overhead. When the bus started up again, he was the only passenger except for a man with a moustache and beetle brows wilted by the heat. The man held on to a violin case. He was the new Kurhaus violinist, he informed, lisping strongly; his predecessor was in the mainland hospital with yellow jaundice; and was it a tipping crowd at the Kurhaus or the ordinary proletariat?

'When you think what the intelligentsia earns,' Hiller answered matter-of-factly, 'I'd say they tipped much less than the working people.'

The man seemed to need time to adjust to this. He stared moodily out of the window. Hiller set his rucksack on the empty seat beside him and settled back into his thoughts. It was the child really; the boy Julian was at the bottom of it; a nice kid, trying to adjust to the upset of everything he'd been accustomed to, trying hard, poor little fellow, with insecurity driving him to stick to Julia like a papoose. Hiller wondered at Eskimo lovemaking with a baby face forever looking over the woman's shoulder; he guessed privacy was beside the point for the Eskimo; what privacy could you have in an igloo with half your clan looking on while you're having a go at it? Or maybe you pulled the fur cap down over the kid's eyes and stuffed his mouth with a piece of blubber. But I'm no Eskimo, he thought, and Waltraut Greve's great-uncle or whatever he was hadn't soundproofed his cottage.

The bus was lurching cruelly. To the right and the left, the boarding houses bounced by, most of them in need of a paint job, the awnings faded on their balconies. People in various stages of undress were ambling on the sidewalks; screaming children were eternally chasing one another; you sensed the sea beyond the sparse green on top of the dunes. The violinist was talking again. Tipping was relative, he said; a small tip from a big man was more than a big tip from a small one; he had grown his moustache to make himself look more like a gypsy . . . he went from table to table and played into his prospect's ear, hardly anyone resisted that. He leaned over and lisped, 'Art must be personal, Mister, to be appreciated. All this mass stuff you get over the loudspeakers, nobody listens; who looks at your statues in the park, or your murals? You're an artist?'

'Of sorts.'

'You paint a nice bunch of flowers or a nude with meat in front and back, and people will buy them and hang them in the bedroom, and publishers will print copies and sell them for good money, and you'll have your own car and won't need that rucksack. That's what I call realism!' He slapped his violin case as if it were a woman's behind. 'And I've had a penchant for realism all my life.'

The bus stopped. 'East-Kleinmallenhagen,' said the driver. 'Kurhaus. End of the line.'

The violinist touched Hiller's knee. 'All right, mister.' And with a nod at the Nightmare Medieval of the Kurhaus with its pointed turrets and its jutting oriels, 'You come here, yes? No tipping. I'll treat you!'

Hiller laughed. The encounter had lightened his mood; he walked on, the rucksack slung over his back, the warm sand caressing his sandalled feet. Maybe part of the trouble was that his character tended toward the sociable; being a recluse was all right as long as the experience was fresh, but for weeks he had talked only to Julia and the boy; to Waltraut, twice; and a few words with the policeman, the doctor, the postman, the driver, the store people on the mainland. It did something to you, made you stir-crazy, that was the expression for it; you grew touchy, hard to get along with. He would tell Julia they must go out, see people – in the Kurhaus, on the beach, even the post office. They

215

didn't need to hide; there was no law against a man and a woman loving one another and living together, even if the Kurhaus was full of friends and acquaintances whose tongues would start clucking. He knew Julia wouldn't take his advice. The boy wouldn't let her. That kid was a ball and chain around her foot. A mother was a mother, not a mistress, that was it.

The Kurhaus was the last building on the street. The re-modelled peasant cottages began farther inland. Straight as a Prussian army road and just as hard on your feet, the boardwalk ran toward the abandoned lighthouse; to the left the dunes fell off to the beach, which was pockmarked as if by moon craters; in the centre of each crater stood the family's wicker beach settee, shielded against outsiders by a surrounding sand wall. The walls, in turn, were decorated with stones or seashells: in their designs, Hiller suspected, lay the origins of some of the friezes that now ran across the buildings of World Peace Road. There were also the wall inscriptions lettered in pebbles – last year, before fate involved him in more serious matters, Hiller had spent whole afternoons collecting them: *Villa Bismarck; Happiness Comes to the Smallest Hut*; and, a testimonial to the impression Brecht had left on the minds of the more sophisticated, *Mahagonny*. What his home was to the Englishman, his fortified beach settee was to the German.

Ordinarily, it was no more than ten minutes from the Kurhaus to the ochre-coloured rock on which the lighthouse stood; Hiller dawdled, stopping to shake out his sandals; then he gazed out at the sea which sparkled back at him, numbing him with its unbroken indifference. The craters grew less frequent; the beach became rocky; only a few Kleinmallenhagen women in working clothes and rubber boots knelt at the water's edge, gathering by the bucketful a stone that, so Hiller had heard, was used in the making of porcelain. Then the lighthouse, like a black finger raised to lecture the waves, loomed up, its door off the hinges, its base defaced by the scrawls of tourists.

Hiller thoughtfully pulled at his earlobe. At the lighthouse the path forked, one branch curving along the naked beach, the other cutting through the pines, straight toward the cottage. Then he hitched up the straps of his rucksack and, whistling loudly to himself, marched off along the shore.

His step now had zip. He felt neither the sand in his sandals nor the sand flies at his ankle; he was playing hooky; revolt within revolt, plain anarchism. The beach once more changed from rock to sand. In the distance pink spots materialised, some quiescent, some dancing against the slate of the sea, without pattern or purpose, somewhat like atomic particles in a bubble chamber. Hiller squinted – he could honestly say that this had not been the reason for his detour; he wasn't the sightseeing type and God knows he had all a man in good physical condition could take care of.

'Yoo-hoo!'

A woman's voice. Hiller didn't bother to look toward it. They yoo-hooed each other, on the beach, all day long.

'Yoo-hoo! John Hiller!'

Beyond the dip of the dune, out of a cluster of pink shapes, one had risen and was waving her arms toward him. She was naked but for a pair of binoculars dangling between her breasts.

The dunes were planted with a particularly tough kind of reed that whipped against Hiller's calves and bruised his feet as he strode down to the beach. The woman had stopped waving and sat on her haunches, watching his progress; two of the men rose lazily; one slipped the binoculars off the woman's neck and focused them on him. Heads raised from behind a long mound of sand fell back again as if the effort had been exhausting. One person, hard to say if man or woman, crawled on top of the mound and remained there, squatting like a Buddha.

Hiller began to recognise faces.

'Well, it's actually him,' said Axel von Heerbrecht. 'In person. The fugitive from justice.'

'And where's the Sundstrom girl?' Comrade Warlimont wondered, scratching his fleshy chest.

'Can't be far,' said Heerbrecht, and to Hiller, 'Greetings, young man. We've been hearing of your bucolic idyll with Julia. But this is the first we *see* of it.'

'Who told you?' said Hiller, trying not to look at Käthchen Kranz and trying to disregard the fact that the use of her titian hair dye was not limited to the hair on her head.

'Waltraut Greve,' said Warlimont. 'She was at the Kurhaus this morning.'

Hiller's mind mechanically registered the information. Professor Kerr was emerging; sand clung to his buttocks and his scrotum. From the top of the mound, the poet Karl-August Mischnick surveyed the scene; despite the few steps' distance to the sea, the skin covering his fat, misshapen body seemed dirty.

'Take them off,' said Käthchen Kranz.

Hiller winced.

'Yes, you,' she said. Take your clothes off. You're making us self-conscious.'

Comrade Warlimont laughed. 'Self-conscious!' The idea, in context with Käthchen, seemed absurd.

'I'd better get going,' Hiller said with a tinge of embarrassment. 'I'm expected.'

'You've hardly said hello,' protested Käthchen and held out her hand. The gesture brought her pink-tipped, pointed breasts into sharp outline.

Hiller swallowed.

'Help me up!'

He took her hand. With one graceful motion she was standing before him, her body close to his, her face, her lips. 'Take those things off,' she insisted. 'Since when are you a prude? Since . . . *her*?'

Again Warlimont laughed. Heerbrecht was sneering openly.

From his mound, Mischnick proclaimed in his high-pitched voice, 'You ought to bring *her* here, Comrade Hiller.'

'*Her?*' enquired Mrs Kerr, from behind the sand pile. 'Who is *her?*'

'Julia Sundstrom,' said the Professor from above. 'You know.'

'Ah, yes,' said Mrs Kerr, 'the architect's wife who ran away with that terrible young man.'

Nobody spoke. Hiller stripped off his clothing and piled his things on his rucksack.

Käthchen Kranz studied him. Then she tapped his chin and said, 'That's better,' and, sighing contentedly, let herself drop back onto the sand.

Warlimont and Heerbrecht sat down at her feet, watching one another like two dogs guarding the same bone. Käthchen stretched in the sun. The bitch, thought Hiller; and then, try counting sheep, or cardinal numbers, get your mind off her.

'John,' Käthchen was saying, 'I want to ask you things. Come here,' a lazy gesture, 'here.'

He lay down beside her. Actually he felt relieved; by rolling over on his stomach he could avoid embarrassment. Käthchen's clasped hands rested on top of her head; he saw the white of her shaved armpit and the tiny drops of sweat on it. Bitch, he thought again, I ought to straddle you right here; that would teach you.

'How long have you been in Kleinmallenhagen?' she asked, her half-shut eyes wandering over him.

'Nearly a month,' he answered.

'In that old fisherman's cottage, they say! How lovely.'

'Yes. Ten minutes from here. Straight through the woods.' Julia has the finer body, he thought. But this one uses hers as if her limbs, curves, skin had a single purpose. Every one of her languid moves proclaimed it.

'If it was a secret speech, Comrade Warlimont,' Mrs Kerr had raised herself and become visible down to her flat, pendulous breasts, 'how come you know of it?'

Secret speech, Hiller thought idly, what secret speech? Warlimont was lovingly kneading Käthchen's toes. 'One hears things,' he said meaningfully. 'There were several thousand delegates and guests at that closed session of the Congress. Several thousand!'

'I'll come and visit you in your cottage,' said Käthchen. 'All of us will.'

She was stroking her belly. So there had been a secret speech at the Soviet Party Congress, thought Hiller; you could hook your mind into that; it was better than listing cardinal numbers or counting sheep.

'Poland,' said Heerbrecht with a sneer, and took hold of Käthchen's other foot and gently massaged it. 'I hear it came out through Poland. They were selling copies of it, black, to Western correspondents. Poland! What can you expect?'

'I can't stand it!' Käthchen moved her legs, denying her feet to both of her admirers. 'They've been talking about nothing but that speech all morning. So Khrushchev told them about Stalin, and nobody actually knows what he said, I mean, *really*!' She took Hiller's hand, 'John, do you want to race me?'

'No,' said Hiller, 'not now. I want to hear about the Congress.' He did want to, that much was true, but it was also an excuse to permit him to remain prone.

The poet Mischnick had finally given up his Buddha indifference. 'Cult of the personality.' He lifted both arms and let them fall again. 'Perhaps they want me to rewrite my poems? Did Stalin ride to Potsdam through Bismarckstrasse, which is now World Peace Road, or didn't he? Well?'

'He's worried over his prize,' Käthchen said to Hiller. 'I kind of liked Stalin; he looked so calm, always lighting his pipe. You've got to have *someone* to believe in, don't you?'

Professor Kerr sadly compared Käthchen's solid flesh with the ribs that showed through his wife's skin. 'But if it were true,' he asked, 'that innocent people were tried on manufactured evidence and tortured and put to death?'

Hiller raised himself on his elbows. The Professor had become a careful man after the public castigation he had received for stating that politicians should adjust their theories to the facts of nature and not ask the scientists to juggle the facts. 'Have you any proof?' Hiller asked. 'Excuse me – but this is important.'

'Did it happen to anyone you know?' said the Professor.

Mischnick slid down from his mound. 'Imagine the books that would have to be pulped,' he said, his boy-soprano voice coloured by anxiety. 'The films that must be shelved! The cities we would have to rename! . . . They'll never let it happen.'

'But if it's true?' said the Professor.

Käthchen turned on her side, facing Hiller. 'John,' she purred, 'they bore me. Let's race, yes? Along the beach, far, far.'

'There is no truth as such!' Mischnick took a deep breath and held it in like a frog about to croak. 'That's pure objectivism, undialectical.'

Both Heerbrecht and Warlimont had switched their positions to get a better view of Käthchen. Heerbrecht, adjusting his thick-lensed glasses, said, 'It would create a crisis of confidence. I hope they don't call me back to the station. I'd hate to have to write a commentary on the subject.'

'Oh, you'd manage,' Warlimont said. 'I've heard you churn yourself out of worse spots.'

I suppose,' Heerbrecht was giving as good as he got, 'you would like to face the young people in your organisation with that thing hanging over your head?'

I don't think it will come to that.'

'What makes you so hopeful?'

'The fact that we can't afford it.' Warlimont laughed and playfully slapped Käthchen's nicely rounded, nicely tanned buttock. 'And I don't know if the Russians can. For a party in power, public self-criticism is a dangerous luxury; that's the one thing we learned in June 1953.'

Hiller scooped up a handful of sand. If there was such a speech at the Soviet Congress as seemed definite, and if its contents were spread, as was likely, and if some of them dealt with frame-ups and tortures and killings of innocent men, it was thoroughly possible that the Goltz case would be reopened from that end, too. Hiller let the sand run through his fingers. Where would that leave Sundstrom and Julia, or, for that matter, himself?

Käthchen yawned. 'John! You're daydreaming!'

'Self-criticism . . . ' Heerbrecht absently rubbed his flabby chin. 'I don't see how you can avoid the issue.'

Mrs Kerr had crawled out entirely from behind her sand pile and lay there, her spindly body stretched full length, her feet pointing at Mischnick, her surprisingly sensitive face appearing between Warlimont and Heerbrecht. 'Why don't we ever have peace?' she asked. 'As far back as I can remember, gods were erected for us only to be publicly smashed, ideas were touted only to be proved lies!'

'Peace,' said the Professor, 'is death.' But he said it with compassion for his wife, perhaps for mankind. 'As a physicist, my duty is to doubt. I've explained that to you, my dear. And if that Congress speech, provided we ever learn what it said, helps us to make doubting legally permissible . . . '

'What did I tell you?' Warlimont called out, cutting off the Professor. 'How do you propose to square doubt and discipline? Am I to put in my function to educate a generation on doubters?' He turned to Heerbrecht. 'Issue! . . . There is no issue unless we admit it. That's how you avoid it. If you keep on not answering people, they'll stop asking . . . Race, Käthchen?'

He jumped up, quite agile despite the premature fat on his body, and motioned to Heerbrecht.

'John?' Käthchen's breasts brushed Hiller's shoulder as he sat up.

Hiller half turned. His mind still reeled from the constant zigzag between the two levels on which it had been operating; either one, the portent of the speech and Käthchen's nude presence, was enough to dizzy a man; or maybe it was the sun and that he hadn't eaten since a very early breakfast.

'Race!' said Käthchen. 'Come on!'

Then she was off, wildly. Hiller was in no hurry; he gave the two middle-aged men prancing after her their head start and waved back at Mischnick and Professor Kerr and his wife. The moist, cool sand at the water's edge felt good to his feet. He ran with long, even steps, preserving his breath, not thinking, but also not blocking the flashes of thoughts that criss-crossed his mind – impressions more than ideas: Käthchen streaking along, hair flying, arms spread, buttocks grinding; Julia kissing him sleepily, lingering aftertaste of last night's embrace; oh, yes, the doctor was due today, always running a temperature, the boy; don't step on that jellyfish, the Baltic's full of jellyfish; Heerbrecht and Warlimont, sounds like a firm of jewellers, they were getting winded; people cheering them on, one big fraternity this naked beach; nudity was the ultimate leveller, very democratic; it reminded him of a painting – who had painted it? Hieronymus Bosch – little nudes spread on rocks and stuffed into crevices, devils spearing, whipping, goring, burning them, while high above the trees and the mountains, in a baby-blue sky, God and the angels and the sainted souls looked on piously; several thousand Congress delegates in shirt and tie; somehow, the horrors appeared more frightening when you heard of them with nothing between them and you but your naked skin and a naked woman shoving herself at you; World Peace Road running straight through Babylon, the great whore; oh, dialectical materialism, where is thy sting; oh, revolution, where is thy victory?

He heard the two men puffing. Heerbrecht strained, his head at an awkward angle, his arms going like pistons; Warlimont gasped, he was flecked with sweat like a horse, his knees buckled. Up ahead of them, uttering shrill, small cries of challenge, capered Käthchen, setting the relentlessness of her youth against the hearts of the chair-borne.

223

Hiller, beginning to feel the thrill of the chase, prepared to pass Heerbrecht and Warlimont. He was closing up on them; another ten seconds, or fifteen, and he would be past them. He saw the sea, a flat dish, to his left; to his right, the undulating grey-green-yellow of the dunes.

'Hey, fellows—'

His call died in a mouthful of sand. He had stumbled, and they were pressing his face into the sand, their moist, sticky arms and legs choking him, an octopus of hate.

'Hey don't—'

They couldn't hear him, or wouldn't. From somewhere, far off, sounded Käthchen's laughter. Bitch, he thought. And then: they'll kill me, the slobs. They will. By God.

With his last breath, he reared. His elbow went into something soft that gave. Warlimont groaned and fell back. Heerbrecht had lost his glasses and groped more than gripped. Hiller, cursing, pushed him off and rose and surveyed the battlefield. Heerbrecht, on all fours, was searching the sand; Warlimont, swaying like an old woman, held his groin. From the water came Käthchen's laughter. She was lying on her back, occasionally kicking her legs. Her hair floated like seaweed; the foam of the tiny breakers lapped over her breasts.

Hiller dove in.

She swam away from him. She was a fast swimmer, her sturdy legs splashing the water, and she was rested. Whenever Hiller thought he had hold of her, she twisted herself free. They were far out beyond the sandbars; he began to worry; there was a strong current hereabouts, he had been warned.

'Come back here!' he shouted.

The sea glistened. Somewhere among the lights a face, like a white ball, bobbing.

'The current!' he shouted. 'D'you want us to get caught in it?'

This time she had heard. She tried to turn back, but whether she was carried by the current or had overtaxed her strength, she made no headway; Hiller saw her raising her arm, a mute call for help.

He stuck his head far out above the water: no boat, no other swimmer, only, way off at the shore, two miniature figures black against the sun. The damn fool bitch, he thought, wouldn't it be a joke if I was to drown out here because of her playing hard to get; Sundstrom would have a laugh over that one. Sundstrom would have the last laugh anyhow; or maybe that secret speech would spike him; too bad those two hadn't come across with the details, the bastards; they surely knew more than they had given out, especially Warlimont. Hiller pumped his lungs full of air and, with swift strokes, set out for Käthchen. He felt tired; his legs wouldn't kick as they should. That was quite a beating they gave me, he thought as he measured the slowly shrinking distance between himself and the struggling girl. Wasn't it stupid; his obligation was toward himself, and Julia, yes, toward Julia; but here he was doing the honourable thing; more men have given up the one life they have for honour than for money though what can you buy with honour absolutely nothing . . .

By the time he reached Käthchen she was grey-faced and her eyes were popping out of her head like big blue glass marbles. 'Now you take it easy,' he panted, fearing above all that, panicked, she would latch on to him and pull him down with her. But once she felt his hand on her she grew meek as a kitten; her body convulsed as she retched out some of the water she had swallowed; but she didn't resist his hold on her head and shoulders; she was thankful not to be alone in that waste of sea.

Hiller didn't know how long he had been swimming back-stroke one arm supporting Käthchen, feeling her body, her shoulder, her breast and yet feeling nothing except the effort it took to force one more stroke of his legs and his free arm. Then he grew conscious of the difference in the ripple of the sea: the

225

sandbar. He tried for bottom, found he could stand; a few steps
on the rising sand; he dropped her.

She stood head and shoulders above the water, her lips blue,
her teeth chattering. He wondered what a man said at such a
moment – *Oh it was nothing at all*, or *Glad to do it again, anytime*.
Her hair hung stringy and her face was bloated from the strain;
she looked the dumb broad she was.

Suddenly her arms were about his neck, her cold body clinging
to his. 'Oh John, John, John.' She whimpered, shaking hysterically
as her imagination caught up with her fears.

He slapped her face.

Hiller pushed open the door. Inside the cottage it was fairly cool,
light and shadows dissecting the big couch, the scrubbed wooden
table, the bench. He dumped his rucksack on the floor, spread
his arms. 'Julia!'

'Sh-h-h! Julian's asleep.'

She kissed him. She smelled of fennel or some other herb, very
fresh, very clean; she wore a checked shirt and dungarees and a
pink flower behind her ear, and she moved with that grace that
still excited him.

'You were swimming?'

'It was so hot. And after the bus ride . . . ' He caressed her
throat. Her shirt was open down to the cleft between her breasts.
'And I met some people on the beach.'

'Who?'

He told her; she only half listened as he conscientiously listed
the names, including Käthchen Kranz's, and she seemed un-
responsive to his embrace. Her eventual question, 'And did you
enjoy them?' sounded preoccupied.

'Well,' he said, 'they're not the most enjoyable people. But
anyhow . . . people.'

'Oh,' she said. And leaving his arms, 'I'm glad you ran into
them.'

226

He turned to unpacking his rucksack. 'And how *is* Julian?' he asked, his emphasis a demonstration that he had wanted to ask this from the moment he arrived and that he knew she had a right to expect the question.

'The doctor was here.' She nodded toward the blue-painted narrow door that led to the cottage's other room. 'He's asleep now, thank goodness.'

Hiller set the cans he had bought on the table; then a special drill, some nails and screws wrapped in pieces of newspaper, towelling, and, a rare treasure, a roll of toilet paper. 'He had a bad night, poor kid,' Hiller said, 'and you, too. What did the doctor say?'

'He thinks it's . . . it's psychosomatic.'

Hiller looked at her. Her eyes were worried, perhaps over him as much as over the child. 'Psychosomatic?' he repeated.

'You know: the upset, the new life, another man with his mother.'

'They run a fever from that?'

'Apparently they do.'

Hiller took her hand, stroked the fingers, down to their tips. 'It couldn't be a simple bug? Or a virus? Viruses are hard to detect. Why not try sulfa, or penicillin?'

'This man has thirty-five years of practise. He's one of those small-town doctors who take a real interest. And he made it a point to come here though ordinarily I would have had to take Julian to his office. He likes the boy.'

'So do I.'

'I know.'

He let go of her hand. He thought of Käthchen shoving herself at him. Käthchen had no Julian, no encumbrance. Just a dumb broad who warbled dumb songs and was the dream girl of a half-million puberty-stricken youngsters. 'Would you have something left to eat?' he asked.

'Oh, dear!' Julia jumped up. 'You haven't had your lunch.'

She rushed to the propane burner in the corner and took off the pot that simmered there. 'I'm sorry. It's this constant worry. And then, on top of the doctor, Waltraut . . .'

'She was here, too?'

'Didn't you meet her? She said she'd walk toward the lighthouse.'

'Missed her!' he said, and thought, another broad, but with intellectual pretensions.

'She mentioned something about a secret speech at the Soviet Congress.' Julia put the soup plate before him filled with a sort of goulash, potatoes and boiled-out carrots and beans. Then she saw the box that he had taken from the rucksack and unwrapped and placed on the table, saw the colourful print pasted on top of its cover. 'John—' she said, and it was as if the light in the room were at this moment concentrated in her, 'you bought . . . that for Julian?'

'You don't play with blocks, do you?' He chewed, thinking: if it's *that* easy! And wryly: I'll be getting into the father act yet.

She had opened the box.

'It's rather intricate,' he explained. 'See those rubber links? You stick those into the holes in the blocks, and you can make a tractor, or a truck, all sorts of things . . .'

'Julian will love it!' Julia tenderly closed the box and put it aside. 'It's the first thing you ever gave him.'

He sensed the unspoken question. 'Hell,' he said, 'I felt like it. Spur of the moment, I suppose.' He listened to the faint rumble that came from far off. 'Why shouldn't I?' he said grandly. 'I would do it for any kid.'

'You see,' Julia lit cigarettes, for him and for herself, 'the doctor said what Julian needs is a father.'

'Thirty-five years of practise taught him that?

'John!' The plea sounded through her voice. 'I was prepared to ask you that we return . . .'

He shoved the empty dish aside. The speech, he thought, the

228

trials, the camps, the executions. 'You . . . want to go back . . . to Arnold?'

The reflection of distant lightning momentarily lit up her pained face. 'No . . . oh, no. I just wanted Julian to see him. Occasionally. So he knows he *has* a father. Arnold was always good to him.'

'I understand he was good to you, too.'

A roll of thunder, closer by, made her wince. Then she said 'But now . . . this . . . ' The glowing end of the cigarette was pointed at the toy box. 'John, I love you very much.'

'I know you do.'

'Sometimes I'm frightened, though.'

'Of what?' He listened. A wind began to stir outside; an open window creaked in its frame. Then all was still again. 'You needn't be.'

She took his hands and held them to her face. 'Do you think this storm will pass us by?'

'It might.' He felt her closeness, her breath tickling his lips. 'But I'd better shut the window.'

When he returned to her she stood, hands limply at her sides, waiting. 'Anyhow,' he said, taking her into his arms, 'we can pull the blankets over us and pretend there's no weather, no lightning, no world outside.'

She gently resisted him. 'The thunder is sure to wake Julian.'

'Julian . . . ' he repeated hoarsely, not letting her move away from him. 'Always Julian. It'll destroy us.'

The pink flower slipped from behind her ear. 'Not now, John. Tonight, I promise.'

A flash of lightning. Thunder. Her body struggling against his made him insensible to argument, his own, hers. This was something other than Käthchen the teaser; this went to the marrow of your bones; this was tinder crackling into bright, steep flame.

'Now,' he said, 'now,' half carrying her.

'This is insane,' she objected weakly. 'My God . . . his sleep is so light and he's afraid of thunderstorms.'

He saw her eyes close, felt her thighs press against him. He ripped the spread off the couch, threw open the cover. The white of the tightly drawn sheet glared in the semi-darkness; tanned skin against the glaring white, and honey hair dancing as her head moved up to him, lips, full, seeking him, drawing him to her; lightning flashes silhouetting, then bringing into relief windows, table, shelves, books, pillow, shoulders, breasts, hips, haunches.

Then the crash and the roll of the thunder.

The cottage shook. The blue-painted door flew open. Damn it, thought Hiller. I should have locked it, how could I, no key, no lock, well, then, jam chair against doorknob; let the brat yammer, there we have it, oh, hell.

In the doorway, pale small ghost numb with fright, the child.

Hiller felt Julia tear herself from him. She hastily pulled the top sheet over herself and him, but there were the clothes piled in disorder on the floor.

'Julia!' Hesitantly, the boy's feet groped toward the couch. 'I want to . . . to be with you . . . '

'Yes, darling, yes, right away.' Julia sat up, her eyes wildly searching for her robe. The robe was somewhere behind the curtain in the corner that served as the clothes closet.

The boy stopped. He looked at the two bodies outlined under the sheet and, with a puzzled frown, at his mother's face.

'Tell him to go back to his room,' hissed Hiller. 'For Christ's sake!'

The part of the sheet with which she had covered her breasts slipped. She put her feet on the floor and, naked, picked up Julian and carried him out through the blue-painted door. The rain was a strange, muffled beat on the straw-thatched roof, set off by the staccato of drops splashing into the puddles. Now he'll ask questions, Hiller thought, squirming with annoyance as his ears strained through the static of wind and rain to hear her answers. But only whispers came through the open door, cooing, caressing, calming.

Then Julia returned to fetch the box with the building blocks. Hiller watched her. She was as unsexual as a Gothic Madonna in her concentration on her motherhood. 'Why don't you put something on,' he sneered, propping himself up. 'You might give me ideas, you know!'

'John, darling—' It sounded haunted. She fled back to the boy's room. Through the open door, Hiller heard her voice. 'John brought this for you, Julian. Wasn't that nice of him? You can build a tractor from the blocks, or a truck – look at the picture – a baggage cart, or a monoplane . . . '

The receding thunder mildly punctuated her account. Hiller threw off the sheet, padded barefoot to the window, tore it open, and stuck his head out into the freshly washed air. Spreading the moisture of the last raindrops over his face, he thought, life, how many years is that, another thirty or so – with *this*?

He turned back into the room and slipped into his shirt and trousers. Then he fetched Julia's robe from behind the curtain, went into the child's room, and put the robe over her shoulders.

'Thanks,' she said, with a slight tremble in her tone, and, more firmly, to Julian. 'Say thank you to John, darling, for that lovely game.'

The boy glanced up at John from deeply ringed eyes and shook his head.

'Why should he?' said Hiller. 'I don't believe in all that thank you business from kids. But I would like to talk to *you*.'

'I don't want her to talk to you,' said the boy with sudden, high-pitched determination. 'You hurt her.'

'But, Julian,' Julia protested, 'John doesn't hurt me.'

Julian's face darkened. He had something of his father's stubbornness about him now. 'I saw him hurt you.'

A slow crimson flooded Julia's forehead. 'You've got to believe me, Julian. John is always kind and good to me.'

Hiller forced a brief laugh. Then he leaned over in an attempt to ruffle the boy's hair.

'I want my daddy . . . ' Julian said, his chin quivering.

'Julia,' said Hiller, 'please come into the other room.'

The boy clung to her hands. Julia looked pleadingly at Hiller. 'Later, John,' she said, 'later.'

'No, now,' he demanded and to Julian, 'I'm not your daddy. Your mother has left your daddy and she's with me; that's why you must obey me now. You stay in your bed like a good boy while your mother and I talk about something important. You can play with your blocks—'

A sweep of the thin arm and the box flew off the bed, the blocks tumbling and rolling across the floor. 'Now you will pick them up, Julian,' said Hiller, 'every one of them. Let's get going . . . '

'No,' said the boy, 'I won't.' He sounded at the point of tears, but his eyes were stone dry.

'You will.'

Julia seized Hiller's arm as he reached over to take hold of the boy. 'He's *my* child . . . ' And, placatingly, 'Don't you see he's not feeling well, John! The shock . . . '

'All right.' Hiller's narrow shoulders hung. 'So I'm a heel; I fight little boys. That's what we've reached.' He paused, squinting. 'Then I must tell it to you in here. You'll have to choose, Julia. I can't have a child run my life.' After a second he added, 'Our life.'

Julia slipped into her robe. She knelt down to pick up the blocks; one by one, she collected them in the box. 'Our life,' she finally said, her tone caressing the words. And then, without looking up, 'He's not quite five years old, John. Can't you laugh at the thing?' She rose, handed the box to Julian. 'Try laughing, John . . . for me.'

'Haw-haw,' he said.

'Now you're the child. It seems I have two children requiring special handling.'

'Don't be silly. And don't expect me to jump over my own shadow.'

'Aren't you letting your spite run away with you?' Julia sat down on the bed; she had to; her knees gave as the questions that had been nagging at the back of her mind suddenly jumped the threshold of her consciousness: how flimsy was this cottage, this idyll, how much security was there with this young man to whom she had fled? She saw Julian gaze at her as if he were trying to understand her quandary, and she said, 'Will *you* help me? Will you be my brave little boy and get well soon, and then we'll all play at the beach and be happy? . . . '

'And then we'll go back to Daddy?' said Julian.

'I don't think your mother will want to do that,' said Hiller, taking a cigarette from his trouser pocket.

'What *am* I to do?' she said, nervously fondling the child. 'You're forcing me into decisions, John, that I shouldn't have to make at all.'

'Life's doing that,' he answered, leaning against the wall and blowing the first smoke through his nostrils. 'Life, my dear, not I.'

'You'd want to give up my child? Take him back to – to his father?'

'He's obviously unmanageable. What do you want to do about his fever? It's psychosomatic, you were told.'

'Then I would have to go back, too.'

Hiller killed the cigarette on the heel of his sandal. His glance fell on Julian: the child's lips had tightened; his jaws worked, the only moving part of a mask of hate. 'I should be very sorry,' said Hiller.

The boy slowly turned to Julia. She took his face in her hands. 'He's burning,' she said.

Hiller groaned with frustration. 'Where's the medicine?'

'Over there . . . ' pointing to the small cupboard.

Hiller fetched the bottle and counted ten drops into a spoon. Julian swallowed obediently.

'It's not his fault,' said Julia, her voice small with distress. 'Or mine. Or yours. Help me, John.'

'To make up your mind?'

'Just help me.'

He watched her shake up the boy's pillow and smooth his forehead. 'Tomorrow, darling,' she was saying, 'if you feel better and your temperature is down, John and I will take you to the beach and you'll play in the sand . . . not too long, because the sun might be hot . . . but half an hour or so. Won't that be lovely?'

Hiller felt miserable, like a doctor who had cut open the patient and failed to find what he searched for and who kept on carving because somewhere must lie the root of the evil. 'What did Waltraut tell you about that secret speech?' he said.

Julia stroked back the child's moist hair. She needed a moment to catch up with the switch: was he making an effort at conciliation, withdrawing the choice and the threat? 'Not much, really . . . ' she said, still sounding uncertain. 'But you know Waltraut; she'll talk whether you listen or not. And I wasn't listening properly. I was waiting for you to come home . . . Not much, I believe, beyond the fact that there had been a secret speech at the Congress. What of it? Why did you ask?'

'Because at the beach they had it that Khrushchev spoke of terror and torture, of false arrests and false evidence, of innocent people executed.'

'At the beach . . . ' she said, quite meaninglessly. She pulled up the boy's blanket and mechanically tucked it in place while one after the other, like parts of a chain, Hiller's comment linked up in her mind with her father and mother with Arnold Sundstrom with her life with Julian who lay there, his thin lids bluish over his eyes his hand holding on to hers.

'Of course,' said Hiller, 'there were the telegrams. Granting that innocent people were ground in the mill, I'm sure the land of socialism was infested by genuine enemy agents, too.'

'John!' she begged. 'Stop it.'

'You asked me to help you. How else can I help you but by giving you all I know?'

She buried her face in the blanket next to the small body of her child. Julian had opened his eyes. 'I want my daddy,' he said.

Hiller turned and walked out.

Despite the cloudburst the sandy soil of the path through the woods was nearly dry. The birds warbled with an enthusiasm that deepened Hiller's annoyance with himself. He cut a birch rod and hit at the air. Where the switch touched the branch of a tree the raindrops that had gathered fell in a glistening shower.

The choice he had put before Julia was his choice, too, and he didn't like making decisions. When she had come to him with the child, he had had no choice, just as he had had none in pulling Käthchen Kranz out of the water – so that was all right. But how long could you go on avoiding the points in life where the road forked? Julia, he thought; it had looked so easy, and he had loved exploring her body, her emotions. You could blame the boy, of course, for the difficulties, but it wasn't the kid's fault that he existed and claimed his rights. Or Julia's: Julia expecting all or nothing of a man. As it turned out he wasn't that kind of one hundred per center – though there were moments when he could give all he had, and *had* given: his job, his comfortable mode of life. Well, Voukovich had warned him. When it came to having staying power, it seemed he wasn't ready, at any rate not yet, to settle down with wife and child till death do us part. He bore as much guilt as anyone for having spoiled what looked like such a sweet and juicy melon. And so he piled it all on Julia.

Hacking the defenceless air with the switch in his hand was no relief. He suspected that Julia saw through him finally: a petty scoundrel in her life, following upon a big one. A petty scoundrel with a merciless mind that analysed and protected itself and its pretences before everything.

He discovered Waltraut before she noticed him: she wasn't wearing her glasses. She walked briskly, almost joyfully, her skirt swirling about her legs; when she was alone, thinking herself unobserved, she seemed to lose the painful self-consciousness that emphasised all that was sharp and ugly about her.

Then with the keen ear that the blind and semi-blind develop, she sensed more than heard a man's presence and stopped.

'Hello, Waltraut,' he greeted, coming up to her, 'on your way to see us again?'

Her face, which had been entirely relaxed, took on its usual disdain and distrust. The glasses, hastily fetched from a pocket in the skirt, masked the eyes and completed the change in her face. 'See *you*,' she corrected.

'Is that so?' he said, sounding less indifferent than he had intended. They were now walking side by side, slowly, but in step, in the direction of the lighthouse. 'Aren't you sick of me yet?'

Her laugh jarred a little. 'Listen,' she said. 'I waited in your love nest as long as I could stand watching Julia flutter about that kid. Then I thought I'd meet you on your way from the bus stop, but no luck. I escaped being drenched by squeezing through the busted door into the ground floor of the lighthouse – it was dark and dusty, but at least dry. Well, and here I am.'

'Here you are,' he repeated, as if it were a new discovery. He felt flattered; there's no one so low-down, he thought, that some other creature won't run after him.

'You're in a mess, John, aren't you?' she asked, finally.

'I am,' he confirmed.

She stopped and faced him, her body almost touching his. 'Why don't you come to Mama,' she said, her ordinarily grating voice dark and velvety. 'Mama has got exactly what you need.'

Her forehead underneath the black bangs was beaded with sweat; her glasses had misted over; but her voice was full of mystery and promise. And he knew her body and its potential.

He stepped back from her. 'We're all in a mess, it appears,' he said, feeling the beat of his heart in his neck.

She took his hand and then hooked it around her arm, and they walked toward the lighthouse. Come to Mama, he thought with a grin, and looked at her flat, unmotherly chest and at her thin but, he knew, extremely capable lips. At least she was no teaser, and she made no claims on you: advantage number two.

'I've had a talk with Sundstrom,' she said, in her usual nagging pitch.

The information, out of the blue, threw his thoughts off their track. He was conscious of her cold, moist fingers on the hand he held over her arm.

'In fact he sent me,' she stated.

'To me?'

'To you.'

He frowned. 'Why didn't he send Voukorich?'

'I guess Voukovich refused the mission.'

'But you didn't.'

'Why should I?'

'That's right,' Hiller said, 'Why should you?' This time it was he who stopped and turned her to face him. Putting one hand to the small of her back he took hold of her hair with the other and pulled back her head. 'I don't trust you, you know,' he said, his mouth almost on hers. 'What did Sundstrom tell you?'

'He says you can have your job back,' she said, moaning softly.

'Ah. And Julia?'

Waltraut attempted a shrug, but his hold on her made it impossible. 'He only said I should see how the boy is and tell him.'

Hiller let go of her. That was Sundstrom's way of doing business: no big stick, no pressure, not even what you might call corruption; and yet he could kill his two birds with one stone. But Sundstrom wouldn't proposition a man unless he had to; he must feel it was high time to swallow his humiliation and patch up matters; perhaps that speech, which had penetrated the thick walls of the Kremlin session hall, had its share in the forces propelling him.

Waltraut had gone a few steps ahead and was waiting for him. The trees were thinning, and above their tops, against a white-fringed cloud, stood the lighthouse cupola, its thick glass grown opaque and burst in places.

Hiller spread his arms. 'Mama,' he called, laughing in disgust at himself, 'where do we go from here?'

She led him through the broken door into the interior of the lighthouse. As she had said, it was dusty there, but also dark and dry.

CHAPTER ELEVEN

The police lieutenant was an elderly man, square boned, with hands that had retained their work-roughened skin. He looked at the young woman before him and at the child who had her soft hair and fine, almost too fine features, and said with something like regret, 'This is the third time you've come to us, Mrs Sundstrom.'

'You said you would let me know if you heard anything,' Julia defended herself. Somehow, she had confidence in this police officer who wore his uniform without strutting, and in the woman sergeant who sat hefty and good-natured at the next desk, a clattering typewriter before her. 'You said a man doesn't disappear without traces.'

The lieutenant patiently folded his hands. 'As I've tried to explain to you, Mrs Sundstrom, we're the registry department. We've checked as far as we could. A Daniel Wollin, residing at Schiller-Strasse 13, care of Mrs Schloth, was duly reported at his local police station as having moved from the city.'

'I know that.' Julia uncrossed her legs. 'I now live at Mrs Schloth's.'

The lieutenant kept his face expressionless. 'We know you do.'

'But in registering your departure, don't you have to state where you're headed?'

'There's a line for it on the form,' confirmed the lieutenant. 'Wollin wrote in: will travel.'

'Oh . . . ' Julia realised that Julian had left her side. 'Julian!' He was standing at the woman sergeant's desk, hands behind his back, studying her. 'Why don't you carry your gun?' he said.

'Because it pinches me when I'm at the typewriter,' said the sergeant. 'Do you want a piece of candy?'

'Thank you.' He held out his hand and received a lemon drop from a little paper bag that lay in the drawer next to the gun. 'I get all the candy I can eat. Julia wants me to grow fat. If your gun pinches you, will you let me have it?'

Julia wanted to break in, but the lieutenant smiled and shook his head.

'Why do you want the gun?'' said the woman sergeant.

Julian sucked on the lemon drop, his mouth pursed in silence.

'Is it a secret?' said the sergeant, her brows raised. 'Do you have many secrets?'

'Two hundred.'

'Well, then . . . you keep your two hundred secrets and I keep my gun.' She turned back to her work. Julian rested his hands on the desktop and watched her crossing off names on a ledger.

'Is he a relative of yours,' the lieutenant resumed, 'this Daniel Wollin?'

'No,' said Julia. 'A fellow architect.'

'Then why doesn't your husband call up, Mrs Sundstrom? He knows the Comrade Colonel – it would take things out of this department and ease them considerably.'

'My husband,' Julia hesitated, 'no, I don't think I would want him involved. I would rather—'

'Will you give me your gun if I tell you some of my secrets?' Julian was saying, his voice bright with hope.

'That depends,' said the sergeant, from her ledger. 'I don't want to promise. I bet you want my gun to shoot with.'

'Of course.'

'But only the police are allowed to use guns, and only in special cases.'

He was whipping excitedly on his toes. 'This is a *really* special case. And my daddy will buy me a uniform . . . ' He turned to Julia. 'He will, Julia, won't he?'

'Perhaps,' said Julia uncomfortably. And to the lieutenant, 'But wherever he goes, he must register. Couldn't you simply send out a tracer to all registry departments in the Republic: please report on so-and-so . . . you know what I mean.'

'The missing persons bureau can, or the criminal police. But is Wollin properly missing – do you suspect foul play? Or do you allege he committed theft, robbery, murder?' The lieutenant paused. 'Or is it political? . . . Why *do* you want to find him, Mrs Sundstrom . . . or is it a secret, like the young man's over there?'

Julia tried to relax on the hard, straight-backed chair. Whichever way she sat, she felt on the rack. How could she tell this man, even though he seemed kind and understanding? She herself hardly knew more than that she needed this lodestar, all other stars by which you could direct your life having sunk behind clouds or having turned out to possess no light of their own, no warmth; specks of cold, dead matter.

Julian was urging the woman sergeant. 'If my daddy buys me a uniform like yours, will you give me your gun?' He swallowed the last of the candy. 'I'll let you have it back afterward.'

The woman sergeant pulled Julian close. 'You're such a nice boy,' she said, and stroked his hair. 'You don't want to shoot anybody.'

'Yes, I do!'

'Who?'

'Uncle John Hiller.'

'Julian!' cried Julia.

Sergeant,' said the lieutenant with a grin, 'you better keep your pistol out of that boy's reach.' And, suddenly serious, he turned to Julia. 'Who is John Hiller?'

'A fellow architect.'

'Another one! . . . ' The lieutenant sounded startled. Then he rose. 'I'm sorry, Mrs Sundstrom, that I can't be of help. But suppose you think over some of my points. You know where I can be reached.'

Julia looked up at him. She wondered how much he really knew; whether he, too, was drawn into the surge of the crisis released by that Congress speech; if anyone could stay unaffected. She felt how lonely she was, how lonely they all were, and suddenly she realised that this loneliness was no new thing. It had always been there, hidden, necessitating the constant protest and display of collectivity; always that terrible loneliness in the face of vast, nameless forces; a despair that went beyond any grief over the individual case of an individual victim.

'Another piece of candy, Julian?' said the woman sergeant. 'For goodbye?'

'Thank you,' said Julian, taking one, but his tone made it plain that he was being polite.

It was like another city: the same landmarks, the same street names; but everything took on a different perspective when you rode the streetcar instead of your husband's automobile, when you lived in an old tenement building that still showed the shrapnel scars on its sooty façade. The people, too, were different, nearer to you; you had another feeling about them when you were hustled by them, smelled them, listened to their lingo, were helped by them – some man lifting Julian up the steep steps to the platform of the car.

Julia sighed. There had been no formal break with John Hiller, just the quiet agreement that after the Kleinmallenhagen experience his reconditioned one-room flat wasn't the place to hold the two of them *and* the child; he was to look for a larger apartment; he *was* looking, he assured her on his visits; you needed patience if you had no one to pull strings for you; and he would wait around at Mrs Schloth's, making half-hearted attempts at a caress while he looked at Julian, who looked back at him, making small talk about this person or the other but never touching on the essentials: work, their relationship, Sundstrom, the dead and why they had died. He waited for her to tell him that she would come to him and when; sometimes he telephoned, sounding contrite, or exaggeratedly cheerful; she always told him it was hard for her to leave Julian alone in this furnished-room atmosphere; who would look after him while she spent the evening out – Mrs Schloth?

The streetcar stopped, then rattled on and crossed World Peace Road. Julia recalled that Arnold had wanted the streetcar line to be run through an underground passage, but the city transit authority, backed by Mayor Riedel, had balked at the cost, and for once Comrade Tolkening seemed frightened at the huge outlay and had sided against his chief architect.

Julia stared through the grimy car windows. Arnold Sundstrom's presence was everywhere – a street being laid through the ruins: *his* plan; trees being planted in a park: *his* suggestion; a bridge being widened, a foundation stone laid for a kindergarten: *he* had fought for that. She had kept out of his way, had avoided the house, the City Architects' Bureau, and the building sites; but his hand was in evidence wherever she turned – in the industrial construction office, where she had applied for work as a freelance draftsman, they had welcomed her as if she were expected and had obligingly paid her a generous advance; the hundred and one difficulties that stymied the ordinary citizen trying to establish himself, and the cobwebbed walls of bureaucracy, were smoothed away for her. And he was there, a dark figure in her darkest fears, when the unanswerable question formed in her mind and the unthinkable problems posed themselves.

She put her arm about Julian protectively.

'Are we going to sec Daddy now?' he asked, as if by some special antennae he had picked up the central subject of his mother's thoughts.

'No, darling.'

'Why not?' His voice had hit that relentless tone common to children that makes adults look up and listen.

Julia looked around in embarrassment. Then she explained, 'This streetcar doesn't take us to where Daddy is. It takes us to Mrs Schloth's.'

'Why don't we ride in a streetcar that takes us to Daddy?'

'Some other time we will,' she said uneasily.

'But we've been here two hundred days!' he stated.

'Two hundred . . . ' she repeated. Two hundred was his conception of the infinite. 'Come, Julian,' she said, 'we get off here.'

They walked the rest of the way. Julian was talking to her and she was trying to reply; he was being very good despite his bewilderment at this new stage in his life; his fevers had let up almost entirely; he insisted on washing himself and keeping his things in order and helping her with the room; once, when she praised him for it he had answered: I'm now the man in the house, am I not?

Wollin, she thought. She longed for Wollin because she longed for clarity.

Mrs Schloth received her at the door. A man was waiting for her. Wollin, she thought, her heart beating in her throat; then: Arnold; then: John Hiller. But with any of the three, Mrs Schloth would have given the name.

'I've taken him into my living room,' Mrs Schloth informed, and to Julian, 'why, little man, you're growing an honest-to-goodness pair of apple cheeks,' and back to Julia, 'You can talk to him in my living room if you wish; maybe it's more comfortable, with the big sofa, and if you want to serve something . . . '

'Thank you, no,' said Julia. Mrs Schloth's overstuffed living room meant Mrs Schloth's black eyes scrutinising your face for whatever you left unsaid. 'Perhaps you'll be kind enough to send him to my room, in a minute.'

She had hardly hung up her things and Julian's when the visitor knocked at the door. At her 'Come in!' he opened the door but remained standing in it, a huge man in a business suit that spanned his chest, carrying a large, flat package.

'What is it, please?'

'Don't you recognise me?' he said awkwardly and advanced into the light. 'On second thought, Mrs Sundstrom, you've only seen me in denims, with cement dust on my face.'

'Comrade Barrasch!' The images joined. It was as if the man had brought with him some of the clatter and smell of the construction site. Julia extended her hands. 'You're the first person I've seen from World Peace Road . . . ' And to the child, 'Comrade Barrasch helps to build the great big buildings that were designed by . . . ' She broke off: Arnold Sundstrom's presence again. 'He's a foreman!' she abruptly concluded the introduction.

Barrasch leaned his package against the wardrobe, shook hands with Julian, and asked him what he wanted to be when he grew up – a bricklayer or a plasterer, a carpenter or a steam fitter, or maybe an architect?

Julian looked him over. 'I'll be a foreman.'

Barrasch roared. He sat down and lifted Julian on his knee and proclaimed, 'You picked the right job: caught between everybody, the bureaucrats on top of you and the men under you; no piece rate, no extras, just complaints . . . ' He turned to Julia. 'I'd better prepare him . . . ' He smiled. 'I had a job finding you, Mrs Sundstrom. I finally got your address at that industrial construction office . . . What I came for is to deliver this package to you from Comrade Wollin.'

He stood Julian on the floor, got up, fetched the package, and, with a solemn grace, placed it on the table.

'Wollin . . . ' repeated Julia. Wollin existed; he had not vanished; the package, nearly covering the top of the table, was witness. 'Where is he?'

The foreman's brows rose on his wind-burned, leathery fore-head.

'Well, when did he give you this?'

He watched her long, tapered fingers expertly deal with the knots of the strings. 'The day he quit,' he said.

'Quit?'

'He came to me and said he had thrown up his job in the office and he needed money, about a thousand marks, and fast. So I put him on as a bricklayer, and he was good at it, nice straight work and at a respectable clip once he got into the swing of it; he did about a hundred and forty per cent of quota, plus premium; and when he had his thousand marks he wrapped them in a handkerchief and pinned them in his inside coat pocket . . . learned that in Russia, he said . . . and told me, goodbye, Comrade Barrasch, it was a pleasure being on your team, and will you give this to Mrs Sundstrom as soon as you can find her, with regards and my love . . . '

The package lay open. Inside was a set of large drawings, each sheet neatly backed by cardboard. Barrasch looked at Julia, the expression of her eyes; beautiful eyes, he thought, a man could lose himself in them.

'Wollin's design for the extension project,' she said, a catch in her voice. She passed the top sheet to the foreman. 'Remember?'

He squinted as he always did when he had to read blueprints. He remembered the drawing; he thought he understood what moved men to fight over the shape of a building that was, after all, just sand and water. A house was more than a man; it out lasted him; it spoke of him, if you knew how to listen, long after the dark earth stuffed his mouth.

'Did Wollin say where he was going?'

Barrasch raised his huge hands.

'Or when he would return?'

Again the gesture. She probably hadn't expected an answer. She was putting the drawings together and rewrapping them and announcing that they still needed additional work.

'I thought they were finished,' he remarked.

'And the detail?' she asked. 'Where are the floor plans, storey by storey? The plans for the technical installations – heating, plumbing, what have you?'

'But that's done by a whole bureau. You want to tackle that by yourself?'

'You like the design?'

Barrasch rubbed his chin. Again his eyes squinted, though there was nothing for them to read but the spots on Mrs Schloth's wallpaper. 'It would be like a part of the future.'

'Then we should prepare everything for its construction,' she said.

The doorbell rang. Julia heard Mrs Schloth in the hallway, heard the apartment door being opened, Mrs Schloth's voice and then another . . .

'My husband.' Julia's voice was unnaturally steady.

Barrasch rose. 'I guess I'll go now.'

Julian had stiffened. His face was working; two red splotches showed on his forehead.

Julia went to the wardrobe. Shoving some clothes to the side, she stowed away the package.

'I had better leave . . . ' said the foreman, unbuttoning and buttoning his jacket.

The steps outside, familiar and yet with a new hesitancy to them, approached. There was Mrs Schloth's obsequious 'Jawohl, Herr Professor' and 'Of course, Herr Professor,' and then the knock at the door of the room.

'Daddy!' cried Julian.

Arnold Sundstrom, framed in the doorway. In the background, visible over his shoulder, the face of Mrs Schloth, like that on an old Dutch genre painting: half curious, half knowing. Then the face disappeared, the door closed.

'Daddy . . . Daddy . . . Daddy . . . ' Julian was near sobs.

Sundstrom lifted him up and hugged him. 'Now, now,' his voice clogged up, 'everything will be all right now, son.' He set the boy down but held on to him. 'You look fine, Julia . . . suntanned, clear-eyed, a little tired perhaps . . . '

'Julian and I were out all morning.'

'I see – then that's why.'

'I had better leave,' said the foreman again.

'Why, Comrade Barrasch!' the usual salute, outgoing, full-voiced, 'now don't feel you're intruding! I'm glad you visited Mrs Sundstrom; nothing worse than being lonely, you know . . . ' He laughed. 'But if your time is short, don't let me hold you; I suppose I'll see you around; and thanks again . . . '

The door closed behind Barrasch. Julia looked at her husband. He has aged, she thought; the grey has risen above his temples, or he needs a haircut. He has let himself go: his shoulders are slack, his face is flabby, his suit hangs.

'Why haven't you ever come?' said Julian. 'Why have you forgotten me?'

The hand on the boy's shoulder twitched. 'I didn't forget you. I was waiting, waiting for you and your mother to come back.'

The boy's eyes, serious beyond his years, were trying to grasp why his father had been visiting and why his mother had not come back.

'Try to be fair for once, Arnold,' said Julia.

'Fair?' he asked.

'Do you consider it fair to use a child's feelings as a pressure point on his mother?'

He frowned. 'You've become very explicit. The independent life, eh?' And, after a pause, 'May I not have a seat?'

'Sit down, please.'

He took a chair but did not let go of the child. Julia observed him as he gazed about the room, disgust curling his lip. 'And do you propose bringing up Julian in this place?' he finally enquired.

She was amazed at the calm that had spread inside her. 'I hope to find a flat.'

'With John Hiller?'

Something in his tone hit her. She suddenly knew that she would never have a decent place to live unless he allowed it, or the food and clothing she needed for herself and the boy unless he granted it. 'With or without John Hiller,' she said warily. 'What skin is it off your back?'

He kept on caressing Julian. The calm within her, so useful to her, became ruffled.

'I would have come sooner, son,' Sundstrom said, with his sixth sense for people's moods and for Julia's especially, 'much sooner.' And to Julia, 'But I was afraid I had disqualified myself. That scene I made was disgraceful. And then,' he shrugged: part bitterness, part resignation, 'life interfered. It created new conditions, new relationships . . . '

And not a word of the reasons for the scene he had chosen to describe as disgraceful, or of the past that cast its shadows over all of them! Julia instinctively reached for Julian, but fearing resistance from the child drew back. She was floundering, and Arnold was aware of it.

'Why don't you two come home,' he was saying. And, fondling Julian, he told him, 'You have new toys waiting in your room for you: a cowboy suit with a real cowboy hat and two guns in real leather holsters; new tracks and new cars and a freight locomotive for your electric railroad; and a tricycle that we can convert into a bicycle as soon as you've grown a little bigger; and—'

'Arnold!'

'Still unfair? My God, Julia, I love the boy. He's my flesh and blood as much as yours, and you took him away. Just let *him* come to me once in a while. Any court would grant me that much.'

'Julia—' said the boy. The one word contained everything: his longing for the cowboy paraphernalia and the electric freight locomotive and the convertible tricycle, and for his room, and for home and security.

Julia hid her face in her hands. After a while she felt Julian's hands trying to pull hers down. She gave in to her son, smiling at him as he smiled up at her, and then looking over his head at the man sitting there whose bland expression seemed to be saying:

That's nice; what a nice little family; and wasn't it a shame to have let those unpleasantnesses come between us; but I'll forgive you, I'm not vindictive.

Julia rose. She went to the door and called out, 'Frau Schloth!'

The landlady popped up, all smiles and eagerness. 'Can I help you, Mrs Sundstrom? A cup of tea, perhaps, for you and the Herr Professor? Or a cool drink, lemonade? There were lemons at the state store, which is rare enough, and I bought a few . . . '

'I mean, Frau Schloth . . . ' Julia sounded awkward. 'My husband and I . . . ' She stopped. She saw the landlady's mouth widen into a grin of consummate understanding.

'Ah, the young man? We need the young man taken care of for a while? Why, certainly . . . ' Mrs Schloth clapped her hands. 'I'm so happy for you, Mrs Sundstrom. Even if it means losing one of my best tenants. Whom God hath joined let no man put asunder, and where do you get another gentleman like the Herr Professor these days and in this country; many's the time I've lain awake at night and thought, now here is this lonely young woman with this lovely child, and if I could help them back to their proper home it would be the biggest thing in my life, something a soul could pride herself on for years to come . . . '

Sundstrom's approach interrupted the flow. A banknote changed hands. 'You tell my driver downstairs, Frau Schloth, to take you and Julian to the zoo. Julian likes the monkey house best. Buy him the biggest portion of ice cream and have yourself a good cup of coffee with cake or whatever you like. I'll see you within the hour?'

'But, Daddy—'

'Yes, son?'

'I want to go to the zoo with you and Julia. I haven't seen you for,' the boy paused, 'for two hundred days.'

'Won't you tell him, Julia?' said Sundstrom.

Julia hesitated. The child, with his hand already in the grip of Mrs Schloth, appeared smaller than ever, and his eyes pleaded

250

with her. 'Your father and I must have a talk,' she finally said 'and it's a talk only for grown-ups . . . '

'And if I promise to be very quiet and not ask questions? Julia . . . ' He tore himself from Mrs Schloth and clung to his mother, one hand, at the same time, reaching out for Sundstrom.

'Perhaps, Julia, we won't need this talk,' suggested Sundstrom. 'You can see for yourself . . . '

Julia saw. In a sudden eerie transference, the image of her child became the image of herself clinging to father and mother, against the echo of boots tramping and of hoarse orders. 'I'm afraid," she said, the vision fading out as fast as it had come, 'since you found it necessary to inject yourself in our lives, we'll have to agree on drawing a line somewhere.'

'As you wish, Julia.' With a somewhat strained smile, he shrugged at Mrs Schloth and turned to the boy. 'Don't you want to help us, Julian? The talk that Julia and I must have will be about . . . yes, about your coming home, and when, and how . . . ' He disregarded Julia's objection. 'Don't you want us to arrange for that?'

'Yes.'

'Well, then you must go with Frau Schloth.'

'Yes.' But once more the boy stopped. 'Only this once, though! Next time you come with me . . . won't you, Daddy . . . and Julia?'

'Hop along, little man!' urged Mrs Schloth. And, raising her hands, 'Now, you remember, Mrs Sundstrom: whom God hath joined . . . ' She swept out, dragging the boy with her.

Julia sat down on her bed, a wave of fatigue, physical and emotional, engulfing her. ' " . . . about your coming home, and when, and how," ' she quoted after a while, bitterness in every word. 'And how shall I explain to the child that he won't?'

He leaned against the wardrobe as if he, too, needed support. 'But he will,' he said, 'Julian and you both will.'

She saw his eyes, the white in them that had yellowed, his puffed lids. He wasn't a man given to tears; so it was the sleepless

251

nights, the endless cigarettes, vodka. 'You can't be serious, Arnold,' she said.

'Why can't I?' His hands moved slightly. 'Though the scandal is beyond recall, I'm a mature man: I can understand emotion getting the better of good sense.'

Julia half reclined on her bed, propping up her pillows behind her. In the wardrobe against which he was leaning stood the package with Wollin's extension drawings; she wondered what kind of face Arnold would make if she told him. But she said, 'You mean *you* are prepared to forgive *me*?'

'If that's how you wish to put it . . . yes, of course.'

'My God!' Her face went blank. The brain, Julia knew, was a remarkable organ, capable of playing the oddest tricks, but that Arnold's could entirely repress the real issue between her and him was incredible.

He realised he had pushed himself out on a limb; he pulled a chair to the side of her bed and sat down. Taking a magazine from his pocket, he said, 'Have you seen this issue of *Crocodile,* by the way?'

'*Crocodile*! . . . ' She frowned. 'What brings that up?' In her Moscow time, she hadn't much liked the heavy-handed satire of the magazine or its cartoons; during her German years and these last months particularly, it never occurred to her to look at a copy of it.

'It's got a picture of a streetcar here.' The pages rustled as he unfolded the paper and handed it to her. 'Won't you have a look?'

'I'm so tired, Arnold. And this is so futile.'

'Look at it!' he said gruffly.

She opened her eyes and reluctantly gazed at the drawing. It actually showed a streetcar – but a streetcar gone mad, an artist's nightmare of a public conveyance with turrets and battlements, its frilly ornaments and architectural bric-a-brac leaving hardly room for the conductor and the none-too-tidy lot of passengers.

'Come on, laugh!' he finally said. 'Why don't you?'

'I don't find it funny.'

'Ah,' he said, 'but you must know when you're permitted to laugh. Laughter can be a great liberator.'

When you're permitted to laugh, she thought. His sarcasm fell flat – perhaps he wasn't being sarcastic. She knew as well as he the way this press worked: what – or whom – they lampooned had long ago and quite elsewhere been weighed and found wanting; the writers and artists in these papers weren't the prosecutor or the judge, they were the executioners; and this ridiculous streetcar was the death warrant for World Peace Road and the architecture she had been taught to believe in, and nothing remained but to plant ivy.

'And what do you intend to achieve by showing me this documentation of our bankruptcy, yours and mine?'

'Bankruptcy?'

Julia thought of how she had stumbled on the Nazis' Charlotten-burger Chaussee design, another such streetcar with medieval trappings, and she began to feel ill.

'Bankruptcy?' he repeated. 'That streetcar documents the fact that finally we can start building as we always wanted to: better and more gracefully and at less expense. Aren't you interested?'

'You . . . always wanted to?' Nausea filled her. 'Shall I quote back to you a few of the things you taught me . . . and others?'

'You mean: I'm a cynic. I tailored my theories to fit require-ments.'

He reflected. 'Perhaps you're too young to understand how a person's mind operates. Uncannily. I ask you: was the cause right – socialism, the revolution?'

Her silence implied: yes.

'Then how could its architectural expression be wrong? Or so the mind argues when you have to decide whether to build in a certain manner or not build at all.'

'In other words, Arnold: if your cause is just, all the injustices committed in its name become just?'

He sighed. 'I was only trying to point out the dialectics of the thing.'

He isn't even play-acting, she thought. He probably saw himself in the context of historical development, its dialectics furnishing him with any rationalisation he needed. What super-elasticity of conscience on the part of a man who brought her up in the spirit of revolutionary rigidity! Or was there no contradiction between rigidity and a rubber conscience; did they complement one another?

Not for her. She refused to accept that the crystal-clear words of the great teachers contained this built-in opportunism; that the streaming red of the revolution was always tinged with the yellow of the toady. Rigid: she was what she was due to the man who now sat, aged and tarnished, before her; what he had implanted in her turned against him.

'Couldn't we try a new beginning?' he suggested. He took back the magazine and slapped the page with the streetcar cartoon. 'Now that we're free to work—'

'Free?' she said.

'What do you expect . . . the sky? Listen, Julia: once we start working together again, everything else will fall into place. We'll build an extension of World Peace Road that you and I can be proud of.'

'All right . . . *you* build it.'

His head began swaying from side to side. 'You still have illusions about the possibilities of the Wollin project?'

Julia involuntarily glanced toward the wardrobe.

'We'll incorporate any of its features that prove acceptable,' he was saying. 'Hiller will help us on that; he has kept some of Wollin's roughs.'

She sat up. 'Hiller?'

'Hiller, yes.' Sundstrom's head stopped moving; a slow smile crept across his face. 'Didn't you know? He's back working with us.'

254

'Excuse me.' Julia got up; walked, her knees cottony, to the washbasin; poured herself a glass of water; drank. John, she thought, and then: at least he had shame enough not to tell me, and then: he had to find work somewhere, and then: this ends it, definitely.

'I'm sorry,' she heard her husband say, 'I didn't know he had failed to inform you.'

The hurt, she thought, wasn't as big as she had feared it would be; it wasn't the knifelike pain of something tearing inside her or a burn searing her heart; it was a dull ache, nothing fresh, rather the pain of a blow that had already fallen, perhaps because she had been expecting it. Her decision carried no grief. Easy come, easy go, she thought, with a bad taste in her mouth; rigidity, ethics, tatters wherever you looked. 'No,' she said, 'he didn't inform me.'

'Come home,' said Sundstrom. 'We'll call it even.'

She went to the wardrobe, opened it, touched the package. It was there, containing the only unsullied thing left: the chaste lines of Wollin's structures – despite everything, the future.

'What are you looking for?' Sundstrom saw that her face had changed: it was calm and set, with none of the softness in it that he had loved.

'Nothing.'

He noticed she was crushing a handkerchief. Keeps her handkerchiefs in that wardrobe, he thought; not even a dresser for herself.

'Come home,' he repeated with real warmth in his voice. 'You've had your fling. One lives and learns. Many marriages work out the better for the rock they once hit.'

'Do you really believe I left you for the sake of a fling?' She waited, and as he did not reply she added, 'Did Comrade Tolkening tell you to patch up things with me?'

He rose, but somehow he failed to be impressive. 'I don't need Party instructions on how to settle my personal affairs . . . Julia,

Julia,' he stepped to her, his hands reaching out for her, 'please, listen to me . . . '

She twisted her shoulders; his hands fell.

'If it isn't Party orders,' she said, 'what is it? I may not have much dignity left . . . but you have none at all.'

'Dignity . . . ' He shrugged. 'I love you. If you're beautiful and strong-willed and high-minded and think you can set yourself up as a judge over me, it's because I fashioned you. I took the child and watched her grow and directed her growth, and I love in you a piece of my life . . . the woman, the child—'

'*Whose* child?'

His eyes seemed to recede into their hollows. 'All those years we gave to one another,' he said, 'they count for nothing?' And, after a pause, 'What *will* you do?'

'Work, probably,' she said. 'Bring up Julian.'

'All right.' He turned to his chair and clutched its backrest. 'I'll make a deal with you. You come home. You take one floor, I take the other. You live your life, I live mine. I won't touch you. But we'll keep up appearances.'

How low can you sink? thought Julia. 'You want me home that badly?' she asked. 'Why?'

'Because of Julian,' he answered.

'That was the initial move, wasn't it?'

'Haven't you noticed how the child looks? He's suffering.'

'Julian was ill. He's much better now.'

'What kind of mother are you . . . dragging him through your kind of life, with that fellow Hiller whom I can buy or sell at will, in that shack in Kleinmallenhagen, or in this dump of a rooming house.' His voice rose, outraged. 'The child needs a home and both parents!'

'Both parents . . . ' Julia repeated, exactly duplicating his tone of voice. 'That's what a child should have. I can confirm it.'

The veins of Sundstrom's hands were swelling.

'And Julian is to grow up in that house,' Julia went on, 'with the two of us living on different floors. And how am I going to teach him to have pride in his father?'

'I wouldn't want you to exert yourself,' he said. 'I'll attend to that.'

'Just as you succeeded in making me believe you were the best, the noblest, the most wonderful man on earth?' Suddenly the magnitude of her loss confronted her: a huge black wall, no end to it, no crag through which a ray of light could break. She sat down on the side of the bed. She had no tears. 'You fetched the orphan and took her in. Who orphaned her? You were father and mother to her. Why did you have to substitute? You married and made love to her. Didn't you ever think of *me*? What it would do to *me*?'

'You miss the essential point, Julia! There is such a thing as a class enemy and collaboration with him. And there is loyalty to the Party and the revolution, which transcends all other loyalties. In my spot, you would not have acted differently. We're all prisoners of the time we live in; we didn't choose it, nor did we form its laws.'

What he said was true, and involuntarily he suited his posture, his expression, to the words he had spoken. For a moment, he again seemed to Julia the old Bolshevik, the perpetual soldier, spartan, his life rigged along immutable principles, unstintingly sacrificing himself and expecting sacrifice from others according to their part in the struggle and their ability.

Then the image collapsed. 'That may be so,' she said, 'and again it may not. I no longer know.'

'What do you mean?'

'If I heard rumours of a secret Congress speech, you must have heard them, too. But even without all that – the laws you claim to be binding have somehow acquired a hollow ring, at least to my ear. I've told you: I don't accuse you, Arnold, I hope and trust you did the right thing, always. But I just can't go on living under the same roof as you. You'll understand that, I'm sure.'

He heard nothing beyond mention of the speech. Something

shrivelled up in him; within seconds, the whole man had run to seed. Only one thought kept him going: control. Re-establish control. When the full story broke and with it the details in all their horrible connotation, he would have to be ready – all leaks plugged, all fences mended. He cursed the weak moment in which he had let Julia slip from his hands; the damage done was bad enough; he had to see that the irreparable was avoided.

'Well, Julia,' he said, 'you'll admit I've done what I could.'

'Yes?' she said. It was not his tone of voice – normal – or his eyes – bare of hostility – that alerted her. There was an expression about his mouth, an ugly sort of resolution: you or me – all right, then it had better be you.

'I begged you,' he went on, 'I pleaded with you, I made my offer without conditions . . . you refused everything. You leave me with no alternative.'

She felt an agonising pull on her heart. That's how he must have looked, she thought, when he decided that certain loyalties transcended others: murderous.

'You don't want to come home . . . neither as my wife nor as the mother of my child. You insist on separation. Very well, Julia, then let's have a clean cut. You know Professor Rothenstrauch the Party lawyer. I'll have him draw up the necessary papers for divorce, and I'm certain he can expedite the matter with the courts. Though I'm not compelled to, under the circumstances, I will agree to a financial settlement that won't leave you penniless. I suppose you will be kind enough, in return, not to insist on delays as regards Julian. I would like to take him with me as soon as Mrs Schloth returns with him from the zoo . . . '

You want to take Julian with you?' Her heart seemed to have hit the bottom of the vacuum forming inside her. 'What makes you believe I would let him go?'

'I'm afraid you'll have to. Do you think that any court in this Republic would assign custody of the child to a woman who runs out on her husband, flaunts her depravity by openly cohabiting with her lover, spoils the child's morals, sets herself up against the collective—'

'And suppose I did?' Holding on to the brass knob of the bed, Julia rose. 'Suppose I tell the court why?'

'You forget I'm not alone in this,' he answered, looking straight at her.

'Oh, God!' She sank her teeth into her knuckles. And, turning to Sundstrom, 'It would have been kinder to let me rot in that children's home.'

'Whining doesn't help,' he said. 'No one wants to punish you. But you simply must learn where you live and that you must keep in step. I've had to learn my lesson. We all have to.'

'No,' she said. Sobs rose in her throat. She fell on her bed and tried to muffle them in her pillow.

Finally she grew conscious of his hand on her shoulder. 'I hear Julian coming, and Mrs Schloth. You had better wash your face.'

He helped her to the basin, let cold water run on the washcloth, and stood by as she dabbed at her eyes and her forehead and her temples. 'Now, now,' he consoled, 'you feel better already,' like the surgeon at his patient's bedside after the operation, or the interrogator resuming his victim's questioning after the beating.

Mrs Schloth knocked elaborately. To Sundstrom's 'Come in!' she ushered in Julian, who looked hot and tired but full of anticipation. 'I couldn't hold him any longer,' Mrs Schloth informed. 'Up to the monkey house it was all right, but after that he started worrying, poor dear. *Do* you think we'll all go home, he kept asking, and is it *really* true?' And wouldn't finish his cake. A sensitive child, Herr Professor, quite like his mother. I can see you've had your little cry, Mrs Sundstrom. After rain comes sunshine. Why, little man, I think everything's turning out for the best,' she patted Julian's head. 'May one congratulate, Herr Professor?'

Sundstrom picked up Julian. 'One may, Frau Schloth,' he said. 'I'm sure one may.'

CHAPTER TWELVE

There was something of a prison to the divided household – she in her cell upstairs, he in the guard room on the ground floor.

At times Julia felt it with special intensity: at breakfast, as she and Arnold watched one another across the table, mentally turning over every word despite their innocuous conversation, or when he came home and dropped up to see Julian and play with the child. His greeting to her would be an aside, too casual not to have been thought out in advance; he would mention this or that about his work, trivialities interspersed with offhand enquiries about her day.

But the veneer was cracked by suspicion. Although, like a good warder, he never turned to look, you could be sure that he knew what went on behind his back. He probably paid Frau Sommer, Julia thought, to check on her visitors and to listen in on her phone calls. When he wasn't busy with meetings or conferences, he spent his evenings in the downstairs living room, just sitting, as far as Julia could discover, not even reaching for a book or a newspaper. When he did come upstairs, he never went beyond the boy's room, which she had set like a fortification before her own.

He was as tied to the prison as she was; the jailer always is, she thought. Every morning when he left for work, he was tense and nervous; his jokes with Julian couldn't hide it; he relaxed only when he came home and saw that nothing had changed, that all were on hand, the bars up, the gates locked; even then, traces of his unrest remained. Mainly, Julia believed, because within her own cell she was able to keep to herself. He knew she was working; he had hinted as much in his questions; but he didn't know on what and it vexed him. And there was another snag: he wasn't through with her, despite her affair with Hiller, despite the cleavage between them. Sometimes she caught his glance: hunger; sometimes his hand touched hers: desire. It froze her.

Day followed day with nothing developing, nothing changing, the weekends having their particular horror. Once or twice he offered to drive her and Julian to the Red Trumpeter, a state-owned restaurant on a hill outside of town, or to the reservoir for a swim. Once or twice, she had accepted and was sorry she had because the pretence of gaiety for Julian's sake, sandwiched between the silences, was self-punishment.

At night, she would awaken from a deep sleep and find herself listening to his pacing downstairs. Then she would ask herself how long this state of suspended hostility would last, could last – weeks, months, years? How would it end – an explosion? The worst was that neither how long it took nor the way the end came depended on her, on what she did or didn't do. She was really like a prisoner, except that she could make the effort to keep her balance, to keep busy. In this, she had two advantages: her work and Julian.

And an obstinate hope that centred on Wollin.

This day, over his cup of coffee, Sundstrom suddenly announced, 'It can't go on.'

Julia continued buttering her roll. Julian was noisily drinking his milk; some of it drooled onto the napkin tied around his neck.

'This cutting ourselves off!' he continued as the expected query failed to come. 'It is no good for you, or me. We must re-establish some . . . well . . . normalcy.'

Julia wiped Julian's chin. 'Normalcy?'

'It's not normal for two healthy, married people to sit in their house night after night, see no one, talk to no one, forget that such a thing as life exists outside their four walls.'

'I'd like another cup of milk,' said Julian. And, while she

poured the milk from a small pitcher, 'Will you play cowboy and Indian with me, Julia? You can be the Indian this time.'

'I'm always the Indian, it seems,' said Julia.

'And it's not good for the child to grow up without playmates,' said Sundstrom. 'He'll become an individualist, asocial. I've been thinking. Perhaps we should enter him in a kindergarten. There is one for the children of special government people; it just means a call to Elise Tolkening. What do you think, Julian . . . wouldn't you like to play with other children part of the day?'

Julian looked at his mother.

Normalcy, thought Julia. First he used the child to force her back into this house; now he was taking the child away from her. 'If it just means a call to Elise Tolkening,' she finally replied, 'why didn't you call her when I lived at Mrs Schloth's? There would have been no need, then, for this . . . ' A vague gesture embracing the breakfast table, the room, the house.

'You know your argument is specious.' He wasn't even angry. 'Parents *and* kindergarten is quite something else for a child than kindergarten *without* parents. But I won't insist.' He turned to the boy. 'You'll play cowboy and Indian with Julia as much as you like, and if you want other children to play with you, we'll invite them. Won't that be nice?' And back to Julia, 'We'll invite some playmates for you, too. That's what I had in mind when I mentioned normalcy . . . ' His mouth grew bitter. 'I only want the best for us, for all of us.'

'You want to show the world a happy family life?'

'The people I thought of inviting know better. I want voices in the house, company, for you, for me . . . '

He sounded contrite enough. Perhaps this jail was getting the warder down sooner than it did the prisoner. 'Whom did you think of inviting?' she asked.

'Voukovich.'

'Voukovich,' she repeated. Voukovich was neither here nor there, just pleasant. And you didn't need to pretend before Voukovich.

'Waltraut Greve.'

This went closer to the skin. But maybe you couldn't be choosy if you wanted to crawl out from under this self-imposed isolation.

'John Hiller.'

No, it did not hurt, thought Julia. She saw Arnold toying with the salt shaker. He wanted voices in the house; that's what he said. And to show her that he had his creatures lined up and could make them perform on command. 'Anyone else?' she asked.

'Not unless you can think of someone. For a starter, a small party is enough. Tonight? You'll talk to Frau Sommer?'

She talked to Frau Sommer, who left at once to do the shopping. Julian tired of the cowboy game and settled down with a book. What he called reading was really a memory exercise; after the story in a picture book had been read to him two or three times, he knew it by heart and told it back to himself, the illustrations serving as a crutch. It enabled Julia to return to her drawings.

The work was not progressing even though it didn't require too much concentration at this stage. She caught herself dreaming: no set patterns, a restlessness bordering on premonition – she had come to distrust what looked like a random event; everything was connected as if by threads, and some thread was always being pulled somewhere. Arnold's party tonight might be a whim, but why this night after so many empty nights, and what had caused his whim?

The ringing of the doorbell broke the quiet of the house. Julia rose apprehensively. Julian looked up from his book, then returned to his story: of the little elephant with the uplifted trunk who got lost on the way from the railroad station to the circus and who joined a little boy named Bimbo and their adventures till the circus clown found the little elephant parked high up on the fourth-floor balcony of little Bimbo's parents' flat and the fire department spread a net and Bimbo and the elephant jumped together because neither of them dared do it by himself. Like Julian, she knew the story by heart and worked her way through it as she walked down the stairs, her hand on the banister, and crossed the sitting room into the hallway, and stood at the door. And the net bent and the firemen strained and the little elephant and Bimbo bounced in the air three times and the people cried, Hurrah.

It was the man from the waterworks come to read the meter in the basement. Julia walked down with him to switch on the lights, and watched him take his readings and enter them into a ledger, and followed him up the cellar stairs, laughing at herself and her worrying.

'Thank you, ma'am,' said the man and opened the door.

In the doorway stood Hiller.

The man passed Hiller and was gone. 'Surprised?' said Hiller, and tried to laugh. He looked haggard; his collar was wilted; his eyes shone feverishly.

'I thought you were to come tonight,' said Julia, supporting herself against the doorjamb.

'Tonight? . . . ' He remembered. 'Ah . . . tonight.' A gesture did away with that. 'I've got news for you . . . for us. Won't you let me come in?'

'News?' she said. 'From Wollin?'

He stared, then understood. 'Wollin . . . ' he said disparagingly. 'This is a lot more important than Wollin, than any one man. And it affects everybody, you particularly. For heaven's sake, Julia, don't keep me here like a pedlar. Think what you like about me . . . and I imagine none of it is pretty . . . but listen to me . . . '

She showed him into the sitting room. He fell into Arnold's big chair and closed his eyes.

'I'm listening,' she said, and remembered his head on her pillow. She had loved the expression about his mouth, soft, for once not centred on himself, not on the defensive; now, the

264

corners of his mouth turned down and the shadows on his sunken cheeks made his nose appear large and crooked.

'I could do with a drink,' he suggested.

She went to the cupboard. 'Vodka?'

'Anything.'

The cupboard always had been well stocked, but Arnold must have gone through the supplies on his lonely guard. She found a remainder of gin and poured it into a glass.

Hiller drank gratefully. Putting the glass aside, he sat up and contemplated her. 'Jesus, Julia,' he said, 'you look as beautiful as ever.' Then, 'You're not wearing your hair differently, are you? Sometimes I think if you were a nun and I could see only the triangle of face between your brows and the tip of your chin, I still would get that feeling.' He broke off, frowned. 'How's Julian?'

'Fine.'

'He's a fine boy,' he said. Then, his head sinking between his shoulders as if he had been whipped, 'I did look for a flat, Julia, for the three of us . . . and I kept on looking long after . . . ' He stopped short. 'You can verify that with every housing authority in every miserable district of this miserable town. There's only one man who could have gotten us that flat, and he had other plans.'

'Is this what you came to tell me?'

'Oh, no.' He plucked briefly at his earlobe. 'I just thought I'd tell you before I show you this.' He reached into his inside coat pocket and took out a long envelope from which he carefully removed a much-folded sheet of onionskin paper. 'This is it!' he announced, pointing at the close print covering both sides. 'The secret speech.'

'Where did you get it?' Julia asked, too quickly. Then she sat down on the nearest chair. Even without his having said so, she knew that the contents of this speech would have an impact on her life like a meteor rushing in at her from space, screaming at white heat.

265

'Where did I get it?' He raised a significant hand. 'I got it.'

'How do you know it isn't a fraud?' Her voice sounded as if it came from the other end of the room. 'A secret speech, held at a Party Congress, would stay secret.'

'Murder will out.' He snorted. 'Always.'

'Murder . . . ' She felt her hands go icy, her heart. 'Let me see the speech.'

He raised himself out of Arnold Sundstrom's easy chair and walked over to her, but held on to the paper. 'You can read the full text later,' he promised, 'at your leisure. It's edifying: the origins of what they call the cult of the personality, the psychology of it, a character analysis of the man they advertised as the great leader and symbol of all that's supposed to be good and ennobling and progressive in this world, the theories that were distorted and the doctrines that were cockeyed, the truth about the muddle they made of the war, the senseless liquidation of entire minority peoples, and the debunking of much-touted history books and novels and films and statuary . . . '

'Stop it,' she whispered. 'Please, stop it.'

'There's more, lots more.' With his hanging shoulders and his sweaty face he looked repugnant, a negation of everything she had believed worthwhile. 'But this is what's of immediate concern to us.'

'Us?' she repeated.

'You, Sundstrom, myself.' He spread the paper on the low coffee table before her. 'I've marked the lines. No, let me read to you.'

She couldn't have read it. The black of the print and the red of his markings flowed into splotches; only his finger, pointing mercilessly, was in focus, the nail uneven, the cuticle almost covering the half-moon.

'Here . . . here it is: *Many entirely innocent persons, who in the past had defended the Party line, became victims . . . Mass arrests and deportations of many thousands of people, execution without trial and without normal investigation, created conditions of insecurity, fear, and even desperation . . . '*

'How is it possible,' Julia said hoarsely, and knew that it was not only possible but fact, and still repeated, like a prayer mill, 'how is it possible how is it possible?'

'Listen to this, my dear . . . doesn't this strike a chord . . . *Many Party, government, and economic activists who were branded . . . enemies, spies, wreckers . . . were always honest, Communists. They were only so stigmatised and often, no longer able to bear barbaric tortures, they charged themselves . . . with all kinds of grave and unlikely crimes . . . '*

Julia stared. The finger pointing at the printed lines grew unbearably, a sausage pink with brown tobacco stains, until it occupied nearly her entire field of vision.

'*Now*,' she heard him read on, '*when the cases of some of these so-called spies and saboteurs were examined it was found that all their cases were fabricated. Confessions of guilt of many arrested and charged with enemy activity were gained with the help of cruel and inhuman torture . . . '*

The finger grew to such a distended size that it became semi-transparent and she could see faces beyond it. The faces, though blurred, seemed familiar and beckoned to her.

' . . . how is it possible how is it possible,' he aped. 'Don't keep saying 'how is it possible'; it's explained right here. The accused were *deprived . . . of any possibility that their cases might be re-examined, even when they stated before the court that their 'confessions' were secured by force, and when, in a convincing manner, they disproved the accusations against them . . .* Deprived, my dear, by directive to the Commissariat of Internal Affairs *to execute the death sentences . . . immediately after the passage of sentences.*'

The finger was back to normal; she could even make out the print. He had ceased reading.

'Well?' he said, searching her face for a sign of what she felt. Her skin was the whitish grey of powdered cement, her eyes large, opaque, almost like a blind person's. If she would weep, he thought; maybe I picked the wrong quotes, too much abstract reporting; to women you must hand the truth in three-dimensional terms.

'Why do you do this to me?' she said.

'Julia,' he said, 'these were *people*, people with hands like yours and mine, with eyes to see and hearts that beat and nerves and brains. There's one man named Eikhe who wrote in a letter to Stalin: . . . *finding my two feet in the grave, I am not lying . . . the most disgraceful part of my life, my confession . . . not being able to suffer the tortures . . . Ushakov . . . utilised the knowledge that my broken ribs have not properly mended and have caused me great pain . . . I have never betrayed you or the Party . . .* '

'Enough,' she pleaded. 'I've heard enough.'

'You think you have. There's Comrade Kedrov, writing to the Central Committee. *Today I, a man of sixty-two years, am being threatened by the investigative judges with more severe, cruel, and degrading methods of physical pressure . . . They try to justify their actions by picturing me as a hardened and raving enemy . . . But let the Party know that I am innocent . . . Everything, however, has its limits. My torture has reached the extreme. My health is broken. My strength and my energy are waning, the end is drawing near. To die in a Soviet prison, branded as a vile traitor to the fatherland – what can be more monstrous for an honest man? . . . No! No! This will not happen; this cannot be – I cry. Neither the Party, nor the Soviet government . . . will permit this cruel, irreparable injustice . . . I believe deeply that truth and justice will triumph. I believe. I believe . . .* '

'I believe . . . ' she repeated, an echo. Her lids shimmered moistly. 'There is no letter from Julian and Babette Goltz?'

'None was quoted.'

She closed her eyes. 'Why did you do this to me?'

The question, put a second time, could no longer be brushed off. 'Because I felt it better you heard it from me than from someone else . . . Julia, that pain that's bottled up in you . . . let it out. Let go. Cry.' He made an attempt at caressing her hair but gave it up as he saw her wince.

'You haven't answered me,' she said, once more looking at him. 'Why did *you* have to come and read this to me?'

'Didn't you *want* to know? Your father . . . your mother—'

'I'll bury my own dead.'

Hiller tried to draw himself erect; his hands searched for some anchorage; there was only the copy of the speech, and he kept folding it and caressing the folds as he said, 'You want to know why I came to you? . . . Because this about finishes *him*. And you'll do the finishing. What's he going to say when you confront him with this? Talk of those people working for the enemy? Of confessions? There's no more excuse, no more rationalisation. He's through, the great Sundstrom, through, I tell you!'

Julia shuddered. His hatred had shoved his whole face out of joint, and it stayed incongruously on the bias while his voice wooed her. 'And then we are free, Julia . . . you and I. Free to love one another, free to build as one should, free to live. Klein-mallenhagen? Perhaps what we had there was premature. The star that shines for us was not yet over the horizon. Now it has come up. We just have to reach for it.'

Free, thought Julia. A world had collapsed, and he was fishing among the rubble for bits and sticks that might be used to keep a ramshackle life going. Free, he said. As if you could wipe off the past and begin again on a freshly washed blackboard.

'Julia!'

She drearily shook her head.

'I know it's been a shock, Julia. But we've got to live with it. Better not to nurse illusions.'

She wished he would go. One by one, the props of her previous existence had been knocked out from under her until, with this last blow, only mourning was left. She tried to recall the faces of her mother and father, but now that they were cleansed of guilt they withdrew mockingly into dim reaches where she could not

269

follow them. A vague sense of remorse filled her, as if in some way she had been part of the conspiracy to murder them, and she searched her mind for obscure memories of childhood days, for missed opportunities when she could have shown her love and didn't, could have eased their load and had made it heavier instead.

'Are you afraid he'll squirm out of this, too?' asked Hiller, beginning to chafe under her silence. 'I swear to you: not this time! That is – if you say the word. If you stand up and speak out.' He tapped the envelope against his knuckles as his eyes narrowed at a new possibility. 'Haven't you comprehended the scope of this? Here's this exemplary Communist, this architect of the new world, who delivers his comrade and his comrade's wife into the hands of these experienced extortioners of confessions and then, to cover up his tracks, poses as the benefactor, fatherly friend, and, finally, loving husband of the murdered couple's child. I know it's hard to conceive, and hardest when you, yourself, are a character in the plot. But I think I've made it clear.'

'And you are the judge?'

'I? . . . You, Julia. Anyone.' But some of his bluster was gone. 'Oh, I appreciate your situation. He's also the father of your child.'

'And what do you want to get out of it?' She licked her lips, tasted the salt. She had bitten them bloody. 'Position? Me? A general sense of righteousness?'

'Julia!' He sounded incredulous. 'You want to let it ride? . . . I tell you what I want to get out of it. This is bigger than one foul murder, or even a thousand or a hundred thousand. It isn't even the murders. Even if no one had been killed unjustly, the injustice would remain. Read that speech and look at our part of the world . . . at the houses we build and the goods we make, the lectures we hear and the novels we write, shoddy, false, un-satisfactory. It's like a blight that has come over us. It's a way of running things that has nothing to do with socialism or

270

democracy or even the dictatorship of the proletariat. It produces people whose spine is crooked from constantly looking back over their shoulders and whose mind is split from saying one thing and thinking another. It cripples the heart and hamstrings the brain and taints the thought and turns into a snivelling hypocrite a man like myself who once upon a time dreamed of walking straight and proud—'

'Only if you let it.'

Hiller blew out his cheeks peevishly and said, 'A person wants to live, doesn't he?'

'What did you ever risk in order to hang on to your precious integrity?'

'I never put the matter to its final test. I don't claim I'm a hero.'

'But you claim the right to judge.'

'Listen, Julia – we all sit in glass houses, all but the dead. And yet we've got to start throwing stones.' He sat down opposite her at the coffee table, whose rim cut into his shins. He took the silly pain as punishment for the exuberance he had felt at bringing her the documented proof of the treachery. He had hoped to catch her on the rebound; she had rebounded, all right, but in no direction he could take. 'Then what do *you* want to do, Julia?' he begged. 'What do you want *me* to do? Tell me . . . '

'Let me have that paper.'

He gave it to her in its envelope. Her hand shook as she struggled with the flap and the sheet, and he finally had to help her unfold it. Then she found what she was looking for and read, like a schoolchild, her lips unconsciously forming the words and her whine unconsciously giving them sound. '*This can not be . . . I cry . . . I believe deeply that truth and justice will triumph. I believe. I believe . . .* '

Hiller saw her eyes fill. The pain, so long dammed up, broke through.

'You must excuse me now,' she managed to say. She got up and ran from the room.

Hiller saw the copy of the speech lying on the coffee table where she had left it. He decided it was better that he took it with him.

Julia went to bed.

She kept falling asleep and waking up with a sudden, jarring start. A glance at the watch showed that two, at most three, minutes had passed, filled with huge, disconnected dreams of which she remembered nothing but a feeling of horror.

Shortly after five she heard the car drive up and heard Julian's excited 'Daddy! Daddy!' from the open window of his room. Then the heavy footsteps on the stairs, the noisy greetings next door, and Julian announcing, importantly, 'Julia's sick in bed.'

There was a moment's quiet. Julia wondered if she should answer the knock at the door. It no longer mattered, really: she was further removed from him than a thousand rooms with a thousand doors.

He entered, the child in tow. He glanced about uncertainly; it was the first time since her return that he had set foot in this part of the house. Julia lay, white, against the white pillow.

'Not feeling well?' He stepped on tiptoe to her bedside. 'What happened?'

She told him she had a migraine headache that was splitting her skull. She was lying only about the seat of her pain; actually there wasn't a part of her that didn't feel battered. It was the heat, he suggested; the day had been muggy and steaming, not a breath of wind, nor the thunder shower the radio had promised; but he would phone Professor Bauer to drop by. Julia said no. She had taken all the pills the doctor could possibly prescribe; she needed rest, she needed to be quiet, to be alone, the curtains drawn.

'I'll call off the party,' he said, sounding worried and disappointed.

'Please, don't!' Julia feared he might insist on an evening of applying cold compresses to her forehead and pouring drops down her throat. 'Have your guests. The pain will stop, and I don't want you to miss out on a little relaxation.'

'This migraine . . . it came quite suddenly?'

'Yes.'

'But I don't recall your ever suffering from migraine headaches.'

Perhaps I should have picked a cleverer excuse, thought Julia. If John could lay his hands on a copy of the speech, Arnold most likely possessed one, too. But her thoughts were sluggish and she felt indifference waft in on her like soft, boundless fog.

'Well,' she heard him say, 'there's always a first.' It was obvious that he still didn't entirely trust her migraine, but he seemed to lack the courage or the persistence to pursue the matter and restricted himself to solicitous noises that barely penetrated the half-stupor in which she lay.

When she came to, the air was still sultry. She kicked off her blanket, conscious of a disagreeable film of sweat. Darkness had set in and her pains were gone. She sat up slowly, massaging the bridge of her nose. There wasn't a sound from Julian's room next door; Frau Sommer and Arnold apparently had succeeded in putting him to sleep. From outside the window came subdued voices: Arnold was telling Frau Sommer to help him set up glasses and plates on the terrace; very hot for this late in the summer, he was saying; we'll be more comfortable outdoors.

Julia went to the bathroom and let the cold water run over her wrists. In the mirror over the basin an unlovely stranger stared back at her from red-rimmed eyes. Her brain was empty, a wasteland; her heart was like a pump that, once started, went through its appointed motions; but it ached, and nowhere a God to whom to pray.

She showered quickly and put on fresh pyjamas and returned to her room. The lower third of her window was filled with the pink and purple hues that rose from the city lights and obscured the stars; above that, the night was black. The guests seemed to have arrived; she could distinguish Hiller's slurring, self-assured tones, and Voukovich's accent, and Waltraut's pitch was unmistakable.

Julia threw herself on the bed. There was the gurgle of wine being poured, the scrape of silver against china, the squeak of the garden furniture, the jarring of steel table legs on the flagstone of the terrace. Arnold was apologising for her absence; migraine, you know; women are prone to it; a regretful chuckle. Small talk: the weather, terrible, this heat, but it's bound to break soon; the food, delicious, Frau Sommer does it all, you're lucky to have a good housekeeper; Julian? – fine, couldn't be better, a child has his problems like any grown-up; and repeated warnings to keep it low, we don't want to wake the boy, or Julia.

Julia rose with a groan, stumbled to her desk, and switched on the work light. From the drawer she pulled her half-finished floor plan for Wollin's proposed shopping centre; he had once talked to her of the proportions of sales space to storage facilities to delivery ramps, but she had trouble reconstructing it from the few hazy pointers she remembered and had debated with herself whether to try finding her own solution. She tacked the sheet to the drawing board; the pencils gleamed, their points sharpened to hairline precision; the slide rule lay handy.

Outside, talk meandered to work, but they were treating it lightly. How many variations of the extension project had they done by now? When your client can't make up his mind, the architect ends up minus his job. Or his head. Laughter. Don't wake Julian. Or Julia. She seems to be awake, there's a light upstairs. In the end, they'll have to approve *something*. They should have approved long ago, we'll fall behind plan. The vanguard can't march too far ahead of the people. That was Arnold. The vanguard, in this case, was the architects, he explained; you've got to see things historically; we must take matters as we find them, do the best under the given circumstances. Waltraut, laughing unpleasantly – well, then, the usual

274

mishmash! No – from John Hiller – more mash than mish; times are changing.

Julia dug her hands in her hair. The white of the floor plan bit at her eyes; the lines she drew, thin, ascetic in their abstraction, seemed unreal against the voices and the subdued chortles and the mishmash and the ivy that in the end would cover their buildings like so many tombstones and so hide the architects' sins. A fat, greyish brown moth threw itself with suicidal persistence against the bulb. Julia tried to deflect it with her slide rule; the moth was too dumb to learn. Its singed wings continued to beat feebly, trying to hurl the hairy body against the glowing hot glass.

Julia turned off the light.

The moth hit the desk with a faint plop. Outside, they had disposed of architecture and had moved on to jokes and anecdotes. A successful evening, Julia thought and, in the darkness of her room, groped for her pencils and snapped off their tips one after the other. Voukovich was telling of some fastness high in the mountains of Croatia, a veritable eagle's nest, that dated back to the Middle Ages, that had survived every siege, that once more did service as a partisan outpost in this war. He spoke of daring raids in which men who seemed like folklore giants swooped down upon the Nazis, and of the ghosts that haunted the empty galleries.

' . . . practically a Hamlet story,' Voukovich was saying. 'The lord of the castle deviously murdered by his best friend who then marries—'

'—the wife,' Julia heard Hiller say.

'No, not the wife,' Voukovich corrected. 'The daughter.'

'The murderer marrying the murdered man's daughter?' This was Arnold, his voice strained. Then, with a snort, 'Pretty gruesome!'

'At least it wasn't incest,' Waltraut threw in, her voice an insinuating whisper.

Arnold chuckled.

'The Greeks, my dear,' Waltraut rejoined, 'would have made it incest!'

Julia felt for the thumbtacks and removed them one by one from the drawing board. Since when was Waltraut whispering to Arnold and my-dearing him? And was Voukovich's tale of the murderer marrying his victim's daughter coincidental, or had Hiller put him up to it?

'Where does the ghost come in?' pursued Waltraut.

'The ghost appears one night—'

'—one stormy night,' corrected Hiller.

'One stormy night,' Voukovich agreed. 'I don't see that the weather really matters. The ghost appears to the young woman and calls on her to avenge the foul deed. She is torn between filial duty and loyalty to a husband from whom she has experienced nothing but love; also, there is some doubt in her mind as to the ghost's authenticity; the mountains are full of evil spirits masquerading in many shapes, with many voices . . . ' Voukovich's tone became pensive, almost solemn. 'But the ghost returns a second time, a third . . . and each time its demands become more urgent.'

'And where's the husband during all this?' demanded Waltraut. 'Strikes me the man would have an eye on his wife and keep her from getting social with ghosts and other strangers.'

'All right,' an angry growl from Arnold, 'let's get through with the story!'

There was a pause. Voukovich seemed to be collecting his thoughts or was undecided about continuing.

'Sorry . . . ' Arnold punctuated his apology with an awkward laugh. 'I'm really very interested.'

'I'll make it brief,' said Voukovich, and then thanked someone for the drink that had been handed him. There was another pause while Voukovich downed it. 'You'll see the parallel to Shakespeare,' he said finally. 'The function of the actors' troupe is taken by a wandering minstrel who is instructed by the girl to

276

compose a ballad containing the details of the murder as she has learned them from the ghost. The singer does the actors Hamlet rehearsed one better. He does such a great job that when he reaches the critical point, the story of the actual killing, the murderer cries out, smashes the minstrel's lute, and, trapped by his fears, prays to his wife to take the curse off him; when she turns from him, he staggers up the stairs to the highest turret and throws himself from the battlement to the rocks below.'

Julia heard a slight clink: Voukovich was setting down his glass.

'They still show you the spot he jumped from,' Voukovich concluded. 'I've been there myself – the rock falls off straight; at the foot of the cliff a small brook runs like a white thread.'

Someone coughed slightly.

'Mrs Hamlet,' Julia heard Waltraut say, and then her laugh, tight and cutting.

'Mrs Hamlet,' Arnold repeated noisily. 'Not bad at all! You didn't make up that story, Voukovich, did you?'

'Why should I make it up?'

'Oh, just to be entertaining!' A chair was being shoved back, Arnold's apparently, because Julia heard his familiar pacing. After a while he said, 'There are no ghosts, you know.'

'There must have been murder, though,' said Hiller, tapping his foot. 'Shakespeare based his tragedies on fact.'

'Ah, well,' said Voukovich, yawning. 'It was all so long ago, or some ballad singer invented the story and someone else pinned it to the fortress in the mountains . . .'

Without switching on the light, Julia put the draft back into her desk and returned to her bed. It was futile to try to work. Outside, they were silent but for an occasional word; a chill seemed to have frozen the conviviality; Waltraut's spasmodic efforts to revive it elicited no more than a brittle laugh. Julia could almost hear the relief which greeted Arnold's comment that tomorrow was another day, with much work requiring a

277

clear mind and bright ideas; yes, he would convey their best wishes to Julia, and let's get together again, we must do this more often . . . The words faded as Arnold walked his guests to the garden gate. Julia pressed her lids closed. Even if she wasn't asleep she would be asleep to him. She thought of locking the door, but that would lock out Julian. The minstrel had told his story and the lord of the castle would want to come a-begging his wife to take the curse off him but there were no ghosts, Mrs Hamlet, or you would have known long ago.

There was whispering on the terrace. Then they hadn't all gone . . . Julia supported herself on her elbow, and listened. They were pouring drinks, striking matches, settling back in creaky chairs.

'I'm glad you stayed on.' That was Arnold, keeping his voice low. 'I'd feel rotten if I had to be alone, now.'

'And Julia?' Waltraut's voice, just above a whisper.

'Julia . . . ' A glass fell, but was caught before it could break.

'Be careful,' Waltraut warned. 'Here's my hand.'

'Tell me, Waltraut: why do they hate me so – Hiller, Vouko-vich? What have I done to them? I've furthered them, helped them, given them position, money . . . '

'I suppose they hate you as the young males hate the chieftain of the tribe and wait for his downfall.'

'You think it's that atavistic?'

'It's many things.'

'You're a smart girl, Waltraut.' He grunted. 'Let them wait for the old chieftain's downfall. Till hell freezes over. Because Stalin was disrobed doesn't mean the rest of us have to start running around naked! . . . Ghosts! . . . What'll they think of next?'

She spoke a few low-toned words that Julia couldn't get but that seemed to calm him. A little later, Julia heard him say, 'Tell you what, Waltraut: I'll get out the car and drive you home . . . '

Julia sank back on her pillow. The garage gate crunched against the gravel of the driveway; the starter groaned a few times before the motor responded; the car door banged shut; the grinding of the tyres, the purr of the engine – then quiet. Mrs Hamlet, thought Julia. John Hiller was playing a childish game; perhaps he hadn't the faculty to grasp her feelings; their whole relationship had been warped by his immaturity; her time was out of joint, but she had no desire to set it right; at present she wanted only to find a firm spot on which to plant her two feet. The quiet was oppressive. Waltraut Greve and Arnold: she tried to visualise the two of them, arm in arm, a couple; ludicrous. But maybe it was just the thing for him; anything that didn't force him to turn upon himself. Julia was surprised at the detachment with which she contemplated her situation and Arnold's; she didn't hate him, or she was too numbed for any clearly defined feelings.

She shrank at the sound of the returning car. No more than ten or fifteen minutes could have passed: so he hadn't stayed with Waltraut. She heard his steps crossing the terrace; he stumbled, stopped; a bottle was being set down, hard. He's drinking too much, Julia thought; I hope he won't get obstreperous and wake Julian; it's a wonder the child slept through the party; he's been sleeping much better since he's home, and the fever is gone, too.

The stillness was intense, a lasting silence. Then, suddenly, a chair was moved. In Julian's room. Her heart raced; fragments of thought hurtled through her mind. She got up unsteadily and groped her way along the wall to the door and opened it.

Arnold was sitting in the half-dark, hunched forward, gazing at the sleeping child. A slight nod indicated his awareness of her in the doorway, but his eyes stayed fixed on Julian as if he were trying to draw from the dim outlines of the small, curled-up body an answer to some unspoken question.

The child turned in his sleep, mumbled. Julia tensed; then she saw that Arnold hadn't moved, was retaining his attitude of silent dialogue with his son. Time passed; she lost count of the minutes.

Finally he straightened. His shadowy face turned in her direction as he levered himself up from the chair. With the slow, stiff steps of a wind up toy he walked toward her. She wanted to cry out but her throat was dry, soundless. She felt the safety of the doorpost slip from under her fingers; her hand rose before her eyes as if to ward off a blow; she tumbled backward and clutched the nearest support, a chair.

He closed the door behind him.

'How's your migraine?' he said. 'You shouldn't be up. Get back to bed.'

She lay down, obediently, as if she had been hooked onto the same wires that seemed to be giving him movement. He dragged a chair to her bedside.

'I didn't stay at Waltraut's,' he said tonelessly. 'I wanted to. I couldn't.'

Julia shivered.

'Cold?' he asked. 'I'll get you another blanket.'

She shook her head.

'Seems there's nothing I can do anymore,' he said and hunched forward, staring at her as he had at Julian. 'It's like a steel ring around my chest that's drawing tighter. Sometimes I think I'm getting only half the breath I need.'

The paling aura of the city lighted the planes of his face; the rest was cavernous shadows.

'No one can say I didn't try, Julia,' he went on in the monotone of a man defeated beyond hope. 'I fought it. With all the weight, experience, connections I had. But there was one weak point . . . you.'

She saw his hands, broad, capable, open and close nervously.

'A man can eliminate what he feels weakens him. But there was the rub. I had hung my heart on you. Everything was entangled and enmeshed, my wishes and my fears, and we were the prisoners of what we wanted to escape.'

The spasm of his hands eased up. Julia lay motionless watching him. He tugged at his tie and collar.

'But now it's changed. A qualitative leap, you know?' He waited as if he expected her to confirm his dialectical joke. 'One thing comes to the other, quantity upon quantity, till all of a sudden you're faced with the new situation. Fear. All that's left is fear, pressing in on you until every nerve wriggles like a worm. I can't go on that way. You understand that, don't you, Julia?'

She wanted to nod but couldn't. Horror made her rigid except for her pupils, which kept on seeing, and her eardrums, which kept on hearing.

'You don't want me to go insane. You don't want me to do anything rash. There's only one person . . . one in the world . . . Julia . . . help me . . . '

She felt him grope for her, his fingers jab into her flesh. She was stony, and her blood seemed to coagulate in her brain.

'Julia—!'

She screamed.

He stood over her, shaking her, slapping her face. Her scream cut the night, jagged, piercing, without end. Then she saw Julian at her bedside, his eyes wide with fright, his fists beating against his father's thighs. 'Let go of Julia!' the boy shrilled wildly. 'I hate you! Let go!'

Her breath gave out. She felt her head being lowered onto the pillow. She saw Arnold slowly turn to stare at the child whose ineffectual fists were still hammering at him. He grasped Julian's wrists and held on to them until they stopped twitching.

Then he walked out, moving stiffly, his steps mechanical: the giant wind up toy that could stop only when the spring had uncoiled.

CHAPTER THIRTEEN

She was packing.

She had called Frau Schloth as soon as Arnold had gone to work. Frau Schloth had been reluctant but had finally said yes, she thought she would have a room.

The packing went unevenly. Her hands flew; a bottle fell and broke, a dress caught and ripped, a suitcase wouldn't close; there's no rush, Julia kept telling herself, he can't hold you, that's done with and past; but her frazzled nerves were deaf to reasoning.

And there was Julian. The last time they left he had asked why – why this, why that, till she was hard put to explain. Now, no why formed on his pale lips. He tripped about seriously, a busy gnome, fetching clothing and underwear from the drawers of the cupboard in his room and folding them, selecting his most indispensable toys from his shelves, and driving her to distraction by his attempts at being helpful. Sometimes she caught him looking at her with an understanding impossible to a child his age; he was like one of those children in war who could distinguish between the drone of enemy planes and that of their own, who knew when to jump into ditches and when to emerge and once more put their thin shoulders to the wheel of the handcart that held everything that once had meant home. He talked interchangeably of his daddy and his uncle John Hiller; they had faded into one in their relation to her and in his fear of them; and his resentment against them spilled out of him. Julia's hands would drop to her sides and her heart would contract: what right had her generation to inflict its curse upon the young?

Downstairs, the phone rang.

She saw Julian stiffen. And she thought: he'll be free of that curse because I'll free him of it because I *know* and what you know you can fight. And then: if that's Arnold calling I'll tell him we're leaving there's nothing he can do about it nothing nothing nothing.

Frau Sommer came up the stairs. Julia braced herself. Frau Sommer stood at the open door, patting the grey bun at her nape and eyeing the confusion and the disordered suitcases. 'Gentleman on the phone for you,' she announced curtly and folded her hands below her flat bosom.

'Didn't he give his name?'

'No, ma'am, he didn't.'

'Frau Sommer!'

'Yes, ma'am?'

'There is no reason for that smirk on your face.'

'Very well, ma'am.' Frau Sommer straightened her apron. 'Herr Professor Sundstrom always found my face satisfactory.' She turned and with deliberate slowness preceded Julia down the stairs.

Julia closed the door to the living room. The receiver lay on the coffee table, gleaming dully, an outsized punctuation mark finalising unspoken questions from an unknown voice. She hesitated to pick it up. She thought it might be John Hiller calling her, after last night – but she knew, suddenly, that it wasn't John.

'Julia?'

Despite the tinny edge that the membrane gave it, the voice had that essential, unmistakable gentleness.

'Yes,' she said, 'yes . . . '

'It's me. Daniel Yakovlevich. Daniel Wollin.'

'I know.' She swallowed. Her fingers tried to unravel the knots in the telephone wire.

'Julia! You're still there?'

'Yes, of course.'

'I couldn't hear you.'

'I hadn't said anything.'

He waited. She thought she could hear him breathing. Then he asked, with effort, 'How are you, Julia?'

'Fine.' She paused. 'Fine.' And after another pause, 'You've been away an awfully long time.'

'I hurried as best I could. But certain matters had to be settled.'

'I imagine.' She had to wait a second before continuing. 'But not a word from you, ever . . . '

'It was impossible. I thought you would understand.'

'You weren't ill?'

'I wasn't ill. I'm all right.'

Julia didn't comment. Words you spoke over the telephone, no matter what they said, were inadequate. She gave herself up to her sense of relief.

'You'll understand the moment I tell you,' he was saying. 'I must see you, Julia. Soon. Now.'

Her fingers stroked the smooth wire that they had straightened. 'You are *really* here? . . . I have to make myself believe it. Daniel,' she laughed anxiously, 'you're not calling from some other town, some other country?'

'I'm calling from World Peace Road. You know the building workers' shed. I am sitting here, with my feet up on the bench, and drinking my friend Barrasch's coffee.'

'Do you have to finish it? Take a cab. Come here.'

'*You* come, Julia. I'm waiting.'

'Say that again, please. And in exactly that tone.'

'What? . . . Oh, all right . . . ' He was silent, apparently trying to recapture the precise mood of a second ago. Then, 'No. We have to postpone that. We have time. A whole lifetime.'

She listened. She took the receiver away from her ear and gazed at the black disk that had offered her a whole lifetime.

Grating, unintelligible sounds began issuing from it.

'What did you say?' Julia hastily pressed the receiver back to her ear. 'When you could expect me? . . . I can't get away. I can't leave

Julian alone, not after last night . . . What happened? Oh, call it a fight. It's too involved and too horrible to explain over the phone. Mrs Hamlet, you know . . . ' No, he didn't know, she thought, how could he? 'I *must* see you, Daniel. Don't worry: Arnold's gone to work; only Julian and Frau Sommer are here . . . ' Her eyes darkened with frustration. How long had he been gone, how much had developed – and now this silly tug-of-war. 'Don't you believe I would run to you, fly?'

'Now listen, Julia,' he cut in. He spoke in a staccato made harsh by the vibrations of the membrane. 'There is something I have to say to both you and Arnold. I phoned him this morning. He refused to meet me and threatened he would – well – kill me if I as much as got in touch with you . . . Yes, kill me,' he repeated at Julia's involuntary gasp, 'though I doubt he'd go through with it; he isn't the do-it-yourself type. He's due here in the shed sometime before noon for a few technical questions they have to iron out, and Barrasch hasn't heard to the contrary. So you see, Julia, you had better come here. I appreciate your problem with Julian. Tell him you are going for his sake, too. Tell him he can help you by being a man . . . '

'He's trying,' she said. 'Really, he is.'

'I know that.' The voice on the phone was reassuring. 'I'm very fond of the boy.'

Her face grew soft. She tried to check the quiver of her lip. 'Daniel?'

'Yes, Julia?'

'I'll be there.'

*   *   *

He was sitting with his back to the door, at his elbow Barrasch's thermos bottle and the remains of a sandwich. The sun beat on the thin roof and streamed through the windows, striping the shed with diagonals of glare. One of them cut him neatly into a light half and a darker one.

He heard the scraping of the door and turned. His face swung entirely into the light. He blinked.

'Julia!'

He jumped up and, with a few steps, reached her and closed his arms about her.

'You're back,' she said, as if the fact were only now believable. Then she kissed his cheeks, the customary three times. He held her, and she let herself be held; her nerves uncoiled; no more need for strain and apprehension; let go, relax. He smiled, and she smiled back at him. His lips, hard, hot, as if parched, sought hers and found them.

'Julia . . . '

He made her sit down on the bench. 'Was it very bad?' he asked, taking her hand.

'Yes,' she answered simply, her fingers responding to the slight, consoling pressure.

'It's over now,' he said. 'Or will be soon. I'm sorry I couldn't give you advance warning, a chance to prepare yourself. Do you think you'll be ready?'

Ready, she thought, for the final scene. Whatever happened, whichever the decision, there would be no more uncertainty. She saw the line of dusty lockers in which the men kept their clothes; the uneven, scratched-up surface of the pine table; wooden clogs carelessly thrown into some corner; a saw, an axe that needed sharpening, a few other carpenter's and bricklayer's tools in a pile. It was a ragged, and yet fitting, backdrop for a duel fought over how to build the future.

'I mean,' he tried to elaborate, 'this is *your* life; you must say how you want to live it.'

She looked at him. He had good colour, his face had filled out, the net of fine lines that had covered it was gone but for the crow's feet at his eyes, white streaking the tan. His absence, or its results, seemed to have agreed with him.

'We haven't much time, Julia. Arnold may be here any minute.'

286

His eyes narrowed in concern. 'I'm willing to step back, out of the picture; leave you and Arnold to carry on somehow. My suitcase is checked at the station. All I need do is pick up my hat.'

'Arnold and I are through.'

He waited as if to make sure that no qualifying footnote would follow. 'Yes,' he said, then, 'but what we're going to do is more than drop a man. He will be dumped among some pretty horrible refuse, and I don't think he'll be able to gather himself up.'

'Yes,' he said again, and then, with compassion, 'It's worse for you than for people like me who've been living with this thing for years.' He gently withdrew his hand and rose. Pushing open the nearest window, he said, 'You're an architect, Julia; you know how hard it is to find the right solution and turn it into reality. The plaster coat came off the house we always dreamed of building; now we see its stresses and cracks, its structural weaknesses; but we also can determine what must be knocked down and where the foundations have to be shored up and which parts of the building should be reconstructed so it will last, in beauty, as we intended it to.'

Embarrassed at his big words, he ruffled his hair. Julia heard the clatter of the cranes, the hoarse grinding of the concrete mixers, a truck engine roaring up, voices singing out. She tried to discern what it was that made him appear about to pick up hammer and trowel from the pile of tools and go out and knock down and shore up and reconstruct. She wanted to tell him of her work on his World Peace Road extension project, but she feared that her floor plans and plumbing details were too prosaic for his concept of the huge, cleansed structure he envisioned.

He was speaking again. 'Let me report briefly.' His matter-of-fact tone recalled her to the immediate problem. 'You should know where I've been and what I've done, and what to expect now. And why I left without telling you or anyone. There was always Arnold, with his connections . . . '

He shrugged. The cranes had stopped; the truck apparently

had driven off; only one of the concrete mixers kept up its crunching and scraping.

'Two telegrams,' Wollin resumed, 'remember? Two telegrams, one father – it kept preying on my mind. And I couldn't make myself believe that Arnold had entirely concocted his evidence; he's a petty bourgeois at heart, and a Prussian; small-minded sticklers even in crime, always needing the correct pretence, with a notary public's seal on it if possible. But what if there were *two* fathers?'

Julia gripped the rim of the bench. 'Two fathers . . . died . . . in different years—'

'—with two corresponding telegrams sent from Germany to inform the bereaved members of the family . . . So, first stop, Berlin, with daily subway trips to West Berlin and search through record offices and files. And always the worry: how much had been lost through bombings and shelling and fire? Finally, this.'

He pulled a much-handled manila envelope from his jacket pocket and took from it the photostatic copy of a document.

'May I see it?' she said.

'Please.'

It was a bad copy. Or her eyes swam, dimming and fuzzing the greyed-out, official letters. Julia needed a while to decipher that the carpenter Paul Goltz had died on the 17th day of August, 1939, at Berlin-Charlottenburg, of a cerebral haemorrhage.

'Second stop,' she heard Wollin say, 'the village of Rosenow in Mecklenburg. There, a visit at the manse, very simple. The present pastor was glad to talk about his predecessor, Pastor Hohmann; he had assisted Pastor Hohmann when diabetes and a kidney ailment tied the old man to his bed from before Christmas, 1934, until the day after Pentecost, 1935. That's when Pastor Hohmann had passed away in his sleep; a good man, mourned by his congregation, and leaving behind three grown-up children – the youngest, his daughter Babette, had gone off and married a known Communist and was out of the country at the time of her father's death. I've brought photostatic copies of the entries certifying his death in the village register and church records.'

He passed the papers to Julia.

'Two deaths, two cables,' he went on in the somewhat dry, factual tone he had been using. 'Though the one telegram probably was addressed to Babette and the other to Julian Goltz, their wording must have been about the same: *Sorry to inform you father died* – or something close to that. What else should the senders have wired?' His voice picked up. 'Third stop, Moscow. It took a lot of managing to get there, but I succeeded, and it wasn't easy to find the men I had to see, but I found them and—'

He turned as the door to the shed was pushed open. Hastily pocketing the envelope with the remaining documents, he was about to reach for those in Julia's hand but desisted as he saw it was Barrasch entering. To Julia, Barrasch's greetings booming against the low roof seemed exaggerated, as did the noise of his men bursting in after him. What was this, she thought, a bodyguard arrangement? But the presumptive bodyguards relaxed over their sandwiches and smokes – a breakfast break had been called, that was all. Her mind reverted to Wollin: *Moscow* . . . Whom, and what, had he found in Moscow?

The sudden quiet caught up with her. The concrete mixer had stopped. Then, just outside the shed, the voice – vibrant, throaty, resonant, the tones of a man conscious of his power and position.

Arnold.

For a moment, he paused in the door; behind his shoulders, like minor apostles, rose the heads of John Hiller, of Voukovich, of several other junior architects.

'Well, Barrasch—' The voice broke off.

'Hello, Arnold,' said Wollin. 'I thought I'd wait here for you.'

Sundstrom glanced behind him. His own entourage was blocking his retreat; besides, there was no retreat. 'I have nothing to say to you, Wollin,' he tried to bluster.

Julia felt the strain it was for him to speak. She saw Wollin take a step toward him. Wollin wasn't looking at him but at the photostats still in her hand. 'What I have to say, Arnold,' he stated quietly, 'will take at most a few minutes of your time.'

The change in Sundstrom was frightening. His face had collapsed about his jutting nose; his eyes flickered and his skin was mottled, an old man's skin. Then Julia sensed that he was discovering her although his glance, unseeing, had already rested on her. He started toward her but checked himself. 'What're you holding there, Julia?' he gibed. 'Secrets?'

Julia shook her head, clutching the papers.

'Secrets,' he insisted. 'Everybody has secrets . . . my wife, my friend . . . ' He turned, round-shouldered, his jaws twitching. 'You've been travelling, I hear, Daniel Yakovlevich?'

'Yes,' said Wollin, 'on business.'

'Architectural?'

'Well . . . structural.'

'I told you on the phone I wasn't buying. I'm not interested in your discoveries. I'm not interested in blackmail.' His voice rose, 'Neither yours,' and cracked, 'nor my wife's.'

Julia saw him coming at her, slowly, awkwardly, like an automaton. Then he was lunging for the papers, and she was bending over them protectively, and surrounding her were Barrasch, the men, John, Voukovich. She heard Wollin's calm 'This is ridiculous, Arnold. Even if you tore these papers, they're just copies.'

'Copies . . . ' Sundstrom stared. 'Copies. Structural.'

'There's no secret about them,' Wollin continued evenly. 'Julia will be glad to let you read them.'

She needed a moment to collect her thoughts. Then she rose, straightened, handed Arnold the papers. She shivered. This was the man she had loved and admired and believed in, and what she was turning over to him was his sentence. She covered her face.

290

Sundstrom absently gazed at the photostats. As their meaning penetrated, his mouth slowly came open and a thread of saliva drooled down his chin.

'Wouldn't you prefer to talk this out in private?' asked Wollin.

Sundstrom stood mute.

'Please!' demanded Wollin, with a slight motion of his hand. At a nod from Barrasch, the workers left; then the junior architects; then Voukovich and Barrasch. Only Hiller remained. 'Come, Julia . . . ' he said, his fingers hesitant on her elbow.

She didn't seem to have heard.

'Julia!' he urged. 'Haven't you had enough?'

'I want to stay.' She removed his fingers from her arm. 'This case concerns me.'

Wollin smiled briefly.

Hiller shrugged. Julia watched him pass through the diagonals of shadow and light, out of the door. One of the cranes outside screeched and rumbled as it started to operate; a few seconds later, as if on command, it stopped again.

Julia turned. Arnold was sitting on the bench, his back against the rim of the table, his head inclined, his eyes closed. The photostats lay beside him, discarded, no longer a matter of argument. 'Well,' he began finally without opening his eyes, 'What else do you have?'

'I'm not enjoying this, you know,' said Wollin. He took the manila envelope out of his pocket. 'This document is an original,' he explained as he extracted it, 'but a copy can be had in Moscow. Do you want to read it?'

'Not necessarily.' Sundstrom opened his eyes and fixed them on a screw joint linking braces and roof beam. 'What is it?'

'An official statement of the Moscow District Court completely rehabilitating the accused Julian Pavlovich Goltz and Babette Hugoovna Goltz, née Hohmann, and exonerating them from the charges of high treason, espionage for a foreign power, and collaboration with agents of same, further from the charges of

291

subversion of the Soviet power and active propaganda against institutions of the Soviet state and against the Communist Party of the Soviet Union brackets Bolsheviki brackets close.'

Wollin breathed deeply and flattened the paper as if he were about to offer it in evidence to the court of justice, exhibit A in *Humanity v. Sundstrom*. But where sat such a court, hearing such a case? . . . He pocketed the document and lit a cigarette.

Sundstrom's interest in the roofing of the shed seemed to abate. He turned heavily and studied Julia. When she averted her face, he retreated further into himself: a huddled figure, elbows on knees, head low.

Gradually, words emerged from him, then sentences. 'You don't understand . . . No one does . . . No one who hasn't himself gone through it . . . ' His head came higher. 'The slow corrosion of a man beginning with a silence where you should have spoken, a nod where you should have objected. When did it begin? Who knows. When did you first say: this is too small to raise a fuss over? Or: let someone else open his big mouth? . . . Conformism . . . ' He nodded. 'But where do you draw the line between conformism and discipline? That great virtue, that revolutionary must that subordinates the individual's pretty ethics to the collective's huge commandment and cloaks in its convenient shadow the servile and the lukewarm, the timeserver and the self-seeker, and furnishes excuse and rationale to every slimy bureaucrat and every stool pigeon . . . Don't you see the logic? It's mathematical. Put a minus before your value and it turns into its opposite: the informer becomes a positive hero; the tyrant's sclerotic brain, the mainstay of your state.'

'Your minus is simply perversion,' said Wollin coldly.

'How small-minded you are!' Sundstrom grinned. 'You think I'm trying to find excuses for myself. I'm explaining a phenomenon.' He straightened, and a glimmer of the man he had been showed itself. 'There are also the rewards of being on the right side of things. Money is the least of them – status counts, security, being part of the establishment; you lift a receiver and something starts moving somewhere, gets done, your accomplishment; and freedom; within your set of people and of circumstances, fenced in – but freedom.'

'Corruption,' said Wollin. 'You're describing corruption.'

'Of course,' said Sundstrom with an edge of annoyance at any possible doubt of his meaning. 'But even this isn't one-sided. That I could sustain you in Moscow, Daniel, that you didn't starve to death there was part of it, too.'

'Except that I didn't give anything in return but my work,' replied Wollin.

'And what does that prove?'

'Nothing,' said Wollin. 'I didn't say it to prove anything. All the proof needed has been furnished.'

Sundstrom collapsed again, his shoulders hunched over his folded hands. A feeling of revulsion shook Julia. The broken, seedy individual on this bench had a frighteningly large number of features in common with the man she had considered a giant among men and whom she had embraced and caressed; but the person on this bench differed from the one she had loved as the corpse differs from the body living, and for a moment she believed she caught a waft of the heavy, sweetish odour of decay.

'Discipline,' resumed Sundstrom. 'They're your own people, your own class, your own functionaries. Even where you think you should oppose them . . . should you? Where do you draw the line between conscious subordination and meek subservience? When do you follow orders out of conviction, and when out of weakness? In effect, it amounts to the same thing, and the subtle moral differences tend to fade. Ah, and they have a fine sense for when you're ripe for them. They can smell it, as jackals smell a carcass . . . '

'They,' said Wollin. 'Weren't you part of them?'

'You are and you aren't.' Sundstrom squirmed slightly. 'One

293

day yes, one day no. That's also a form of dialectics: you're both victim and pursuer, both hunted and hunter. You're caught between your fears and their saying: but this is so little; you've said *a*, *b*, *c*, and *d*, Comrade, and now you want to balk at *e*, or *f*, or *g*? And you know what they can do to you; you, of all people, know it best; you have seen your share of what there is to see, and you know that a single stroke of the pen can push you from one side of the ledger to the other; and you want to live, just live. When the boots come at dawn, you want them to pass your door; when the lights of their cars skim along the road at night, you want to be able to tell yourself that they're headed the other way. And sometimes, in the middle of your sweat, with your skin crawling from anxiety and your toes freezing from fear, you say to yourself: you, a Communist – look what you've come to, look what you've permitted them to make of you! And you rush to the window and tear it open and want to throw yourself down onto the empty, glistening pavement. But you don't. This can't last forever, you reason. This is still a socialist country; there were Marx, Engels, Lenin, and now there is Stalin; it can't all be insanity; you've just got to survive; this is your highest Communist duty. And so you go on. You try to be a human being part of the day. You save a little girl—'

'After you had her father and mother killed,' said Wollin. The concrete mixer began grinding.

'There were two identical telegrams,' said Sundstrom. 'I wasn't in charge of the investigation and—'

Wollin cut him off. 'And what telegrams were there,' he asked, 'when you put the finger on your friend Wollin?'

From outside, Barrasch's voice was shouting instructions; chains clanked as they were laid about a load of bricks; then the bricks swayed past the window, upward. Julia could no longer bear standing alone. She moved through the diagonals, to Wollin, and put her forehead against his shoulder.

*

The building was finished but for the inside work. On the stairs, Sundstrom passed a few workmen who were plastering over the gaps torn by the electricians, the usual muddle; you planned and planned, but something always went wrong somewhere; a few yards of cable were missing or a subcontractor mixed up an order, and your fine finished walls had to be chiselled open and broken through; twice the work and twice the cost; you railed and ranted, but everybody had his valid excuse, and you never got to the root of the evil. Perched on their ladders, the men greeted him civilly enough. He returned the greetings mechanically; a lifetime in the working-class movement had reduced his smile and the few personal words that went with it to a matter of rote; not even hypocrisy, just habit.

None of it reached through to him: not the work or the workers. As he mounted the stairs, brushing against scaffoldings or abandoned buckets of whitewash or a forgotten bag of cement, he grew increasingly insensible to his surroundings. Only the stairs remained, zigzagging skyward, each landing an additional tax on his heart.

He felt for the slip in his pocket. Torn from his notebook, a few lines scrawled on the page; his hand had trembled, but he thought it was legible enough: *To Julia – the child is yours, the house and everything in it, also alimonies in cash and in the account in the City Savings Bank. Try if you can to have Julian remember me as I would want him to. I always loved you. Always.* And the signature. All he need do was leave it on the roof, on top of his jacket, with a piece of brick to weight it down. There would be plenty of that about; the men were paid for producing square footage of wall, not for clearing away rubble.

He wondered at the human mind, which even at such a moment could revert to the annoyances of petty problems never solved. Probably, when he streaked by the outside wall, plummeting toward the final collision with the uncleaned earth, it would still worry over the durability of the tiles or the excessive breakage of the windows.

He paused on the top landing. He *had* become winded: his heart wasn't what it used to be; he remembered climbing the Caucasus and how he had left far younger men behind; this chair-borne office life was slow but sure murder, and the constant upset of emotions could be more damaging than any amount of wear and tear.

He looked at the steel ladder that led to the trapdoor; it had the finality of gallows stairs: only the hangman descended them, and he an outcast. Julia's parting words rang in his ear; her voice had been soft, sad rather than condemning, but it cut deeply. Wouldn't it have been kinder, she had asked, to have let her drudge through life in some out-of-the-way Soviet village, or to have let her perish, than to have taken her from that orphanage and raised her in elegance and used her for his bed and his conscience. Used her . . . That was the one thing he had not done. Not consciously. He had visited the orphanage because he had given a promise, and his heart had gone out to the thin little thing, forlorn and forgotten, and he had taken her to him – nemesis in a cheap, ill-fitting brown cotton smock, with large grey eyes and two tight blonde pigtails sticking out from her head. 'Julia,' a groan more than a name; and again, 'Julia,' this time carrying a reflection of the feeling he had held for her. Death came to everyone in a different guise: for him, Death wore pigtails behind the dark hollows of its temples. Sundstrom gripped the steel rung of the ladder; step by step, he pulled himself up; the trapdoor came open easily.

Then he stood on the flat of the roof, behind him a group of chimneys like a posse ready to spring; to his left the square, cabin-like structure that held the pulleys of the elevator. The heat of the day had softened the fresh tar on the roofing; his own tracks, cut into the tar, were like the footprints of an invisible man in soundless pursuit of him. He began to sweat: sticky, large, fear-produced drops clinging to his pores before they united into trickles that stung the corners of his eyes. He tore open his collar and, as though someone had shoved him, he stumbled toward the parapet.

There he stopped, frowning at the profusion of knee-high columns supporting a tar-papered rim that was good for nothing. The columns, swollen about their middle, reminded him of the calves of a muscle-bound strongwoman he had seen in a side-show at a village fair; hundreds of such calves, a parade of obesity, topped by this good-for-nothing ledge – no, it was good for something: you could step onto it and jump off from it. Maybe someone would mark the spot, between columns fifty-seven and fifty-eight, south wall; and the children of the people who would move into the house would feel a shudder along their spines when they told the neighbours' children who hadn't been favoured with a suicide from their roof: that's where he stood, and that's where he threw himself down, and that's where he landed, plop, and boy what a mess, bones and entrails and brain splattered all over you should have seen it my mother vomited but my mother can't even look at a dead chicken without half fainting; and in the course of time a legend would arise like the mountain fastness tale that Voukovich had told, it had been a plot against him, all of it, from the day he first met Wollin back in the old Bauhaus and sketched out his first design, Wollin helping him with a line here and an angle there, to this day and this minute on top of this last completed building on World Peace Road with the view on the ground broken for the extension he would never see . . .

Sundstrom took off his jacket, folded it neatly, and laid it next to the parapet. He caught himself immediately: why that? He had no reason for not jumping with his jacket on except for his innate sense of tidiness that kept him from ever leaving his office without having his desk clear for the next day's work. Or was it because of that American newsreel he had seen years ago somewhere: the man trying to hurl himself from the skyscraper had been in shirtsleeves, thus setting a subconscious pattern for God knows how many of his disciples.

Sundstrom felt better with the jacket off, less narrowed in, less sticky. He fished in his pockets for the slip he had written to Julia, placed it on top of the jacket, secured it with a good-sized chip of brick. For a moment he eyed the pile: the last structure ever built by Arnold Sundstrom, who might have become a great architect in another time.

Then there was nothing more to be done, nothing more to be said, nothing more to be thought. Awkwardly twisting his hip, he climbed the parapet and stood in precarious balance.

Just one more prod, he thought, the touch of a finger, a small gust of wind. Down there, the earth started slowly to circle, its movement carrying along the bugs that were the people and the cars on the road, and the cranes and the buildings. He felt himself sway, the depth at his feet had a pull of its own, God God God, he thought, someone must come, someone always does at the last moment, they can't let me die like this, they can't. With an effort that strained every nerve and squeezed renewed sweat from every pore, he checked his swaying. No one on the ground had noticed him, no one had come out onto the roof. He saw the road stretching, World Peace Road, his road, against the score of ruins beyond. So much remained to be done. Like anything else, he thought, life was a dialectical process: one must weigh the evil a man does against his achievements. And he hadn't made the world, that inexorable maelstrom down there that threatened to suck him into its vortex. He was as much a victim of circumstances as were Julian Goltz and Babette, or Wollin, or the countless others; but while in the final account they had nothing to show for themselves, he had built – huge buildings, whole roads, socialism . . .

He thought he heard footsteps. The dizziness rushed back at him; the earth was a giant wheel, spinning faster, faster, with himself in the hub; the footsteps came closer; his legs buckled, his arms beat the air, his eyes wanted to pop from their sockets; he yelled out, something, a cry of fear, out of the ages, out of the darkness of birth, and threw himself backward onto the tarred roof.

Later, much later, he picked himself up. He crawled to the pile topped by the piece of brick. His breath came in gasps, he was filthy, his shirt clung to his back. He took the slip of paper and with trembling fingers tore it to bits.

Then he looked up. 'How long have you been here, Barrasch?' he asked hoarsely.

'I saw you standing up there,' said the foreman, blinking against the light.

Sundstrom tried to get up, but his knees refused him. The son of a bitch, he thought; he saw me all right, and he would have let me jump.

The foreman shuffled his feet. 'I thought I'd better not startle you. I've had a man fall off a scaffolding once because some joker came up on him from behind.'

Sundstrom fingered his jacket. 'That was considerate of you, Barrasch,' he said. 'I suppose I should thank you?'

'Well . . . ' Barrasch slowly shook his big head. 'You never can tell what a person really wants.'

The remark allowed for any interpretation. Sundstrom realised he was growing angry. It was like a miracle, like life returning into a dead limb, like rebirth. 'Help me up,' he demanded, and as he stood on his feet, he said with an attempted laugh, 'If I hear any stories circulating, Barrasch, I'll have your skin.'

CHAPTER FOURTEEN

Fall, with its faint tang of winesap, was very much in the air. Its clear, mellow light made even the Wilhelm II Gothic of City Hall somehow bearable.

On the stairs to the entrance, Julia hesitated.

'Nervous?' asked Wollin.

'That, too,' she admitted. 'But it suddenly struck me: here's where it all started. Here's where I stood one night last winter. Arnold had parked the car across the street. We were going to a reception.'

Wollin waited.

She shook her head. 'Not even a year ago . . . and the world has changed for me.'

'Not just for you.'

'Do you really think so, Daniel?' She turned toward him, searching his face for the answer behind the answer. 'Do you think we've got a chance?'

'I'll tell you.' A slow smile crept from his eyes to the corners of his mouth. 'Socialism is such a logical, sensible thing that no one, not even the biggest knave and fool, can murder it. There are always the others: those who create. And they're in the majority, irrepressible.'

'I was really referring to our project,' Julia replied after a pause.

'Ah, that . . . ' He opened the entrance door and held it open for her. 'We'll know soon enough.'

A fairly large room, fairly well lit, had been set aside for the display of the scale models and drawings submitted for the jury's consideration. A beautiful lettered sign stretched across the length of one wall: WORLD PEACE ROAD, and underneath, in smaller type, the line *Built By The People For The People.*

Arnold Sundstrom frowned at the sign and then at his model, white plaster, clean, neat to the last papier-mâché tree, on the large table in the precise centre of the room. Tacked to one end of the table was a card that stated, *Project Sundstrom–Hiller.*

For a while, he stared at the model, his mind a blank. Gradually, the blank filled with fragments of thought, none of them cheering. There was no other model. Project Wollin–Sundstrom consisted only of drawings, and not too many of those, hung on the wall with the least favourable light. He tried not to look at that wall; he knew the shape of things that Wollin–Sundstrom imagined; he didn't like it, but something in him felt drawn to it, a last truncated remainder of the Arnold Sundstrom who in his Bauhaus days had nibbled at the fruits of the tree of the knowledge of good and evil.

He was alone in the room, and the quiet, the waiting began to wear on him. Where was everybody? He glanced toward the door from the hallway and then at the door opposite, which led to the jury room. He knew that Krummholz from the Academy in Berlin was in town, as were Pietzsch of the Central Committee and Wilezinsky of the Planning Board; they were to serve on the jury along with such local notables as Comrade Mayor Riedel and Comrade Bunsen, who spoke for the press, and Elise Tolkening, who represented the city's women.

He began to pace. In the past, pacing had helped; it no longer did. Jitters, he thought; will I never get my nerves back into decent condition? By degrees, the pacing led him closer to Project Wollin–Sundstrom; he controlled the swerve of his eyes; a disagreeable heat rose behind his forehead; his collar seemed suddenly tight.

'This is stupid!'

He stopped. He had spoken to himself. He shook his head and resolutely turned to the first of the drawings. *Project Wollin–Sundstrom* – the hand that had entered the three words at the lower right-hand corner of the sheet was painfully familiar, the curves of the capital and lower case *s* – he had given that name to her and she had learned to sign it, in Roman and Cyrillic script. God oh God, will I never forget?

Footsteps.

He swung about. They stood in the door from the hallway, relaxed, happy, self-contained. They hadn't yet seen him, apparently.

Sundstrom coughed.

'Oh, hello,' called Wollin, guiding Julia into the room, toward the table with the Sundstrom–Hiller model.

'Hello,' said Sundstrom.

Julia said nothing. Her lips looked very red in her pale face.

'You were early,' said Wollin.

'Seems I was,' Sundstrom confirmed. And, after a pause, 'I was just looking at your designs.'

'Were you?' said Wollin.

Julia leaned against the table, her fingers spreading across the model's access to a side road and a driveway to a collective garage.

'The plaster will dirty your skirt, Julia,' said Sundstrom. 'Watch it.'

'Thanks,' she said, stepping back.

'Your project has merits,' Sundstrom went on, in the direction of Wollin. 'Especially your solution of—'

The door had opened again.

'Comrade Tolkening!' said Sundstrom.

Tolkening beamed at the three of them. 'Ah, our architects! Waiting? Well, this is the day! You look a bit strained, Julia . . . ' He took her hand and patted it in his father-of-the-people manner. 'And you, Comrade Wollin, everything is all right? Getting adjusted again with us? No better place to get back to yourself and over the old wounds than in your own country . . . ' He raised his brows. 'I know it's a problem, but you'll master it, and we need the old and tried comrades, need them badly, especially in view of—'

302

'Yes, Comrade Tolkening,' said Wollin, breaking the oratory.

Tolkening's eyes narrowed, part amazement, part suspicion. Abruptly, he addressed Sundstrom, 'I'd like to have a few words with you.'

'Now?' asked Sundstrom, his eyes seeking support from his plaster-cast model.

'Now.'

Sundstrom thought he felt the sting of Julia's glance and Wollin's on the back of his neck; he pulled in his head and obediently followed Tolkening – out of the room, along the hallway, past innumerable panelled doors; it was like being caught between parallel mirrors repeating the same reflection endlessly.

Finally there was a larger door, and Sundstrom realised where he was; from the files of his mind his architect's memory culled the ground plans of City Hall and the detail of its interior as he and Julia had designed them; this was the mayor's suite: ante-room, reception and conference room, and private study, all of it planned with the sort of largesse that would lend stature to the figurehead job of Comrade Riedel.

'Please, Comrade Sundstrom!' With a commanding gesture Tolkening ushered him through the doors of the anteroom, of the reception and conference room, into the private study.

Comrade Mayor Riedel, who had been leafing through the day's papers, jumped up from behind his desk and, chins quivering, effusively greeted Tolkening. Tolkening made no pretence of listening; he wore the slightly bored expression of a landlord come to dislodge his dilatory tenant as he said, 'I'm afraid the jury is about to meet, Comrade Riedel. You don't mind if Comrade Sundstrom and I take advantage of the privacy of your office?'

'No, no!' Comrade Mayor Riedel assured Tolkening; he gathered his papers and hurriedly left the room. Tokening, with a slight sigh, dropped into the seat still warmed by the mayor and motioned for Sundstrom to sit down facing him. Sundstrom pulled up a straight-backed chair; it would not do to appear too much at ease; besides, he felt anything but relaxed.

Tolkening seemed to have noticed his uneasiness. With a knowing smile, he leaned back, his fingers caressing the sphinx heads that decorated the armrests of Comrade Mayor Riedel's chair, and gazed thoughtfully at Sundstrom. Sundstrom pressed his hands flat against one another and squeezed them between his knees: his face, his shoulders, everything about him narrowed; he was supplicant and sinner, self-criticism personified; had he planned it, he wouldn't have gone that far in abasing himself, but his instinct for self-preservation had taken over.

'I'm glad we have this opportunity,' Tolkening began. 'You and I haven't had a heart-to-heart talk since—'

'Since this spring,' Sundstrom aided the Party secretary's memory. 'Since the first news came of the Soviet Party Congress.'

'Yes,' Tolkening nodded. 'And the first doubts about your first project.'

Sundstrom permitted himself a brief, courteous laugh. 'You were so right, Comrade Tolkening, when you pointed out the dialectical connections between political developments and architecture.'

Tolkening hadn't the haziest notion of what he had told Sundstrom so many months ago. For a moment he felt flattered that the man should have treasured his words through the ups and downs of this hectic year; then his caution, sharpened by experience, warned him against letting himself be sidetracked. 'Of course I was right,' he said in a tone that precluded his having to add: and I don't need you to tell me. 'But that wasn't what I intended to discuss with you.'

Sundstrom listened into the pause. His back ached from the tense way in which he sat, and he didn't know what Tolkening expected him to say, if anything. A slow hate welled up in him against Tolkening and against the apparent joy with which the

Party secretary was protracting this game. Tolkening knew the decision; why didn't he say yes or no and be done with it?

'How do you feel, Comrade Sundstrom?' enquired Tolkening.

'Thank you,' said Sundstrom. 'No nearer to infarct than last time, I hope.'

'I hear there was some trouble. My wife told me – about Julia?'

As if Tolkening got his intelligence through Elise. For a second, the desire flooded Sundstrom to bang his fist down on the mayor's desk, to tell Comrade Tolkening to go to hell, and to walk out and keep walking. But this was suicide – like his jump from the roof; and he hadn't jumped because he had built and wanted to go on building, go on living. 'Julia left me,' he said.

'Most unfortunate.' Tolkening produced a sympathetic noise. 'For you, for her, for all of us. We have enough to contend with as it is.'

Sundstrom pulled his hands out from between his knees. 'Really, Comrade Tolkening . . . I've done my best. I took her back after her escapade in Kleinmallenhagen. I know scandal doesn't help the Party—'

'It rocks the boat.'

'It rocks the boat,' Sundstrom agreed. 'But she's headstrong. I couldn't chain her, could I?'

'I suppose not,' Tolkening said absently. He wasn't happy. He disliked having to disappoint people; he much preferred giving them glad news; at bottom, he had a good-natured streak; that all-embracing beam, which his calumniators called sanctimonious, originally had a genuine impetus. 'But that accident?'

'Accident?'

'It was reported to me that you had a near accident.'

Barrasch, thought Sundstrom. The foreman had blabbed. Naturally – seeing your boss about to kill himself and then renege was too good a story to miss telling. 'Accident?' Sundstrom repeated. 'No, Comrade Tolkening. That was no accident. I was at the point of no return. There's something we architects

305

call tensile strength. It has a limit. When this limit is reached, something snaps. You understand, Comrade Tolkening, that limit *was* reached. But then, as I looked down on World Peace Road lying below, I thought that my death would do great harm . . . to the Road, to the extension project, to the Party. It would,' he looked at Tolkening, gauging mood, intentions, situation, 'rock the boat.'

A momentary narrowing of the eyes, then a slight guffaw, then the famous beam of kinship and understanding: you're indestructible, Comrade Sundstrom – or at least you think you are. Actually, Tolkening felt something close to admiration for the man. Minting political capital out of emotions that drove one to the point of suicide was an achievement hard to equal. But again, his caution asserted itself, and he said, 'And would you wish me to thank you for that much consideration?'

'Oh, no,' said Sundstrom, taken aback.

'Well, then,' Tolkening advised, 'let's not claim credit for what is a Communist's first and uppermost duty: to live.'

Sundstrom nodded in agreement.

'Let's take a comrade like Wollin, for instance,' Tolkening continued. 'Do you think it was easy for *him?* How often, do you think, did he feel like giving up and lying down to die? But he didn't; he had faith in the Party, faith in people. I have great respect for such comrades. Haven't you?'

'I have,' assured Sundstrom.

'Then you will understand, Comrade Sundstrom, that we do everything in our power to help him and men like him.' Tolkening waited for Sundstrom to confirm his understanding.

'I've done what I could all along,' Sundstrom said finally. 'I took him into my house; I gave him his job . . . ' Suddenly he straightened, and the outrage that had been done him made his voice screech, '*Wollin–Sundstrom* . . . am I *not* supposed to have feelings, Comrade Tolkening?'

Tolkening stared at him.

Wollin–Sundstrom, thought Sundstrom. But that was impossible. They couldn't do that. They couldn't fall from one extreme to the other, from World Peace Road to Wollin's cosmopolitanism. 'I'm sorry,' he said. 'I'm sorry I lost control of myself. Perhaps this hour before the jury decides wasn't the right time for a calm assessment of—'

He broke off. What was to be assessed?

'—of where you and I stand?' asked Tolkening quietly, but the threat was unmistakable.

Sundstrom readied himself to receive the blow. It would be the final one. Honour and love were imaginary values; you could easily find substitutes for them or numb yourself to their loss, but power and position were something else, and the axe that cut the ground from under your feet was merciless.

'This morning, before I came here,' said Tolkening, 'I had them bring me your cadre file.'

Sundstrom sat motionless. That cadre file would have some recent additions – the knife blade at his jugular vein, the pistol at his head.

'Also, there've been some opinions on World Peace Road, in the light of new developments. No censure, mind you,' Tolkening raised his hand, 'no denying the achievement, but enough differing viewpoints on this angle and that to preclude your receiving the National Prize.'

'The National Prize . . . ' Sundstrom repeated mechanically. God, yes, he had completely forgotten about the prize; the bauble had been promised to him when life still proceeded in orderly channels and top was top and bottom bottom, and a man knew what another would do. How quickly your own values changed: what did he care about the prize if only he wasn't thrown to the wolves, to the Hillers, the Voukoviches, the Wollins . . .

Tolkening shrugged. 'I know it's a minor annoyance, but it must be mentioned.'

Sure, sure, thought Sundstrom. Then, with a new wave of fear flooding his chest: so much preparation for so small an effect? 'Comrade Tolkening . . . ' he said.

'Yes?'

'Comrade Tolkening . . . ' Almost at a whisper.

This was abject submission, utter surrender. He was like a small animal with all four paws in the air, offering its soft underbelly to the powerful enemy, praying the big beast would pass him up in contempt.

Tolkening didn't even bother to put on his smile. 'The jury naturally will pick the Sundstrom–Hiller project,' he said. 'As for the other points, I think we understand one another?'

Sundstrom sat motionless, every nerve drained of energy.

'Well?' said Tolkening.

'Yes, of course, of course,' stammered Sundstrom, his tongue too slow for the haste of his assurance.

Tolkening glanced at his watch. 'The jury,' he said, 'should be through in a minute.'

Sundstrom needed a while to realise that he had won – won by default, by chicanery, by force of habit. The reasons didn't matter; what mattered was that out of the welter of breakdown and defeat one rock emerged to which he could cling: the Road, the extension project.

Bloodied, bespattered, bedraggled – the victor. He shook hands with Hiller, who seemed to know although the jury's decision had not yet been announced: Mayor Riedel, who was to speak in its name, was cleaning his glasses and coughing. Immediately upon the relief and the sense of triumph came anger, anger at himself – why the anguish, the humiliation? There hadn't been a chance of *Wollin–Sundstrom* being picked; psychologically, politically, architecturally, no jury would have dared, no functionary would have approved; he had let himself be bluffed by Tolkening, he had whined and whimpered before a man who was as responsible as himself for every contrived décor and dishonest pronunciamento.

308

Hiller was grinning. Nodding at their model, he said, 'Didn't I tell you, Comrade Sundstrom? . . . the right mixture. *This* has the proper ingredients for a National Prize. Pietzsch of the Central Committee hinted at it. Two years or three, and the extension will rise for everyone to see . . . ' His grin vanished. Julia, standing beyond the model, had frozen him out: a stranger, with a stranger's eyes.

'It isn't the prize,' Sundstrom said abstractedly, 'it's the work, the people, the socialism.' These things again came by rote; he was back in the old groove, outwardly at least. Elise Tolkening, curls fresh from the hairdresser, was noisily addressing Julia, small talk kept consciously small: how was little Julian, a fine child, gifted and beautiful, why don't you bring him around sometime.

Entering the room, Waltraut Greve, then Voukovich; then photographers and press; then unknowns pressing in, the public. The air became heavy. Sundstrom felt it laying itself about his throat and chest; there was a crush toward the Sundstrom–Hiller model. Somewhere, far off, Wollin's 'hypocrisy in plaster.'

Sundstrom felt like crying out, but he had no voice. He suddenly caught sight of Julia, and the need for a word from her grew till he thought it would burst his heart. But it wasn't the Julia of now whom he saw; it was the girl in the sequinned dress, patting her loose hair in place before the mirror: her white elbows, her breasts, high, pointed, making his tongue cleave to the roof of his mouth.

' . . . Project Sundstrom–Hiller . . . ' How long had the mayor been talking? Sundstrom looked at the pudgy hands clutching the manuscript, at the red face, the blubber of chins. ' . . . combines the best of architectural tradition with a healthy approach to all that is desirable in modern trends and recent technical developments, while following, in its varied features, the principle of greatest economy and the spirit of socialist realism . . . '

His eyes met Tolkening's. Tolkening was beaming. With his shiny, thick hair and his shrewdly narrowed eyes he looked like one of the saints Sundstrom had seen on an old icon at Zagorsk Monastery; and something in Comrade Mayor Riedel's voice reminded him of the ritual chant of the monks.

' . . . the jury's duty not to omit mention of the striking ideas and innovations of Project Wollin–Sundstrom. The jury feels that, although the project would be misplaced within the ensemble of World Peace Road, some of its elements can be incorporated in the greater context of the socialist reconstruction of our city; and the jury therefore recommends that this promising team of architects be employed for the design of the modernisation and extension of the Karl Marx Spinning and Textile Mill in the suburb of . . . '

Comrade Tolkening's fixed smile seemed to embrace the whole room, model and drafts, the jury, Herr Professor Krummholz, Comrade Pietzsch, Department Counselor Wilezinsky, the architects, the journalists, the people. No, this wasn't a balancing act, thought Sundstrom – this was the synthesis growing from thesis and antithesis; he, Comrade Sundstrom, found his place in it as well as Wollin–Sundstrom, and above them, unshakable, beyond good and evil, Comrade Tolkening, the keystone held in place by the convergent pressures. Nothing had changed. And everything.

Polite applause marked the end of Comrade Mayor Riedel's speech. His chins came to rest; his face paled out; he melted into the jury. Sundstrom found himself in a whirl of people; he lost sight of Julia, of Wollin; cameras upraised, silver moons ready to flash; men pushing him, the same requests repeated over and again. 'Here, Comrade Professor . . . more in the centre, please . . . that's better . . . smile.' A corner of the table was jabbing his groin. Behind him, he heard the laboured wheezing of Mayor Riedel; to his right were Tolkening and Elise; to his left stood Hiller, a satyr caught among a herd of beef. He glimpsed Krummholz of the Academy and Pietzsch of the Central Committee

310

and Wilezinsky of the Planning Board somewhere in the vicinity. 'Comrades, comrades!' The requests again: 'Will you please group about the model . . . examine it, please . . . kindly say something to one another, anything . . . that's better . . . smile.' Sundstrom saw the silver moons rise higher. The pressure against his groin grew unbearable. The room was overcrowded; the damned public wouldn't give the photographers a chance. He saw Wilezinsky lose his footing, or maybe it was Pietzsch; the man reached out wildly; his hand slipped among the twelve-storey buildings of the World Peace Road extension; the roof cafeteria tumbled, the bachelor tower, the hotel; Sundstrom lunged out, trying to save what he could—

Then the flashbulbs went off.

Time out.

How do you feel with one part of your life ended and another not yet begun? Was there a pattern? Julia shivered, wrapped her coat about her, and reached for Wollin's arm. She was acutely sensitive to these breaks in continuity: the hissing of the engine stopped on the open track, factory sirens greeting an uncertain peace, a nurse's monotonous count as the ether takes over.

These are the moments when you need the other person, warmth, love. You're without a shell, vulnerable; the suspended motion makes any balance precarious, but the support nearest you may not be the best; and there are things like pride, and the scars, and differences of age – trying to cuddle up with Father again? – and look before you jump, and you don't want just to keel over; it isn't that sort of relationship; this one must stick; how many experiments can you afford without getting scuffed and tarnished?

'Shall I tell you what you are thinking?' he said as they walked along the gravel path that cut through the green behind City Hall. One day it would be a small park; now it was a meagre planting of naked, trembling twigs in reddish loam and patches of struggling grass.

Perhaps he did know, she thought, and remembered Arnold, who had made a point of not leaving a corner of her mind unexplored. But to her surprise, Wollin said, 'I feel as helpless as you do. I had wanted to sweep you off your feet, *Wollin–Sundstrom*, this promising team of architects,' he looked at her and smiled, 'but I couldn't find the starting point for the great rush, and, maybe, with people like us it shouldn't be done one-two-three-hurrah and kiss and embrace, but carefully, feeling our way with each step.'

Wollin–Sundstrom, she thought. Whichever steps they took, whatever way they chose, this would be the only project ever signed in this manner.

'We're both growing a new skin,' he went on, his eyes seeking hers. 'It's still raw to the touch. But, frankly, do you see anyone else, for you and for me, but the two of us?'

'Doesn't that make it sound like a pairing-off of convenience?' she said.

'Sure,' he said, suddenly decisive, 'as much as Adam and Eve's.'

For a moment, she was awestruck. Then she objected, 'The world is peopled; this country, this Republic, this city aren't paradise or wasteland: and we're part of them.'

'But any new beginning,' he said, 'is Adam and Eve.'

'Yes,' she said, and knew that the intermission was over and with it its anxieties.

'I think we will love each other very much,' he said.

His eyes held hers; their blue was no longer pale and tired, it had an incredible depth; Julian, she thought, and knew in the same moment that her child would be no problem with him; and she said, 'Yes,' and again, a first tinge of joy colouring her voice, 'Yes.'

Wollin took her hand. Briefly, he caressed her long, tapered fingers; then, with a sudden passion hardly constrained, he kissed their tips.

312

AFTERWORD

Every German Communist fleeing Hitler in the 1930s had a natural destination: Moscow. But life in the shadow of the Kremlin was just as evil as it would have been in Nazi Germany. In November 1936, for example, the German Communist Ernst Ottwalt was arrested and quickly found guilty of 'anti-Soviet agitation.' He was sentenced to a Siberian labour camp, where he died in 1943. His fate was typical of many Germans who found in Moscow not Soviet protection but a climate of fear and, after the famous show trials of 1936, mutual suspicion. As the purge of German Communists accelerated, there were soon instances of denunciation of colleagues and even friends in the interest of personal survival. It was not until after the death of Stalin in 1953 that the full nature of this treachery became clear. In 1956, along with many others, Ottwalt was declared to have been innocent.

This, one of the principal sources of inspiration for *The Architects,* would seem prime subject matter for a novel, but hardly an easy one in a society where censorship was rigid and where those in power actually had been the survivors of this Moscow tyranny. Fiction on this subject could be attempted only by someone whose desire for truth was absolute and who could publish his work in another country and another language. In the 1950s only one writer in the German Democratic Republic was in this position. His place of exile had been the United States.

Stefan Heym was born Helmut Flieg into a Jewish family in the southern German city of Chemnitz in 1913. His first published poem was pacifist, and the poem for which he was hounded out of school was an attack on German military policy. He left Berlin for Czechoslovakia in 1933, immediately after the Reichstag fire, his father having been taken hostage by a Chemnitz police force determined to make an example of him. He was probably Hitler's youngest literary exile. Taking the name Stefan Heym, Flieg made his way in Prague as a journalist and then, in 1935, won a Phi Sigma Delta scholarship to the United States (for Jewish students whose education had been interrupted by the rise of National Socialism). He studied in Chicago, learned English, became the editor of a German-language newspaper in New York, and published his first bestseller, *Hostages,* in 1942. He joined the US Army in 1943 and, after considerable bravery in the Normandy campaign, where he worked in psychological warfare, returned to the United States, where he used his wartime experiences to write his second bestseller, *The Crusaders* (1948). From this point until his death in 2001, Heym was to publish a succession of novels devoted to questions of revolution and its aftermath, fascism, anti-Semitism, the structures and problems of socialist government, and, most important, Stalinism and its legacy.

From his early youth, Heym had been socialist in his outlook, and this position was firmly maintained in the United States. His American wife, Gertrude, whom he married in 1944, was a member of the Communist Party. Fearful that they would fall victim to the McCarthy Communist witch hunt that was sweeping the States, the couple decided to leave for Europe in search of a safer home. The reviews of Heym's 1951 novel *The Eyes of Reason* (a positive treatment of the Communist 'takeover' in Prague in 1948) confirmed that the decision was wise: one critic declared that anyone who reviewed the book positively should be jailed for blatant Communist sympathies. The Heyms settled in the German Democratic Republic around the turn of 1951–2, and after initial difficulties Heym was generally celebrated as an important antifascist author who had chosen a Communist lifestyle over the 'immorality' of American capitalism.

This favourable position was short-lived, however. Although the author heartily disapproved of numerous aspects of the United States, in particular its role in the Korean War, he soon began to question aspects of life and politics in the GDR. After the half-hearted East German uprising on June 17, 1953, he took on a high-profile role as an advocate of socialism and a castigator of those who were failing it. His regular newspaper column, in which he boldly exposed inadequacies in local and national government, may have won him wide acclaim, but it also brought him into disfavour. The knowledge that he was writing a novel about the June uprising gave the authorities even greater cause for concern. Heym completed the novel in English in 1958 and then set about translating it into German so that he could have a response from the so-called cultural functionaries – those in charge of cultural affairs and responsible for overseeing all aspects of book production. Their response was negative and angry. Heym decided to leave the novel and wait for better political times. His view of the events was shifting anyway, so he turned instead to newspaper articles, short stories, and a novel on an earlier German revolution, that of 1848.

Novels on historical events have been a standard form of escape for writers living under censorship, but in this case the author put surprisingly little between the lines. Possibly because it was his first historical novel, Heym held closely to his sources and, through extensive and detailed research, brought alive an earlier epoch in which widespread hopes of liberal reform had temporarily flourished and then had been crushed. In the course of composition, however, momentous events were taking place in Germany. On August 13, 1961, the East German authorities built a wall across Berlin, ostensibly to prevent infiltration of 'capitalist agents' but in reality to block the ever-increasing number of East Germans seeking a better life in the West. Heym held ambivalent feelings about the Wall in its earliest years, although he later called for its removal. It did, however, raise further unease in his mind about government policy and the future of socialism. Before the publication of *Lenz* in 1963 he had embarked on the study of a subject that was to retain his interest for the following four decades: Stalinism.

Stalin may now be recognised as one of the most brutal dictators of the twentieth century, but for many years after the Second World War he was celebrated in East Germany as the heroic figure who had liberated the country from Hitler's tyranny. All the members of the Politburo, the centre of power in the GDR, had been in exile in Moscow and were indebted to the USSR for their survival – and, moreover, their *continuing* survival, since it had been the Soviet army that had quelled the uprising in 1953 and that maintained a substantial presence in the country. The most famous street under reconstruction in East Berlin carried Stalin's name. His death in March 1953 was thus greeted with widespread official mourning.

By 1956, however, the situation had changed dramatically. Nikita Khrushchev, in a supposedly secret speech to the Twentieth Congress of the Communist Party of the Soviet Union, denounced Stalin for incompetence and a succession of crimes against the Party. His brutal purges, previously regarded as necessary, were branded as monstrous and completely unjustifiable, and so began the rehabilitation of numerous prominent individuals, many of whom had actually 'confessed' to their supposed crimes. Most of them had already been executed or had died in labour camps, but some did return – including to East Germany.

The government of the GDR clearly knew the nature and something of the scale of Stalin's brutality, but admitting that knowledge was not in their interests. All of them had been shaped by the Stalinist approach to dissent, and their own domestic policies were repressive and inflexible. Now forced into following the lead of their Soviet masters, they allowed a modest liberalisation, especially in the arts, but this 'thaw' proved short-lived. The relative freedom permitted in Soviet society, which culminated in Solzhenitsyn's shocking portrayal of life in a camp, *One Day in the Life of Ivan Denisovich* (1962), did not take place in the GDR. Even when Gorbachev began his reforms many years later (and full-scale rehabilitation of those falsely accused under Stalin took place in the Soviet Union), the GDR maintained an unapologetic stance.

Heym heard of Khrushchev's revelations before most others. Details of the speech were suppressed in the GDR (it was never officially published), but Heym had access to the *New York Times*, which provided the key details. Not until Heym's private diary becomes available – thirty years after his death – will we know the point at which he became determined to write against the perversions of Stalin's megalomania. In view of the space he was later to accord aspects of Stalinism in his work, it is surprising that he wrote nothing substantial in the late 1950s. It may well have been Solzhenitsyn's novel that proved the spark, for Heym's first questioning of Stalin's legacy comes in an unpublished essay of late 1962, followed by an outline of a novel, *The Architects*, early in 1963.

Heym presented his massive personal archive to the University of Cambridge, England, in 1992, and we therefore can follow the precise stages of composition. First, there is a rough, handwritten sketch of the plot, probably written around May or June 1963. The essence of the story is all here, and the author clearly had heard the fate of the writer Ernst Ottwalt by this point; there is then a longer, typed version that carries a date of July 30, 1963, and finally a substantial outline dated November 1. The archive carries cuttings from newspapers on aspects of modern architecture from around this time, a list of books on the subject borrowed from a Berlin library, and a list of the prominent Berlin architects of the day, together with their phone numbers. There are numerous cards with detailed notes on

317

Berlin architecture, comments by architects, and criticism of mistakes in construction, but, in addition, there are comments by victims of Stalinist oppression and six pages of notes, in English, from Khrushchev's 'secret speech.' Composition probably took around two years, the normal period for Heym's novels at this stage, but it was interrupted by separate speeches and articles on Stalinism, the GDR's failure to deal with it, and the need for writers in particular to write honestly. These articles include some of the best short pieces Heym ever wrote, including 'Stalin Leaves the Room' and 'The Boredom of Minsk.' Neither of them was published in the GDR.

Heym's outspoken remarks were carefully noted by the authorities, and indeed by this point the secret police followed all his movements. The government decided on a plan to prevent him from having an even greater impact on the populace, and in December 1965, together with several other dissidents, he was denounced by Erich Honecker at the Eleventh Plenary Conference of the Socialist Unity Party. In a decision the following February, the Politburo agreed to 'smash his ideas and isolate him,' putting pressure on his friends and all other writers to break off contact. For the following few years his work was effectively banned in the Republic, the study of his work forbidden in universities; no publishing house could accept his novels, nor could newspapers accept his articles. Although he did publish two short stories for children, there was obviously no hope for *The Architects*.

Heym therefore turned again toward history for less controversial material: to the figure of Lassalle, the founder of the German Workers' Association and the man in whom he identified the origins of modern totalitarianism and the 'cult of personality.' By the time this manuscript was completed in 1969, another partial thaw was in progress, but Heym's new work still could not be published in the GDR. It was not until the mid-1970s that publication was possible. But publication of *Lassalle* went ahead in both West Germany and England, and Heym, encouraged, returned to the manuscript of *The Architects*. He sent it to his old friend Desmond Flower, managing director of the London publishing house of Cassell, but was disappointed by the response. Flower's reader clearly worked in haste, misunderstood aspects of the plot, and failed to grasp several of the essentials of theme. Flower therefore declined the novel. Heym responded, pointing out the reader's mistakes but accepting that he would make changes and asking for examples of points where he might make them. He also added that there was no great hurry since he was at work on another novel, on the biblical King David. *The King David Report* was to prove Heym's masterpiece; it marked a turning point in his acceptance and celebration by the West, and the years that followed proved politically tempestuous. It is no small wonder, then, that *The Architects* remained unpublished.

One curious feature in the novel's history is the fact that Desmond Flower claimed not to have read the manuscript himself but to have assigned the task to another – someone whose report was hasty and careless. Flower had known Heym since the publication of *The Crusaders,* which had proved a great success for his company, and he had published a collection of Heym's short stories in 1963 as well as the English version of *Lenz* in 1964. Private conversations have recently revealed that Heym's wife, Gertrude, may have attempted to dissuade Flower from taking on the novel, and if he had indeed read it, he immediately would have recognised the risks for the author. By this stage the secret police had established a massive dossier on him, and, in retrospect, it is remarkable that they did not prosecute. One can only assume that they hesitated in view of the consequences of such an act. Heym was, after all, Jewish; he had fought against Hitler; he had been acknowledged as an important antifascist writer; and he was well known in the West. Prosecution would have proved an international embarrassment.

This was not self-evident, at the time, however, and Flower's rejection of the novel may thus have been a means of protecting his old friend.

In 1999 Heym fell seriously ill; his doctors were obliged to put him into an induced coma for almost two months. The event undoubtedly convinced him that he needed to address certain matters for posterity. His life had been long and often turbulent, and he had enjoyed numerous successes as a novelist, a journalist, and an orator. The last decade had been particularly eventful, for he had been centrally involved in the collapse of the Berlin Wall, had despaired of the East German stampede for capitalism that followed, and had therefore stood for Parliament – where he had become Father of the House. His massive novel *Radek* (1995) had been his most intensive investigation of Stalinism, yet his very first study remained unpublished. He therefore made the decision to translate the English manuscript into German, and *Die Architekten* was published in 2000. Heym was to die on a visit to Israel in 2001, and the present publication of the novel in its original form is a fitting tribute to a man who fought fearlessly throughout his life for what he believed in.

PETER HUTCHINSON